CW01502134

Contour

Jon Beattiey

Contour

Entrancement Redefined

Matador
9 De Montfort Mews
Leicester LE1 7FW, UK
Tel: (+44) 116 255 9311 / 9312
Email: books@troubador.co.uk
Web: www.troubador.co.uk/matador

ISBN 978-1906221-430SB
978-1906221-447HB

This is a work of fiction. Characters, companies and locations are either the product
of the author's imagination or, in the case of locations, if real, used fictitiously
without any intent to describe their actual environment.

Typeset in 11pt Book Antiqua by Troubador Publishing Ltd, Leicester, UK
Printed in the UK by The Cromwell Press Ltd, Trowbridge, Wilts

Matador is an imprint of Troubador Publishing Ltd

To the recollection of Annette, a slim blonde girl who stirred an early imagination and who never knew how much

Valete

Author's Note

Though there is denial that the places or the *persona* as described exist in anything other than the mind's eye, nevertheless the concepts of the Manor and its environs have roots in rural Bedfordshire, and a Brewery may once have stood on a site now occupied by a Supermarket. Who knows, maybe an Interior Decorating Consultant does exercise her professional talents somewhere out there in an old Manor House? I wonder if she has such an involvement in life as Roberta? Certainly the backdrop to a lovely week in Ireland is genuine...

There is a stong possibilty that this tale may have a sequence, as all the characters are too much alive in the imagination to fade into insignificance.

ONE

She'd flounced out, not looking back. He watched her go, unemotionally, in that old coat, baggy trousers, strange woolly hat and pondered yet again on how she had become so cold, so distant, seemingly uncaring. The low growl of the diesel faded and the quiet wrapped itself round him. He shrugged, went back into the kitchen and moved the kettle across on the hob.

Outside the early morning rain had eased, clouds breaking up into straggling wisps of things that blew away over the treeline; the first glint of watery sun gave flashes of luminescence to the hanging drops of water released from grateful shrubs. Coffee mug full, he went out into the sodden garden, the lawn squelching under foot. The air felt good, cool but fresh, renewed; he felt his spirit lift as the first daffodils bounced their heads in greeting and the hen blackbird swooped down from the apple tree to stand, head poised, waiting for morning crumbs. With a laugh, he retraced his steps to find the box and scatter crumbs on the grass. At least the bird appreciated the attention, unlike his wife. She'd made her own breakfast, her own coffee, eaten in a hurry and given precious little regard to the suggestion they ate sitting down, and together.

'You know how much I have to fit in today,' had been the rejoinder. His early morning attempts to show affection, a hand brushed across a thigh, her breasts, stirringly soft, had been rebuffed with her grunt and move to crush his hand beneath her. Then she'd slid out and got dressed before him. So many times had he waited for some hint she might relish a cuddle, just a kiss even, but the moon was crying, crying, crying . . .

1

The glow of the ashes had dimmed, the last crackle of sparks extinguished, the cold was getting to his very bones.

He'd go for a long walk. She wouldn't be back for hours, going from one minor necessity to another, taking strange pride in being so disorganised. Once they had walked together, arm in arm, laughing and chattering, stealing the occasional kiss, the fondle, and even once or twice had lain in the long grass and made love, achingly beautifully. Not now. Time had moved on, taken away and stolen the essence of togetherness, that indefinable thing called love. Now it was like maintaining a business, keeping the wheels turning, day running into boring day. At least they didn't actually quarrel, not really. The odd spat, nothing untoward, but just that sad indicator of things no longer as happy as they'd once been. He drained his mug, tipped the dregs away and returned to the house. Ten minutes later, suitably clad in old Barbour and stout shoes, and with his indispensable favourite walking stick, he was making his way up the lane.

The wet spring weather hadn't done the lane any favours. The ruts were deep and brimming with last night's rain; it was as much as he could do to advance along the edges without getting sopping wet feet, all clagged up with mud. As it was, the longer grass brushed his trouser bottoms and the thick socks to start damping the fabric. Long straggles of thorn and blackberry springing across the path he snipped away with the shrub-pruners he always carried, making reasonable progress towards the open fields. The whirr and alarm cackle of a cock pheasant were startling; the pigeons' wings beating on the tree branches as a dozen or so took flight were annoying, breaking into the stillness. Otherwise there was just the dripping moisture and the distant sound of occasional traffic; scarce any vestiges of a breeze but the last of the clouds were disappearing. It was, eventually, going to be a fine morning. Swinging his stick, he turned into the pasture. The ground sloped away, running down into the small valley with the tree-lined brook. Behind the lower wood the old Manor House was just visible, the church spire from the next village appearing over its roof, but he knew it was still a couple of miles away. He'd never been close to the Manor, always found it easier to walk along the old road. Maybe today.

Now the going was easier and he was able to rid his shoes of the encrusted mud picked up from the lane, wiping them sideways on the longer tufts. The hedgerow was beginning to green up, first buds opening, nettle shoots showing darker green frilly leaves above the winter yellowed grass. This was more like it, out in the open, only country sights and sounds. No phones, no idle chat; let the tension unwind. Coming to that strangely placed seat, he took a few minutes respite; reached for a chocolate bar out of his capacious pockets and relaxed. Peace and serenity, no one to interfere with thoughts or actions. He allowed the spirit of the place to ease his mind, take away something of the perpetual greyness of his days.

Surveying the lie of the land below, his eye caught the emergence of a solitary horse rider, out from the lower wood and along the old track. Nothing unusual; there were all sorts of horsey people in the neighbourhood, from youngsters, usually girls, to the gruff old foxhunting type he couldn't quite get on with. He often met one or two riders while he was out, always careful either to stay out of sight or to be easily visible from a distance, so as not to startle the horses. This one seemed to be having difficulty, the animal rearing up and not wanting to move. As he watched, the rider managed to pull the horse round, but it bucked, and suddenly, he, she, he couldn't tell, was off, and the horse had gone. Stupid animal, he thought, and realised he was going to have to go and see what was up, for no one else was about.

Striding briskly along the field edge, doing half-jumps from tussock to tussock, covering the ground rapidly without running, it took near five, ten, minutes to reach the lane. A struggle with the slope of the ditch; a briar tore at his hand as he forced his way through the hawthorn. No sign of the horse, but its rider lay sprawled out on the grass of the lane edge, seemingly unconscious. Oh Lord, he thought, and I've come out without my phone. Damn!

3

Kneeling down, he saw the girl, - it had to be a girl - had a bruised forehead, her jodhpur clad legs sprawled akimbo, an arm twisted under her, the other flung wide as though clutching at the grass. Her helmet was askew, the strap cutting at her chin. No obvious bleeding, no signs of anything broken. She was breathing, thank God. With some diffidence, unused to such demands on his rusty first aid skills, he straightened her legs, released her helmet strap, and half turned her as best he could to the so-called recovery position. Her pulse was okay. In her thirties, maybe early forties, oval features, longish dark hair. Attractive, in a strange way, rather Italianate. Now what? No kiss of life required, but he couldn't just leave her, neither could he summon assistance. And it was a mile and a half to the village, cross-country, longer by road. The Manor House lay three-quarters of a mile up the track. So what to do? That thump on her head, must have been where she'd landed; that would have knocked her out. Maybe she'd . . . and just as he thought, hoped, she'd come round, she did. A flutter of those eyelashes, a stir, and then eyes wide open. Panic, alarm, maybe fear, and she struggled to sit up.

'Bouncer! He threw me. Blasted horse! Where is he?' She made to get up, then held a hand to her head, touched the graze and winced. 'Ouch! I'm sorry. Bloody horse!' There was a trace of a smile, a wry smile, and she held out a shaky hand. 'Roberta. Smiley. Pleased to meet you, glad you were here. Help me up?' It was a plea, not a command.

He stood up, took the gloved hand and held it firmly as she pulled on him to get her feet underneath her. She wasn't all that tall, and reasonably slim. Her dark hair, released from the helmet, flowed back onto her shoulders and she brushed it away from her bruised forehead.

'I'm going to look a sight, aren't I?' Another wry smile. 'I suppose I'd better find that stupid animal. He's probably gone back home.'

'Home?'

'The Old Manor. Up there.' She pointed. 'You are . . . ?'

'Oh yes, sorry. Andrew, Andrew Hailsworthy. From

Trellam. I saw the battle, from the hill. Out walking to get some sense into my lungs. I think you may be right; I saw the animal go up the track. Can I give you a hand?'

'You have.' She grinned at him. He was still holding hers.

'Sorry!' He made to release her, but instead, surprisingly, she pulled him towards her, and kissed, lightly, quickly, on the cheek. Then she let go.

'Just a small token of appreciation. For being around, and being concerned. It makes a change.' She turned half round and stared up the lane. 'Will you see me home? Just in case I faint or something?'

'Surely. Kill two birds. I'd been meaning to walk round the Manor anyway. I didn't know who lived there; it's always looked semi-derelict.' Then realising that sounded like a criticism he attempted to redress his mistake, 'It blends so well into the scenery.'

She laughed again, and her laugh was happiness itself. How little laughter he'd heard lately; and she had smiled and she'd *kissed him?*

'Please don't talk about killing birds. This bird nearly got herself killed. Then your morning might have taken on a different light. Come on, I'll organise us a drink.'

'You sure you're feeling okay?'

He was concerned, she could feel it, and her insides did a little skip. How long since anyone had been concerned about *her?* Maybe that bloody horse had done her a favour, apart from giving her a fright and a gi-normous headache. Nothing an aspirin wouldn't cure. She'd have to own up to the headache. 'Apart from the head, yes. Stiff, and probably bruises where bruises oughtn't to be, but a good hot bath will help.' *I was always used to bruises anyway,* she thought, wryly.

They made their way slowly up the lane, Andrew holding her arm with his free hand. He stole a glance at her a time or two, but she seemed to be lost in thought. Reaching the five bar gate to the Manor gardens, she paused and whistled, then whistled again.

'Bloody horse!' She stepped back and peered over the hedge into the adjoining pasture. 'There he is! Well, he can effing well stay saddled for a while. I'll get Mary to see to him.' He wasn't entirely used to hearing a woman swear, but somehow it didn't seem out of character with this one. Forthright she was, but not unpleasantly so. She lifted the gate latch and ushered him through. 'You're not pushed for time?'

'No. Not at all; my own master. At least, while I'm out,' minding all the 'Do this, do that, why haven't you done the other?' instructions he'd get from Samantha.

'Good. Then stay for some lunch.' She expected no refusal, evidently, and strode on up the drive. So she wasn't as badly shaken up after all? He shook his head, blinked, and followed.

The Manor, seen at close quarters, oozed that sense of sublime indifference to age, the weathered stone matching the time-worn woodwork, and from what he could see, still in good repair. The immediate garden was tidy, not at all flamboyant, with close cut lawn and well trimmed edges. She opened the wide plain oak panelled front door and preceded him inside. A feeling of warmth and peace enveloped him with the scent of old timber and wax polish. The hall carpet was a deep crimson and blue, hand woven, the centre table solid walnut and gleaming, a vase of fresh daffodils in its centre. Two old landscape paintings hung on the panelled walls and there was a fireplace all set with logs. It could have been pure National Trust.

'Mareeee!' She called, not loudly, but with an authoritative voice. She unbuttoned her coat, unzipped her riding boots. He stood, unsure, until she looked up at him. 'Take your coat off? Then help me with these things.' Again, authority, but with a different edge.

He unzipped his Barbour, laid it on one of the oak chairs. She sat down on the other one and stuck a foot out for him to pull the one boot off, then the other. Coat removed, she was slimmer than he first thought, but . . . she caught his glance and grinned at him.

'I do look a bit of a fright, don't I? Well, take those shoes off, I don't mind stocking feet; and I'll show you into my sitting room. Then I'll clear off upstairs and improve things a bit.

Where is she? Mareeee!' She called again, louder.

A door opened at the back of the hall and an apron clad buxom woman, fiftyish, appeared.

'Mary. This is Andrew. He saw Bouncer chuck me off and was good enough to come and make sure I hadn't been hurt. When you get a moment, can you get Bouncer in from the Home Paddock and unsaddle him for me? I'd only call him names if I did it, and I'm not in the mood. After lunch will do. Andrew's staying. Least I can do. Look, you show him the sitting room, and I'll nip up and get changed.' She picked up her boots and jacket and ran lightly up the staircase and disappeared across the open landing above.

Mary was shaking her head. 'That girl, she'll never stop. Fell off again, did she? That 'orse she got be too big for 'er. Hurt hersen?'

'I don't think so, apart from her bruising. But she *did* get knocked unconscious, so perhaps she'd best be checked over – concussion and all that?'

'You be right. I'll have her see Dr Knowles tomorrow. Landed me sorting Bouncer again; Bouncer by name and nature, that one. She'd best get rid, but don't ee tell 'er I said. This way, young man.' She led the way through the rear door into a corridor and from there into a delightful room, with cosy armchairs, a couple of occasional tables and through the leaded window a view down the valley beyond the garden. More flowers, hyacinths this time, in bowls, and another fireplace, cosily warming the room with the logs flaming as she stirred them.

She replaced the poker on its stand. 'Make yoursen at home. Dare say she won't be long. Chicken sandwiches orlright for 'ee?'

'Fine, yes, anything, er, I. Roberta – Mrs Smythe – she on her own?'

Mary gave him a sideways glance with her correction. 'Smiley. She be. Since himself ran off with his *personal assistant.*' She sniffed; her tone full of derision and contempt. 'Near a year, that be. Cost him, that did. Still, not for me to say. Back in jiff.'

She left him alone, allowing him to browse the books in the half-wall of a bookcase. The titles always gave away a person's interests, and he was pleasantly surprised at the diverse collection. History, people, adventure, a nice collection of art catalogues; the odd book on birds and trees; fascinatingly, a few novels, mainly, from what he could see, romance. Hardbacks and originals, not your book club cheapies or three for two's.

The door opened and he turned to a delight. Her long hair now tied back in a twirled sort of knot; a plain and revealingly close fitting jersey dress in a linen colour, with a wide leather belt. At her breast a simple brooch in silver and marcasite. She'd evidently powdered over her bruise, but it still showed up as a florid red. Simple shoes, but raised heels. And a slight waft of scent; a real treat of a girl.

She caught his eyes as soon as she entered the room, and held them. Deep brown, he noticed, and a firm gaze.

'Well, that feels better.' She dropped into what must surely be her favourite chair with a large plumped-up cushion; a book on the side. 'It's a bit like the lunatic banging his head on the wall.' She paused, waiting, but then a trifle disappointed he didn't respond, finished the phrase: 'It's nice when you stop. I'm not sure I really enjoy riding, but as I have the horse, the gear and the country, I keep up appearances.' She crossed her legs, smoothing her skirt over her knees. 'Do sit down, Andrew; Mary will be here shortly with a bite of lunch. Would you like a drink? I've beer if you care for it at this time of day?'

Now, there's a trap if ever there was, he thought. 'Thank you, no. Whatever you're having, tea, coffee . . . '

She interrupted him. 'Sherry?'

'Fine. You're very kind.'

'It's you who's the kind one. So long as you don't feel obliged. How come we've not met before? Have you been in the village long?'

He smiled. Often the way, you see someone new only to discover they've been around for ages; it's just that you don't move in the same circles. Samantha would likely know her, or of her, she knew everybody, from school or church or Women's

Institute or Farmer's Markets, fingers in every pie. His own accountancy job that kept him behind the home office desk most days lessened his chances of meeting local folk and his lack of interest in meaningless social functions didn't help.

'Only ten years. Before that, in town. I'm afraid I don't get involved with much locally. My wife does, you may know of her. Samantha.' As he answered her question, she'd lifted herself out of her chair in a simple fluid movement that he found strangely appealing, crossing to a cupboard on a table that was evidently the drinks cabinet. There would be a name for it, he knew, in the antique furniture trade, but he couldn't for the life of him remember.

With a half turned head towards him, she raised a delightful eyebrow. 'Dry, medium or sweet?' She smiled. 'I'm showing off. Sorry. I may know your Samantha, but I can't place the name. Since my former husband ditched me for a different flavour I've kept a bit out of things. Embarrassing, finding you're not quite the bee's knees anymore. At least he paid for his mistake. Well, perhaps not such a mistake. My good fortune in a way. Mary said?' She obviously knew her housekeeper's foibles. 'She's always been on my side. A treasure, as the books say. What do you do, Andrew?'

'Accountant; my own business. Medium would be fine, thank you. Used to work for a large company, but got bored, so now I work for myself, from home most of the time. Has its compensations and its downsides. How about yourself?' He took the glass she proffered, relishing the feel of well-cut crystal. She returned to her chair and he tried to ignore the fleeting but tantalising glimpse of thigh as she crossed her legs.

'Me? I do some interior design consultancy, off and on. More off, lately. I'm too choosey when it comes to clients, I suppose.' She sipped her sherry, levelled her deep brown eyes at him, and there was a hint of another smile. 'I'm my own person, I decide. Too forthright for some, that included my ex. He didn't like women who stood up for themselves. Maybe one reason he wandered off. At least he left me this place - for the time being.' She put her glass down on the side table. 'I have to spend a fair few days in town now and again, to earn enough to pay the bills, but it's nice to come back into the country. Do you go walking a lot, Andrew?'

Before he could answer, a light tap on the door prefaced Mary's arrival with a tray. He got up to help her move an occasional table into the centre. In this room you wouldn't call it a coffee table, he thought. There was a plateful of assorted sandwiches, neatly arranged, lettuce and tomato trimmed; a few bridge rolls with chicken slices, a small bowl of mayonnaise, china plates, little silver knives and proper serviettes. Charming, utterly charming, and a far cry from the 'get it yourself' routine back home. If Mary had been wearing a black dress, white cap and pinny he would have thought himself back in the 1930's. But then Roberta would have been in a longer dress . . . Mary looked at her mistress, who merely nodded and smiled dismissal.

'Please, help yourself.' As Mary closed the door behind her, Roberta destroyed the illusion. 'She only does this to impress the guests, Andrew. I don't get this treatment on my own, I assure you. It's what's called 'keeping up the standard.' She laughed, briefly, quietly, more a musical chuckle. 'No bad thing, I suppose; better than eating on the hoof. Go on, don't stand on ceremony. Another sherry?' She leant forward, piled sandwiches and a roll onto a plate, put a dollop of mayonnaise on the edge, and sat back.

Andrew copied her, shook his head at the sherry. Any more and he'd start talking silly. Sherry on an empty tum was already making him feel fuzzy edged. 'This is nice. I could get used to being pampered. 'Eating on the hoof' is probably more my norm, regretfully. In answer to your question, I don't walk as much as I would like to, but the country round here isn't all that brilliant for proper walking. Too many hedges and ditches and farmers who plough up field-edge pathways. How about yourself – do you walk or is it always horseback?' He couldn't help himself adding, light heartedly, 'when you can stay on!'

There was a bit more of a laugh from the girl. Lovely, it was, to hear some laughter; the humour was missing more often than not in his world. Her sandwich disappeared before she replied, narrowing her eyes at him.

'Are you disputing my riding skills, Mr Hailsworthy?' Then another laugh, 'you're right; I should be able to manage him better. I think it was a bit of polythene flapping in the hedge that spooked him, and I haven't quite got the strength I should have for his size. My ex. used to ride him, but his new model didn't care for horses, so he got left.' She paused. 'I'm sorry, Andrew, to intrude on your morning like this. But I am grateful, really, and it's nice to have company. Another sandwich or two? Perhaps we ought to have coffee. I'll ask Mary,' and she was out of her chair and across to the door, that same sinuously appealing fluid movement, before he could politely protest.

While she was gone, he finished his plateful and another sandwich, before taking another glance around the room. Yes, the interior decoration skill was tastefully evident. Curtains in such a lovely deep blue; the soft furnishings looked – to him - generally all in tune, the furniture well chosen, not really old, but certainly no veneered chipboard here. She must know what she wanted, and, importantly, where to find it – usually half the problem. Better than mooching round a DIY store where he was dragged more often than not to give credence to Samantha's concepts of décor. He liked the room, he felt at home; there was a lovely comforting atmosphere and it wasn't just because he saw Roberta as an interesting person, either. The hyacinths, a Wedgwood blue, were scenting the room. He'd picked up another sandwich and taken his first bite when Roberta reappeared, percolator in one hand and a couple of mugs in the other.

'Sorry,' she said, gaily, 'Mary's cross with me, not using a proper coffee pot and the 'right cups" She imitated her helper's accent. 'But I guess you don't mind mugs, so long as I haven't spoilt the effect. At least its proper coffee – Taylor's best . . . ' The coffee was poured and she passed him a mug. 'Black, no sugar? I'll fetch milk and sugar if you like?'

'No, this is fine, thanks. You're too kind. Nothing like this anticipated when I left home. I shouldn't overstay my

11

welcome. Samantha will be back mid afternoon.' They were still standing up and he began to feel uncomfortable beside her; that subtle scent and her close proximity were powerful interactions. The coffee was hot, so he could only sip.

Silence; then, 'you're welcome any time, Andrew. You're good company; really. I miss having friends here. Most of mine are in town. What few people we knew properly round here seemed to think I chased my ex away.' She perched on the arm of her chair, swung a shapely leg. 'Why don't you and your wife come to dinner one evening? I can always rustle up someone from town to give the right impression. I'd love to show you the rest of the house, if you're interested, that is. And Mary's a very good cook.' It was for all the world as if she was beseeching him to come back. Well, why not?

'You're very kind,' he was repeating himself. 'I think we'd love to. So long as you're sure?'

Her expression hardened. 'I wouldn't invite you otherwise. Of course I'm sure. How about next Friday? I'm in London until Thursday. Give me a call to confirm, if you have to discuss it with your wife, Andrew.' He noticed she didn't use other people's Christian names, just their role. Her ex, his wife. She slipped off the chair arm and moved to the door. He was being dismissed. He finished his coffee; put the mug carefully down on the tray. Suddenly conscious he was just in socks, he felt embarrassed. She followed him out and into the hall, where he slipped his shoes back on and felt better.

She picked up his old tatty Barbour and handed it to him, gravely. 'Seen some service, hasn't it?'

He shrugged it on, struggled a bit with the zip, and looked for his stick, finding it propped up by the door where he'd left it.

'Thank you for looking after me,' she said. 'Mary's suggested I look in the Doctor's Surgery tomorrow. I'll do that, just to set your mind at rest.' She was standing in front of him again, arms at her sides. He bent down and kissed her cheek, warm, soft, breathed more of her scent. She turned her head only slightly. He could have kissed her properly, held her, hugged her, but he didn't. Was that disappointment in her eyes? She moved, quickly, to the door, and once opened, he was gone, walking steadily up the gravel drive and away.

A deep breath, watching him, but he didn't turn or wave. The door closed; in the empty hall there was just the sound of the clock ticking, otherwise the silence of the house had folded itself around her once more, as though she was smothering in velvet.

* * *

Andrew strode on, his mind churning the events of the day. Now the middle of the afternoon, the sun had given up the struggle in front of the oncoming cloudbank. It was turning cool, so all he wanted to do now was get home. What sort of a welcome he'd get was another matter, but the interlude with Roberta had boosted his morale and as he felt her invitation to return was no mere polite social gesture, maybe, just maybe, there was somewhere he could go now and again to break the monotony, so long as he didn't upset Samantha. He stepped out; taking the road back was going to be the better option, he didn't fancy the field route now the light was going. The damp of the night had gone, the few puddles remaining had shrunk, but with the rising wind the chill factor increased and so did his pace. The local farmer's beaten-up old Landrover clattered past him, he thought he got a wave but wasn't sure. Then the local bus lumbered past on its rounds, leaving a waft of diesel smoke. The afternoon had markedly deteriorated and the morning evidently far the better part of the day. He turned the corner, reached the start of the kerbed tarmac path, ducked under those pendulous yew branches he'd promised himself he'd prune but hadn't yet plucked up enough courage to do, and pushed open the side gate. The car was back. Well, at least the kettle would be on. He heaved a sigh, and opened the kitchen door.

Samantha was standing over the pile of groceries heaped on the kitchen worktop, checking the long till list in her hand, item by item. She barely looked up. 'The flour's gone up again.

13

And they haven't taken those vouchers off. It's a nightmare!' Everything was a nightmare to Samantha. 'Wretched car park was full up with mothers and toddlers. I didn't get your batteries, sorry, couldn't park round by the Mill. If you want some tea you'll have to get the kettle on.' She didn't ask where he'd been, if he'd had a good day. She'd be out again by six, some Committee meeting or other. 'I'll have to grab a pizza or something. There's some of that stew left, or you can get a piece of chicken out the freezer.' She started to put the shopping away. 'Oh, by the way, the interior light's gone on the car. Get it fixed, will you?'

There was always something. No greeting, no acknowledgement despite the twenty odd years they'd been together and he'd been the only man in her life. Taken for granted he'd always be there, servicing her every need without regard for his feelings, his own wishes for his life. Even in bed, he doubted she'd know if he wasn't there, some nights. Yet he still loyally stayed by her, perhaps because it was the soft option, or the memories of what had been, or even what could be again. The two children were almost past history with her, the one married and out of sight, the other stuck in endless studying at University.

'I met the owner of the Manor today.' It was something to say.

'Right, that's all I need for those cakes for Friday.' She closed the cupboard door, swept the bags under the sink unit. 'Who was that?' There was no avid curiosity, just a need to ensure she knew who was who. She moved into the other room, only half-listening.

'Roberta Smiley. She came off her horse, so I helped her home. Nice girl. We've an invite to dinner.'

'Oh?' There was the sound of papers being shuffled about. 'I'm sure I left my list here somewhere.' A pause, before she came back into the kitchen. 'Dinner, you say. When?'

'Friday. At the Manor. Dress up job.'

'Don't think Friday's a good day. The Church Bazaar, I shan't get done till gone six. Still, if you want, I'll try and get finished early. Right, I'm going to eat.' Not, 'Would you like to have dinner,' he noticed, which would have been nice. Andrew spun round and retreated to his office. She wouldn't care. Sitting down at his desk in front of the computer, he stared at the screen saver. 'Worthy Accountancy Services' floated by in front of its background of blue sky. The business was good, no doubt over that, but the domestic day to day monotony was driving him to desperation. How could he inspire Samantha to return to her vivacious former self? Take her away? Move? He couldn't see how he could change the way in which he looked after her. She had everything she wanted, within reason. The house was fine, the garden tidy. Okay, she moaned about the height of the shrubs occasionally, but she'd also moan if he cut them down. They did manage to get out together every now and again, but it always had to dovetail into her frenetic social calendar. Like tonight, after a committee meeting that would no doubt work its interminable way through a stuffy agenda and get next to nowhere, she'd come home and treat him to a half hour diatribe on how inefficient everyone was, that she would have to do this that and the other because no one else would, and so it went on. He thumped the desk and the screen leapt into life, the page telling him what work was still to do. Well, get on with it, he thought. Not a lot else. He'd eat when he'd finished.

About an hour and a half later, he'd broken the back of the end of the year calculations for one of his latest clients, an internet vegetable marketing company; knocked out a preliminary balance sheet and finalised two other quarterly accounts for the more regular clients. Time for a break and he stretched, climbed off his chair, mooched into the kitchen and found half the pizza Samantha had left. It would have to do; at least he'd had a nice lunch.

Once having eaten, he dropped into his chair in the lounge and vainly tried to get interested in a television programme. Never much to stretch the mind these days, he surmised, idly hopping from channel to channel. Blowed if he was going to spend money on satellite telly, so much of it was either repeats or sport. Even the new digital Freeview system had its limitations. Bored, he cracked open a can of beer from the fridge and thought of Roberta: 'I bet she's not watching telly' - and pondered on how she did pass her time, all on her own. It would be very pleasant to have some good company and stimulating conversation for a change. When Samantha was at home she was always on the go, baking, ironing, sorting out her papers, hardly ever sat with him, let alone showed him any affection, not even the passing kiss. Putting his feet up on the low table, he finally found a passable film, albeit half way through, and inevitably, ten minutes later, fell asleep.

When Samantha did arrive home, she was in a foul mood. Apart from being talked down by that ponce of an overbearing Chairman, she'd spilt half-time coffee on her blouse – nothing unusual but annoying none the less – she'd had to take old Mrs Jones home and then some half-baked twit had nearly run her off the road at the junction. She slammed into the house and Andrew woke, with a headache.

'Sleeping in front of the telly again? I don't know how you can stand it. I'm going to bed. Turn off the lights.' And she was gone, thumping up the stairs. 'Oh God, what a disaster,' he thought and winced at the prospect of climbing into bed with her in that sort of mood. He waited until silence reigned, gave it another ten minutes, and crept upstairs. Gentle snoring sounds suggested she'd gone to sleep, thank goodness. He undressed carefully, slid gently into the bed and doused the bedside light. He might have read for a while, but he had some care for her, in that the light might have eventually disturbed her slumber. Could have been worse, but it could also have been a damn sight better if she'd been in the right mood. The thought of what should end the day between loving couples manifested itself in physical stirrings and he contemplated some exploration, but discretion or the knowledge a rebuff was worse than no attempt at all gave him second thoughts. He closed his eyes and called it a day.

TWO

During the course of the ensuing week, Andrew had plenty to do to keep his mind occupied. A call came in from the local Brewery, surprisingly, suggesting that he might like to sort out the ailing accounts from the Thistle and Thorn pub in the next village. This surely could be the start of more good business, for if one pub used him and found it was worth the few hundred he'd charge, then maybe others would follow suit. He didn't mind dealing with that sort of client; it was when you had so many different personnel to deal with in the middle-sized companies life got tedious. Everyone thought they were geniuses with figures, from the M.D. down to the warehouse man, and the end result was chaos. He'd had to unravel just such a problem with that glass company; it wouldn't have surprised him if they weren't trying to dodge v.a.t, judging from the peculiar way the invoice figures went up and down. It had taken him the best part of a day and a half, with several hours on-site, before a 'missing ledger' suddenly appeared and solved the problem. Talk about creative accounting! He mentally reminded himself to up his own invoice this next time round. Blowed if he was going to get them out of trouble for mere peanuts.

Then old Mr Ramworthy gave him a call to ask for some guidance on his tax returns, now his wife had died – she'd always sorted the finances out, so it seemed, to the extent the dear chap was 'flummoxed'. That took him the best part of an afternoon, in that strange building that was half cottage, half two storey house, full of old books and peculiar paintings. It turned out the couple had been wheeler-dealers on the side; no wonder Ramworthy had asked for help. Once he'd got the hang of how his wife had kept her books though, fortunately, it became plain sailing, and at least Andrew felt he had been appreciated when the old man gave him tea and toasted buns.

Samantha had unhelpfully caught a cold, at least a sniffle, which put the dinner date into jeopardy. He'd rung Roberta, asked after her well being, received re-assurance that the Doctor thought no harm had been done and was given what to him was good news, the wayward horse had been 'sold to a good home'. He'd confirmed acceptance of her invitation, and although she was very correct in her conversation, was he deluding himself that her 'oh good' was just that teeny bit more enthusiastic than one would have expected? So when this wretched sniffle made itself evident, annoyingly more so in the evenings, he went out of his way to ply Samantha with hot blackcurrant and aspirin. On the credit side at least it meant she didn't go gallivanting off to that remote Farmers' Market on the Wednesday, so at least he managed to get a decent lunch that day.

To cheer himself up, he went into town on the Thursday morning and spent a fair bit of time looking at the latest computer hardware in the I.T chain store, eventually giving way to the enthusiastic salesman's blandishments and buying one of the new generation of monitors, so flat and lightweight it was a delight to handle after that big antediluvian monster that took up so much desk space. Samantha snorted. 'You don't know what to spend your money on next!' No more than you, he privately thought, as she was contemplating purchasing a new pair of slacks she'd seen in the mail order catalogue. She hadn't got the figure for trousers, not now, but that didn't seem to deter her one bit. True, she was cosy enough to cuddle whenever the unexpected swings of mutual need coincided with a less sleepy moment in bed; alas the demonstrative semblance of marital bliss usually faltered again in the following daylight hours, but in trousers, no, really she'd no shape to show off.

When in due course Friday came and the indisposition had waned to the point of social acceptability, luckily, he was privileged to be given the option, to a small degree, on what she should wear. The wardrobe was inspected, an older dress or two dragged out, spurned, and re-hung (instead of referring them to the charity shop bag), before a newer, and, let's face it, he thought, a quite suitable an outfit was chosen. He left her to polish and preen, having taken all of ten minutes to put himself into something not too formal but sensibly upmarket. Her eventual emergence, with a whiff of the expensive perfume he'd given her last Christmas, wasn't too bad an effect at all. Quite good, actually; after all, she was who she was. It wouldn't do for her to outgun her host.

There were some little low lights on the side of the driveway at the Manor; he hadn't noticed them before, and in the reflected glow the building presented a quite mysterious and semi-romantic appearance. A car was already parked on the gravel in front of the house, a newish dark blue Audi. He'd no idea what Roberta drove, more than likely this would be another guest. He remembered she'd mentioned 'rustling up someone from town, to give the right impression'. The wee tinge of jealousy that crept through his gut, as though he was the only one with the right to her company, he did his best to ignore – she probably had a whole string of male friends, considering how an attractive divorcee she was.

Mary took their coats. Samantha nodded familiarly at Mary as though she was an old friend, but then it was highly likely she'd met her somewhere else. The hallway was just as he recalled, but tonight seen in evening dress; she'd put candles out and even though the faint drift of some aromatherapy type scent caught at his throat, it seemed tantalisingly evocative of a century long gone.

She was greeting them; a wonderful vision of feminine perfection in a long blue dress of some swishy silk material, hair in that complicated swirl and a brooch in the height of it; a simple gold chain in the shadowed vee of her neckline. Andrew's pulse skipped at her smile, the dimples in her cheek adding allure. Inwardly he tried to concentrate on anything other than how lovely she looked, and formally introduced his wife.

'Roberta – Samantha, my wife. Samantha – Mrs Smiley, the lady who tumbled off her horse.' Roberta gave Samantha a peck on the cheek and a cool hand to Andrew.

'Lovely to see you both. Thank you so much for coming. Samantha – your husband was extremely helpful to me, a real Good Samaritan.' The bruise on her forehead had virtually disappeared, but she touched it, briefly. 'I took a proper tumble and knocked myself out. It could have been a lot worse, I guess, but I was certainly fortunate in having someone so caring nearby to pick me up. Do come through – I'd like you to meet a couple of other friends of mine.' She led the way into her cosy sitting room. The log fire was burning well, giving the room the same warming welcoming feel. The bowl of hyacinths was at its best and the subtle scent drifted across Andrew's nose. He nearly sneezed, but caught it in time. 'Marjorie, Martin. Mr and Mrs Hailsworthy. My knight gallant and his wife. Samantha, Andrew – my indispensable solicitor and her husband, without whom I might not be quite as well placed as I am.' Roberta's slight grin was at Andrew's facial expression; he'd blinked at the unexpected role announcement. 'Marjorie may look unlike your typecast family solicitor, Andrew, but she got my ex. on the run. Martin – get Samantha a drink. I'll just pop and see how Mary's getting on.' With a swirl of skirt, she went, leaving the foursome to get on with it.

Martin, a tall, slightly stooped thin-featured man with a sad expression, gestured vaguely. 'A sherry, Mrs Hailsworthy? And Mr Hailsworthy? What can I get you?' The drinks cupboard was already open.

'Oh, thank you. A dry sherry would be lovely.' Samantha wasn't as overtly overawed as she might have been, Andrew thought, as he moved to collect her glass.

'Please, we're Samantha and Andrew. Pleased to meet you both.' The correctness and politeness was a trifle suffocating. Marjorie was a pleasant, plain-faced girl, slightly older than Roberta, he guessed, with a typical hair-do and a simple two-piece costume. Neither would have been out of place at a Church social, and he mentally heaved a sigh of relief. Why had he anticipated some high-flyer and a snooty trophy wife from an urbane city acquaintanceship who may have been high in Roberta's regard? Why should he care, anyway?

Samantha with her glass was politely sipping, eyeing Marjorie. She was going to enjoy her evening, now she'd found her level. 'May I call you Marjorie? I'm pleased to see the legal profession is not a purely male preserve! How long have you known Roberta?'

My, my, thought Andrew, she's going to sparkle, thankfully. With Marjorie now linked in her explanations, that left him with Martin. Oh dear. 'Martin. You don't live locally?' As good an opening gambit as any. Better than 'it's not been a bad day, has it?' 'May I have a gin and tonic?' This Martin was not going to be the life and soul of the party, he could tell. He received his glass, with overmuch tonic. 'We're close by, Trellam. I'm an accountant. Self-employed.'

'Yes. Roberta said. We're from Court Hamden.' He wasn't going to be very forthcoming, it seemed. Then, surprisingly, he gave a dry smile. 'She's an attractive girl, isn't she? You know, her former husband was a real cad. He had no idea - didn't appreciate her at all. But my Marjorie made him pay, oh yes. Real cad.' He looked around for his own drink. 'She's damn good, you know.' Was he referring to his wife, Andrew wondered, or Roberta? 'Did the girl a favour, did you? Well, she'll not forget. Good woman, that.' He picked up his glass from the small table. 'Fills her skirts well, don't you think, heh?' He'd lowered his voice, but his wife, still in conversation with Samantha about, guess what, home baking, turned and glowered at him. 'Ah, well. Yes. Another drink?'

Andrew changed his opinion and began to like the old chap. He had a droll sense of humour beneath that lugubrious look, probably having about as much fun at home as he did, poor fellow. Still, you never knew, the Marjorie girl might be quite energetic once you got her going. Stop thinking like that, he told himself. 'Thank you, but no – this is fine.' Liar, he added to himself, not liking tonic quite as liberal. There was *some* gin in there, somewhere. Where *was* Roberta?

Roberta was still in the kitchen, adding her own touch to the sauce, for despite Mary being a very good cook, she sadly lacked the patience to tweak flavourings. She'd purposely abandoned Andrew and Samantha to make their own running – not wanting to be the centre of attraction. Getting Marjorie and Martin in had been a risk, but far better than being on her own. Anyway, she owed Marjorie, and Martin liked eyeing her up, dear old chap. Why shouldn't he enjoy her company? There was nothing wrong in that. It was Andrew she felt sorry for. Samantha looked as though she was going to decide who won the next election, all on her own. Pleasant enough, but not sufficiently feminine; too macho, that was it. At least she knew Marjorie melted every now and again; she could tell from Martin's humour, dry though it might be. She smiled to herself. One of these days she'd get back in the saddle, and no falling off. Mmm, one of these days. She supped at the spoon again, the final taste, yes, that would do. 'Shall we serve up, then, Mary?'

'Aye, reckon. You go and play Mistress now; I'll get this lot onto the table.' Mary, dear good as a mum Mary, what would I do without you, Roberta thought, picking up her skirt to traipse through into the sitting room to rejoin her guests.

Martin looked up from his discussion with Andrew on the dubious merits of self-assessment, while Marjorie evidently welcomed the interruption to the dissertation on farm-gate sales. Oh dear, Roberta thought again, this looks a trifle grim. Well, let's see what avocado and chilli will do. 'Would you like to come through? Bring your drinks.' She spun beautifully on her high heels and held the door.

* * *

Dinner was superb. The dining room, rich brocade wallpaper, decorative plasterwork ceiling, the chandelier sparkling, the old mahogany table with the saddle back chairs glowing with loving polished care, a carpet that evidently had come a long way from its hand worked craftsman's loom, and candles setting their steady glow on the silverwork. Samantha had all but gasped at the setting, Andrew not unduly surprised but impressed none the less. Roberta's other guests – he still didn't know their surname – must have been here before. She'd placed Andrew on her right, Samantha on her left, so the other two were opposites. It worked well, and with the wine in those long stemmed glasses flowing freely, conversation improved to a great degree, bringing out reminiscences from Martin, discussions on theatres between Marjorie and Roberta, and Samantha managing to hold her own on the subject of how little the modern youth knew about etiquette. Mary served perfectly correctly and with aplomb, taking great care with the Minton plates and silver cutlery. It was abundantly clear she loved handling nice things. Andrew watched her, taking in the wrapt expression, the lightness of her movement, and was intrigued. He would love to discover more about her involvement, her connection with Roberta; they evidently went back a long way, almost a sort of uncanny but impossible mother/daughter feel. That lovely lady was playing the perfect hostess, not giving anyone too much or too little attention, keeping her guests well plied with wine, bouncing the conversation around. Finally they were into the choice of the mouth-watering desserts, raspberry meringues, lemon soufflé, little chocolate pyramids with minty centres and it was much as Samantha could do to decline a second meringue.

'Coffee in the sitting room, I think. It's cosier. Samantha – if you would like to use the facilities at all, it's the last door on the left. Martin – be a dear and ask Mary if she's got some more logs handy – we're sure to need them. Marjorie – if you could possibly show Samantha where . . . ?' It was a neat bit of military style planning.

Roberta had Andrew to herself, albeit briefly. 'Enjoy?' She gave him a lifted eyebrow look.

'Roberta; magnificent, truly magnificent, an absolutely marvellous evening; wonderful setting.' He was far too close to her. A waft of the same scent she'd worn that day after her fall; he wanted to kiss her, hold her, and his heart was thumping. She knew, he was sure, and with the look in those deep brown eyes mischievous, her steady gaze seemed to say 'You're mine, aren't you?' Dangerous, this one.

'I'm glad. I love to entertain. Don't get much of the opportunity. Mary loves it, showing off. Quite like old times,' and her eyes went all dreamy and far away. 'Well?'

Conversation stopped, the gap between them charged, palpably emotive. He clenched his fingers, digging his nails into his palms, trying hard to stop making a fool of himself. She closed her eyes, briefly, to make a kissing gesture with her lips, her hands close to her sides. A whisper, just a whisper, 'thanks, Andrew. Just stay caring . . .' It might have been 'sharing', whatever, but enough for him. 'Always,' he said, unwittingly, automatically, not thinking straight. Then a door closed down the passage and the tension broke.

Coffee, the chance of brandy, the little mints Samantha loved, the conversation continuing to flow, and Andrew felt lulled into euphoria, just drinking her in, fixing her image firmly in mind. He was making unfair comparisons, the slender vivacious Roberta, the solid uncontentious always-consistent Samantha, with her abundant womanhood that had all but ceased to excite the maleness in him.

Marjorie noticed, and professionally filed her impressions away. Martin only saw Roberta as a picture book girl and the Hailsworthys as not bad people, really. Ultimately the evening drew to its close, and Marjorie took Martin home, leaving Samantha and Andrew.

'I didn't show you the house, you two. Would you like a quick tour? Or is it too late? You can always come over again.' She was still playing the perfect hostess.

'No, I'd love to see it now, that's all right, isn't it, Andrew?' Samantha was in good spirits, full of cheer and good wine. Andrew nodded. If the truth were told, he wanted to see where she slept, to fix her in his mind. Roberta took them into the kitchen first, where Mary had cleared and washed up and gone, the vast area, or vast to Samantha, with gleaming enamelled Aga, pine panelled cupboards, oak worktops and a large upright stainless steel fridge/freezer. Then quickly through to the other side of the hall, past the dining room, to a proper drawing room, with plain carpet, elegant settees, a pair of glass fronted display cupboards with a collection of porcelain figures, rather too formal, too 'National Trust' for him. Up the stairs, the house divided into two, one side where without ceremony they saw three other rooms, each with a different colour scheme; Roberta had evidently exercised her talents to the full. The doors were opened, they peeped, then on to the next. Then across the landing to her room, and it was beautiful in cream and white; deep shag pile rugs on cream carpet, wide bed, swaged half canopy, scatter cushions, the works. The surprise was concealed lighting, but with spotlights on three paintings on the walls.

These were originals, Andrew could see, ethereal landscapes, almost Turneresque. 'Those are good, Roberta.' He couldn't make out a signature.

'Yes. I'm quite proud of those. Italy, those two, Southern Spain, that one. My early work.'

'You did them?' He couldn't hide the surprise in his voice.

'Hrrmmmm. When I was twenty, twenty-two. Then I got married and I stopped painting.'

'That's a shame. But that must have been, what ten, twelve years ago?' Roberta pulled a face at him, Samantha didn't notice; she'd gone over to have a closer look. Andrew wanted to know how long she'd been married and in his curiosity, nearly prodded her. 'How long, Roberta?'

She gave in. 'Married at twenty four, lasted seven years, almost. What was that about a seven year itch? He'd got itchy pants long before that. Good riddance. Now are you satisfied?'

'Just as well you had no children, then.' He was being too pushy, and frowned. 'Sorry, Roberta. I didn't mean . . .'

She put out a hand, touched his. 'No offence, Andrew. You're right. Though if there had been things may have been different. I don't know. You have children?'

'Yes, two. Both away from home, one married, June, she's the eldest at twenty, then Peter, he's a perennial student, at Durham. We don't see much of them, do we, Samantha?'

She'd come back across the room, curious as to what her

husband was talking about. 'No, we don't. But then, they lead their own lives. Shouldn't we be getting home, Andrew? Roberta has had a long day.'

'Don't worry about me, Samantha. I've got no one after me in the morning; I can have a lie in.' She moved back to the door. 'It's been great having you over. You must come again.' She led the way back down stairs and only moments later they were in the car and gone.

The door bolted, the down stairs lights off, she retreated back to her room, unfastened her hair from its clip, taking out the brooch carefully, stripped her dress off and returned it to its hanger. The last time she'd worn this dress had been to Michael's final dinner party, the night before he and that slip of a thing had vanished off to Spain. She'd nearly thrown it out a couple of times, but now she was glad she hadn't. Andrew had seen her in it, and she'd welcomed his visual approbation. Why were all the nicest men married? She did a mental sum. Elder girl, twenty, so married twenty-one years – she couldn't imagine Samantha letting him loose before – he would have been over twenty, so he's over forty. Forty-five max and she thirty-two. Then she shook her head crossly and peeled off her slip. What was she thinking of, silly girl! He was just nice to have around. Her reflection stared back at her in the cheval mirror. Still trim, still slim, still got a tight tummy, not bad for coming to mid thirties. Getting past the children stage, she told herself, and there was a tug at her inner bits. She would have loved a daughter or two.

Samantha and Andrew drove the short distance home in silence. It had been a good evening, a lovely dinner, and in beautiful surroundings, but something of a slight strain; they'd both been a little on edge, and for such different reasons.

Once indoors, Samantha deigned to comment. 'She's nice, Andrew, not at all the snobbish type. Beautiful house, too, and so well kept. I'm sure I know Mary, but I can't place her. She does a good job. Meal was just right. She likes you?' It was a rhetorical question.

'She says I care.' He didn't want to be drawn, uneasy about his feelings towards the girl, realising he was spell-bound, but still highly sensitive about his allegiance to his wife. 'Shame she had a husband who didn't care about her – at least as a person.' He took his coat off and hung it on the door.

Samantha eased her feet out of her dress-up shoes, and reaching for a glass, filled it with cold water. She was so very sensibly conscious about diluting wine to prevent headaches in the morning. 'Can't fault you there, Andrew, I know you care. Sorry if I don't seem as appreciative as I should. She's very attractive, isn't she?' Samantha collapsed onto a kitchen chair and slurped her water. She eyed her husband and waited.

'Ay, she's attractive. She's also intelligent and a good conversationalist. But apart from what we gleaned tonight and knowing she has a – profession, I suppose – as an interior designer in London, I don't know much else. Look, dear, are we going to bed, or what? It's late.'

Samantha wasn't going to give up. 'Would you see her again – I mean, socially – or is this a one off?'

Andrew shrugged. 'I don't know. There's no reason to just 'go round', is there? Would you want to keep up an acquaintanceship, Samantha? Do you think the Manor garden is good for a Church fete or something?' He was waiting at the hall door. 'Come on, girl. I'm tired.'

Samantha heaved herself off her chair. 'No bad idea, that. Perhaps you – we – should maintain contact then. Well, it saved us a supper, I suppose. Liked the chilli sauce on those avocados.'

She stretched, and Andrew winced as her skirt waist popped its zip button. 'Steady on, girl, you'll have your skirt round your ankles. That dessert was too fattening.'

She eyed him, suspiciously. 'You'd like that, seeing my skirt fall off?'

Andrew decided to wink at her. It wouldn't do any harm, but it wouldn't do any good, either. She wasn't the sort to drop her skirt in the kitchen, but then, he wasn't sure he'd want her to anyway. She pulled a face at him, stuck her tongue out. The problem with being an old married couple, he thought, too darned used to each other, no surprises any more. He turned away and climbed the stairs. She put the lights out and followed.

* * *

Roberta lay, on her back, in the middle of her wide bed, and just couldn't get her mind to settle down. As her dinner parties went, it had been a moderate success, though Martin and Marjorie could have been a little bit livelier. At least Samantha didn't look out of place, and Andrew seemed comfortable enough with them. He'd liked her paintings. Why she hadn't kept it up, she'd never really thought. It just seemed to stop of its own accord, rather like writer's block or whatever it was; maybe because her life had changed with Michael. After those first few months it had lost its colour, its zest. Damn him! She longed to get back to those carefree days, when the sun always shone and the boys always wanted to take her out. But now she had this house, at least until the ex. got his finances sorted, and a business to run to fund the upkeep, and what would Mary do without her? Dear Mary, such a treasure, naturally dedicated to her, so she was. Roberta stretched out, pointing her toes and pulling on the small of her back, feeling the muscles arch round her shoulders as she flexed, and flexed again. She rolled over, buried her head in the pillow, slid her hands under and gripped the mattress edge, pulled, pretended she was teasing a lover, widened her legs apart, and rubbed her tummy on the sheets, up and down.

'It's been a long time!' the thought went through her mind. 'Should I find myself a lover? Someone who would care for me? Make me happy again? Without strings?' She flung herself on her back again. 'Care for me? Like Andrew? But he's married, and Samantha's a nice girl, even though she's gone stodgy.' Her nightdress was all rucked up under her and uncomfortable, so she tossed the covers off and straightened herself out before pulling them back. She thumped the bedside light switch and plunged the room into darkness, closed her eyes, and in a dreamy girly way imagined Andrew asleep alongside her. Within minutes she was herself asleep.

* * *

Away, across three countries, on the Swiss/Austrian border, Michael climbed into his bright blue metallic Audi Sports and waved goodbye to Fiona. It was mid February and the snow was lying heavily. 'See you soon!' he mouthed, and blew her a kiss. Silly bitch, he thought, as he took off. Whatever did she want to ask him about getting married for? It was expensive enough getting rid of Roberta, so blowed if he was going to risk another relationship going bust like that. No, take 'em and leave 'em. If they wanted him, then on his terms. At least that Aleida seemed willing to chance her luck. Lovely pair, she had, and he was sure she was going commando. Only twenty miles or so across the pass, then hey ho, he'd jolly well find out what she'd got. The Audi was running well, and if Fiona thought he was going for a spin, just to try out the new tyres, she was as dim as her current sex appeal. Roll on Aleida – let's go! He reached the start of the climb and put his foot down. 'Let's see what she'll do!' The roar of the exhaust echoed up through the mountains.

THREE

He knew it could be a mistake as soon as he entered the room. Mary had answered the door, with one of her most lugubrious expressions, and not much more life in her tone of voice either as she gave him a 'good evening, Mr Andrew', but there was something else, in the additional 'she'll be the better for the seeing of you.' Curious, that, and he would have preferred to have interrogated her more on how Roberta actually was, but it was too late. The now familiar hallway had absorbed him into its embrace, the redolence of age and quiet comfort. Mary opened the sitting room door, ushered him in, bade her mistress a 'good night, I'll be off then', and silently, for a woman of her size, vanished down the corridor. Those beautiful deep blue curtains were drawn against the February twilight and he had to pause a moment to adjust to the low light, a small table lamp by her usual chair; other than the predominant firelight which gave him a flickering vision of her smiling warmth of welcome. An open box of chocolates and her latest book with silk marker lay on the table alongside the lamp.

She was ensconced, akin to the Anderson Mermaid, on the deep pile rug by the blazing log fire, hair tied back, with a silky sort of blouse and a full skirt spread round, a glimpse of naked and shoeless ankles, bare footed, like a set piece of seduction? This was dangerous ground. She made no effort to rise to greet him, merely patted the rug. 'Dear Andrew. Good of you to come, it's lovely to see you again. I've been a trifle despondent; I need someone to cheer me up. Do you want to fix us a drink?' She could have been tearful, her voice low and soft. He crossed over to the drinks cabinet, aware she was following him with those lustrous dark eyes. He met her gaze with raised eyebrows.

'Brandy and soda, please.' This wasn't the normal her, of that he was sure, but made no comment, taking his time, deciding he would share her choice, keep her company. She'd got the room so warm he had to take off his jacket, laying it carefully on the arm of a chair. She wouldn't mind, he knew. He carried the glasses over to the fireplace, put one glass on the mantelpiece, then leant down, touched her cheek, offered her the other.

'Sit down, Andrew. No, not there, with me.'

Halfway into the fireside chair, he had to crouch down on his heels, then wriggle to sit, legs sideways, to copy her position. He'd brought his glass down, and lifted it to her. 'Your health, Roberta. This is cosy.'

There was a vestige of a smile as she clinked his glass. 'Yes, it is. I'm glad you're here. I've needed this.' She sipped. No answering salutation; then, 'Sorry if I seem a little sad.' Another perceptibly emotive silence. Curiously he scrutinised her downcast face, and waited. She raised her eyes to him, plucking up the courage she didn't feel. 'I've just heard – before I rang you – from the ex's girl friend. That silly child he ran off with.' A further pause. 'At least Fiona had the courtesy to let me know. He's been killed, Andrew.' The tears welled up, and she carefully put her glass down on the fireplace, pulled out a scrap of a handkerchief to dab at her eyes. 'It's daft. A year apart, hardly a word between us, and I'm being a silly girl. Why should I cry, Andrew, when he was nothing but a pain?'

He could feel no grief, no sadness, he'd never known the man, but whatever else the guy had been, he had lived and loved with this girl, once. Then deserted her, for another. 'You loved him, Roberta.' He spoke softly, feeling his way. 'You must have, at some time. Otherwise you surely wouldn't have married him.' Dare he? 'Do you want to talk about it?' He reached for a hand, and squeezed, gently. 'You don't have to, but it might help. Not that I'm a qualified counsellor.'

That made her smile and she gripped his fingers. 'I'm past the counselling bit. I suppose you're right.' The fire flickered and a spark spat at them; she turned her head to gaze pensively at the flames. 'We used to do everything together, long before we married. Part of a group, doing all sorts of crazy things. It just seemed the right thing to do. His parents were great friends of my father, went on cruises together, that sort of thing. Then he simply said 'we'd best get married,' Rob, he called me, and we had the best wedding out, cost my father a fortune.' She paused again contemplatively, sipped her glass. 'I landed here, he started doing his own thing, took on a girl to help with the office work, she flashed her eyes or her knickers at him, and off he went. Now he's dead.'

'How?'

'Took a bend on an alpine road too fast – four days ago. So she says. Lucky for her she wasn't with him. P'raps he was chasing after some chalet girl.' She tucked her handkerchief away and took another sip. 'There's going to be complications. Andrew. The house, the estate, all still in joint names – part of the divorce settlement, why I don't know. Something to do with taxation, according to Marjorie. Luckily the London end is all mine, but glory knows what will happen here. I don't know if he's altered his will, if *she* will benefit, whether I'll get chucked out from here. It's a disaster, all round. The strange thing is, Fiona the girlfriend didn't seem to be too distressed.' Yet another reflective pause as she stared into the fire. 'Maybe she'd had enough of his shenanigans. He did get around a bit, even when he was with me.'

Andrew was consciously aware that all had not been well between Roberta and her former husband from things said or just hinted at in the three weeks he had come to know her. From his point of view, he found it incomprehensible, for there was nothing he saw in Roberta that would make him look away. He felt privileged, being party to her concerns and what distress she felt.

'The man must have been mad, Roberta, leaving you.' There, he'd said it, expressed something of what he was beginning to feel, not just a regard for her, but something indefinable and infinitely hazardous.

Her dark eyes swivelled round, firelight reflecting, and took his statement with a suggestion of an enigmatic smile.

'You don't know me, Andrew. Not that well.' She sipped again, put the glass down to move her legs from under her; brought her knees up, adjusted her skirt and wrapped her arms round them. His glance had to take in the way her movement allowed a glimpse of thigh and more. Her eyes were still on him, and she knew what she was doing. The skirt slipped back as she lifted her arms clear to reach for her glass again. 'I was quite demanding at times. It's been a long time, Andrew.' This time she took a deep swallow, emptying the glass. 'How good are you at comforting damsels in distress? You've picked me up before, Andrew. Can you do it again?'

The overtones were plain and all the vibes suggested there was going to be an inevitable outcome. Their eyes met and held for that long decisive moment of time before he nodded. He wanted to be the comforting of her, for he cared for this girl, and his weakness was caring, even when it meant risking the normality of social convention. Roberta was wanting, he could see it in her eyes, her body language, in turn he had the need to feel the wanting, to assuage the coolness of a wasting marriage.

She knew this was not right, that she was risking her reputation and his, but the need was too great, the emotions running too high. Slowly, as she kept her eyes fixed on him, she was putting her glass down, and lay back, resting her head on the cushion of the chair, leaving her knees in the air. Her skirt rucked up to her waist as she slid down . . .

The kiss, the brush of hand on breast, another, deeper kiss, before the first tentative touch on thigh, the gentle stroke, the softest feel imaginable as he reached for her, the embrace, the withdrawal of the scrap of cotton, her sigh and clutching his waist at the parting of her, the feel of sheer heaven in velvet, then movement, delving the depths, her rising to meet him, ecstasy and then the passion; a heaving, frantic necessity to culminate in gasps and such desire to achieve completion, satisfaction, and in her case, absolution . . .

In the flickering light of the fire they lay, stretched out together, warm and satiated, she with rucked up skirt and opened blouse, breasts all his to kiss and suckle, lips full for him, hair astray and glowing face. He, barely shirt clad, was aware for the first time in ages of what it felt like to possess such lovely feminity. She was beautiful. He could tell her he loved her, but he was married to Samantha, she was his wife, and he loved *her*, albeit without the depths of passion that had once been there. But this? It had been a rekindling of his ego.

Nothing had been said, Roberta had taken all he could give, had murmured, sighed, and gasped when he must have triggered in her a reaction; orgasmic feelings of whatever depth, felt or imagined. His achievement had been too easy; now in more thinking mode, he should have been less demanding, more in tune with her. Lifting himself onto his elbows, gazing at her, flushed and rumpled though she was, until eyes opened to him. He raised his eyebrows, in question.

A smile; coy, maybe; then almost a chuckle. '*Yes*, Andrew, I believe I've found a lover. You've been too good to me; I told you I was demanding. Have I been naughty, seducing you like this?'

Just looking down at her made his heart pound. The vagaries of the whole episode trundled through his mind, the impossibility of it all. Yes, he cared for her, but who wouldn't when she'd seemed so vulnerable? Had she *used* him, planned to seduce him, taking advantage of his weakness and his own vulnerability, or maybe it had been something beautiful between them? Naughty? She wasn't a teenager, to be punished when she'd overstepped the mark, she was a grown woman with responsibilities, position, able to choose – and she'd chosen him!

'Take me to bed, Andrew. Please?' She struggled and he moved to let her flex her limbs. To bed? She managed to scramble clear, stood up, skirt falling back, and he was looking up at her, all of her. 'I *need* you to make love to me, Andrew. Properly. Nakedly!' She pulled him to his feet, held his hands; waiting for a response, now unsure and nervous. 'Do you mind?' Her eyes had more of a curious look to them, reflecting with that fire lit glow, but he sensed her trembling. What should he do? He couldn't abandon her, say 'No' and walk out. He ought to, he knew, but he couldn't.

He felt embarrassed, standing there in just a shirt and socks. 'This isn't quite what I expected, Roberta?' He couldn't call her 'Rob', nor 'Bert'. He wouldn't call her 'darling', either. 'You're a temptress. You have me at a disadvantage, girl. I'm all male, and you're a very desirable woman.' It sounded so inane, after making love. To recover, to lessen the tautness between them, he attempted a more light-hearted response 'It's better than riding horses then?'

Her hands slipped under his shirt and pulled him to her. 'I'll ride *you*, Andrew. I'll make your hair stand on end. Really. I know. Come up stairs.' She tugged him, by the hand, out to the hall, and then, seemingly wild with childish enthusiasm, raced on up the stairs. She posed, briefly, at the top, and waited for him to start climbing, before disappearing down the corridor. When he got to an open door, the lights were on and she was sitting hunched up, arms round her knees, on that most gorgeous bed.

He'd seen all this on their dinner date those weeks ago, he and Samantha. She'd not stinted her interior design skills here, remembering the room in creams and off whites, deep pile carpet, king size bed, large cushions, mirrors, dressing table to die for. Her skirt and blouse lay in a tangle on the floor. He got rid of his embarrassing socks and took off his shirt with his back to her, not really believing all this was happening to him; it had all the hallmarks of a cheap paperback romance. He sat alongside her, all but willing her to change her mind, to tell him it was a big mistake, but she pushed him over to convince him that it was for real; this was no fanciful dream. Her face with its rapt expression, 'Need you. Need you. Feel me? *Love me!*' It was all happening, within her, the feel, the openness, the longing, the desire to be *possessed*. This time she was in command, and using him.

Marvellous though it was, he couldn't help but think of Samantha. She'd never have loved like this, only the one way, and mostly no reactions, just a passive acceptability of him, his need. This girl, though, was like a wild cat; there was a pull and a thrust to her that made his hackles stand on end. Those breasts above him, the surge of gut rending spasm, and she cried, once, falling back on her heels, leaving him still proud but wilting, damp, the admixture of their passion running across his thigh. In the pause, craning his neck, he could see all of her, soft thighs, curvaceous contour, smooth stomach and shadows of breasts, pert and erective nipples standing proud. Swan neck, firm chin, those lips he'd kissed, dark eyes, mischievous now, glinting and revelling in the use she'd made of him. All of her.

'*Andrew!*' The way she called him came like a caress, as she rolled forward and sideways, that sinuous way she had, to lie alongside him, first taking his kiss and then reaching down to touch, gently stroke. Samantha would never have touched him. 'Thank you.' Her words weren't trite, or facile, but softly spoken with meaning beyond the simplicity. 'You don't mind?' She was relaxed now, the passion spent, the fervour fading, but all woman and the feminine scent of her, musky, mysteriously intoxicating, enveloped him.

He turned his head to her, took her kiss, reached down and laid his hand on hers, to cup all that mattered. 'Mind? Madness, you, but *bloody* marvellous! I'm rather glad you fell of that horse!'

She laughed. 'You're my new Bouncer. I shan't fall off you. Never, ever.'

They lay, side by side, quiet now, absorbing the strange sudden togetherness and that all pervading sense of mutual satisfaction. He could reach a hand and stroke the silk softness of her inner thigh, run it back to cup a breast, and feel her joy in his movement, a half turn to tighten that togetherness. Another long, ensnaring kiss, stroking her hair, feeling his return and this time his possession.

As he looked down, her hair spread across the pillows, breasts less prominent in their gravity flattened state, she looked totally wanton, still desirable, but time had run its course.

'*Three* times, Andrew? My, my. Does she not demand as much?' She was teasing him now, more confident in her custody of his feelings. He had to fall back alongside her and she straightened her legs. 'You'll make me pregnant.' That wasn't a tease; rather it was a bald statement of potential. 'You could, you know. You, me, getting physical. You got all the way, my lover.' She reached over and touched.

This was a totally new experience; Samantha used to roll out of bed and go straight into the shower, as if she couldn't bear to feel the loving around her. Roberta took his hand. He wasn't quite sure, Samantha never let him experiment on 'winding her up' as she put it, but this girl had no such inhibitions.

Finally she seemed to take deeper breaths and an even deeper sigh. 'Well done. That's me. God, but it's been a long time!' A meaningful, reflective pause, and the quiet and the comfort of the room and their togetherness enveloped them.

'Shower time, Andrew. Come on, I'll scrub your back!' Before he knew it, she had flung herself, all naked five foot four of her, off the bed, and was pulling him up. 'Bathroom – bet you've never seen one like it!' She opened the door to a dream. The large round tub was half sunken, the shower had a wall of glass, the room was carpeted like the bedroom, there were mirrors, the lighting hidden in the ceiling, and it was nicely warm. She dragged him into the shower and the strong jets of water coming from all directions took his breath away. True to her word, he just stood there and she made all the running, before turning her back on him and demanding her turn. It was sheer heaven, and after the ten minutes or so, he couldn't tell, they were laughing and towelling each other and kissing again.

'Roberta.' Her name-calling was like a gift. 'You know you're a witch? I thought you might be dangerous, but I didn't know *how* dangerous. I think I'm under your spell.' He was holding her again, kissing her again.

Those dark eyes were searching his face, with such softness and warmth in her look. 'You're good for me, Andrew. I know you are. Don't lose me?'

'I shan't lose you, Roberta. Keep yourself warm for me. So long as we don't hurt anyone.' It was an obvious statement, and a rashly inevitable one from the moment he had crossed the line from the correctness of skirt draped legs to being party to wanton nakedness. Samantha. Would she know? Feminine instinct? 'I'll have to go. I'd better be home before . . .'

She touched his lips with a finger. 'I know. I'll think of something, Andrew. This evening has been the best one ever. You knew, didn't you?'

'Seeing you sitting by the fire, asking for a brandy. Showing . . .' he paused. 'Yes, I suppose I did. And I should have walked out. But I couldn't, somehow.'

'You care, Andrew, that's why. And I have never had anyone who *cared* for me, before, not like you, even risking your marriage for me. I'm sorry if I've asked too much, but I'm not sorry you've loved me. It's made me believe I can get over all this mess, if I've got you around. Love me?'

That was a direct question, and standing, nakedly together after so much passionate coupling, copulation, it would have been easy to say 'Of course'. 'I love your body, Roberta. I love the way you talk, the way you move, the expressions on your face. You've done things to my manhood I never knew could happen. And I care for you, that's the important bit. Let's let the rest develop, shall we?'

She nodded. It was more than enough to be going on with.

She'd put a bath robe on, brushed her hair back, and rope sandaled, followed him downstairs to find the rest of his clothes. It seemed bizarre, dressing in the sitting room, watching her stoke up the fire that had died to mere embers whilst they had been upstairs. She'd turned on the wall lights, but dimmed, so the romance of the room was still there. He would always remember the picture of her, ensconced by the fire, feet under her, that skirt around her. Even if no more came of their quirky relationship, he'd remember how he had picked her up, cared for her, and now, how, oh how, they'd loved. He collected his jacket, looked at her.

'Go, Andrew. Just go. Else I'll cry, and you won't want to, and that wouldn't help. I'll be okay. Just go back to Samantha.'

She turned her back on him and poked at the fire. A log burst into flames, sparks flew and the reflection on her gave her an ethereal glow. When she turned round, he had gone, silently closing the door behind himself and leaving the euphoria of the hours alone.

* * *

He was home well before Samantha returned. He'd been gone, what, three hours? Three and a half, then. He wondered if she'd notice the change in him. Maybe the shower gel would have left its scent. He made himself a drink, settled down in front of the television, but his mind was anywhere but on the screen. Roberta, all of her, seemed to be filling his brain. Roberta, Roberta, Roberta. Idly, he wondered if she had been meant to have been a boy. And why him? Surely there were some other hot-blooded males in her life who would have gone running to her bed? Then he recalled her statement 'You'll make me pregnant!' and his mind did a cartwheel, making him feel dizzy. Pregnant? How old was she? Thirty - thirty-five? Well, it was certainly a possibility, he supposed. He'd never thought, had had no choice, and certainly not anticipated. She may have, though. She'd hadn't sounded at all concerned, so maybe *she'd* taken precautions. Unless that's what she wanted? The thought made him shiver, cold with sudden anxiety. He'd love another family, but at what cost? Retribution, disaster, recriminations, dire chaos. What would his two say? The one might say 'I never knew he had it in him!' And the other might disown him; she was almost as sanctimonious as her mother. Sad, really, he'd never really had their love, but then maybe he was to blame, not giving them the parental smothering that seemed so alien at the time. His coffee was cold, and pulling a face, he went into the kitchen, poured the dregs down the sink, and wished he were back in Roberta's bed. That sounded like her car.

Samantha opened the kitchen door, bringing the cold chill of the night in with her. 'Had a quiet evening, have you, dear?'

She put her bag of papers down alongside her desk. 'Anybody ring?' God, he'd forgotten to look at the answer machine. He had to bluff. 'Not that I heard. I've been dozing.'

'Boring evening then. Bit like mine. Really, this lot don't know what they're doing.' And she was away, giving him a debrief of the whole futile meeting. He pretended to be interested, asked her if she wanted a coffee or something in a gap in the flow, but she shook her head and carried on. 'I told them I was going, but it didn't make a blind bit of difference. Then I had to run old Mrs Elliot home. Sorry if I'm a bit late. I'm going up.' And with that she went, annoyingly switching the hall light off in passing so he had to grope around in the dark. By the time he'd been through the bathroom, she was all tucked up and ignored him as he slid in alongside her. How different two women could be, he thought, as he lay on his back and relived Roberta's frenzied pulsating demands. There was a snoring sound from his bedmate and he tried to make his mind a blank. Tomorrow would bring its own problems.

* * *

Roberta had curled up in front of her newly replenished log fire, opening her robe to the heat and warming her body again. Wouldn't it have just been glorious to have gone back to a man- present warmed bed again, had him desire her, ravish her, make her feel wanted? She massaged her legs, reliving the past hours. So the ex. had gone, tumbling off after another floozy, and her achy sort of sadness at his demise had been eclipsed, as she had unwittingly expunged his part in her life by taking Andrew to her bed. So long as she could keep him. Well, she'd damn well try. Tomorrow, what have I to do tomorrow? See the solicitors, I suppose. Check if the Will is still valid. God, what a mess she'd have if the house was no longer all hers? And she'd need to get those accounts right. Then it hit her. Andrew was an accountant! She'd ask him, and he could come here quite openly, and, and . . . She got quite excited. Think of it! He could check her figures. Figure! She laughed. Check her figure! He'd do that all right. She raked the fire together, put the guard up, picked up the brandy glasses and put them on the small table. Then, with a sudden decision, sloshed

some more brandy into a glass – his, hers, it didn't matter – and tossed it
back. The fire of it hit her throat, made her eyes water.

'Silly girl,' she said out loud, then giggled. 'I'd better not be starting a baby, at my age!' That more rational thought sobered her and she made a mental note to take a morning after pill.She had two or three left from before, and hoped they were still viable. Getting back to her bed, she lay on the top for a while, taking in all that had gone on earlier, delighting in her body's response, before finally pulling the covers over and falling into a dreamless sleep.

FOUR

The morning brought its awareness of uncertainties, as Andrew struggled into wakefulness yet again. Three times he'd woken during the night, gut wrenchingly mindful of his actions and what they would mean. Once he'd crept quietly to the toilet, desperate not to waken his snoring wife. He felt strange, down there, taut, achy, but then it could be expected, over indulgence after abstinence. Lying on his back, reliving the conversations and then the way she'd opened up to him, seeking, seeking what, absolution? The memory brought its own problems into hard reality and he'd had to wriggle around to relieve the tension. Finally he thought he might have managed three hours uninterrupted sleep, but now it was dawn, past, and his stomach demanded breakfast. Last night's brandy was sour in his mouth.

Carefully laying the covers back, he rolled silently off the bed, seeing Samantha's tousled mop all but buried in her pillow. She was still asleep, judging from the slow and stertorous breathing. He picked up his pile of clothes and tiptoed out of the room. He'd dress downstairs; get some coffee down him, maybe a slice or two of toast. The kitchen smelt of yesterday's cooking, some unwashed plates and pans still on the draining board. He should have cleared those up before she came home last night. He shivered, and dressed hurriedly, checking the boiler had gone on; wretched thing was always playing up; then set to to eliminate the debris. Washing up cauterised his mind, producing clean order out of chaos. He even scrubbed the sink clean, polished the top, finally dried and put away all the dishes. The toilet flush from upstairs heralded her waking and eventual descent to impinge on the quiet of the kitchen. The kettle had boiled, gone cool while he had cleared up, so he flicked the switch down once more, and the noise broke into that quiet. He tried to compose his thoughts; would she interrogate last night's events once more?

Outside, the morning had deteriorated into grey rain, chilled the early spring day and dampened scenery and spirits. Would that he was back in the cheery brightness and laughter of the Manor kitchen, fielding the curious glances from Mary and holding his arm over Roberta's shoulders while kissing her long neck and murmuring nice thoughts into delectable ears, then sitting with her to savour croissants and cherry jam, hot dark coffee, discuss mutual use of the day ahead, maybe to take her back to bed before dressing her, taking their time, quoting poetry at each other, listening to Rachmaninov. . .

'Andrew! I didn't hear you get up. Whatever time was that?' He almost jumped, and the room crashed back into solid familiarity, shadows of his reverie thinned and wisped away. The last echoes of Roberta's 'Love me?' dimmed out.

The sigh was tangible; he stood up and stretched. 'Oh, an hour ago. You were sleeping soundly; I didn't want to wake you. I've cleared up.' He didn't anticipate praise, nor was he disappointed. He watched her immediately busy herself, taking one bowl from the cupboard, reaching for her favourite cereal. No 'would you like?', nor 'shall we have breakfast together?' He tried – 'Do you want some coffee? Shall I make some toast?'

'No, I'll have coffee later. I'm due at the Day Centre at ten. Are you out this morning? There's the rubbish to put out, and we still haven't decided about a holiday. Maybe you can sort something out? So long as you check my diary. I shan't be back at lunchtime – I've got to see Joan about the W.I accounts.' She was munching away at her cereal, standing with her back to the window, her mind not really with him.

He rinsed his coffee mug under the tap, decided to have his toast later, once he had the house to himself again. 'Yes, I'm out this morning, an invite to discuss looking after more pubs in the Brewery chain. It seems they're happy with the way I got them out of a hole over the Thistle and Thorn accounts. It will be a nice steady job, that, if I can persuade them I'm worth the money. At least I'll get a proper lunch.'

That wasn't meant as a snub, or a criticism, just a plain statement of fact, and she shouldn't worry, seeing as she would be rabbitting away with Joan what's her name. Strange in a way; he'd never been asked to have anything to do with the W.I. accounts, despite his profession. Maybe it just hadn't occurred to them, or maybe it was too close to home. Prophet in his own country and all that. Not that he was particularly bothered as he was sure he wouldn't have been paid and any mistakes were sure to be laid at his door. Samantha snorted, turned her back on him and rinsed out her bowl. That made a change, he thought, instead of dumping it and leaving the remnant cereal to dry. She pulled a heap of washing out from the basket and stuffed it into the twin-tub, muttering something about rinse-aid as he beat a retreat to his office room. She rarely crossed the threshold so it had become rather a sanctum. Ten minutes later, just as he was into printing out a resume of what he thought Brewery accounts should look like, he heard the door slam and the little car's diesel rev up. When would she realise it didn't need foot flat down to take off? Silence descended, apart from the distant 'my toe hurts, betty, my toe' from the wood pigeons in the trees opposite. Leaning back in his chair, he stared at the screen. 'Looks good,' he said to himself. 'Will it impress?' He pulled the copy off the printer, studied it close to. 'Damn!' He noticed a spelling error, corrected it on the screen and reprinted the page.

As the printer's whirr subsided, the phone rang. 'Worthy Accountancy. How can I help you?' Standard format reply on this line, not the domestic phone plain 'Hello.' He tried to keep the business out of the rest of the house.

'Andrew?' His heart did a bounce.

'Roberta!'

'That's me-eee. On your own?'

'I am. How's things with you?'

'Not bad, considering the rough time I had last night.' There was mischief in her voice.

His brow creased. 'Rough time . . .?' then he twigged, and chuckled. 'I thought I was very considerate!'

'You were. Three times, as I recall; are you sore?'

'Roberta! Not the question a lady asks!'

There was a charming little giggle down the phone. 'Am I a lady?'

'In my eyes you are. A very charming, very lovely, very sexy lady.'

'Well, in that case . . . come and see your lady again. She's in desperate need of advice.'

'Roberta. I have to earn a living.'

'I know. That's why I'm asking. Come and see me.' The phone went dead.

'Damnation!' He swore, unusually and out loud. His Mistresses Voice! Well, he hadn't got time this morning, and goodness knows how long lunch would take at the Brewery. How would she take it if he didn't rush at her command? He shrugged. This time yesterday he would have consulted his diary, agreed a date and time. He would have been pleased to go, happy to see a charming woman and visit a lovely house. Today, no niceties, just a command, and he had to ask himself, was he pleased to go? The image of her, naked, her abandonment, then the remembrance of the feel of her, hard and soft, tantalised him and he squirmed in his chair to relieve the sudden pressure. 'Damn the girl!' Of course he'd go.

The Brewery offices were on the other side of town, alongside the strange miscellany of buildings that made up an elderly brewery. Sheds and structures housing the incomprehensible collection of tanks and vats and pipes that turned barley and hops and whatever else into beer or lager, a process that he didn't know much about; all he knew was that it was supposedly profitable. He often wondered about the possible dilution of life and talent that washed about on the tide of misuse that could flow around the innumerable pubs and clubs on the grubby High Streets Saturday night after Saturday night; the occasional inevitable struggle of yellow jacketed police with ill-dressed open shirted young men and barely clad girls with more sex than sense. All the potential criticism in him had to be bottled up if he were to succeed; at least he had no teenage daughters left to worry about. His car parked in the 'Visitors Only' bay, he squared his shoulders as he went up the steps to the heavy mahogany door with its brass fittings, pushed open to enter the Victorian hallway.

'Mr Hailsworthy! Thank you for coming. This way please.' The middle-aged lady had been waiting for him; that was a good sign. 'We haven't got a receptionist anymore.' Was he expected to query the obvious statement? He let it ride, following her ample plain costume clad figure down the green and cream corridor, past frosted half glassed doors variously labelled 'Accounts'; 'Production'; 'Premises', before reaching the one she'd opened ahead of him, no glass this time, just the cachet 'Board'. The mental picture of dark green carpet, mahogany desk or tables and dark-varnished pictures of long dead Chairmen didn't disappoint him.

A florid faced chap in a tweedy suit, yellowish grey receding hair, stood up from behind his desk, and repeated his gopher's comment. 'Mr Hailsworthy! Good of you to come! Take a seat. My Finance manager – Mr Skipton. Mrs Rollason you've met. She's our Office manager.'

Mr Skipton, a thin man in his late thirties, with a scared expression that looked permanent, did at least shake hands. Andrew began to wonder if he was on a time warp, mysteriously catapulted into the nineteen twenties. No wonder they had called for help. They sat, formally, round a separate table, on heavy chairs to match the rest, one on each side, as Mrs Rollason pushed a set of papers at him. 'Last year's Accounts, for our southerly tenanted houses. You'll see why we're a bit concerned.'

'Yes, yes, Ida, let Barry explain.' Andrew only knew the Chairman – his assumption – as Mr Howard by the letter of invitation. Introductions were evidently superfluous for a

Chairman. 'Ida' suited her, as 'Barry' did the young so-called Finance Manager. Was he the problem, or was it just endemic incompetence in this historic stage set of an outfit?

Barry did a quiet resume of the layout, explained the salient points, as Andrew took the figuring on board. Then the Chairman, in those fruity tones that so matched his features, leant back in his armed chair and pontificated. 'See the problem? Blasted tenants can't give us the gallonage we need! No point in kicking them out, takes ages to put new fellas in. Need some clever suggestions, d'see. Thought p'raps new eyes, eh, give us some clues. Barry here, does his best, but mebbe . . .'

Mrs Rollason intervened on Barry's behalf, in a matronly role. 'We have had the same accounts format for years, Mr Hailsworthy, very traditional, breweries; and perhaps the tenants don't feel rewarded for their efforts, so . . .'

'Quite, quite, Ida.' Howard needed to maintain his control. 'What d'say, Hailsworthy? Willing to have a look-see and give us a clue how to get things on the upturn? I don't mind telling we have a fight to maintain our independence now a days, and we don't want our beer going down the drain! Ha. Hah ha!' He was laughing at his own joke. Andrew smiled politely and reaching into his document case, produced his own accounts format, which, given his lack of briefing to date, just had to do. Pushing a copy across to each of them, he then sat back as they studied the three pages. It was difficult to imagine, having walked in off a twenty-first century street, that he was dealing with one of the town's notable businesses. Just as well he hadn't produced the laptop and a projector, given them a presentation some of his business rivals in major accountancy practices would have done. Maybe old fashioned was beautiful in their eyes, and his hand written notes on the 'Thistle & Thorn' accounts had done the trick.

'Hmmph.' Howard pushed the pages aside, as though he couldn't soil his hands with *figures*. 'Barry?'

'I think Mr Hailsworthy has given us a clear idea, Mr Howard. If we interpolate some of our own figures, and then do a projection, we may find our margins are too thin for our tenants, along the lines we may have considered. If I might suggest we let Mr Hailsworthy work on these, then assess what benefits may accrue?'

This Barry was not as dim as he might appear, thought Andrew. Maybe I'm home and dry. 'I would be able to produce some comparative balances for each tied house within a day or two, Mr Howard, and if you can let me have a feel for the current take on a week by week basis, maybe I can offer the projections on profit and margins as Mr Skipton suggests. I certainly would be keen to help keep the Brewery as an independent. I don't relish having to switch to a conglomerate brew myself.'

'Ah – you appreciate our efforts then?' Howard's face creased into a semblance of a smile.

'Indeed I do.' He waited. This was crunch time. He noticed Mrs Roberts give a sort of discreet nod. Was she the power behind the throne? Daringly, he smiled at her.

'Right. We'll give you the job, Hailsworthy. For a half year. Work out your fee with Mrs Rollason. Barry'll give you all the information he can; mebbe you'll want to talk to the tenants themselves, eh? Our area sales girl will give you the intro, just arrange things with Ida – Mrs Rollason.' The decision made, he became quite affable, pushing his chair back and going over to a panelled cupboard, opened it to reveal a well stocked bar. 'You'd like a snifter? Seal the pact, eh?' He produced a bottle, apparently whisky, and a collection of small glasses, adroitly holding them with a podgy finger in each one. There was no choice in the matter, and Andrew found himself toasting the Brewery's continued prosperity in a unique malt that Howard had pleasure in telling him 'came from the best distillery in Scotland, brewed and bottled on one site, y'now'. At least it was only a small glass, though indeed it was quality stuff. Maybe he'd get a bottle at Christmas; he could imagine the Brewery doing that sort of thing.

'You'll want to see round, Andrew?' So it was 'Andrew' now, was it? He must have passed the initiation test. Mrs

Rollason - 'Ida, please' - ushered him out of the presence. 'I'll get young Andrea to show you round. She's a cheeky madam, but she knows her stuff. Then you'll join us for a bite of lunch? She'll bring you back in time.' They had reached another of the glass-doored offices.

'Andrea? Mr Hailsworthy. Our new financial consultant. Give him the tour, please, and back to Mr Howard's office for half past twelve. I'll leave you with her, Andrew.' She turned on her well shod heels and departed for whatever sanctum she possessed. Andrea turned out to be a very well presented young lady, in a good jacket and skirt, neat blonde hair, a smile to charm and a figure to match. He'd put her at twenty, twenty two, and probably extremely competent. Quite what her role was he had to guess, unless she was the area sales girl Howard had mentioned. She shared the office with two others.

'Mr Hailsworthy. Your wife knows my mum. We hear a lot about you! I'm very pleased you are going to be able to help us. Barry's all right, but he has a job to get across to the boss. Would you like to leave your case here? It'll be safe enough. I'll get you a coat; it's a bit dusty in some places.' She opened a cupboard and pulled out two warehouse style buff coats, offered one to him and slipped into the other.

He wondered quite what it was she'd heard about him from 'her mum', but whatever it was it can't have been bad news. He left his document case sitting on a convenient chair and put on the coat. It was a bit of a tight fit, but better than nothing. The girl preceded him back down the corridor and out into the yard. She had a delightful sway on her, though the warehouse coat didn't do her any favours. Andrew found her utterly charming, confident, unassuming, and very knowledgeable; by the end of the tour, he would have cheerfully taken her on as a daughter of his own.

She led him back to her office, where she helped him out of his coat and handed him back his document case. 'Hope you enjoyed your tour, Mr Hailsworthy? Any time you want another look round just give me a ring, please?' It was if she was pleading with him. 'Now, if I can take you back to the boss's office?' He was sorry to lose her, but at least it wasn't as if she'd been the sole purpose of his visit.

Ida was waiting for him in the corridor. 'Andrea treated you well?'

'Superbly, thank you.' She'd smiled at him, a lovely deep smile, and gone. 'Lovely girl.'

He couldn't help it, and saw Mrs Rollason look sharply at him. Oh dear. He tried to soften his imprudent comment. 'Not all our youngsters have the same self-confidence, do they?'

'She certainly has that. Knows her stuff, too.' She opened the office door, ushered him in, to see the table laid out with a buffet, and inevitably, the bottles and glasses of the Brewery's best. It was a pleasant interlude, but he had to ration himself to a mere half pint. He had to get himself home – or rather, on to the Manor – without going over the limit. At least Howard had appreciated the point and gave him a bag with four bottles as a parting gift.

'Don't think we won't value any help you can give us, Hailsworthy.' He showed him out, shook his hand; though Andrew wasn't sure he liked his hand being swallowed in a big pastry.

Ida followed him down to the office front door, catching up on her commission to agree the fee. 'I'm sure whatever you charge will be well worth it, Andrew. Just send me an invoice, if I've any doubts I'll talk things over with you on the phone.' She winked at him, surprisingly. 'I'll tell Andrea you enjoyed her tour. My regards to your wife. Thank you again.'

What was it that made him appear as if he had an eye for the young girls, he wondered, and Mrs Rollason winking at him like that? Well, she probably was no saint either, with that rapport between her and Howard. Not that she was, well, anything special. No, Andrea was just a delightful young lady and a pleasure to be with; there was nothing untoward in that. It wasn't as though he 'fancied her' as that horrible expression went. Would that all girls of her age were as polite and well turned out, instead of slouching about in tatty jeans and scruffy hair, pretending they were grown up with excessive make up and cigarettes dangling from pieced lips. Yuck! Maybe he was just growing old. Well, not that old. He'd 'scored' with Roberta, using another detestable expression, though it wasn't anticipated, nor intended. It was just two human beings seeking solace in mutual need, as they had since time whenever. How was he going to reconcile that with Samantha and his relationship there? As he drove the half hour out to the Manor in answer to his summons, the question flitted back and forth. Would he abandon either girl? Could he keep Roberta happy and still stay effectively married and living with Samantha? How could he best inspire his wife to recover her old poise and vibrancy that he had originally fallen in love with, regain her looks and yes, damn it, sexiness? 'For better, for worse' – well, it wasn't getting any better, despite him doing his best to keep her happy. He swung into the Manor driveway, and pulled up on the gravel with a raunch of the tyres. She'd heard him and had the door open, stood waiting with eyes bright and a lift to her toes. Informal sweater top and a plain cross cut skirt, moulding well to her hips. It didn't seem like the one she'd worn last night – was it only last night? It could be, he couldn't remember. Half expecting her to fling her arms round him, he was braced to respond, but she took his hand and tugged him indoors, shut the big old heavy door with a push of her foot, *then* she folded herself round him, searching for a kiss.

'Andrew. Darling man. Hmmmm.' He found her lips intoxicating; her warmth a comfort; her scent, subtle, definitively her, a heady attack on the senses. After the weird morning it was like a prelude to heaven. Under her sweater his hold on her rose to her shoulder blades, finding straps, pushing the woollen thing up and baring her midriff. Hard up against him, she could feel his response to her, and loved it. For two pins she'd let him take her on the hall table, but sense had to prevail and she pushed him away, pulling her sweater back into place. 'I've missed you.' A hackneyed phrase, that, but true. 'Come.' Her command, leading the way with a coquettish swing of skirt and hair, took them into her sitting room. This is where it started, he thought, picturing her again on the rug in total disarray. This time she sat on the high window seat, back to the view, her face against the light. He couldn't join her, so stood by the table, watching her swing her legs, hands under her thighs, like a twenty year old, like an Andrea.

'You said you were in desperate need of advice.'

'I did. I am.'

'So?'

They were sparring with each other.

'I need to employ an accountant. I wondered if you could recommend one.'

'*An accountant?*'

'Yes, you know, someone to sort accounts out.'

Because she was against the light, he couldn't see her expression, but from the tone she was laughing at him.

'I know what I do. Haven't you got one already?'

'No.'

'You surprise me.'

'I thought I did. Will you?'

'Will I what?' Oh, no, he thought, she wouldn't, she couldn't!

'Be my Accountant. Come and inspect my figure-uress.' She giggled.

'Why me?' As if he didn't know, scheming little madam.

'Cos.'

She was still swinging her delicious legs. He was trying hard not to yield to the temptation to put her over his knee and spank her, just as he would have an errant child before the days when the State interfered in parents' God given right to bring up their own children. Just as he moved towards her, she slid off her perch and ducked under his outstretched arm.

'I'm going to make us some tea. Think about it.' She waltzed out of the room and slammed the door behind her. This was a different side to the girl, seeing her being mischievous like a gamin fourteen year old. Mary mustn't be about either, so he was on his own with her, dangerously so. He walked round the room, taking in the essence of her again, reading the book titles once more, seeing the eclectic array of bottles in the drinks cabinet, sticking his nose into the new bowl of hyacinths, this time some pale pink ones that scented beautifully. Outside the afternoon was wearing on, and the grey of impending rain was darkening the garden, hiding the shrubs in gloom. An erratic flight of birds – pigeons most likely – scurried across the sky. He'd come to a stand still, looking out over the deserted countryside, the empty lawn, and wondered what he was doing here, at the beck and call of this impossible female. Time ticked on, measured in the slow beat of the wall clock, and still no tea. Where was the girl?

Eventually he had to go in search of her, for he couldn't risk not being back home after Samantha. She would expect him to be in the home office, as was his wont after a client consultation. There was no sign of her in the kitchen, apart from the tea tray made ready and a steaming kettle on the Aga.

'Roberta!' He called, loudly. '*Roberta!*'

'Up stairs, darling!' A faint answer, as though she was miles away. With some trepidation, he followed the voice. The bedroom – *the* bedroom – door was open, but no sign of her there, thank goodness. Where then?

'Row-BERTA!'

'Here.' The voice came from the end of the corridor. He pushed open a half closed door, to discover a sort of box room unshown during the whirlwind tour he and Samantha had had those weeks ago. She was on her knees, grovelling amongst some old boxes of papers, looked up as he entered and then back to the pile. 'I'm sure I had some old balance sheets up here. Sorry, darling, I got carried away.' Scrambling to her feet, she dusted off her skirt and shook out her hair. 'Let's go and have that tea. Did you think I was all stripped off and ready for you?' Another mischievous grin. 'Sorry if I disappointed you. I think I'm over that particular hill. Come on.' She pushed past him, ducked again as he made to kiss her, laughed and ran down the passage. He closed the door on the rubbish and followed her down into the kitchen.

'You can carry the tray in. I'll find some biscuits or something.'

Once ensconced in the sitting room again, she became the proper hostess, asked about sugar and milk, offered the biscuit plate and then relaxed back into her chair. No crossed legs, no tantalising glimpses of thigh. The earlier rush of passionate embrace seemed a dream.

'Have I offended you, Roberta? What do you mean, over that particular hill?'

With a flick of eyebrows, and a quizzical look, as if to say 'none of your business', she settled back still further and sipped her tea. It was if he'd never been her lover, but merely a business guest, which in truth, he was. 'Well, Andrew? Will you be my accountant? Sort out my finances; help me plan for life as a widowed divorcee? At the going rate?'

Of course he would, he'd not dream of doing otherwise, not for this girl.

'Then that's settled. Come and look at that heap of rubbish and sort it all out for me. Come to London and see what happens there. You can have one of the back rooms for an office here, if you like. I'll rent it to you, to offset your charges!' Again, there was humour in her voice, and he relaxed a little. 'You do have time for me, don't you?'

'You know I do.' There was a push me, pull you aspect to this conversation, leading him on, then shoving him back. At least it wasn't going to be all sex for the sake of it, thank goodness.

'Okay.' They lapsed into silence; Andrew finished off another biscuit and emptied his cup. He poured himself another, as she eyed him from her chair. This was going to be fun, she knew it was, and her whole being suddenly sizzled with anticipation. 'Would you have made love to me, Andrew?'

Startled, he nearly dropped his cup. Now where was she going, in all this? 'Should I have?'

'Hmm mmm. I'd sent Mary home, didn't you notice?'

'Could have been her day off.'

'True.' No, she wasn't going to rush things. 'Never mind. I can wait.' Which wasn't strictly true, but she had the promise of him being about quite a lot in the future, and she wasn't one for rushing her fences. She laughed, almost to herself, and then giggled at the look on his face. 'Oh Andrew, dear, I do love your expressions. You know I've fallen for you, don't you?'

'Silly girl.'

'Yes, I know. I'll try and be good, sometimes.' She giggled again, got up from her chair, did a twirl and then flounced down onto his knees, slung an arm round his neck and sought for a proper smoochy kiss. Tempted, his hand found her skirt hem and slid upwards. Nearly, but not quite, before her free hand caught his and stopped him going any further. She just held him where he was, so he felt the warmth and softness of her, soaking up the deliciousness of contact.

A murmur in his ear. 'Don't rush your fences, Andrew. That's what I laughed about. We don't want to fall off, do we?' Another kiss, then she de-clutched and he was bereft of his comfortable handful. 'Hadn't you better go?' Struggling back to reality and the awareness of the deepening darkness of the room that heralded a wet evening, he got up. She stood close to him, put up her face for another kiss, and reaching to hold a hand, placed it over a breast. 'Feel me, Andrew. Take the feel home with you.'

It was as much as he could do, to tear himself away, but it had to be. The heavy door shutting behind him sounded like a cannon shot at a distance. The onset of a battle, between reality and dream emotions.

No, he didn't want to drop back into the tedium, fighting to retain his sanity, or more to the point, his husbandly position. It was if the sun had peeped out from between these sodden wet clouds that heralded a soaking, flashed up his spirits, woken latent senses, then disappeared to leave him doubly disappointed. Grey, grey, all grey. Nothing but hard decisions, to keep a semblance of normality and work at the increasing business and hold Roberta at bay, or was he to come clean, declare how much he'd been tempted by the girl, confront Samantha with an ultimatum, risk wrecking everything, and all because of a wretched horse shying at some rubbish polythene bag? He sat in the car, hands on the wheel, staring at the driveway, for what seemed like a whole bloody hour, before starting the engine, crawling away to hide himself away in the office, to idly construct a new client profile. Not a Brewery, not a comment on the hidden wasted talents neither of a Barry or an Andrea, nor on the superfluous Howard and organising Ida, but on a London based Interior Design business, with a Principal who would stir the imagination of any red blooded bloke. He tapped away on the keys, the words flowing, the paragraphs filling the page, before hesitation over stupid spelling brought him up sharply, and he re-read his text. God, what *was* he doing?

> *'Roberta Smiley is the sole owner of a London based Interior Design Company, a delightful young woman who has a strong desire to succeed in this extremely competitive business. She has a strong personality that becomes very evident when one becomes closely involved with the lovely lady. Her sense of humour and her wonderful figure provide great incentive to the desire to spend more time in her company which may mean that her business acumen is sharper than that for which one could originally give credit.*
>
> *Though the circumstances surrounding her interest in seeking a local Accountancy service are entirely circumstantial, her subsequent actions involving the Principal have meant that there is a tie that may prove extremely difficult to disconnect shuld nessecity arise.*
>
> *There will an inevitable desire to wish this charming girl every success, especially so after the stultifying life she must have led whilst married to a man whose only wish was to dominate and gratify selfish needs. The country home that occupies most of her time and finances is probably her greatest asset, other than her looks, and should be preserved if at all possible. Maybe the London business should be re-located, so that . . . '*

Well, that was all true, but not what he would have written ordinarily, not about a client, the words *'delightful'*, *'lovely'*, '*wonderful figure*' and maybe even '*charming*' - he did use adjectives, yes, but - damn it, why shouldn't he tell the truth? So long as he didn't add '*sexy*', '*provocative*', '*wanton*', then it would just about pass muster. But who was going to read it anyway? It was only his accustomed practice to put background notes into the file, and maybe it would be the only reminder of an incredible episode. The girl had him all at sixes and sevens and there was a sneaking feeling at the back of his mind she might well be stringing him along, after she'd apparently satisfied her immediate wants. He'd just been vulnerable, that's all. Drat the girl. But those images of her wouldn't go away; try as he might, he couldn't just slam the door shut, forget all about her. He leant back in his chair, hands behind his head, watched the computer screen dissolve into the blue sky then images of *her*.

Two days later, after he'd had a very successful meeting with the Brewery's property man and been taken to be introduced to three of the 'irksome' – not his description – tenants, he had the bones of a good provisional re-draft of their trading terms, and could see it was looking good.

He couldn't neglect his other established clients, though, and on Thursday morning was resigned to a solid morning behind the desk, finalising two sets of quarterly returns and another provisional balance sheet for his first original client, an old friend of his who did a lot of small building work around the village. He'd almost forgotten about Roberta, having dropped back into his old self-protectionist routine with Samantha, despite her building up steam over his failure to book a holiday. Somehow, he just couldn't work up much enthusiasm about two solid weeks in her company if all she wanted to do was mooch around and carp on about the standards of catering in the hotel. He liked to walk, meaningful walks covering lots of ground, but she had no interest in scenery whatsoever. Now she was out of the house until mid-afternoon again, doing her monthly stint at the old folks' home. Then the phone rang to interrupt his reverie. He'd meant to get one of those caller display things, so he could vet the caller and choose whether to answer or not. So many people seemed to assume they had a right to use *your* phone to interrupt *your* day to try and sell some totally unwanted product or service. Perhaps he ought to get an 0870 number so they at least had to pay him something for the privilege.

'Worthy Accounts.'

'Andrew? It's Roberta.' Of course, he recognised her voice, and waited. 'You're not cross with me, are you?'

'No. Why should I be cross with you?'

'You were ages in the car, in the drive. You haven't phoned.' He still waited, not replying. 'Andrew. I'm not playing games. I do need an accountant. I don't want to employ just anyone. Please, Andrew. It will work, you know. If you don't want me, that's . . . ' Was that a sob? 'I just want you around, Andrew. Please?'

He sighed. 'Roberta, I haven't made up my mind. I'm sorry I haven't been back to you before now, but I've had a lot to do on the Brewery contract, bit preoccupied on that. I'm sorry,' he repeated, then relented, for she sounded a bit down, and having gone so far with her, he couldn't back off, not now. 'Look, maybe I ought to spend a couple of hours with you working out exactly what you need. Would you like to have lunch with me? Then we'll thrash out some detail? How does that sound? If you can spare the time, that is?' He waited, listening to the silence that was her thinking. There was a high level of tension in this conversation, which sent sudden shivers down his spine and into the back of his scalp, a weird feeling.

'I'd love to have lunch with you, Andrew, if it won't compromise you. The last thing I want do is to make life awkward for either of us. Don't think you just have to be nice to me because we . . . ' It was very much as though she didn't know how to say they had made love in such extreme circumstances, or was it because she found it embarrassing that they had? Then came the decider, softly spoken. 'Andrew, I might not be able to go on without someone to talk to.'

'You're stronger than that, Roberta. Meet me in the Royal

George, lounge bar, in say . . .' he looked at his watch, 'three quarters of an hour? Look pretty.' He dropped the phone back on the pad and wiped his forehead, wondering what exactly he was doing with this girl. He didn't even know quite why he'd been so blunt and forceful over the timing, whether or not she would turn up. Staring at the screen, the almost finished balance sheet, he tried to get his concentration back on line, get this wretched thing finalised. 'Damn the girl,' he said, out loud, 'why did I ever take her to bed?' He leant back in his chair, saw the mistake, swore again, and dealt with it, finished the column, cross checked, let the spread sheet programme do its thing, saved it and exited the screen. 'Why did I, why, why, why?' he asked himself. 'Because she was vulnerable? Because she was – sexy – or was it because I just felt for her? Did she *seduce* me? Or was it because there's something missing from my life that *I* needed – was I being selfish?' Questions, questions, no bloody answers. Well, I might just as well take her up on the offer of sorting her accounts, see what materialises. 'Be professional', he told himself, talking to the now silent computer.

The car park at the George was more than half empty, not surprising for a Thursday, and he couldn't see a car that could be hers. The lounge bar didn't evince a Roberta, either. Maybe she just wouldn't respond to a truncated phone call and a virtual command. He bought himself a half, as a stopgap, and checked there was a table in the dining area. At least he'd get a lunch on expenses, provided she turned up. A casual search round the less than a dozen people in the bar area didn't elicit any familiar faces, thank the Lord. Not that he should have qualms of conscience if she was seen with him, it was all above board, but, as he reminded himself, what the eye don't see, the heart – damnation, whose heart? Samantha's?

The armchairs in the bar area were all covered in that atypical red velvet sort of material, stained, worn and dusty in the crevices, the carpet pattern incomprehensible and the wallpaper yellowed and stained. What a grubby place this was, why had he suggested here, off the top of his head; suggested

59

that Roberta, the interior designer Roberta, should meet him here? Perhaps she wouldn't come here anyway, because it was run down, or maybe she doesn't know it as run down, has never been here? The beer was a touch warm and went well with the décor, the glass on its ancient beer mat blended with the rest of the stains on the worn table. The saving grace was the restaurant's good reputation, though, which was what mattered. Would she come? He'd give her another ten minutes, and no, he couldn't stand another beer. He crossed his legs, sat back and watched the byplay around; the business meeting in the corner, the elderly couple on a day out, the three scruffy young men who could be contractors, the solitary rather tarted-up woman leaning up on the bar and looking hungry – for what was anyone's guess – and here he was, on a sort of assignation. Was this an *affaire* or the start – continuation – of one? Briefly he considered where Samantha was and if she ever thought of what he was doing for lunch. That was a laugh, or it would be if it weren't so pitifully sad. No, he was entitled to a bit of pleasure in an otherwise humdrum life. He hoped, against hope, that she *would* come, that she wouldn't be long. Another couple came in through those sticking grubby doors. Really, the establishment should pick itself up and realise it was going to the dogs; just as well it wasn't part of his remit, at least, not yet.

Then she came, through those tatty doors, and suddenly the place didn't seem so bad, for she was smiling at him, in that mischievous gamin sort of way, and he rose out of his chair to reach for her hands, gently pull her to him and offer a chaste kiss on her cheek that seemed so appropriate. She had a smart, well-cut little mustard coloured jacket over a swirly flowered silk dress, a strangely patterned leather belt pulling in to her slender waist, and looked lovely.

'I came, Andrew.'

'So you did.' Their eyes met and held. He noticed, perhaps for the first time, those amber flecks in the mid brown iris, how clear they were, but what depth of mystery? 'You look lovely, Roberta. Thank you for coming. Brightened up my day.'

'Really? You told me to look pretty. Am I pretty enough for you? Not spoiling your preoccupation? Making life too complicated?'

He had to smile again 'Roberta, you complicated my life when you fell off that horse, but at least I can say you didn't plan to – did you?'

Her turn to laugh. 'No, I *did* not! Just say the fates conspired. You, where you were, that stupid bit of plastic.' Still holding hands, she turned to look around, and wrinkled her nose. 'This the best you could do, Andrew? It's a bit, er, seedy. Not ideal for a romantic lunch, is it?'

'Spur of the moment, R. Not designed as a *romantic* lunch, was it? I think it needs a woman's touch. A *particular woman's* touch. The restaurant's okay, though. Hungry?'

She nodded, let go his hands, and then said 'R, Andrew? You called me R? No-one's called me that since I was a little girl; my father called me that.'

'You don't mind?' he replied, quickly.

She shook her head, and her long dark hair bounced in a fascinating way. 'No, Andrew, I don't.' The tenor of her reply seemed rather profound, there was silence between them for an equally profound moment, before she broke the spell. 'You mentioned lunch?'

He laughed at her. 'That hungry? Then we'll eat. Oh – would you like a drink?'

'I thought you'd never ask. Tomato juice, no ice, a dash of sauce. Big one!'

He moved over to the bar, decided to join her, ordered two, and then beckoned her towards the entrance to the restaurant. Seated, in a corner by the window, with fresh white tablecloth, a small vase of what looked like freesias, and a clean menu, and her subtle scent, life became a lot, lot brighter. Only three other tables were occupied, and, thankfully, still no one he recognised.

'I want to . . . 'he began, just as she started to talk.

'Have you . . . ?' They both grinned at each other.

'You say.' Andrew deferred to her.

'Have you decided? To look after my figure –ss.' There was

that mischievous look again. 'I want you . . . to, so much, Andrew. It would . . . mean . . . a lot to me.' The pauses were palpable.

'Do I understand you, Roberta? I might be *very* expensive. There's a strong risk factor you recognize, don't you?'

She looked down at her tablemat, as though seeking inspiration, before he saw her eyes lift towards him. 'I realise that. I've thought about – us. You'd be very good for me. I suppose I'm really rather selfish, but I've missed you, Andrew. Since *he* died, and that evening you rescued me, I've missed you. Bloody silly, isn't it?'

He still couldn't quite accept the swearing, that schizophrenic side of her, so much a demure girl but with brash undertones. 'New name for it, R, 'rescuing.' I thought it would be more like 'hazarding'.'

They were still sparring with other as the waitress came for an order, a pretty little thing with nice legs under that badly made uniform dress. 'I'll have prawn cocktail, then the lamb, please.' Roberta was decisive; Andrew hesitated, then went for the same starter and the beef.

'Any wine, Roberta?'

'Not at lunch, Andrew, thank you. A nice jug of water will do fine.' The girl gave a lovely smile at them both and Andrew watched her hips sway as she headed for the kitchen. 'Like her legs, do you? She's pretty, but a little young for you!'

He found a leg under the table, and nudged it. 'Is it that obvious, R?'

That grin was still mischievous. 'I don't blame you, Andrew. Life's too short not to appreciate the finer things, is it? I've got nice legs too, you know. *And* you've seen them. All of them.'

This was getting them nowhere in particular, but the *frisson* of innuendo was exhilarating.

He took the plunge, suddenly reckless, or was it abandonment? 'Can I see them again, sometime? All of them?'

It caught her off balance, but just for a second. 'If.'

'If what?'

'You take up the job offer. *Then* you can.'

'Done. When do I start?'

Her smile deepened, and with her head coquettishly on one side, there was the merest whisper 'This afternoon?' He felt a shoeless toe against his leg, moving up.

'Hey. The girl is coming back.' The toe went. 'Sure?'

'Very. If you can spare the time, Mr Hailsworthy. I have all the papers ready for you, and last year's accounts.' The girl would hear all she said, as the prawn cocktails were set down. They did actually look very well put together, with a good proportion of prawns vis-à-vis lettuce and pink mayonnaise, and a sprinkling of cayenne. The jug of water, iced with lemon, came with two chilled glasses. The restaurant manager knew his stuff.

Andrew glanced at his watch. Two o'clock. Samantha would expect him back home by five, if she got back first. Another hour, outside, here, so, three-ish back at the Manor. Just under two hours. Hmmm. There was nothing else pressing, but he would have to concentrate tomorrow.

'That would be fine, Mrs Smiley. I shall be glad to be of service.' The waitress girl, still hovering, asked if 'everything was all right?' and heard his reply to Roberta, got a smile and a nod from him, returned her smile, and went. Roberta concentrated on her prawns, looking quite smug. She'd accomplished what she'd set out to do, and felt a tiny, tiny, little shiver of anticipation running round the small of her back.

* * *

After he had left her, she lay stretched out on her bed, happily drowsy with a glorious afterglow percolating through all her being. Never, ever, had she had these sorts of feelings after that man had had her; it had always been for him, banging away at her as though she was a sort of horizontal punch bag. Andrew was so different, careful, gentle, teasing her, stroking her so temptingly that she just had to react beautifully. Even now, and he'd been gone half an hour, she knew she could welcome him again. With one hand feeling her softness, her scrunchy little mound, she dreamt, and dozed.

* * *

'Andrew? You're late back? I thought you were behind the desk today!' Samantha was putting a meal together, surprisingly.

'I had a call. Mrs Smiley, at the Manor, wants me to sort out her accounts and advise on the profitability of her business. I thought I'd better see what was involved; it could be a good account to have.' He didn't feel too bad, considering. He needed a shower, not having risked staying on at the Manor. He reminded himself, he'd have to ensure his brand of shower gel was on the shelf in *her* bathroom.

'What's happening over at her place now that her former husband's killed himself?' She was putting out the knives and forks on the kitchen table and he nearly said he wasn't hungry, after that superb beef casserole at the George. 'I would have thought that place was too big for her, and with a business in London, surely she'd go back there?'

Andrew was surprised, pleasantly surprised, at the interest. 'She's a country girl at heart. She's more likely to sell out in London and concentrate her business here. It's easy enough to travel back into town to see her clients as and when, and it would save on her overheads. We still don't know how she stands on the ownership of the Manor yet, as hubby kept it in joint names for some quirky tax reason – so it's all a bit complicated. Luckily her solicitor girl – you know, the one we met at the dinner party – has it under control, hopefully. What's for dinner?'

'Beef casserole. Your favourite.'

* * *

Waking up, feeling decidedly chilly, with goose pimples on sticky thighs, she rolled off the bed and padded into the shower. Under the streaming water, hair carefully tucked away in that dreadfully un-sexy shower cap, she sluiced the vestiges of the afternoon's passion away, and idly wondered just what it would take to get herself pregnant. Should she, would she – could she? He would, she was sure. He got there, she'd felt him, all of him, and it was bloody eff-ing marvellous.

* * *

He was replete, more than replete, and it had been as good, if not better than the George, and again, nearly said so. Samantha was looking at him quite happily, as though she was working up to something. 'Would you like a sweet?'

Goodness, what ever has come over her? Andrew couldn't face another thing. He opted for a coffee, and took it into the lounge. Time for the telly. She followed him in, with her decaff.

'You haven't asked me about my day, Andrew.'

'Sorry. How was your day?'

'Well, I met Andrea's mother. She was telling me how much her daughter admired your approach. She's apparently a very clever girl, and knows a lot about what goes on, including, would you believe, that there's talk about the Office Manager woman having an affaire with Mr Howard, silly woman. You must have made an impression.' She sunk into her armchair. 'Was Andrea interesting?'

Leading question, he thought. Well, she could make a useful red herring. 'Hmm, well, she fills her skirts well, if that's what you mean,' unwittingly he'd borrowed Martin's expression. 'Quite nice to look at, and certainly a pleasant person to get on with. Why?'

A glimmer of a smile, heavens, as she sipped her mug. 'Your cup of tea?'

'Samantha! As if!' Whatever was the woman leading up to?

'Well, I know I haven't been too, er, accommodating lately. Time of life, you know. I'm sorry; it's just the way of things. Do you miss me?'

Well, this was a turn up for the books. 'I miss the times we used to have, Sam.' She wanted the truth, then so be it. 'You've been more than a bit distant of late. I sometimes feel I don't exist. Sorry, but you did ask.'

There was a silence, as Andrew took a couple of swallows. Samantha put her mug down on the carpet alongside her and seemed to go into a trance. Andrew reached for the television remote, but she put out a hand. 'If you need to look elsewhere, Andrew, I'd understand, provided you were careful. And discreet. And it didn't affect *us*. I'm still your wife, you know, even if I can't feel I can express those feelings in the same way.'

'You want me to have an *affaire*? To make up for not making love to you? That's not very chapel, is it?'

She shook her head. 'Chapel's not where you make love, Andrew, only where you declare it.' Then: 'If you want to – if you can find a girl who doesn't mind a middle aged bloke!' There was a chuckle, and he wasn't sure whether she found the idea of *him* pulling – dreadful expression – or whether the whole idea of him having an ex-marital relationship was funny.

'If I did, er, find a girl, would you want to know?'

'Oh yes, all the sordid details. You never know, it might turn me on again.'

Now, there was an opportunity, if there was ever going to be one, to describe what wonderfully interesting concepts he and Roberta had managed to come up with. But no, what went on between them was precious, even if it –possibly – would be condoned. At least it wasn't going to be as dangerous as he thought, or so it seemed. 'You mentioned Andrea. You think she's a candidate then?'

'Oh, yes, from what her mother said, she thinks you're really sexy. Mind you, her mother wasn't to know I'd tell you, and I doubt she'd approve of her daughter having a fling with a married man, not at all.' Samantha was now really smiling, and he recognised the flirty girl of old.

'I still love you, Sam, especially when you smile. If I did find another girl, you know it wouldn't mean anything?'

She nodded. 'Not while I know you would if I wanted you to. Like now.'

Goodness, he thought. Two women in the same day?

* * *

Now she was warm again, and still with that lovely glowey feeling, she went back downstairs, totally and happily naked, back to the slumbering fire in her sitting room. Curling up in the same way when she'd first seduced him, she again allowed her thoughts to wander. What if she got him to make her pregnant then? Would he

divorce Samantha, marry her; become the father to the child –
children – she craved? Or would it all go pear shaped? Did she really
want a few months of hell, carrying a baby, and then be saddled with
all the responsibilities of parenthood? Could she afford it? She could
ask her accountant, couldn't she, and laughed out loud.

* * *

Samantha lay still, with her husband's rather comforting hand resting over her damp and somewhat sweaty passion place. Her nipples were a trifle sore, but then that was only to be expected. Andrew was fast asleep, so she was reluctant to stir. It had actually been rather good, if somewhat prolonged; she'd taken quite a pounding before he finally came. Maybe he was out of practice, she thought. Why she didn't feel this way more often was a bit disappointing. Maybe she'd have to give something up, spend more time at home, doing wifely things again, if her other exciting new project didn't come to anything. Then he wouldn't need to flirt with another girl, how disappointing for Andrea, but then if she was successful . . . She smiled inwardly, and allowed herself to fall asleep.

FIVE

'Wake up! Miss Roberta! It's gone nine o'clock!' Mary, with chilled orange juice glass in her other hand, gently shook her protégé. What ever had she been doing to stay asleep so long? Normally she'd be up and about long before this. The girl hadn't even got a nightie on! She'd hadn't had a man here, had she? If she had, well, no bad thing, but he'd better be a good one.

Roberta stirred, coming out of a peculiar dream.

Children playing, the sunlight streaming across the lawn, a handsome man coming towards her, taking hold of her, shaking her . . .

'Mary! What time did you say? Oh, sorry, I should have been up ages ago!' She swung naked limbs out and realised. 'Ooops! Where did I leave my nightdress?'

Mary tactfully looked away, not that she wasn't used to seeing her girl *au naturel*.

'Here, Roberta, still folded up.' The girl had either been gallivanting about nude, or it must have been warmer than she thought last night.

'Oh well. Thanks, I'll be down shortly. Can we get started on the document room today, Mary? I've got organised with an accountant.'

'If you wish. I've still got the ironing to do, but I can always take that home.'

'No way, Mary! I'm not having you working at home – you do more than enough, as it is, bless you. I don't know what I'd do without you.'

'Well, Miss Roberta, I'd not leave you, and that's a fact. Not unless you gives me the sack!'

'Unlikely.' *Mary was part of her life.* 'Tell me, Mary, what do you think to Mr Hailsworthy?'

After a pause, and the thought, so *he's* the chap, she said what she knew her girl would want to hear, and in truth. 'He's a gentleman, Roberta. Very pleasant sort of a chap. Reckon he's been good for you. Pity he's married.' *So she did know. Well, not surprising, really.* 'You will take care, won't you? He's got a lovely wife, other than she's let herself go a bit. Shouldn't like things to go wrong, like.' A gentle warning from her precious Mary.

She stood up and stretched. Mary eyed her, a trifle envious though proud of her girl's younger, taut yet curvy figure and the fulsome bust. 'You're a mite too tempting, even if I says so. Shame the other one didn't appreciate what you had on offer.' She sniffed, and left the room, closing the door behind her with a bit less than her usual quietness.

Roberta grinned at her departing housekeeper. If only she knew, well perhaps she did, who cared, she was the natural soul of discretion. She enjoyed her dressing, taking care over selecting her clothes, watching herself in the long mirror, and finally spent longer than usual brushing her hair till it shone. Going on down to breakfast she was in a good mood and started to whistle, a habit she'd brought with her from early school days that the former husband had really hated, he said it was so unladylike. Him – at the time he'd divorced her he'd forgotten what ladies were. Other, cruder definitions of the female, maybe he was more familiar with. Now Andrew – he really knew how to treat a lady, yes sir!

Mary looked up from the stove. 'It's nice to hear you whistling again, Miss Roberta. Is it the company you've had lately?'

'Uh huh. Just to let you know, he's coming to sort out the books for me, and maybe, just maybe, he'll use that back room as an office. A tame Accountant. And if Marjorie can unravel the problems over the late unlamented's Will, we may begin to see daylight.' She parked herself on one of the kitchen stools. 'Should I bring my London business here, Mary?'

'Not for me to say, Roberta, but if it saves you the hassle of the journey, then it must be worth it, provided there's no loss of clients. Some likes the London address, you knows.'

'True. But it would save me a lot of money, and there's space enough to have plenty of samples about. Who knows, it may bring *more* clients if this place offers country charm.' She reflected, head on her hands, elbows on the table. 'What if we went into bed and breakfast, Mary? Ran a sort of design school here – weekends in the country? Used the spare rooms? And I've got the barn and the stables, too.' She jumped up in a fit of inspired enthusiasm, did a sort of spin round and Mary was treated to what looked like a teenager's expression of joy. 'Yes! Yes! I must ask Andrew!' She would have impetuously rung him then and there, but Mary put out a restraining arm.

'*Miss* Roberta. It's not that I don't want to stifle any ideas, but shall us just think things through a mite? Have your breakfast, now, and let the idea simmer, there's a good girl. There's some of your favourite streaky bacon, look, and fresh grilled tomatoes. Scrambled egg as you like it as well – so just you sits down again. Here.' She put the laden plate down on the placed tablemat, poured out a mug of freshly brewed coffee.

'Oh, Mary! I shall put on more weight if you continue to feed me good breakfasts.' Roberta plonked herself back on the stool, and started to tuck into the plateful. True, she had put on a bit of weight, though still within her limits, and if she were going to work the day through sorting the debris in the box room she'd likely not have any lunch.

* * *

Andrew hadn't had the advantage of a Mary to cook his breakfast, but Samantha had gone out of her way to ensure he at least had the fresh brewed coffee. And she was still smiling this morning, so her rare night of womanly enthusiasm hadn't quite worn off. Today he *must* do some more work on the Brewery figures and get them over to the Offices so the tenants could have them before the end of the month. He'd see that Andrea girl, and try and avoid Mrs Rollason if he could. He'd best not give her the glad eye, though, else who knows what would happen. It wasn't as if he intentionally set out to do so.

'How's your day planned, darling?' He didn't always ask, for most often he just got told.

'I thought I might change the bed and vacuum through. I've nothing organised.'

Good Lord, he thought, I don't believe it. 'Then I might ring the children. See if June and William can come over for a meal sometime during Easter. Peter might come down from Durham? It would be nice to have them all here, wouldn't it?'

Another turn up for the books; she hadn't gone out of her way to invite June over since their daughter had made scathing remarks over Samantha's increasing weight and the way she'd let her figure go. Andrew had privately agreed with June, but couldn't have gone public otherwise his life would have been even more unbearable. So if June was out of the dog-box, what other miracles might occur?

'Well, if you think they'd come, fine. Always assuming they aren't skiving off to Spain or somewhere. And Peter'll always come for a free meal, knowing him, provided he can doss down here for at least three days!' He was under no apprehensions about their younger son, who glided from one freebie opportunity to the next with uncanny ease. June he had some conscience over, aware he should have behaved more like a father towards her when she was still a trendy teenager, so he would welcome any opportunity to try and redress that omission. William he could just about tolerate, but then maybe that was because he happened to be a whiz kid on computers.

Samantha beamed at him. She *did* have a lovely smile when she tried. En-route for the office, he put an arm round her waist, and pecked her cheek. She inclined her head towards him, rested a moment, and then pulled away. Nothing was said, but he felt a wee bit closer to her than he had for a long time.

Later that morning he rang the Brewery, the direct dial to Andrea's phone, and heard her pleasant very girly accent. She recognised his voice, and did he just imagine a change in tenor?

'Nice of you to call, Andrew. How can I help?'

'I've some completed tenants' projections and wondered if I should drop by with them?'

'If it's convenient for you, then I'm sure we'd be pleased to have them, Andrew. Would you care for lunch, if that's about your timing? Mrs Rollason has given instructions to us to look after you. I'm free about one. We can go to the Jam Butty Bistro – we've an account there.' Her chuckle came down the line as quite melodic and inviting. Well now, that's an invitation that sounds tempting, he thought, and said so. Another pleasant laugh. 'Then I'll see you later. Please park in the office spare space – I'll look out for you.'

When he explained he'd be out for lunch to Samantha, and where he was going and with whom, she raised an eyebrow, and *grinned!* This was unnerving, and he wondered if he was being set up.

The Jam Butty Bistro hadn't been going all that long, but it had established a fair reputation for innovative menus. Not pricey, and a very pleasant bunch of lads ran it well. He had parked as instructed, and true enough, Andrea was waiting, looking very spick, span and assured. How old was the girl? He'd put her at twenty two or so the last time, but today she seemed more like a twenty-five year old, so confident and lovely with it, beautifully dressed in a different lightweight costume than when he'd been before. She had put her hand in his arm as they crossed the road to the Bistro, and the smile was utterly charming. This was a business lunch with a difference. When he inadvertently commented that he was glad she was lunching and not Mrs Rollason he was treated to another girlish chuckle, and maybe, unless he imagined it, a slight blush. She was a lovely lunch companion, no one could gainsay that, and though the conversation did concern the tenant projections, it was so well handled by this chit of a girl that he almost felt she knew what he was going to say all along. Back at the car, he handed over the file, and from the way in which she'd been so companionable he might well have expected a chaste kiss on departure, but all he had was a cool handshake and an eye contact smile. Well, what else? He watched her swing back into the office door. Nice, very nice. He'd just have to wait and see what developed.

* * *

Roberta was feeling a trifle cross. Having, in a rather silly girl moment, dressed to show off this morning, just because she'd felt so happy, she'd near ruined a quite nice skirt by kneeling on the dusty floor of the box room. Mary had tut-tutted, typically, which didn't help. Three large boxes, those funny storage boxes so beloved of office minions, had been emptied, and piles of papers now littered the passageway. Thoughtfully Mary had brought up half a dozen black plastic sacks, and Roberta was now sitting cross-legged sifting through pile after pile, getting rid of her temper by venting it on screwing up anything that didn't seem important. Mary was really very patient with her, picking up the crumpled balls that missed the open bag, before going off and returning with the vacuum cleaner. Then it was lunchtime, and despite the gorgeous breakfast, Roberta felt pangs.

She unfolded herself, and her back nearly froze. 'Ouch!' She rubbed the small of her back and grimaced. 'Not good; I thought I was more supple than this.' Mary grinned, but did not voice her thoughts. 'Don't you laugh at me, Mrs! I know what you're thinking!' Then she had to laugh herself. So what if it was because she'd been over indulged, she'd get her suppleness back in fullness of time. 'Coffee and a biscuit, just one, Mary, honest.'

It wasn't until they had cleared one whole shelf and started on the next that Roberta realised the enormity of the task she set herself. So much rubbish! Accumulation of literally every bit of paper from the last goodness knows how long. Nothing of what she'd gone through seemed in the slightest way of any importance and she got the impression that rubbish husband of hers had just kept paper for the hell of it. Between them, they had filled two whole sacks of scrumbled paper and flattened four boxes.

Suddenly Roberta tired of it. 'Enough! I've had enough. Let's go make some tea, Mary. Thanks, you've been a brick.'

'Brick, Miss Roberta? That sounds like an upper class public school girl! Gym slip and navy knickers!'

Roberta gave her housekeeper a sly look. 'I was an upper class public school girl, as well you know. *And* I wore navy knickers; you used to buy them! Not any longer!' She waltzed off, and had a sudden yen to phone Andrew.

He was back behind his desk, still with a degree of euphoria from his interlude with the admirable Andrea. Samantha had gone off to do some shopping, so he could feel quite relaxed about putting his feet up on the desk and thinking. Should he have some fun and go on an ego trip with the girl's emotions? All down to Roberta, to be honest, because he doubted if he'd have had either the courage or the bravado to give any girl the glad eye if it hadn't been for her forwardness. Time for tea. He swung his legs down and was just about to visit the kitchen, when the phone went.

'Andrew?'

'Roberta.' *That girl – woman – again. A sudden flip of internal panic.*

'That's me. You alone?'

'Yes.'

'I miss you.'

'Hmm. You okay?'

'I've got a stiff back. Mary laughed at me.'

'Why's that?'

'Don't ask awkward questions, Andrew. It's all your fault.'

'*My fault?* Silly girl, how can it be my fault?' Then he twigged. Whoops!

'You'll have to put it right. And I need some advice.'

Cautiously, he replied, 'Advice comes within the framework of the accountancy remit.'

'Don't be pompous! I've been cleaning out the box room and there's mountains of paper. I need you to tell me if I can throw it all away. And I've had a super idea. When can you come?'

Andrew was alarmed. Roberta shouldn't be throwing paper away without supervision. 'Woman! – Do you want me to spank you? You shouldn't throw *any* paper away until at least six years after the date. Look, I'd best come over in the morning before you do anything else mad. And keep your knickers on!' The expression slipped out without thought, and he grimaced, asking for trouble, that was, but she didn't take umbrage.

'Yes Andrew. Sorry Andrew. If I keep my knickers on you can't spank me. Mary thinks they're still navy ones!' She laughed down the phone. 'See you tomorrow then.' The phone went down.

Andrew shuddered. She was going to be a trouble, that one.

* * *

Andrea, having looked carefully through Andrew's tenant projections, was impressed. If the Brewery could get all the tied houses to work to this framework, the spectre of a takeover would be pretty well exorcised. It just proved that the outside eye could be the more perceptive. Well, time to go home. With the file safely tucked away under lock and key, the girl shrugged on her jacket, picked up her handbag and closed the office door behind her. She was always the last to leave. With the main door locked, she went, as normal, out across the yard and through the dray gates, and bumped into an old college acquaintance she didn't much care for.

'Fred! How's things with you?' She'd never been over confident about this one, somehow, especially as she'd stupidly egged him on ages ago when she'd felt desperate and far too easy. He fell into step alongside her and she had that scary feeling he'd been waiting for her.

'Okay, Andrea, okay. You?'

'Yes, fine, thanks. You going my way?'

'Well, looks like it, d'unt it?' They walked in silence along the road, to the point where Andrea crossed to go through the park. Fred kept up with her, and she was less than happy.

'Look, Fred, I'm sure you don't need to keep me company. I've got to be home before six. So I'll say cheerio.'

'Thas allright. I don't mind.' he bumped into her, and she nearly fell over.

'Hey, watch it!' She was getting frightened. 'Look, just push off, Fred.'

'That's not very friendly. I want you to be friendly, Andrea.' He grabbed her arm, and started to hustle her down a side path. 'I've always wanted you to be *friendly.*'

'Leave me alone! You're not like that, Fred. Just go away, *please!*'

'Come on, you know what I want.'

She screamed, tore her arm out of his grasp, and ran. She wasn't sure if he was after her, but she ran for her life, and collided with a woman with a pushchair, sprawled, grazed her knee, her head hit the pavement, and everything went dark, and nothingness.

The first person she saw when she came to was the ambulance Para-medic, a girl with astonishing ginger hair. She was inside an ambulance, on a stretcher thing, and she felt incredibly stupid.

The ginger haired girl was smiling at her, holding her wrist. 'Welcome back. What's your name?'

'Andrea. Andrea Chaney. Look, I'm fine. Sorry to have wasted your time.'

'Not a problem, Andrea. I'm Irene. Glad to hear you say you're fine. Let's check you out again. May I?' The girl ran her checks, and seemed satisfied. 'Now, we'll run you to casualty if you want, but I agree, you're okay, apart from your head and your knee, which we've patched.' True enough, Andrea saw her knee had a plaster, and felt her bruised forehead. 'There's a police guy wanting to talk to you. Okay?'

'Sure. Thanks, inadequate, but thanks.'

'Just glad you're safe and sound. Just as well the woman you crashed into had common sense and a mobile phone.'

'I was running away from a bloke.'

'So we gather. Look, we need to get back on the road if you're sure you're okay.'

Andrea swung herself off the stretcher bunk and smoothed down her muddied skirt.

Irene helped her out of the ambulance and into the care of the waiting policeman.

She found herself transported by the patrol car to the local police station and into an interview room. This was something she could do without. 'I need to phone home. My folks will be worried. I'm all right, you know.'

'Yes, we just need a few details. Shouldn't take long, then we'll run you back.'

By the time all the forms had been completed and the system satisfied, it was way past eight o'clock. Being delivered back home was easy, getting her parents to accept she hadn't been physically assaulted was another, but eventually she escaped back to her room. It was time she found a place of her own.

The tom-toms had been beating well and fast. The following morning Samantha broke into Andrew's morning reverie, a period when he mentally ran through the tasks for the day. Yes, there was Roberta, but the business wouldn't survive on pandering to her quirky needs, however pleasant and egotistical they were. So thinking, would he hear from Andrea – and here was Samantha, talking about the self same girl. 'What did you say, Samantha? Andrea was attacked?' He sat up and was all ears.

'She got waylaid by some freak of a bloke, managed to run

off, but tripped over in her panic. Luckily the woman she fell over managed to call the ambulance.'

'Is she all right?'

'Apparently, apart from a bruised forehead and knee, so her mother says.'

'She's still living at home then?'

'Well, yes.'

'Poor girl. Time she was independent. She's confident enough. Is she back at work this morning? I was going to ring her.' Samantha merely sniffed. What Andrew did with his day was no immediate concern of hers, but she did hope that Andrea wasn't going to be too much of his, not just yet. She'd still to hear more about that other opportunity.

Roberta's morning started a good deal earlier than on the day before. She was in the kitchen before Mary turned in, even if all she was doing was drinking orange juice and reading her current novel.

'Good morning, Miss Roberta. You're an early bird. What's afoot?'

'Oh, nothing specific, Mary. What's on your plan today?'

'It's dusting and polishing day, hall, your sitting room, dining room. Then if you need a hand upstairs?'

'Not until Andrew's been. It seems we may have been a bit premature in clearing the debris.' She shrugged. 'What's done is done. He says he'll call this morning.'

'Ah. That explains the bright and cheery expression. I'll not be in the way?'

'Not at all, Mary, business visit. Bless you for thinking.'

Once Samantha had left for her day on the market, Andrew reached for the phone. Andrea's extension was engaged; well, that was a good omen. In the meantime he had a go at Roberta's number. That rang and rang too, but just as he was about to give up on her, she answered, in a breathless voice.

'You been running, R? You sound puffed!'

'Don't ask, Andrew. Personal. Sorry. When you coming?'

'Around half ten? I've got some telephone calls to make, then I'll be over. Let me guess, you were on the loo.' He laughed at being called a rotter. 'Sorry, dear. At least if you were running you didn't collide with a pushchair.'

'What's that supposed to mean?'

'Tell you later. Look pretty.' That phrase again! He pushed the phone rest down, and then re-dialled Andrea's number. Success. 'Andrea. My dear girl, I'm sorry to hear you were molested, or something. How are you this morning?' He was genuinely concerned.

'Good morning, Andrew. Thank you for phoning. Shaken but not stirred. A bump on the head, an unpretty knee, a messed up skirt and wrecked tights. I won't talk about the rest.' And there was that bubbly tone in her voice that was so easy on the ear. 'Come and see me, if only to hear what we think to your projections.'

'I don't need to – oh, sorry. I didn't mean that. I'd love to come and see you again. This afternoon, three o'clock. On the dot.'

One good reason for being one's own boss, the ability to be totally flexible. Well, that's sorted today's programme. He returned two files to the cabinet, gave a shrug. Well, he could only do so much, and one uppermost thought was the state that girl was in.

When he rang the bell at the Manor, it was Mary who opened the door.

'Good Morning, Mr Hailsworthy. Miss Roberta's in her sitting room. I'm doing the dining room. Would you like coffee with her?'

'You're very kind, Mary, and please, call me Andrew. I may be a frequent visitor from now on – and yes, coffee would be nice. Thank you – you're a brick.' He was totally unprepared for the bust-wobbling laugh from the normally staid Mary, unaware of the previous day's exchange about gymslips between Mary and her employer.

Roberta rose from her armchair with the now familiar fluid movement he found so appealing, stood on tip toe and kissed him, with arms wrapped round. She smelt – and tasted – wonderful, and the linen dress was the one she wore that first day, weeks ago. She got back kiss for kiss, all her senses tingling, and wished life was simpler, so her dreams, her lovely dreams, could become reality. A knock on the door, oh how tactful Mary was, bringing in the coffee. Andrew managed to reach the window seat, as Roberta gently smoothed her hair down. Mary wasn't fooled, but if it made her girl happy, then, provided no harm was done, fine. She left them to it, hoping sanity would prevail.

'R – I said Mary was a brick when I came in, and she howled with laughter. What was so funny?'

Roberta nearly creased up, making Andrew more intrigued. 'Oh, Andrew! I called Mary a brick yesterday, and we had a giggle about upper class schoolgirls, gymslips and navy knickers. I was one, you see.'

He couldn't resist it. 'Bet you don't wear navy knickers now.'

She gave him an old fashioned look. 'Andrew. You do *not* need to look at my knickers! You're here to help me with my figures.'

'Don't tempt me then. Where do you want me to start?'

'Now who's tempting who?' Then they both smiled at each other, knowing full well where this could end. In the meantime. . .

Roberta was duly chastened by Andrew's revelation about the six-year rule, albeit also relieved that the boxes she and Mary had disposed of pre-dated the cut-off date. Then he went through the essential invoices she'd need to establish who paid the bills, and finally, she flung her idea at him.

'Design school weekends? Brilliant, R. The Manor, ideal. Are you sure you want to, though? It'll make a deal of difference to your way of life. What about Mary? You'd need other staff, methinks. Let me do some costings. There is one other thing – the London end. It would help if I had a look at it. Fancy taking your accountant on a day trip?'

'Now that *is* an idea. Will she let you?'

'R, it's a business trip. Of course she will 'let me' – I don't have to have my passport stamped! When are you going next?'

'I could go at the weekend. Sure a day is sufficient?'

'Mmmm. I'll think about it, R. You're a great girl, you know.'

Mary saw him go, and went to find her girl, ensconced in her armchair, legs tucked up beneath her, reading. 'Sorted?'

'Sorted, Mary. What should I have for lunch?'

* * *

Andrew called back in at home, made himself a sandwich, looked at his watch, gave himself half an hour to finish off another small client's half-year figures, and then shot off into town. Three o'clock and Andrea.

The route to her office was now familiar territory, there was confidence in his step and just a tap on her office door before going straight in; no standing on ceremony. The younger girl smiled at him as he entered, and inclined her head towards the other end of the office, partitioned off. Andrea heard his footsteps, and appeared in the doorway, beckoned him over. Today she was in a dress, plain, yes, but well made, and a simple necklace and brooch to match. She certainly knew how to wear her clothes and make the most of herself, maybe that was her undoing, being too nice to look at. Backing off the doorway and thereby ensuring he followed her, she offered him a cheek, out of sight of her junior. The room was pretty well full of archive boxes, just one desk stuffed into a gap.

'I know, it's a mess, Andrew, but I can retreat in here and pretend I'm not about. It's good to see you. Good news on your projections. Ida had to ask me to interpret this morning, but both she and Mr H reckon they're onto a good thing, and poor old Barry's feeling a trifle unloved, poor man. He'll get over it – but it would be nice if you drop in on him and polish his ego a bit.' She sat on the desk and pulled her skirt up over her knees to do so. Nice legs, he thought, and she caught his eyes. 'Sorry, Andrew.'

'Sorry? What about?'

She tugged at her hemline ineffectually. 'Showing my bent knee.'

'I'm not complaining. Nice knees, and a shame about the damage, but you're a lucky girl, Andrea. I hate to think what could have happened. Will the law find the bloke, d'you think?'

'Oh yes, I should think so. I knew him from college, and he hankered after touching me up then, so I guess this was an encounter waiting to happen, sadly. I'd have kicked him where it would have dented more than his pride, but running away just happened.' She looked down at her toes, swung her legs back and forth, just like a schoolgirl. 'Look, let's forget about it, please? I am quite touched by your concern, Andrew. You're a caring sort of man, aren't you?'

This, coming from a girl near fifteen years his junior, put him a trifle off balance, especially as a certain other girl had told him much the same. So what if he did care, that was just him, and vulnerable females seemed to be a speciality. 'I don't like to see girls damaged, physically or mentally. Especially pretty ones, even if they have bent knees.' The temptation to touch her, show his concern, was overwhelming, but the self control was just about adequate. 'If there's anything I can do – silly question, that, but I mean it. P'raps we'd best get on?'

'Yes.' She pushed herself off the desk and brushed past him to the partition door.

They spent the best part of an hour running over his figures, with Andrea correcting one or two assumptions with best guess figures of her own, and they sparred over the profit margins amicably until a compromise was achieved. Finally, both were happy with the results and Andrew regretted not bringing his disk with him so he could have amended the spreadsheet there and then, and said so.

'No problem. Have one on me.' Andrea made no bones about copying what they had on her computer screen and handed it over. 'At the risk of foregoing the pleasure of your company, Andrew, we can always swap figures over the internet, can't we?'

'Hmm. Not *quite* the same as leaning over your shoulder.'

'No. But then you wouldn't be peering at my bra strap either.' She felt him flinch and pull back and realised her error.

'Oops, sorry, Andrew. Didn't mean that. Don't take offence; I'm not going to sue you for sexual harassment. Not my scene.' The colour flushed up her neck.

'None taken. Isn't time you weren't here?' The other young girl had already wished them a goodnight and vanished. 'Aren't you worried about a second attempt?'

'Not really. I reckon the poor boy will be frightened off. He wouldn't have known what to do if he had got me down. I might have been mauled but not, well you know . . .'

Seriously concerned at her narrow escape, aware that the girl might be over confident of her ability to cope and knowing he was beginning to become more than a little proprietorial, he had to do something. 'Let me see you home. I'd be happier.'

A startled glance up at him. 'Are you that interested, Andrew?'

'Interested? Concerned maybe, as any person should be. Interested has other connotations, Andrea.'

There was no one in the office by now; they were alone. 'That's why I asked.' Her hand came up, stroked his cheek. 'You're nice to have around.'

'Andrea. In the short time I've known you, I've come to like you,' Andrew drew back and copying her earlier action, sat on the desk alongside. 'I don't know what else to say. If I had a daughter like you I'd be very proud.'

She swung round on her chair and faced him. 'A daughter? Is *that* how you see me?'

'I'm sorry, Andrea, We've met as a result of business – we've hit it off, you understand what I'm trying to achieve, I think you're great, as a person, as a girl, heaven help me, you're very attractive – personable – and yes, I could well be said to be interested in you – but how do you see that interest?' Looking down at her, he was aware of the luminous quality of her eyes, almost hypnotic, the curl of her eyelashes and the slight dimples on her cheeks, the fullness of her lips and the clear skin. Oh my goodness, whatever was he doing?

'Maybe I'm being silly. Sorry, am I being too interesting?' She'd got up and was standing in front of him.

He slid off the desk, held her arms and lightly kissed her, seeing her eyes close, and kissed her again, just as lightly, just as gesture. 'There. Am I being silly as well? Do we know what we're doing? Isn't this classed as your sexual harassment?'

Those deep wide eyes opened and a twitch of a grin, then a full-blown smile.'Maybe. I shan't tell. And I'm not tearing off to collide with a pram this time. Again?' Again, and again, as her arms went round him, and it was deeper and more intense, before she gently untangled herself, reached for her jacket off her chair, and he followed her out of the office.

'I'm taking you home, Andrea. Come on, get in.' He opened the car door for her and watched her in.

'You're looking at my knees again.' Another smile.

'Nice knees, Andrea. Why shouldn't I?' He shut the passenger door and moved round to slide in beside her. 'Where to?'

Outside her house, she leant across and planted a 'thank-you' kiss on his cheek. 'Thanks, Andrew. You've managed to repair my damaged ego. We'll be seeing a bit more of each other?' The query could have been a statement and with a depth of meaning. With no further comment, she opened her door and got out, closed the door and he watched her swing away up the house path. She did turn at the door, and gave a single wave. As he drove away, what Samantha had said a couple of days ago went through his mind. Perhaps she was right, but how this would impact on his relationship with Roberta he just didn't know. It was all getting a bit much, and really, Andrea and the 'mending' of her so called damaged ego was inflating his more than was somewhat sensible.

Samantha was home and well on the way to producing a meal; there was even a bottle of white wine standing on the table. She'd changed, brushed her fluffy hair and looked really rather lovely. He felt guilty about the time spent with two different girls during the course of the day. He had to be nice, very nice, to her as a consequence, which led to yet another record being chalked up. Twice, in *one* week!

SIX

The question of going to London wouldn't go away, he knew, not that he, in heart of hearts, wanted it to go away. Roberta rang him just about every day, usually while she was having her morning coffee, and although she frequently described how she was dressed, how she was sitting, flirting on the phone, she hadn't beseeched him to visit her in the same way, no doubt saving him up for the projected investigation into the town business. Quite how he was going to get this round Samantha he hadn't yet worked out, for despite having many attempts at dreaming up all the reasons or excuses he could possibly plausibly offer, nothing had seemed logical.

Then fate intervened, in the form of an irrefutable offer of a place for Samantha at the Women's Institute's residential College, a week away on a Market Cooking course. Did he mind, she asked, if she took advantage of this rare opportunity? He made every pretence of being unsure, having very mixed feelings about it all, but gave in, she'd no doubt think, because she'd been quite *'nice'* to him recently. In fact, life had begun to take on something of its old pleasant familiar feel. When Roberta rang that morning, he was able to give her the good news; with Samantha away for the week, he could easily take two days out, albeit with a twinge of conscience about the deception.

So the following Tuesday afternoon, with Samantha safely away up near Abingdon, he drove to the Manor with a mixture of emotions, uppermost being the interest in getting away from routine. The idea that he was embarking on a dangerous mission didn't really come to mind. Roberta was all beams and smiles. She would drive, knowing the way, and her little overnight bag was already in the back of her car. He'd never been quite sure about two seater sports cars and fast women, but the MGF was exactly right for her, and, he had to admit, she drove very well. The roar of the car's exhaust and the traffic noise, all mixed up in the windage from the open top, denied them conversation; the trip took them just under the hour even with the go-home traffic. Roberta knew her back streets, he gave her that, and by the time they stopped, she happily finding a parking slot not a hundred yards from her front door, he was totally lost. He knew it was a desirable address, but wasn't quite prepared for the cream painted three storey terrace house, black railings and sandstone steps up to the door, with the enclosed little park on the other side of the road. The square wasn't noisy, either. It was a town house with Georgian elegance, complete with an understatement of a little brass plaque by the shiny dark green door. 'Smiley Interior Design', nothing else. Three pots of crimson geraniums stood in a row in each ground floor window.

Hoisting her own bag out of the car, she was evidently very happy with his reaction. 'Impressed, Andrew?'

'I am, R. You're a lucky girl to have a town pad like this. I'd imagined a sort of mews-ish place, you know, just a door and a couple of rooms over the garage. This is nice.'

'Well, don't stand on ceremony. Here, you open up. Then you can carry me over the threshold if you like. Take my bag.' Her eyes were sparkling and she'd gone all girlish, chucking the keys at him and then handing over the little case. He struggled a bit with the Chubb, managed it, pushed open the solid door to reveal a fully carpeted hall, placed her bag inside, and then went back for her. She was quite a solid little girl too, but he managed her fairly gracefully, feet first, and claimed his reward. Then he went back to the car for his own bag.

'Sure the car's okay?'

'We'll pop it round the back later. After I've shown you round.' She twirled. 'Oh, Andrew, this is making me feel desperately happy, having you here, on our own, just us!' The door closed, the silence wrapped itself round them, and he took her in his arms. Three minutes later she came up for air, kicked her shoes off, and taking him by the hand, led him up the stairs.

Somehow, later that evening, seeing her happily naked in this context put a different complexion on their relationship. It wasn't for therapeutic comfort, it was her taking him for what he had to give, and so totally abandoned. She was a *proper* girl, she told him, and consequently he was right to exercise and enjoy her as a girl. And enjoy her he did, till they were totally exhausted and fell asleep, entwined, amongst a heap of tangled sheets on the wide bed.

Waking un-naturally after dark, he had great difficulty in working out where he was, but then with far more light borrowed from the street than he was ever used to, sufficient to see most of the still sleeping lithe figure not a foot away from him, it all came back. Such a gorgeous creature, tousled hair, gently rising and falling breasts, with such a comfortable shape and those deep mysterious contours; he stroked her back, running fingers down her spine, feeling a new desire for her possession.

'Hmmmmm,' she woke, stirred, and rolled over onto her back. 'Darling man, love me?'

'I thought I had.'

'I think you're right. You have. Again?'

Who was it that had asked 'Again', not two weeks ago? That had been very chaste, compared with this. Roberta pulled up her knees and took him.

Taking his delight in her seemed selfish. 'Roberta, *Roberta!*' as though he was punishing her, lying quiescent under him, eyes closed, his the movement. Then it was done and he collapsed onto her, taking a deep kiss and a smile from slumberous eyes.

She whispered into his ear.

'I feel you, darling Roberta, All of you.'

'No, not that way. Here.' She took his hand and whispered instructions. 'Yes. Like that. Now, stroke me.' This was still a new experience, but it felt very good. The relaxation in her meant easy access to that secretive little place for her delight, until, to his enchantment and surprise, she reacted. This time her 'Oh! Oh!'s,' became intense and he saw her tremble.

'Roberta!'

She was breathing deeply, a perceptive pause before her reply. 'Didn't you know, Andrew?'

'Not really, other than . . . '

'Oh!' She struggled up and he rolled sideways. Without looking at him, she explained what it meant to her, far more timely and long lasting than the brief but tumultuous version he'd experience. He was humbled, being told these things at such a time from a woman with whom he'd been so physically involved.

'Poor Samantha. Hasn't she ever . . .?' He knew what she meant, and as far as he'd known, the answer was no. In fact, there had always been reluctance on her part for him to 'touch' her that way. 'Poor girl!' Roberta repeated, saddened, and swung herself off the bed, standing proud and unabashed, just as she could see all of him.

'You're gorgeous, R.'

'I know. I feel gorgeous. Thank you very much, Mr Hailsworthy. Back in a minute.'

The bathroom was across the landing, no such luxuries as en-suites in these houses.

In the privacy of her bathroom, she used the toilet and took a shower, avoiding her hair, and reflected on progress. Having wonderfully felt him within her that evening, no precautionary measures and confidant she was receptive, there was a fair, a very fair chance, she might, just might, conceive. She loved him, he would be a caring father, she was sure he loved her, even if he didn't actually say so in as many words. Towelling her self down, and adding just a dab of scent to her neck, and a mischievous one to the top of her thigh, she went back to see if she could tempt him any further.

Later that morning, after a delightfully simple but exquisite continental breakfast Roberta rightly had a simple pride in producing, they were both very business like, as though last night had never happened. She showed him all that she did; the samples room, the photo albums, the accounts, and the order book. It was a flourishing business, no doubt about it, despite the relaxed attitude she had towards working in London. And she only worked here three days a week! For the lunch break she took him out to the local little bistro not five minutes away, and then they spent a good couple of hours in late afternoon looking at the concept of shifting to the Manor, and still didn't reach a positive conclusion. Andrew was firmly convinced she shouldn't sell the London house, even if she let it. The capital value was likely to increase, and it would be a bolthole if all else failed.

She agreed, and then brought up the idea of running residential courses at the Manor again. They considered the concept in depth and finally decided to give it a try. It was now six o'clock, and with tea and biscuits now a memory of over an hour ago, there was a mutual requirement to eat. 'Dine out again, I think, Andrew. My favourite proper little restaurant is only five minutes walk beyond the bistro. Shall I give them a call? You don't want to do a show do you?'

Andrew wasn't much of a theatre man, but he'd have gone along with her if she'd wanted to, happy to have been seen with her. Eating out was certainly the best idea in his book. The table reserved, it was time to change. She'd worn a neat little costume during the day; he'd been in casual dress. In the bedroom she used she had an intriguing and surprising wardrobe. He was very much in favour of her allowing him to watch her strip down to the basics before the rummage through the collection; the satisfaction of involvement. The dark blue below calf length dress first produced she frowned over, put it back and pulled out a slinky thing in turquoise silk, cut on the cross. 'Nope. Too Chinese-ey. How about this?' A deep burgundy, low cut bodice, fairly full skirt just below knee length, colour wise it was a perfect foil to her hair. 'I always feel nice in this. What do you think?'

'R, darling, you don't need a dress to look extremely lovely to me – but I do like that. Allow me?' Surprised, and somewhat bemused, she handed the dress over. Andrew ran his hands up inside the material, held it on his arms and standing behind the girl, dropped it over her head, let the fabric run down, smoothed it over her bust, pulled the zip up carefully, stepped back and allowed her space to twirl. Certainly, it was superb fit, but then it should be, he'd just seen the label . . .

Roberta's reaction to being dressed that way made itself evident to him forthwith. He found her wrapped round him, face aglow. 'Never, *ever* has a *man* dressed me before; Andrew, which is why you're a super sort of bloke to have around. Why weren't you about when I was looking for a husband? It's a lovely feeling. Oh . . . I can't wait for you to take it off again!'

'Steady on, my girl! We've a table booked and I've got to change too, you know. Anticipation will certainly wet my appetite though; you look good enough to eat.'

'Hmm. Not me, don't think so. Good enough for other things, p'raps, later?'

The innuendos and veiled intentions surfaced and swirled about them for the rest of the evening, the verbal sparring keeping the humour and the senses alive despite the tiring stresses of the day. Her dark eyes were flashing and sparkling at him, the little dimples as she smiled constantly appearing and he felt her toes stroking his leg under the table from time to time. A totally incorrigible and desperately exciting female seated in front of him across the dark tablecloth.

The restaurant was a dream, the menu sublime and the service impeccable, or so it seemed; perhaps having Roberta there put a more than rosy glow on the meal, whatever, the wine was also doing its thing, and a bottle of Chablis between them was a sure-fire way to add to that glow. By the time he had argued with her over the bill and lost – it would go on her business account, she said; if he wanted he could argue with her when he was playing accountant . . . the evening was swimming along and he couldn't wait to get her back to the house.

Once back into the bedroom and he'd peeled off his jacket and tie, she let him unzip her, but this time the dress fell down around her ankles and she merely stepped out of the circle of glowing burgundy to stand, a vision, with her head a little on the side, a half smile in a coquettish manner. 'Want to finish the job, my lover?'

The slight nod, so meaningful, sealed his fate. The captivation, the degree of his acceptability, her wanting, the whole scenario, took them to the point of no realistic return. His involvement in slowly, gently, carefully, taking her to the ultimate passion became the unspoken declaration of a caring love neither of them had previously experienced.

When daylight brought them both back to full wakefulness, she was still nestled close to him, each had an arm entwined, and he very conscious of a deep feeling of responsibility for this girl. He'd loved her, made her his, and there was no going back on his – their – actions.

She stirred, and he kissed her. 'Good morning, my darling.'

'So formal, my lover?'

He chuckled and rolled over. 'Prefer another way?'

Finally, she pushed him away. 'You're too good to me. Let's have breakfast. You know we have to get back?'

'Don't remind me.' On his back, with her alongside him, he had to try and come to terms with the situation. 'Where do we go from here, R?'

Sitting up, leaning on an elbow, she stroked his forehead with a finger. 'Wherever you want to go, my lover. You tell me. You want to keep me secret; I'll be a secret love for you. You want to shout our love out loud; then I'm not going to dive for cover. Anything, anyhow. Andrew, my darling man, you're the best thing that's happened to me . . . I know, it sounds trite, how many women, men, have said that before . . . but you are. I don't think I'll forget you picked me up when I fell over, given me comfort, help, advice even, and now we've shared nights in bed . . . and *how!*' She poked him, and laughed, '*love* you, Andrew!'

'Roberta, my darling, yes, I know you do. Otherwise you wouldn't have let me dress – and undress - you. But I have a problem.' She frowned at him. 'Samantha. I can't – I won't – abandon her, you know. She's my wife, R, and we've had some wonderful times together, two children, and, yes, I still love her, despite all her annoying idiosyncrasies.' He paused, 'I'm wrong. She's not a problem. I'm the problem. I've just a soft spot for damsels in distress. Don't get me wrong, R. I'd not change things for the world. You – me, we fit well, don't we?'

So she wasn't going to get a new husband yet. Not just yet. She smiled, a meaningful smile, and had to agree. 'So I'm a secret, then?'

'I love you as a secret, R. Adds spice to us. Do you mind?'

'Spicy; hmmm. Okay. On condition; we go on holiday together, away from it all, for at least a week. So I can pretend you're a proper husband for a while at least.'

'*Holiday? A week!* How on earth are we going to manage that, for heaven's sake?'

'Don't know. Your problem.' She flung the crumpled duvet to one side, slid lovely legs in her sinuous fashion onto the floor, and stood stark naked, looking down at him. 'What you going to do about *that?*'

Ultimately, after a mutual shower and another Roberta style breakfast, they locked up and drove back to the Manor. An advisory phone call to Mary meant lunch was waiting.

Mary herself was in good form.

'Miss Roberta.' She greeted her girl with a broad smile while Andrew was getting the bags out of the MGF. 'You got what you wanted?'

'Yes, Mary, I did. Well, up to a point. Andrew's a good accountant, pity he's married.'

'Ah. I take it Samantha doesn't know everything?'

'That Andrew spent two nights in London? No, and I don't think she ought to find out either, not just yet. Let's wait and see, shall we?'

* * *

92

Andrea was not quite asleep, though her book had fallen out of her hand onto the bedroom floor through sheer tiredness. Going to bed so early wasn't always a good idea, but what else when she was so bored? Thoughts ranged around in such a strange way. The way in which Andrew had held her, kissed her, was still fresh in her mind and she ached for his touch again. She wriggled round and tried to get comfortable on her back, smoothing her nightdress down, and straightened out the covers. 'Silly girl,' she told herself. 'He's married, and he's a lot older than me', but he had kissed her, not just the once either. And he cared for her; she definitely knew he cared about her otherwise he wouldn't have acted the way he did. What if that horror Fred had raped her? What would have happened then? Would he have cared? Yes, of course he would. That thought was comforting. He wouldn't go away, of that her sleepy mind was sure. Would she still be awake when her parents came home – she couldn't remember if they'd said before or after midnight? Andrew. Andrew. She concentrated, with a strong belief she'd feel him kiss her again if she tried hard enough.

* * *

Andrew was back home, and after the excitement of the last forty-eight hours or so, had to relax on his own. The house seemed so desperately strange, empty, no Samantha. Reliving the two days, so much of a forced frenetic pace that wasn't him. Today's lunch at the Manor, well up to Mary's usual standard, was a de-brief and allowed him to come back to earth. Roberta had seen him off with a cool kiss and a 'see you soon', a twirl of skirts as she turned her back on him and gone back indoors. That afternoon he disciplined himself to put all Roberta's thoughts and plans into the computer, allied to his own ideas, so at least he had something to show for the jaunt. He couldn't bring himself to cook a meal, and resorted to a bowl of soup and some cheese sandwiches, none of which he enjoyed but he had to keep something inside. Then he tried the television and did a stint of channel hopping, but that wasn't at all satisfying either. Toyed with the idea of phoning Roberta, but to what end? No point in ringing Samantha, she'd wonder what he'd done to make him phone her. It was an early nine o'clock, it felt like eight. A real hiatus. Nothing he could do; nowhere to go. Almost like being cast adrift. Not a soul in sight.

Andrea? How would she be, now? She was a sweet person; he nearly said 'child' to himself, but she was no child. She'd make good company, lively and tantalising conversation and pleasant with it, as well as easy on the eye. That afternoon visit to the Brewery had been very pleasant; though flirting with client's staff was very unethical. Just as well he wasn't working for anybody but himself. Her face swum into clear focus, the way she'd part closed her eyes when they'd kissed. No, he shouldn't think that way; he should have been firm and kept aloof. Roberta was more than enough to worry about, let alone an 'understanding' with a younger girl. She wouldn't go away though, the poise and natural grace she'd exhibited, and the clear way her mind worked. Lovely creature. What possible excuse did he have for maintaining close contact with her? What was that Samantha had said about her? Oh yes, her mother, she'd apparently reported Andrea's comment that she thought I was really sexy! Me, really *sexy?* He nearly laughed out loud, and then sobered up, for what he and Roberta got up to inevitably fell into that category. Without really knowing why, he went into the office and looked up the file. Andrea's own notes on the edge of the returned copy of the first draft of his proposals, in that neat, precise hand. He wondered where that Finance guy figured in all this, for if Andrea was so involved it didn't seem he had an effective role. She knew her onions, that one, as he read through the jottings. Turning the page, he scanned down, smiling at one comment about the tenants, frowned at another. Then, on the last page, tucked away, a note he hadn't noticed before. *'Hope you like my asides, A. Feel free to call me, anytime, xx, A.'* and the phone number, all in pencil. Devious little madam! Well, so be it. The phone sat in its sit up and beg holder, daring him to ring. What would her parents think? Her mother would report back to Samantha if he contacted her, of that he was sure. What the hell! He picked the phone up; nearly put it back, then decisively punched the numbers. It dialled; that musical sequence. It wasn't too late, he could drop it – but then it *was* perhaps too late? It was ringing, and ringing. Perhaps they were out, so . . . just as he was about to drop it back in the cradle, a sleepy voice answered, just repeating the number.

'Andrea? Andrew; I'm sorry if it's late – I'll call again.'

'*No!*' Her voice snapped into gear. 'Andrew! Oh, thanks for ringing. No, it's not too late; though I'm glad we don't have videophones . . . I'm a mess and not dressed. But you rang me – what can I do for you?'

'Now there's an invitation. To be honest, I'm not sure, I rang on impulse, forgive me, reading your notes through, and there was your number, which serves you right.'

A bit of a chuckle came at him. 'It worked, then, though maybe the timing's a bit out.'

'I'll ring you tomorrow then. It's just that I'm on my own and had to do something stimulating.' As an antidote to too much Roberta, he thought.

'Am I stimulating? I'm on my own too, till about one o'clock in the morning.'

'So we're a pair of loners then. I'd say come and share a nightcap, but that might be misconstrued. Anyway, if you're not dressed . . .'

Another throaty chuckle, 'you're flirting, Mr Hailsworthy. I don't think single ladies should visit lonely married men late at night, especially if their parents will be home and wonder where their only daughter is.' A fractional pause prefaced the more positive side of her reply. 'I'd love to come. Fifteen minutes. Remind me of your address again?'

'Don't be silly, Andrea, you don't have to take me seriously.'

'I'm not, but I'm coming, if the invite's still open?'

He told her the address, knew it was less than fifteen minutes away by car, and pulled a face after she'd put the phone down. All it wanted was for Samantha to come home unexpectedly and life would become more than interesting.

Still unsure of exactly why he'd rang her, the evening now had a different colour, from drab grey with undertones of shadow purple left from Roberta's part of his day, to a much more vibrant sort of pink, at least, that's how it seemed. Ten minutes, he had, to get something together before her vivacious queries would spin around. Change, certainly, so a rush upstairs to get a newer shirt on and a better pair of trousers, quick wash in between and the merest touch of aftershave. Then put the Brewery file on the table, for appearances sake. A bottle of wine? Why not? Has to be a red, one of the collection kept on the top of the kitchen cupboard.

The glasses clinking as he put them down on the coffee table coincided with the tune from the doorbell, though he'd heard no car. She wouldn't have walked, surely not, so the question was on the tip of his tongue as he opened the door, and vanished as he took one look at her. From the concept of an undressed mess as she'd described herself on the phone not half an hour ago to the smiling vision on his doorstep was miraculous. She *was* Andrea, she had to be, but not the office lass he'd thought he knew. Her hair was piled up with a comb; a low cut dress that gave emphasis to the shape of her, a shorty coat she just held lightly, and semi-high heels added a modicum to her height and posture.

'Aren't you going to ask me in?' The smile was putting dimples in her cheeks and the mischievous look in her eyes emphasised the difference in his and her poise. He was off balance, she supremely confident. 'Andrew? It's me –eee!' A hand waved in front of him as if to wake him up, the coat going into one hand and revealing the off-shoulder style of the dark green silky thing.

'Surely. My apologies; you're a vision, Andrea. Just for my benefit? Do come in. Where's the car?' Going back to his first thought query put him back into the frame.

'Just round the corner. So no-one gets the wrong idea.' She closed the door behind her, and he took the little coat, hung it on the banisters. 'You like the dress, then?' She did a slow twirl.

'Yes.' What more could he say? Was she going to be a

business contact or just a lovely new friend? 'Glad you came.' The door to the sitting room was open and he ushered her through. 'Glass of wine? Or what else can I get you? Have a seat.' All so, so formal, as she sat demurely, legs sideways, skirt smoothed over her knees, on the settee. The smile stayed in place, her eyes still in contact.

'Wine would be lovely. Your usual nightcap, Andrew?' The mischievousness was into her voice, and he returned her grin.

'Well, no, but I'm not averse, especially if there's a good excuse. It's red?'

'Better and better. If you try hard I may even succumb to a second glass.' The lift of leg and crossing was subtly done, with a slight trace of a wink, or was it imagination?

The glasses filled, Andrew raised his to her, as she sipped. 'To a lovely lady. Thank you for coming. To be perfectly honest, I'm not actually quite sure why – oh, damn it – I'm sorry, Andrea – I just fancied some company. Do you mind?'

The eyes still danced. 'Of course not. Delighted. Gets me out of the house for a very good reason. Boring, you know, living with parents, especially when you're twenty eight.'

'Andrea? I'd had you down as less than twenty five?' Four years younger than Roberta. It would have been crass to ask if she'd had any boyfriends, why she wasn't, what was the word, an *item* with some bloke? Another smile.

'You're dying to ask if I've a boyfriend. Answer's no. I haven't. Once or twice, but no one who could tolerate me and my, er, niceties. Thank you for the compliment.' Her glass was nearly empty, and she leant back on the cushions. 'Aren't you going to join me?' She patted the cushion beside her and changed her legs over. Standing where he was he could see most of her cleavage and curiously, didn't notice a bra. Topping up her glass with the wine bottle had given him an opportunity for gazing at her, though there was nothing to suggest she was embarrassed.

Sitting alongside her deepened the sense of tension between them, palpable and vibrant.

Logically, Andrew had to rest his arm along the back of the

settee, the classic move beloved of all back seat cinema goers. Andrea leant forward and placed her glass on the coffee table, and pushed the Brewery file slightly away, a pointed gesture. The turn of her head towards him, and picking up the hem of her skirt to give it the merest of twitches, all contributed to the body language.

'You're a nice man, Andrew. Remember holding me?'

His arm slipped down onto her shoulders and she closed her eyes, anticipating his kiss. It was all too easy, this slide into a deeper relationship, totally wrong and extremely dangerous, and the little voice in the back of his mind was saying no, no, *no*, but his hands and her lips were saying yes, yes, *yes*! Then her eyes were on him, bright and searching, searching for how she was affecting him, looking for the hint she could get closer to him, the warm glow of the wine working its way into the depths of her and banishing the last vestige of her inhibitions.

In his mind the warmth of her closeness, the softness of her never-ending kiss, the subtlety of her scent and her blatant availability combined into a drastic cocktail of explosive emotion; the next move would be a trigger to an inevitability of procreative passion. His hand slipped down, touching her breast above her dress, not intentionally, but in *her* mind she felt it was enough; with a free hand she eased her strap off her shoulder and a simple little twitch sent the dress on its way. No, she wasn't wearing a bra, and his hand had the bareness of her, a dark brown point of a growing nipple within a hair's breath of his fingers. The deep breath she took broke their kiss, and free of their togetherness the rest of her dress just hung on the other strap. This time he moved it, watching the revelation of the proudness of her, seeing the fineness of her skin, the swell and curve, the depth of her cleavage, the flatness of her tummy emphasising the tautness of her body. Those gorgeous breasts were crying for a caress, a tactile appreciation of their beauty, the crown of the glory of her, a mute but demanding invitation for his kiss.

'Like what you see, Andrew?' It was no more than a whisper.

He was lost, and he knew it, for to back down would hurt her beyond sensibility. 'Gorgeous – you spoil me.'

Their eyes met again, and there was a truism in the expression oft quoted that hers were smouldering.

The zip was at her waist, no more than six inches, just sufficient to allow her to lift slightly and push the fabric away, letting the whole dress slide. He was lost, stupidly, weakly, lost. 'Show me, Andrea. Show me your sex.' Why had he said that? Where was that point of no return? Somewhere amongst the fabric of the discarded dress. She was close, now, and kissable . . . her hands on his shoulders, beginning to move gently, feeling her body's response grow, all she desired was happening and the contour of her woman-ness a drug for him. Ripples of sheer pleasure kept coming at her, in waves, then the finality of her climactic feelings hit her and she screamed, once, an animal yelp, and thrust away from him.

'Andrea?' Her possession a need now, and urgently. She shook her head, picked up her dress and ran instinctively for the bathroom. He followed, but she'd bolted the door. 'Andrea! For God's sake!' Common sense had vanished.

'No!' A muffled voice.

'Andrea!'

'I'm still a virgin, Andrew. you've seen me, but I'm not having sex that way.'

'You're a tease!'

Silence then, before a 'Sorry. But I'm not . . . It's just how it is.'

Was that a sob? He gave up. No way would he have forced the girl, but he was totally unused to such a situation. Roberta would never have done this to him. The desire for her began to evaporate, and sanity started to return. The minutes passed.

'Okay. I won't touch you. You're safe, you should know that.'

She unbolted the door and came out, dress impeccably in place. She had tears in her eyes, and suddenly, inexplicably, he felt sorry for her. A crazy mixed up female. No wonder she had no boyfriend, if all they got was a taste. 'Sorry, Andrew,' she said, again, and didn't look at him.

He had to smile then, at her woebegone expression. 'Silly

girl, Andrea. Why didn't you say?' A sense of strange relief in the way this had worked out.

'Say?' She did look at him then, all very surprised, perplexed, even. 'You'd never . . . ?'

'I might have.'

'Would you do it again, then?'

'I might. But there may be a condition.' He'd had a wild idea, and it was mind blowing.

She'd become wary, he could see that. 'I think we'd better go and sit down. This is silly, Andrea. I wanted your company, you wanted something else, and now you've got me at a complete disadvantage. No wonder you've no steady boyfriend. Was this in your mind when you came?'

Coldly aware of what she'd done, and how close she'd come to crossing her self-imposed line, she was getting confused herself. And he'd been good, very good, the glow was still with her. She tucked herself into the cushions and kept her legs together.

'Andrew, please. I'm sorry. I don't know. I don't know what I . . . yes, I wanted you to love me, but I'm not prepared for . . . I mean, I don't . . . please, Andrew, *please, please* don't be annoyed with me.' She felt like crying, but somehow couldn't, because deep inside she was happy, because he *had* loved her in her way, just as she had imagined he would when he'd kissed her in the office. She met his eyes, and found them smiling at her, which made her feel all the more mixed up and foolish. In a way, it would have been better if he'd been cross and kicked her out. He wouldn't have forced her, she was sure of that. 'I'd better go.' She made to get up, but he was shaking his head.

'No. Don't rush away. You're far too decorative, and you're not running out on me – no, don't panic, I won't, though I can understand why you might have been savaged the other evening. Did you ever tease the bloke who went for you?'

She had and didn't want to explain; there had been others too, but she'd never gone this far with anyone else. Andrew had been the first man she'd fully undressed for, ever, so she shook her head.

'You know I'd have made love to you, girl? You've a beautiful body, Andrea.'

The blush came unannounced, leaving her more than a shade embarrassed. 'What are we going to do now?' she asked, as though she was some errant teenager, to cover the discomfiture.

He grinned at her, a wholesome, pleasant happy grin. He would tease her, unmercifully, and she'd know he would always see her with different eyes. 'I could answer that in a very obvious manner, Andrea, but I'm guessing you're not asking the question that way. If you were, you wouldn't have climbed back into that lovely dress. No, you're going to sit close to me, I'm going to put my arm round you; if you want, I might be persuaded to kiss you, and we'll just listen to some wonderful music, then you must go home before there are questions asked you won't want to answer. And when I see you next I shall be just the same as ever, but I shall wink at you and you'll blush, which will make me feel rather special and highly honoured, because I've *seen* you. You'll be a singularly interesting person to know, Andrea.' She was still blushing, and looking decidedly coy. On a whim, and without considering all the implications, he decided to trust her. 'Your mother is friends with my wife?'

'Samantha?' It sounded so strange, mentioning her name to Andrew under these conditions. 'Yes, she is. They spend quite a bit of time together in town, cosy chats over tea in the Supermarket café. Why?'

'Samantha mentioned that you might be giving me the glad eye; your mother's comment, apparently. Sorry, Andrea, but I was primed.' And that really did make her blush, even more, the red going down that lovely neckline. 'Come and sit here, girl.' He patted the vacant cushion on the settee. No hesitation; she did as she was told. He put his arm round her and she nestled into his shoulder. It could have been the start of a re-run, and he fully intended to keep his hand on her shoulder, but she reached up and placed it over her bust.

'I just think you're a lovely man, Andrew. Does that make me sound tartish?'

He shook his head, gently disengaged himself to put one of his favourite discs into the player before returning to her. 'Thanks for the compliment. I wish Samantha's views were as provocative. Shame I don't get much chance to practise sofa seduction nowadays. This is a real treat. We should do it more often.'

'Hmmm,' given the evening's programme so far had been more to her benefit; 'I might agree, especially if you don't mind giving me little thrills and not taking advantage.'

'I might possibly promise that, Andrea.' He returned to his original line of thinking. 'Do you know Roberta Smiley, from the Manor?'

'I don't *know* her, but, yes, I know who you mean. Why?'

'Can I trust you not to let this go any further?'

Her face swivelled up to him and she got the expected kiss, loving it. 'Need you ask? With me showing you all I've got?'

'And well trimmed too.' Their repartee had taken on a new dimension; possibly he'd describe it as clinical. 'Okay. Roberta and I are having an *affaire,* as they say. And as she is rather, er, demanding, to put it bluntly, I'm quite well taken care of, so I can control the primitive urges rather better than maybe I would have done if she wasn't around. See?' It was his excuse, his reasoning.

'Oh.' Her response was flat. He'd expected more of a reaction. 'Is she good?'

'Is that a ladylike question?'

'Curious, Andrew, but you mentioned it. Should a gentleman discuss his *amours?* Sorry.'

He hesitated. She was right, and this wasn't being fair to Roberta. 'She's good. I like her, a lot. Not just . . . ' He stopped; he wasn't going to dissect their relationship with anyway, not even with a girl he'd just seen naked. New territory, all this. A new slant to life, a strange contour.

'I can guess. I like the music. Kiss me?'

* * *

Samantha dumped her suitcase on the bed in the twin bedded room at the college and surveyed her surroundings. *'Typical college,'* she thought, *'bulk-buy beds and duvets.'* The rest of the décor wasn't bad. Obviously *'designed'* and her mind went back to the visit to the Manor and Roberta's job – or was it a profession? Idly, she wondered about her husband's interest in that business and how he'd get on with the woman. She'd seemed nice enough, but maybe too much a high flyer to want Andrew about too long. Still, you never know.

They'd not been apart much, no reason to be, so it was rather akin to a breathe of fresh air not to have him under her feet; she hoped it wouldn't be too much of a drag for him; wondered briefly what he was doing before her room mate breezed in, and after introductions and so on it was time for dinner.

Later that evening, after their first session, she strolled round the garden. Not unlike Roberta's place; her thoughts went back home and perhaps she should ring him to check? After reflection she abandoned the idea. After all, if she was successful in her application there wouldn't be much point . . .

Back in her room and lying on top of the duvet before her room mate returned, her thoughts went back over the way their marriage had changed. With the kids – grown ups now, both of them – off their hands, she knew there had been some change in attitude towards each other. She'd grown away from him; her interests had multiplied in line with her confidence and, ruefully she had to admit, had rather left him behind. He hadn't changed much, apart from taking that revolutionary step of going it alone. Rather boring. Early days – memory bank scratching – had been more fun. He'd had his moments then, as she had, but nowadays it was all the same, day in day out – and the occasional night; well she had to keep it oiled when the mood took her; the medical profession reckoned it was a good antidote to this or that. Her thoughts rambled on and included the chat they'd had over her idea he might find the need to seek pastures new. Poor Andrew, he'd never declutch from the nest, far too staid and timid to launch out. Unlike her idea. Would Andrea fill the role? Her mother thought she needed a father figure. Father figure! She giggled. He'd not make the running, not with her; far to pretty a girl.

Strangely, she still loved him; the love of twenty odd years of very much togetherness had woven an inseparable mesh of comfort ties that couldn't be unstitched by flighty girls born about the time they'd married. Even if her project came to a head, she knew it would be good for them both. New starts and all that, once she returned. It would be fun. Tomorrow she'd ring and get the results of the medical checks.

The door banged open and her musings broke up, to disappear in the excited chattering of her room mate.

SEVEN

She returned home full of good humour, with lots of chat and plenty of new ideas. Andrew had her in full spate for the best part of the evening and quite a lot over breakfast the following morning, before she finally exhausted her repertoire and got round to asking after his week alone.

'I had Andrea round one evening.' She'd probably find out anyway, so he'd be totally honest over that one, with some exceptions. Andrea had finally gone home, still intact, just after midnight, albeit there may have been a tinge of reluctance somewhere in that last lingering kiss. At least it would divert attention away from the two day jaunt into London, though he was quite ready and prepared to stand his ground over that, for it had been 'on business', ha ha.

'Told you she liked you,' was the reply. 'Not a problem. Pleasant girl, isn't she? Her mother thinks the world of her. Make some chap a good wife. Anyone else take pity on you? That Roberta girl, for instance? Not that she's your type, far too upper crust.'

'I've been up to the Manor a couple of times,' Andrew cautiously replied. 'Her late husband – ex. husband that was – left an awful lot of rubbish we need to look at before it gets turned out. Boring stuff, really, but it has to be done.' He ignored the 'not your type' comment. 'What's on your schedule today?' Anything to keep the conversation on a mundane level. She was buttering more toast as she caught his eye.

'I know, you think I eat too much. Well, it's too late to change my figure now. You'll have to make do with what you've got. I thought I'd go and have coffee with my friend Joan, then maybe do a supermarket shop, perhaps pop into the market. I'll get something nice for supper. What about you?'

He knew what he wanted to do, catch up with Andrea in the office, just to see what reaction he would get from her, then go on up to the Manor and find out what Roberta's humour was like. He pushed his chair back from the table and stood up, stretched, yawned, then gave his wife a peck on the cheek before the planned retreat to the office.

'I'll do an hour or two behind the desk, then see what comes up. Maybe we'll catch an early night?' As a suggestion, it was pretty tame stuff, but she raised an eyebrow at him.

'Been missing me?'

'Of course.'

'Okay. Put a bottle out.' That was an unspoken code between them and he felt a little guilty as he left her clearing the table.

An hour later and she'd gone, leaving the coast clear. He rang Andrea's office, and got the girl first ring. 'Andrew – how's the gallonage this week, Andrea?'

'Not bad, Andrew.' She had a lovely mellow voice, a hint of a chuckle that made his hair stand on end. 'Are you looking to see some figures?'

'Is that an invitation or a threat?'

'Hmm. Just be nice to see you again. If you can spare the time?'

'Half an hour?'

'Fine. Steer clear of the dragon.' He knew she meant Ida, the Mrs Rollason.

It was so easy, really, slipping into the Brewery offices like an old hand, catching Andrea on her own – did she organise that, he wondered – and finding a welcome in her that belied the tenseness that he might have expected. There was no doubt about her evident pleasure in his visit, for having risen from her desk on his arrival, offered a cheek for a social gesture, and then led the way into the back room where the files were stored, he found her looking for more than just a return kiss. '*Andrea!*'

'Shhh!' her hands were searching and her eyes were laughing. 'I thought so! I am an inspiration, then?'

'Don't – *don't . . . not here!*' It was embarrassing, but she had the measure of him, and it had to happen. When he could recover, all he could say was 'You're incorrigible!'

'Long words, Andrew. How about . . .' The door to the outer office banged and she raised her voice. 'These are the figures, Mr Hailsworthy. Quite a reasonable set, too. Would you like a copy?'

The rest of his visit rightly turned properly business-like and he managed to escape without further incident. Andrea's office junior was a sweet eighteen year old who appeared not to have any inkling of the *rapport* between her immediate boss and the Brewery's Consultant Accountant. Just as well, he thought. Andrea wrote a few lines on a scrap of paper, folded it and tucked it in his top pocket, then before he picked up his briefcase, shook his hand and winked at him.

'Thank you for your visit, Mr Hailsworthy. I hope you felt it was worth coming.' A girl with a sense of humour, that was for sure.

'Oh, indeed. It's always a pleasant experience to have preferential treatment.' Her slight inclination of her head, a lowering of her eyebrows and that little cheeky grin acknowledged his *double entendre* of a reply.

'See you again soon.'

'Look forward to it. May be we can get a bit further with the concept?'

'I'm sure we can.'

How could he go back to Roberta fresh from the administrations of this creature? He sat in the car for a few minutes, trying to readjust himself to the strange way his business had been abruptly coloured with unexpected relationships that had so heightened his libido. He hadn't looked to start *anything* with Andrea, not really; though she was very attractive and a pleasure to be with, he'd never have thought she would have looked twice at him, fifteen years her senior. How would she fit in with his real affection for Roberta? And what would happen if Samantha caught wind of her involvement? As he drove out of the yard, he thought he caught a glimpse of Andrea at her office window, watching him. He daren't wave.

The Manor driveway was empty. Was she at home? Nothing had been said about her next trip to London. The lawns had been mown that morning, judging from the scent of cutgrass everywhere. He knew she had an odd-job guy up from the village to do the routine jobs, but was also conscious she liked getting her hands grubby in the garden. She made a good job of looking after the place, he gave her that. He rang the bell, tried the door, found it unlocked, and walked in. The same sensation of warmth and comfort enveloped him; he loved the atmosphere, the *ambience* of the place and felt so very much at home.

'Roberta?' No reply. 'Marreee?' No reply. Perhaps she was in the back quarters. He walked on down towards the kitchen, had a peek in the sitting room, no-one, but the fire was slumbering, as normal, so she must surely be about somewhere. He reached the back door, heard steps across the yard, and the door opened in front of him.

Roberta squeaked, and all but dropped her basket of cut flowers. '*Andrew!* What *are* you doing here? You didn't ring!' She put the basket down carefully, shook her hair loose and brushed it back, a gesture he loved. 'Darling man. A lovely surprise!' She advanced on him so he could put his arms round her, pick her up and kiss her.

'You're a lovely girl, R. Can I take you to bed?' The earlier exploits with Andrea had not diminished urges normally kept well under wraps during the working day; the need to overlay the less meaningful with the more precious was paramount.

'*Andrew!* Really?' Her reply was half astonishment, half query. '*Really?*'

'Really. Let me love you. Properly.'

She struggled free, picked up her basket and pushed past

him. He had to turn and follow her back into the kitchen where she busied herself putting the flowers into two vases, taking care over the arrangements and frowning as she concentrated, ignoring him. Andrew just watched her, loving the movement. He caught her sideways glances.

Finally she was satisfied and faced him, hands on hips. 'No. Not unless.'

'Unless?'

'Unless you promise to take me away for a week. Honeymoon style.'

'How can I?'

She shrugged. 'That's your problem. You want me; that's the deal. I'll be your mistress, do whatever you want, but only if we're away together someplace. If you promise, than maybe we'll seal the pact the way you evidently want. Just as well it's Mary's half day off.' She laughed, picked up one of her vases. 'I'm taking this upstairs. Want to come?'

Again, she brushed past him, and led the way. He followed the swaying hips in her old gardening skirt and waited until she had carefully placed the flower arrangement on the table on the upstairs landing.

'Well?' She turned and faced him.

'Well what?'

'Will you take me away for a week?'

'When?'

'As soon as you like. You say.'

'Where?'

'When, where, you're all questions, Andrew. You're the man; you're supposed to make decisions. I'm just the humble *hausfrau*, doing as her master wishes.' She was taunting him, and flicked her skirt. 'What does master require today?' Her eyes were all mischief, bright, and the corners of her lips were twitching with suppressed mirth. He took a step towards her, and she turned and ran for her room.

Later; the word which compresses all the joys and energies of athletic and demanding fulfilment of passion into a simple passage of what, half an hour or so, she lay, sweaty and more than a little glowing, trapped underneath him, twisting her fingers in his tousled hair, staring at the ceiling while he was nuzzling away at her shoulder. Taking a deep breath lifted her breasts below him, and he raised his head, only to kiss each nipple in turn.

'Was I good for master?'

'Wanton!'

'You're the wanting one. I just lay here and let you. Was I good? You're falling out.'

'Need you ask? How about you, are you . . . ' asking about her state and moving to ease the situation.

She giggled, lifting her head sufficiently to view the depletion. 'Like discussing the weather, isn't? Bright and sunny with a hint of dampness? Or torrential downpours followed by sunny spells! As long as there's no depressions or anti-what's-its.'

It was his turn to laugh. She was such fun to be with, no inhibitions and a clear response to both their needs, a totally delightful experience. 'You're looking damp, Roberta, if that isn't an impolite continuation of the meteorology theme.'

'And you've wilted. Too much heat, not enough water. Come on, let's water you!'

When they'd showered, and Andrew had been careful not to get involved with any of Roberta's own scented shower gel, he watched her dress. She kept her eyes on him, loving the way his eyes followed her every move. 'So you will take me away, won't you?'

'Roberta, I'd love to. Being with you, like this. Watching you dress, knowing *all of* what you are. I'll think of something. Love me?'

'Love you. *Oh, Andrew!*' Without warning, he found himself all but bowled over with her arms wrapped tightly round him, and her upturned face seeking the kisses she desperately craved. If the phone hadn't rung she might have found her careful dressing was a waste of time, but the intrusion broke the spell. 'Get dressed, Andrew, while I answer this downstairs.'

'Nothing of consequence,' was her reply when he rejoined her in her sitting room.

'Now tell me why you came?' She crossed to the window and stared out. Would that he lived here, was *her* man, with no complications, gave her a child to nurture and love and *mother*. The utter entanglement of the rights and wrongs of what she wanted, what was Andrew's and what was Samantha's, was fast becoming a child's nightmare of knots and uncertainties. Why had she fallen for him, why hadn't she found some single bloke who fitted the job description? Well, she hadn't and Andrew wasn't going to go away, not if she'd anything to do with it.

'I wanted you.' he said.

'Liar. You wanted a bit on the side.'

Her teasing remark annoyed him. 'Andrea!' The girl's name slipped out before he knew, and his heart missed a beat. Oh, *hell!* Now he'd done it.

'*Andrea?* Andrea? Who's she, for God's sake, Andrew?' She whirled round and stared at him. He was going red, damn him! 'You *bastard!* You've had another girl, haven't you! I'm not just the only one you're fucking on the side then!' She went to hit him, thumped his chest, and slapped his face, making him reel away.

'I haven't *fucked* her! She's only the office girl at the Brewery, she'd been making eyes at me, Roberta, and that's the truth. I saw her this morning, had to get away, which is why I came to see you!' She was standing, legs apart, breathing heavily, glaring at him. 'I wouldn't touch her! Roberta, how could I, I care for *you!*' Would she believe him? He *did* care for her, which was true. And he loved her, in a very masculine way, true, but she was growing on him, and he'd be devastated if she dumped him just because of his lightweight flirtations with the younger girl. He moved towards her, but she backed away.

'How do I know? I don't, do I? I don't *know* anything about you! How many girls have you taken to bed during office hours, Andrew? Is that how you keep the business going, between your clients legs?' Now she was losing control, and with her flushed face and angry eyes, she could be getting hysterical. He went after her, she continued to back away but collided with an armchair and went sprawling, put out an arm to save herself, and he heard the wrist snap.

'Oh – bugger, bugger, *bugger!*' Cradling her broken wrist, curled up with the unexpected hurting of it, she started to cry, with the sudden anger, the foolishness of it all, and now the *pain!* 'Andruuoo – it hurts!' She was a sprawled, crumpled, anguished heap on the carpet.

The anger had gone and now she was just a silly little child of a girl in agony, crying for help, and his heart melted for her. 'R! I'll call for an ambulance. We need to get you to hospital! I'm sorry, my darling, this shouldn't have happened. I'll make it up to you, promise.' He felt his own tears coming, and wished, oh how he wished, he never invited that stupid sex mad Andrea round that evening. What had he been thinking of? Crouching down alongside her, seeing the contorted and now swollen wrist, he cradled her against him. 'I love you, Roberta!' And he believed it, the first time of saying in these clear words.

'Stupid man. Now look where this has landed you. A crazed girl with a bent wrist. What's Sam going to say? No, don't touch it. Drive me, Andrew, *you* take me to hospital. I want you with me.' Tearful eyes looked up at him and he knew he couldn't leave her.

It was true; he did love her, and brushed her lips with his. 'Of course. I'm sorry, my darling. After such a wonderful time, too.'

'At least I've got some memories saved of the day. I'm sorry, too, Andrew. I shouldn't have doubted you. No right to really, what you do is your affair. But . . . '

'All right, R. Come on; let's get you up. Pity Mary isn't about.'

'She'll be back later. We'll have to leave her a note. Ouch!'

'I'll make you a sling. Hang about.' He looked around for something he could use, and saw the cotton runner on the small table by the window. 'Can I use that?'

'Anything.'

Between the two of them, he managed to get her arm supported with the damaged wrist lying in the width of the runner. He wrote a brief note for Mary and went to leave it on the kitchen worktop. *'Roberta's broken her wrist – taken her to Hospital, will ring with up-date – Andrew'*

Getting her into the car was a painful affair; when she sat back in the seat she almost passed out with oncoming shock and the pain. Andrew was concerned, wishing he'd phoned triple nine, but the die was cast. It was twenty minutes to A & E, and the kafuffle getting her out again and into the triage bit, then parking the car and finding change for the machine for the exorbitant fee got him more than a bit hassled. By the time he'd got back, she'd been assessed and was waiting her turn. The information display thing with its racing letters in red was no calming device either – *'Waiting time Two Hours'* it was saying, unhelpfully.

'*Two* hours!Heavens – *two* hours! With you in pain?'

'Look, Andrew – you go. I'll be all right; I'll get them to ring when I've been seen. Really, you don't need to wait. Thanks for bringing me.'

'I can't leave you, R, and I won't, not like this.' He got up from his chair and went to the desk. The receptionist girl was well used to the indignation.

'I'm sorry, sir, but your wife *will* be seen as soon as we can. There've been quite a few major problems this afternoon and we do have to see the serious cases first. As long as she's comfortable; really, we'll always do our best.' She smiled at him, and yes, she was quite pretty. That helped. Very often the sour faced unhelpful people ended up on reception, which always made matters worse. He turned back to Roberta, she'd got her eyes closed and her head fell sideways.

'Roberta?' He was going to tell her the girl thought she was his wife, but got no response.

'Roberta!' Was she unconscious? He turned back to the girl on the desk, but she'd beaten him to it, seen the collapse, and in minutes Roberta was being lifted onto a trolley and wheeled away, almost before he knew what was happening.

'You can come if you like, Sir, while we assess the damage?' He followed, into one of the many side rooms, and sat on the chair by the door while the staff fussed over her. Then she was being taken through into another corridor, and the young guy who seemed to be the one in charge was talking to him. 'Simple fracture, Sir, happily, no complications, so we'll be able to set it without surgery, just manipulation. Your wife will have a plaster on for about six weeks, though, so no more washing up!' He was trying to make light of things, part of the job, Andrew supposed.

'She was unconscious!'

'Nothing to worry about, just a faint, really. We'll get some glucose drip into her and she'll be fine. Now, if you'd like to wait, we'll call you when she's ready to go home. 'Bout half an hour?'

When the straight haired nurse he'd seen wheel Roberta away finally came back to him, and he looked at his watch, it may have been more like an hour. He must have dozed, glad that he'd managed to get a corner seat in the open reception area. He'd not fancied any drinks from the trolley and was now suffering hunger pangs. No lunch, he was ready for a meal. Nearly time he was back home, too. What was he going to say to Samantha?

'I said, your wife's ready to go home, Mr Smiley.' She wasn't smiling, not this one.

'Oh, yes, sorry. Miles away. Where . . .?'

'Follow me.' No please, then. He followed the narrow straight back and shapeless legs to the recovery area. In a cubicle with the young Doctor chap, Roberta was sitting up, with a shining white plastered forearm, just fingers and a thumb showing. At least she was sort of smiling.

'Right, Mr Smiley. I'll leave you do it. She's to come back to see the Orthopaedic Reg. in a couple of weeks, just to check. She's been a good girl. No problems. Just make sure she rests for a couple of days, to get rid of the anaesthetic and the shock. Don't hit him too hard with the plaster, Mrs Smiley.' He smiled at his own joke, and went out through the curtains.

'Are you going to take good care of me, *Mr Smiley?*' She can't be too bad, if she'd picked that one up, he thought.

'Certainly, *Mrs Smiley!*' They both giggled, like two school children. 'I'd better get dressed, then, so you can take me home.'

'Dressed?' He was puzzled. 'I thought you'd broken a wrist?'

'I know. Don't ask me why, but someone had a thrill getting my knickers off. Over there.' She pointed at a hanger, where true enough, her dress and presumably underwear hung. 'You'll have to help, Hubby, dear.'

Andrew pulled a face. He did *not* like being called hubby, not even by Samantha. Roberta swung half naked limbs off the trolley and unashamedly tried to divest herself of the shapeless theatre gown. He had to help, and saw the bruises on her arm. 'What did they do to you?'

'Manipulation, it's called. He did say, and apologised, but it's better than being cut open.'

'Hhmmph. Well, at least your fainting fit got you out of the waiting time. Just as well. Can you stand up?'

'Thought it might. Yes I can. Pass me my pants.'

Between them she got dressed and they walked out into the late afternoon sun. Once clear of the door, she pulled him round with her good hand, and kissed him, hard, on the lips.

'Thank you, Andrew. For caring. I love you. Don't play around with any more Andrea's. Samantha I can tolerate, but I *need* you.'

'I love you too, Roberta. I didn't think I did, but now I know different. Don't knock Andrea though, because she may be useful. No – I mean it. You'll see.'

Mary was concerned and even worried at the note she'd picked up. How on earth had Roberta managed to break a wrist, and why was Mr Hailsworthy involved? That one was getting rather too close to her girl for a married man, despite her evident appreciation of his involvement. Oh, yes, she knew they'd been to bed together, for the bedroom was in a fair old state. In the morning, too! Still, if her Roberta was enjoying life, then it was up to her. Surely their lovemaking hadn't been that frenetic? She went all twizzly inside at the thought. As she stripped the sheet off the bed and bundled it up for the wash, her mind went back a decade or two and how much fun she used to have. Sighing at the deception and the part she still had to play, she took the sheet and the other things out of the laundry basket down to the kitchen.

By the time she'd got the washing machine under way and made herself a cup of tea before starting on the evening meal, it was gone half five. The note hadn't been timed, so goodness knows how long she'd have to wait before she got any news. Maybe she'd ring the Hospital and ask? But just as that thought had surfaced, as if by telepathy, the phone rang.

'The Manor.'

'Mary, it's Andrew; we're just about to leave the Hospital. Back in about half an hour. She's fine – well, as good as, under the circumstances, she says not to worry about her. Which I know you will, but really, it could have been worse. See you soon. 'Bye'

So that's a bit of a relief. Best get some more vegetables done, then, he'll surely stay for dinner. Wonder what tale he'll tell his wife? Mary poured herself the dregs of the teapot, grimaced at the stewed taste, and got on with the peeling.

Roberta also wondered how Andrew would get all this past Samantha, as she sat alongside him driving carefully and sedately back to the Manor. His face was a picture of concern, and she loved the set of his jaw, the strong neckline, the way his hair curled over his forehead.

She could feel his strength and the wanting of her even now, and wondered what making love without one arm, well, hand, was like. 'Love me?' The question slipped out, unconsciously, and hung in the air.

He carefully turned into the driveway and seemingly ignored her. She looked straight ahead, at the wonderful old house that was her's, legally and finally her's, and wished, oh how she wished, she could share it with him and children of her own. Her thighs tightened and her tummy twitched. He turned the car so she could get out nearest the door. He was a caring, thinking, man.

'I love you, Roberta. How, why, when, where, I just don't know. Let's just let time take us along, heh?' As she turned to look at him, he lifted her chin with one finger and reached over to kiss her gently. 'You're a very precious girl. Now we'd better let Mary have a look at you. She won't rest until she knows you're all in one piece.' He helped her out and up the steps. He used her keys to open the big front door, and without thinking, picked her up and carried her across the threshold.

Mary had heard the car and was on her way. She saw her mistress being lifted in, and put her hand to her mouth. 'Oh, Miss Roberta!'

Andrew realised what she'd assumed, and laughed. 'Sorry, Mary, it's not that bad.' He put his precious girl back on her feet, and as she straightened up, Mary could see the plaster.

'Oh *Miss Roberta!*'

'It's not as bad as it looks, Mary. A simple fracture, so they say. No washing up for a week – or two. And housebound, sort of, for a while. No driving.'

'How did you manage to do that, Miss Roberta?' The inevitable question, which Roberta had worried over, but Andrew beat her to the answer.

'She got cross with me, Mary, and fell over the chair in the sitting room. My fault, I suppose. I think we've patched things up, haven't we, darling?'

Oh, so it's 'darling' is it now? Mary took the phrase on board and kept a straight face. 'So that's why a chair was on its side. Hmmph. Are you staying for dinner, Mr Andrew?' At least he was entitled to a Mr Andrew instead of a Mr Hailsworthy if Roberta was his 'darling'.

Andrew looked at a silent Roberta. She was still absorbing his more than tacit admission of their relationship, what with being carried over the threshold and named 'darling' in front of Mary . . . "If you can, Andrew, it would be nice. You'll have to let Samantha know."

Andrew had a strength of resolve beyond his dreams. He pulled out his mobile, switched it back on after its sojourn in the 'no mobiles' area of the hospital, and punched the buttons.

'Samantha. Yes, I've been caught in a bit of a crisis at the Manor, with Roberta. I'm going to stay here for dinner, is that all right? No, not sure. Just you carry on. Yes, fine, see you later then. 'Bye.' He snapped the phone shut. 'She doesn't seem to mind. She's got a meeting tonight anyway, so no real problem. I'm all yours.'

I wish you were, Roberta thought. Well, I'll make the most of what I've got. 'Right, Mary. What have you organised? Get a bottle out, and light the candles. Oh, and we'll eat together. I mean it. I'm going to change. Come and help me, Andrew.'

An eyebrow was raised, but Roberta was unabashed. In for a penny, and all that. She knows, she thought, and she also knew Mary knew she knows, so to hell with conventions. If I come down to dinner with no knickers, then I do. So what! She wheeled round and marched up the stairs. Andrew didn't quite know where to put himself, but his fleeting glance at Mary elicited a wink before she vanished back to her domain. He followed Roberta upstairs.

'Look, she's changed the bed. Oh dear me!' Roberta didn't sound as concerned as her phrase suggested. 'I rather think, Andrew dear, that you've burnt your boats with Mary. Now, what shall I wear?' She was tugging, one handedly, at her dress zip. 'Come on, what are you waiting for? A perfect excuse to strip me naked and you're hanging about? Get on with it!'

Going back to his domesticity with Samantha was going to be harder than ever. The cosy meal they'd had, all three of them, had been very pleasant. Roberta behaved, Mary was quite relaxed as well as attentive, and conversation was impeccably correct. Andrew felt as though he'd been part of the scene for years, which was just what Roberta intended. She managed really rather well, sort of one handedly, apart from splashing sauce on her plaster. At least, as she had said, she could still lift a wine glass, though she did admit that her damaged wrist was painful and ached a lot, despite painkillers. Once the meal was over, and they'd even had coffee and mints, all very correctly, in the sitting room, Mary discreetly bid them a good night, and withdrew. She'd put the dishes in the washing up machine, she said, before she went, but she'd be back first thing to see to breakfast. 'She's a brick,' Roberta had said, 'But a discreet one.' He'd kissed her a few times and seen her upstairs and into bed, resisting the evident temptations, aware he had a very tired and slightly traumatised girl on his hands. She may even have fallen asleep before he softly closed the front door behind him, hearing the dead latch snick into place. But he had a key in his pocket, her last minute gift. 'It's only right, *Mr Smiley,*' she'd said, 'you're entitled,' and smiled a sleepy smile at him.

Samantha was still out. He didn't waste any time, stripped off and climbed into their bed. Maybe if he was asleep when she came home? He didn't fancy a late night interrogation, not after such a pleasant evening. He certainly was tired. And tomorrow he'd have to tell Andrea she was wasting her time. Pity, though, she was a lovely little thing, and. . . .

EIGHT

Samantha appeared preoccupied the following morning. She'd slipped out of bed early and his first waking appreciation was hearing the shower run. His breakfast was already on the table when he came down, unusually everything was in place, orange juice, his brand of cereal, even the offer of bacon and tomato, and the coffee was already brewed. She'd eaten, though; the dish was on the draining board with her glass and mug.

'Nice meal at the Manor?' No undertones either, surprisingly.

'Yes, thanks. Small reward for services rendered. Your meeting go okay?'

'Uh huh. Sort of. Look, we need to have a talk, something's come up. Lunchtime or later this evening?'

'Sounds ominous. I'm staying in the office this morning. Lunchtime?'

She smiled at him. 'Fine. Nothing ominous, as you would say, merely an opportunity that's turned up. I'm doing a stint in the Charity Shop this morning. See you lunchtime.' Before he knew it she'd gone, and left him wondering what on earth she'd got up her sleeve.

It was true he had to spend some time behind the desk. Neglecting the bread and butter clients in favour of playing knight gallant – and more – to the undeniably shapelier and physically rewarding ones was a short road to disaster. He steeled himself, and buckled down to some very mundane routine work. Half way through the morning he fetched a coffee, and with a jolt realised he'd not rung Roberta. Initially the line was engaged, but when he tried again after finishing his coffee, it rang.

'The Manor.' It was Mary, then.

'Andrew. How's Roberta this morning?'

'Oh, Mr Andrew. She's fine. I'll put her on. One moment.' He heard a muffled exchange, then *her* voice. 'Morning, darling. I take it you are still my darling? Not been, er, castrated or anything?'

'No.' He was surprised at her. 'I'm still intact, thank you. How did you sleep?'

'On my own. You?'

He laughed. 'As good as. Samantha's gone charitable this morning, but she wants to have 'a talk' at lunchtime. Wish me luck. How's the wrist?'

'Achy. Mary's not as nice a dresser as someone else I know. When do I see you again?'

'Maybe not today, I'll see. What are you going to do with yourself?'

'Cheeky! As if I'd explain! Think about you, read a sexy book, think about you some more, have a nice lunch, read some more sexy books, you know, all that sort of thing. You?'

'Run my eye over some less than sexy figures, think about you, put right all the mistakes I made while thinking about you, dream of some *really* sexy figures – sorry – figure, then I shall phone you again and tell you how much I love you. . .'

'Enough to want to marry me?' Silence. Had she stunned him? 'Andrew?'

He'd not replied, just found his heart pounding at the thought. Marry her? How could he? 'Roberta,' and she heard the catch in his voice. 'If I could, I would. I love you.'

The depth of silence between them was profound.. She'd proposed to him, over the phone. He'd virtually said 'yes'. 'I mean it.'

'Yes, darling, I know you do. That's enough for me. You have a key. Use it.' The phone went dead.

The rest of the morning went by incredibly slowly, minute by aching minute. It was if he was waiting for his own execution, pacing one step and another step down the road to oblivion, yet it wasn't oblivion, it was infinite infinity. The comfortable world of the day to day, the routines, the identicalness, the boring boring sameness, all that would be swept aside, tipped into a plastic bag of un-recyclable remnants of a useless existence. Nothing would remain. He would have to rebuild a life, a brand new being, constructed on the site of the total demolition of all that he knew and at one time, had strived for and, admittedly, had once loved. Maybe he still did.

Samantha returned at twenty-five past one. Exactly; he would remember the time forever. She was humming, strangely, totally out of character. She flung some bags down on the kitchen table, flicked the switch down on the kettle and reached up for the coffee jar.

'Coffee?'

He nodded.

'I'm leaving you.' It was such a prosaic statement, said without emotion, prelude, histrionics, or even attitude. 'I've got a job with the Charity, flying out next week. Sierra Leone. Looking after the Aid team. Contract for a year, maybe longer. You'll manage, won't you?'

There was a phrase, he recalled, that seemed to fit the bill. Gob smacked, that was it. Gob smacked. 'You're pulling my leg.'

'Nope. Didn't think you'd mind, after all, there's always Andrea. She'd move in like a shot. Sugar?' She stirred his mug for him. 'Sorry about the short notice, but I didn't get the clearance until yesterday. Farmers Market will miss me, but that's tough. They'll survive. You can always visit if you want – they fly dependants out twice a year for free. Do you good, holiday in the sun. Right, lunch?' She pulled some pizzas out of one of the bags. 'Better get used to ready meals; I guess you'll find they're easier.'

'You're serious?'

'Never more so. Real feeling of being needed. All the things I'm good at rolled into one, and anyway, it's a challenge. Challenge for you too, I suppose. Do what you want, Andrew, while I'm away.'

'What about the children? What will they say?' He was clutching, foolishly, at straws.

'I've had words with June. She thinks it's a great idea, working with these people out there.'

Naturally, he thought. 'What about Peter?'

'He'll think it's a hoot, if I know him. He'll be the first to fly out to see me, you'll see.'

Yes, he would, if there's a free meal at the end of it. He knew he shouldn't say that about his son, but it was true, none the less. 'Vaccinations? Visas?'

'All done. While I was away.'

Oh, so she's as devious as I've been, then. Nothing much more he could say. At least he'd get a reduction on his Council tax. 'You'll miss me?'

She laughed. 'More than you'll miss me? Get real, Andrew. We'll both have a ball, and you know it. Then when I've done my stint, we'll see what we feel like, heh?'

He felt drained, totally drained. Here he was, sweating on the concept of trying to explain to her that they may have reached crisis point, that he had fallen for Roberta and he might be leaving her, and she'd handed the whole thing to him on a plate, with a virtual open cheque. Unreal, more than real. 'What if you get taken ill or something?'

'Then the Charity will fly me home. Fully insured, you know. All ayes dotted, all tees crossed. Don't worry about it. Just enjoy life; I know I will.'

'When do you fly out?'

'Tuesday. Spending the night with a girl in West London, flight leaves at half past eight. I'll let you know when I'm there. They do have e-mails, you know. How's Roberta?'

He started. How did she know about Roberta? She shoved a plate in front of him with half the pizza. 'One of Lorna's friends saw you in the Accident reception. What happened?'

'She fell over and broke a wrist.'

'Lucky you were there, then.'

'Yes.' The pizza was actually quite good. 'Is there a can in the fridge?'

'Celebrating, are we?' She opened the fridge door and took a can off the shelf, popped it for him and tipped it fast into his big glass. As it frothed away she sat down and started on her half of the pizza. 'Let me guess. You and Roberta had a fling, she got cross about something and you had an argument. Are you still friends, or was that the end of a beautiful relationship? How about Andrea, don't you prefer her?'

'Catty remarks don't sit well on your shoulders, Samantha. Andrea's a cute girl in many ways, but that's as far as it goes. Roberta gets into tantrums about silly things, and yes, it was as well I was there. We get on well, happily, because we may have a joint business venture involving her interior decorating company.' He wasn't going to elaborate, not now; there was no point.

'Well, you'll have your hands full with that one.'

He concentrated on his pizza, and didn't answer her.

She finished before he did, but then, she'd always been a rapid eater. 'I'm going to start sorting clothes out, upstairs. There'll be quite a few things I'll be taking to the Shop. Shan't need half the stuff I've got and what's left will be out of fashion.' She pushed her chair back and stood over him. 'You've not said I shouldn't go?'

'No, I haven't. If it's what you want to do, it's not for me to stop you. So long as you're sure.'

'Oh, I'm sure, all right. New beginnings, that's me.' She flounced out, and he heard her humming again. Well, that was Roberta's faux honeymoon sorted; suddenly he felt his spirits lift. New beginnings, for Samantha and him both. He looked forward to telling his lovely Roberta the good news, wondered how she'd react. Samantha had nearly scored ten out of ten on the accident, and he cursed the spies that she seemed to have lurking in all the dark corners. At least he hadn't got an irksome holiday to organise now, and he guessed the family party was off as well. He retreated to the front room and turned the television on for company, for he couldn't have gone back behind the desk. Blowed if there wasn't a documentary about the refugee problem in Africa, with stark pictures of children just bags of bones, and she was going out there to try and help. In a way, he felt humbled by her action and strangely proud, seeing that flood tide of human disaster she would be trying to stem. Then his more clinical, analytic mind kicked in, and he considered how such misery could come about in the first place; over population, corrupt administrations, fanatical regimes that no regard for life whatsoever. The sad thing was he believed that often all the aid did was encourage the population to breed even faster because they had more energy. Maybe what they should be doing was encouraging some rationale, so population matched food supplies; after all, that's what happened in other species. Survival of the fittest, without interference. The chaos out there was, ironically, nature's way of sorting the problem, however cruel it seemed. How did we manage before Oxfam or Christian Aid, he wondered? Disasters have been a fact of life – or death – since Adam first arrived. Look at what happened to the Egyptians, the Maya Indians, the Jews, heaven help us. It unsettled him; he switched it off and went upstairs.

Samantha was well into her third drawer, with piles of clothes on the floor in the guest room. 'This lot's going. Packing that lot, or least some of it till I run out of weight allowance. You can deal with that heap, keep or chuck as you fancy.'

Some of the dresses were memorable ones, things he'd loved her wearing, and his emotions began to get the better of him. 'I'll miss you.'

'No you won't. We've drifted apart, Andrew, you know that, I know that. Okay, mutual passions erupt every now and again, but it ain't the love it used to be, now is it?' She stood and faced him, arms akimbo. 'I'm not the girl you loved to take out, go on exploratory trips with, took to bed or shagged on the grass just when we felt like it. We've changed, Andrew, and you know it. So just let's have a year apart and see how we get on. No recriminations please, no pricks of conscience, no worries about who's doing what – to whom – or when.' Then she heaved a huge sigh and stared at the ceiling. 'Maybe I'll miss you, more than you'll miss me, who knows?'

Andrew couldn't help himself, stepped forward; avoiding a pile of old shoes, and took her in his arms. 'I do still love you, Samantha, despite what you say. Maybe in a totally different way.' He held her at arms length and they stared at each other, then slowly, she pulled back and unpinned her hair.

'There is only one way, Andrew.' She laughed, an early, girly Samantha laugh. 'At least, there has been only one way lately, but I seem to remember other versions. Game?' That, too was an early euphemism they had enjoyed using, and he remembered one wedding they'd been invited to when she'd said 'Game?' to him during the reception and they'd ended up in the bride's bed, very nearly being caught *in flagrante delicto.*

He saw the coquettish smile in her and smiled back. 'Game.'

They hadn't lost the knack of pleasing each other, despite the day-to-day coolness. Andrew savoured the obvious difference in her since she'd announced her decision, and it was clear she had enjoyed him. 'So okay, I'll miss you, or parts of you. At least it's something to remember. Don't get any ideas, Andrew, you won't change my mind. But we do have a few nights left, eh?'

He nodded, debating in his mind whether he should say anything or just let matters ride.

Despite the unusualness of taking her to bed in the afternoon, or come to that, taking her to bed at all other than to sleep, he felt peculiarly relaxed. Samantha, with a certain smugness, just lay there, waiting for his next move. He'd take a shower, and then maybe he'd suggest an evening out.

As evenings out with his wife went, it wasn't too bad at all. She'd happily agreed, and so they went to the pictures, enjoyed a historical comedy/romance, had a good meal, talked to some friends they met in the restaurant, and were home again by eleven. Samantha stripped off unhurriedly, watching him watching her. 'Quite like old times, isn't it?' She was teasing

126

him, willing him to react, aware of her body and his inevitable response. Twice in the same day, he'd not known her like this since, not since goodness knows when. Momentarily he thought of Roberta in her lonely bed, then of Andrea and her tease, tried hard to forget the mental picture of her intimacy, and took his frustration out by responding vigorously to what was immediately on offer.

'Steady on. You'll wreck the bed!' Good old Samantha, always thinking of the practicalities. He didn't quite lose it, but she did have the uncanny knack of deflating his ego just when he needed it most. Unlike someone else he knew, who carried him along on the crest of mutual demand and made as much of the running as he did. Seeing *her* in his mind's eye, recalling the feel of *her* brought him to fulfilment, whereupon the actual recipient of his athleticism gave a little snortle and promptly fell asleep. 'Trust her!' his last waking thought before tumbling over onto his back and falling asleep himself.

In the middle of the night, or early morning, he didn't bother to look at the time; he woke up, wide-awake for no apparent reason. Samantha was still fast asleep and making small snoring sounds, and then he remembered, she was going away. He wouldn't have her next to him in bed after, when, Monday? New beginnings, she'd said. Thoughts began to tumble around chaotically in his brain; the why's and wherefores of what she'd done; whether he was the instigator of her machinations to go abroad, or had he played no part in her decision-making? When did she start all this, was it their life style; had it been the children, him bringing his job home, was it the weather, the god-awful way the country was being run, the ceaseless imposition of petty bureaucracy on her interests in small marketeering, the relentless increase in traffic, the bloody mindedness of people in general all caught up in the same web of despair and unable to see proper space and daylight? He was beginning to envy her, ducking out from all this and going somewhere where just to survive another day was a miracle. No one would worry if you sold a chicken with or without its giblets out there, or complain if you drove the wrong side of a white line, if there were any white lines to start with. He thought of the Brewery and its endless quest to encourage pub tenants to tip more gallons down more teenage throats. Well, that could be a problem out there too, as well as lung cancer from over-marketed cigarettes, and Aids from frenetic sex, which was probably a natural extension of boredom or reaction to *their* problems. That thought, that there may be worse problems than we have at home, challenged him, and he started to worry about her, would she be in any danger? No more than here, getting hit by a drunken yob showing off his prowess at speeding in a stolen car to his under age pregnant girl friend. Nothing he could do about things like that, anymore than he could have stopped Roberta's former husband from falling off an Alpine road. That guy probably was near to the drunken yob specification, anyway. He didn't feel any real sorrow other than the guy may have been loved by someone once, even Roberta, bless her, except that now she'd got him well and truly out of the system. At least he'd had the decency to let her inherit the Manor. Then his mind turned to Andrea and how she'd been assaulted by another dropout. If he'd been nearby at the time that bloke may have been less intact by now. She really was a very decorative little animal, with all the right things in the right place, but a shame she acted the way she did. He felt somewhat embarrassed at the way he'd encouraged her and nearly taken advantage. At least she had been *that* strong-minded, enough to stay the right side. Hope she continues to stay *intacto,* which she would if he'd got any influence. Too nice a girl to be messed with. Samantha gave a louder snort and turned over. He lay perfectly still, not wishing her to wake, and fell asleep once more.

Daylight brought him back to the surface with a muddled brain. Something of the disturbed night's thoughts remained, in a jumbled heap, and he didn't feel at all rested. The encounter with Sam hadn't helped, but normally that wore off before dawn. Easing out of bed carefully, he made for the bathroom and the relaxation and restorative powers of the shower. After five minutes or so most of the debris of the night's mental wanderings had gone, to be replaced by the bright new clean golden prospect of waking up to Roberta at his side, with her awesome talent at brightening his day. Towelling his hair, smiling at himself in the dewed mirror, he reached for the talcum powder and relished the smoothness and subtlety of the scent. What to do today? Help Samantha pack, spend another day at the desk, do some client visits, or yield to temptation and go tell Roberta the good news?

A still sleepy-eyed and bedraggled Samantha disturbed his reverie. 'Can I use the loo?'

He managed a light kiss on her cheek as he gave her the space. 'Sleep well?'

'Can't remember. You smell nice.'

'So will you, after you've showered. I'll brew some coffee.' Goodness, this was getting more like the old times every hour. He'd be *really* sorry to see her go at this rate. Choosing a clean shirt with care and a well-pressed pair of trousers improved his humour even more. Decision – go and give Roberta the news, then maybe lunch, and an afternoon visiting other *nice* clients. It was a day for feeling full of *bonhomie*.

Breakfast over, and Samantha still inured in sorting out the debris of her wardrobe, he drove light heartedly to the Manor. A sort of 'returning home' feeling gripped him, and he whistled as he went, full of hopeful anticipation at her delight. The Manor gardens looked good, as ever, and the mellow stonework smiled at him as he crunched the gravel to the *open* door. Open? Then she must be about in the garden somewhere?

'Roberta?'

'Andrew! I'm round here!' That voice, the pleasure in her, it made his heart sing. She was beautiful, so beautiful, and so, so happy. Light summer skirt, swaying in the fullness of it, cotton blouse straining the buttons, open-toed sandals, with two summer roses in the one good hand; he could eat her. 'You're a lovely surprise, my darling, and my, you're looking smart! What brings you here at such an early hour? Have a rose.' He took the proffered rose and dipped his nose in its fragrance.

'Almost as good as you. How's the wrist?'

'Better than last night, but I can't get used to the lump.' She still had her forearm resting in a simple sling. 'Teach me to get cross with you. Kiss me?'

She stood on tiptoe and closed her eyes, as he obliged, one hand round her waist, one holding the rose behind her head. There was surprise in her voice at the tightness of his arm round her. 'Andrew? What's up? There's something, isn't there?' Her intuition was remarkable, or was it?

'Will you marry me?'

Her eyes flew open and he saw the dawning delight in her, and he knew, knew well, this was going to be his new beginning. 'Andrew! You *mean* it! What's happened? Have you left her? Have you told her? How?'

'Hey, hey, Roberta! You haven't answered my question. You asked yours, I gave you an answer, now it's my turn.'

'But we were only playing games, weren't we? Imagination, wasn't it? You *really* mean it, Andrew?'

'*Will* you marry me, Miss Roberta former Smiley?'

Her free hand came up and stroked his face, her eyes alive and singing. 'Yes, *yes, oh, YES!*'

'There's a small catch. I still have another wife. At the moment.'

The light in her eyes dimmed. 'Tell me.'

'Samantha's going abroad. Next week. Sierra Leone, to run a Charity base for Aid there, for a year. It's a sort of separation, and if it turns out as permanent, then no doubt we'll divorce. In the mean time, my darling, I have *carte blanche*. Your honeymoon on account is on. Happy?'

The sunlight followed the drifting clouds and raced across the lawn towards them, bathing her in a warm glow. The shrubs and their burgeoning flowers came sharply into focus, and she pulled him back to her, inwardly cursing her injury. 'Happy.' It was a soft response, but all he wanted. They stood for what seemed ages, a gentle kiss, a pause, a gentle kiss, a squeeze, another kiss. Her head resting on his chest, her hand stroking the small of his back, he could feel the warmth of her so close, and the wanting of her.

'Oh, Andrew, *Andrew!* This is all too, too perfect. I shall keep this rose forever. Let's go and tell Mary.'

'Tell Mary?' He was a wee bit puzzled. Surely she knew the score?

'I've just got to tell someone, Andrew, I'm so happy'!'

So Mary was told that Roberta and Andrew were to be considered mutually in agreement that they would marry when it became legally possible, that she was to regard this as privileged information and otherwise pretend that her mistress and Mr Andrew were 'just good friends'.

She could not conceal her delight. 'Mr Andrew' had passed her acceptance test when Roberta had taken him to London and she'd come back radiant, happier than she'd seemed since before her careless former husband started eyeing that chit of a secretary girl.

She beamed at them both. 'Well, now, there's nought like getting ahead on yer'sen. Mind you, your present wife seems a steady sort of lass, but I guess she's lost her sparkle for 'ee. Shame, that, yer ken, but if you can make a happy life between you, then God bless.' She always seem to lapse into her native northern dialect whenever emotion ran high, as Roberta knew from old, and was that a wee bit of a tear in her eye? 'Now, will you both be wanting a bite o'lunch? There's some real good smoked ham, and I've fresh lettuce, mebbe a few new Jerseys? I reckon a decent bottle of that Chablis, Miss Roberta, so we's can toast you'n future?'

Roberta could only but chortle at her; with that extra bit of colour she always seemed to have whenever she was thinking beyond the hand holding stage. She turned to Andrew. 'How about it? An 'at home' celebratory lunch? Then what's on the agenda for the afternoon, hey? If I ply you with enough wine, will you have to stay until gone tea time?'

His mind was racing ahead, to the time when he could involve her in all the day-to-day things, when they could discuss how their interests could prosper together, and he'd be able to love her to bits. He knew she wouldn't be bored with his business; she'd want to be part of what he wanted to do, as much as he would in hers. All he felt now was the need to cherish her, and the time between now and when Samantha would fly out of his life appeared to be impossibly ages ahead.

'Lunch sounds lovely, Mary. Is it warm enough to have it outside?' He ignored Roberta's invite to stay on this afternoon for the time being, waiting until he could drag her back outdoors and round into the little rose courtyard, where the heat of the early summer sunshine was bringing the fragrance and the colour to life. There was a rather shabby white metal slatted bench, and he sat her down. 'I need to ask, Roberta, whether I should move in with you, or continue to live where I am. You needn't ask which I prefer, because that should be very obvious, but you must decide. Whatever you think is best. If I move in, then the die is pretty well cast, and I'll have an empty house on my hands, though I have an idea about that. If I'm here, we can get down to organising this new slant to your business, and certainly being office based here will improve matters for my side of things.'

With her pretty cotton skirt over her knees and her blouse, top buttons undone and the swell of her breasts very evident, he could have just swept her up and carted her off to bed that instant. The day she came off her horse was eons ago and he felt he had known her forever.

'Roberta?'

'Hmmm?'

'You haven't heard a word, have you?'

'What, darling? Oh, sorry. You want to move in? Sure. I want you to.' The tone of her voice was distant. 'All this, you, it just seems to perfect to be true. Promise me, Andrew, you won't rush off with another girl?'

Andrew felt for her; she was re-living the past and understandably comparing him with her late divorced husband, but it was very hard to sound positive about an answer. What if another twist of fate's iniquitous spirals brought some other factor into play? After all, it was only a stupid bit of plastic and his decision to walk off some depression that had brought them together. Admittedly he had never ever had these sorts of feelings before, the response in body and mind which came when he was with her, not ever. The relationship that had come with Samantha had been built on availability and some sort of concept of compatibility, maybe even just a desire to do what was expected of them at the time; it hadn't been always filled with golden moments from day one. Oh yes, they'd had those moments when it had been good and maybe most of the time they'd rubbed along fine, but nothing, *nothing*, like this.

Roberta was grinning at him, searching his eyes. 'Andrew? Who's in a brown study now?'

He punched her good arm, playfully, brushed her cheek with his hand. 'Which girl would that be?'

'Don't tempt me. Answer me, or no lunch!' Mary was advancing along the path with a tray.

'Are we bargaining then?' He got up to take the tray from Mary while she moved out an equally shabby looking white metal table from the little stone outhouse. He heard the seriousness behind her question; saw the concern in her gaze. 'I shan't run off, Roberta. Not now, not ever. I love you.'

Mary had heard him, he saw her face, and knew she'd be after him if he failed to live up to expectations. 'I'll just be fetching the wine, then. Won't be a tick,' she said, and waddled off again.

Roberta patted the bench. 'Sit down. You make the place untidy. I don't want to be hurt again, Andrew. I've let myself go, given you all I have. I would have rather broken my neck, falling of that stupid horse, than lose you. Will you give me – us – a child, Andrew?'

That took him by surprise, not something he'd given any thought to. *Children?* He sat on his hands, to stare out across the smooth level greenness of the lawn, at the compact mass of flowers in the opposite border and the dappled shadows of the silver birch. A mental picture of a toddler crawling over the grass, a young girl in a pinafore dress, an enthusiastic teenager batting a ball about, superimposed on the very Englishness of it all and what could he do? Still married to Samantha, how could he and Roberta have children? Was she still of an age?

She anticipated his question. 'I can, at least I hope I can. It's all still working,' then she giggled, looked at him with a coy sideways grin. 'It already might be,' then laughed aloud at the look on his face. 'Well, maister, youse have a way's with ee.' Her imitation of Mary's accent didn't do her justice, especially as Mary herself was returning with the wine cooler and a trio of glasses This was a twist to the affair he hadn't anticipated, or had he? It hadn't really entered his head, and being honest with himself, he perhaps should have considered *all* the implications that first time he'd loved her, in the sitting room in front of the fire. She'd been doing the driving, not him. She'd seduced *him,* not he her, willing though he may have been. Oh, Lord! He couldn't make any sort of rejoinder until later, now that Mary had come back and was uncorking the bottle.

She poured out three glasses, waited till they'd each grasped one, and raised hers. 'To you both – happiness in whatever life brings!'

Roberta clinked on Andrew's, not sure if she should reply, but Andrew could.

'To the occupants of the Manor, may they always enjoy each other's company.'

Roberta nodded, that was a really nice way of putting it.

'I'll leave you to it, Miss Roberta. I'll be back after five, if that's all right?'

'Thank you, Mary. For everything.' A meaningful comment, simply said, and Mary just nodded and walked away. 'Come on, then Andrew. Tuck in.' Mary's pre-plated ham and new potatoes with a salad was just right and the cool Chablis well suited. Only when the plates went back on the tray did Roberta return to her question.

'*Would* you like another family, Andrew?'

This time it was an easy answer. 'With you, Roberta, I'd love it, if you want to. I think you'd make a super mum.' The return look in her eyes was reward enough.

'What if I'm already pregnant?'

'Then we'll have a head start, and I'd love you all the way.'

'You mean it?'

'Yes.'

'Even if it messed things up with Samantha?'

'She'd have to understand. Not sure about my existing pair of kids, though. They have their own ideas.'

'I'd like to meet them, someday.'

'Someday.'

'Afters?' She reached for his hand. 'Mary's gone home.'

The implication was obvious, the desire already in place. Andrew was about to gather up the plates, but Roberta stayed his hand. 'Just bring the bottle and the glasses.' She led the way back indoors, skirt swinging, heart thumping. She *wanted* him, oh, how much she wanted him!

He'd actually fallen asleep on her, a combination of the warmth of the day, the lunch, the wine, and the loving. She'd been on top of him, full of exuberance, taking every advantage to work off her enthusiasm, and she'd been sublime, despite the obvious disadvantage of a forearm disabled. It only seemed to give her more incentive. With her hair straying all over the place, and the perspiration drying on her, she was a mess, and a teeny bit glad he'd gone to sleep. Moving naked limbs ever so carefully off the crumpled bed, she had a momentary twinge at Mary's possible thoughts, quickly forgotten, as she stepped into the shower, not forgetting to use that silly plastic bag to keep the plaster dry. . .

Andrew woke as he heard the shower start, and groaned. She was lovely, but a reckless lady once let loose, and he'd honestly meant to go and see other clients this afternoon. Much as he loved her, appreciated her desires, he couldn't let the business slide to pot. Her eyes were closed against the lather as he joined her, and started as he cupped a breast and held her injured arm.

'Eh! Oh, *yes yes yes!*' A natural instinct to caress her, and it seemed to be appreciated.

'I have to go, Roberta, and do some work, much as though I'd rather stay with you. I've promised.'

'Shame. Just as . . .'

'There'll be plenty of other times, R.'

'True. Just a pity to . . .'

'I know – just keep it warm.' He started lathering himself and she moved out to give him room. Their relationship was beginning to season; making allowances for the way things had to be.

Once showered and he'd finished drying his lover girl's back for her, and as he put his jacket on, his mind jerked back to that morning – was it only *two days ago?* – when they'd had the row over Andrea. She'd put something in his pocket. He fished the folded note out, and spread it out. Roberta eyed him curiously.

'What's that, darling?'

'Something that girl Andrea gave me.' He was reading it, and felt a chill.

'Don't be surprised if your wife runs out on you, and I'm here if you want me.' The *want* was underlined twice. How had she – Andrea – had any idea Samantha was going away, unless her mother had talked of it sometime? She must have, the only way she'd know. As for blatantly suggesting she could step into the gap, especially as he'd entrusted her with the knowledge of his relationship with Roberta. He'd been an idiot to ever give her the glad eye.

'So? What's it about?' Roberta was giving him the narrowed eye look.

'She gave me this *the day before yesterday,* Roberta; before Sam told me and you'd had the fall. She *knew* what Sam was planning, the little minx.' He let her read it.

'Hmmph. *Do* you want her?'

'Nope.' He nearly let slip how she'd enticed him on, and then run out at the crucial moment. He doubted if anyone would, well . . . and then he tried to forget her.

Roberta tore the paper to shreds. 'Just as well. I ain't having my man slip into another girl's knickers. Just you remember – or I'll send Mary after you with the kitchen knife!'

He helped her into a clean dress with a buttoned front. 'Then you'd have no chance of a family!' He lifted her hair clear of her collar and kissed her neck. 'Unless as you say, the deed's been done.' Then he coloured up, at once becoming amazingly self-conscious

'I'll let you know, dear Andrew, the moment I think there's any chance. Boy or girl?'

'Girl; another one like you.' With a little effort, he was entering into the spirit of her moment.

'Do my best for you. Maybe it's a case of 'here's one we conceived earlier'?' and she giggled again. 'Go on with you. You said you had more clients to see?'

He managed to get to Orchard Farm and dealt with the problem Jack Allbrother had with his bank's mistaken idea of how much interest was owing on a complicated loan, regretfully declined a cup of tea with him and his delightful little sparrow of a wife, before driving on to the decrepit garage business in the next village that was hanging on to its existence on a bent wing and half a prayer. Poor old Richard Thomas, pushing sixty and still in the dark ages, couldn't connect with modern accounting and the threat of action from Revenue and Customs It would be easier to take the papers home than try and unravel them on site. He persuaded Richard to lend him a big box, and he shovelled all the papers he could find from the old man's roll top desk into it, promised he'd look after them, and endeavoured to reassure him that, no, he wouldn't be taken to court, even if he owed them something, which he doubted. More likely they owed him, judging from the piles of spare parts tucked away. One thing about Richard, he'd always got the bit you needed, even if it took a week to fit. Then he went home; to the prospect of another evening's unsettling description of the uphill task Sam would face in the outback, or whatever the wastes of Sierra Leone were called.

The weekend was a comfortless one. He couldn't face another visit to the Manor until Samantha had left, and had to content himself with phoning Roberta twice a day. She even joked about having another line put in just for his calls, which was something. He left Andrea alone; with no reason to go back to the Brewery until his accounts management plan had had time to work. Samantha herself seemed preoccupied, and didn't offer any creature comforts; perhaps, he mused, she was endeavouring to get used to the celibate life. Then Monday came, and at last she'd finished sorting out her luggage, a stack of cases in the hall waiting for the Charity's van to call – they would be flown out as part of the Aid flights. He stayed in the office all day, working his way steadily through Thomas's papers, a thankless task but one he only had to do the once. As soon as he had a reasonable idea of where they were with the tax he rang the Revenue and Customs office and told them what he thought; unsurprisingly got a promise of a 'nil action' letter in view of the amounts involved; it wasn't worth their time to follow it through, and anyway, he knew they trusted him. So he phoned poor old Richard and gave him the good news. At least one bloke's day had been made to shine.

Somehow the inevitable moment arrived, the taxi at the door, Samantha, in a smart new two-piece costume and with her overnight bag, in the hallway, picking up her travel papers from the hall table, and saying, 'I'm off then. I'll phone you when I'm at Melinda's.' A perfunctory peck on the cheek and she was gone, with the echo of the slam of the front door and the rattle of the taxi's diesel repeating in his ears like a nightmarish waking from a bad dream.

She'd gone. Gone – out of his life, just like that, and then the realisation of it hit him. He crumpled onto the hall chair; stared at the old sixties style wallpaper and all the comforting anaesthesia of Roberta's love and care vanished to leave the stark cold comprehension that Samantha, his wife of twenty odd years standing had walked out on him. He was on his own.

He couldn't help it, his eyes watered, his head suddenly started to pound, and he felt sick. How long he sat there he didn't know, becoming aware he was cold, miserable and cursing the way in which his life had been twisted about, unsure of how to climb back on board reality. It was the telephone ringing that got him stiffly off the chair, massaging his creased thighs. He managed a croaky 'Hello'.

'Andrew? Are you all right? You sound a bit strange. Has Samantha gone? I wondered if I should pop round, cheer you up. I've got nothing on this evening.' It was Andrea. It had to be Andrea, poised to leap into the gap at the first opportunity. He held the phone away from his ear, getting his mind back in gear. He didn't need Andrea. He wasn't sure if he needed Roberta either. He needed Samantha, dependable, boringly nice, sagging tummy and soft, soft thighs and the way she just took him in and he felt so cosy with her. But she'd gone, run out on him, left *him,* and suddenly he was angry. 'Blast the woman!'

'*Andrew? What did you say?*' Her voice sounded tinny in the earpiece, and realising what he'd said out loud, had to make amends. He brought it back to his ear.

'Sorry, Andrea. Sam's just gone. You've caught me at a bad moment.' He heard her breathing and his mind flipped, seeing her naked and all too sexy. Bad idea, when he was so vulnerable. 'You shouldn't be thinking of me. I'm too bloody old and I've just lost my wife. I'm not thinking straight.' Her opening gambit went back round his brain; '*pop round, cheer you up, I've nothing on this evening*'. 'Do what you want. I'm not going anywhere.' He put the phone down and went upstairs. The bed was unmade from last night, and the old clothes Samantha had worn during the day were strewn in a heap on the floor. Everything, even her underwear, she'd stripped off and dumped, put her new kit on and gone. Left the remnants, just as she'd left him. He swept them all up and got a whiff of her, sweat and scent, as he dumped them into the laundry basket. Her knickers fell onto the floor so he had to bend down and collect them, with a twist in his gut and a sudden pull at his genitals. Her, and the picture of thighs, a cotton covered crotch and wisps of pubic hair zoomed wide at his emotions. He flopped back onto the bed, holding the pants and just staring at them, held them close to his face, breathing in the muskiness.

His wife, all that was left of her to remember, a pair of sweaty pants and a futile erection, God help him. Wryly, he imagined her laughing at him, cynically telling him all he wanted was her body. So what? Wasn't that what all men wanted, a body? Rolling over, burying his face in the softness of the pillows – her pillow – and getting another nostril full of the scent of her hair shampoo. How long he'd lain there he just didn't know, but became aware of the doorbell. Who would that be? Oh, no, not Andrea. She'd no sense, that girl. He'd be no company. There it went again, an insistent drone like a bloody mosquito. Drinnnnng, drinnnnnng. He tumbled off the bed and almost lurched downstairs. His head was closing in on him, a heavy, thickening cloyingness of strain.

He held the door open and the girl, with all the vigour of youth and clean and shiny and nice and scented and sexy and smiling, gently took his hand from the door and closed it behind her.

'You're a wreck, Andrew. I'm here to cheer you up. Come on; let's get you a coffee, or something.' Ignoring him, she went through into the kitchen. She knew where things were, she'd been before, remember, he told himself, following her. 'It had to happen, you know.' Her glance at him was full of a mixture of concern and amusement. He was vulnerable and sad, not the self assured confident, competent professional; just a tired middle aged man who'd taken a severe knock in his self esteem. The kettle on, she busied herself clearing up the debris of the day, left just as Samantha had. 'She hasn't bothered to tidy up.' Andrea eyed him, just standing there, watching her. 'Want anything to eat? Had a meal lately?'

He shook his head. A scratch lunch, leftovers. She'd been gone a couple of hours. Andrea pushed a mug into his hand. 'Go and watch the telly or something. I'll rustle up a meal. Go on, shoo. I'll manage.' She turned him round and gently pushed him out of the kitchen, making no attempt to flaunt herself. He'd not really taken on board that Samantha had *left him*, she knew. Surprised and yet not surprised at his reaction. Some of the things her mother had said, the feedback from market conversations, womens' talk, cruel really, exposing a man's foibles to the world like that. Everyone was vulnerable in their own way, not that she was anything other than another female with her own quirks and fancies, but she'd got a soft spot for Andrew now and felt for him. Samantha should have been more alive to his needs, then maybe he'd have been more responsive to hers; and her thinking surprised her.

She hunted around; discovered some chicken pieces in the freezer, put some potatoes in the microwave and found a can of mushy peas. Inside twenty minutes she'd got a meal together, and went to find him. He was napping, in front of the television, poor man. 'Androooo?' His head came up. 'Meal's on the table.' She'd not bothered with a bottle, unsure of his needs in that direction.

'You're very kind. You didn't need to do all this, Andrea.'

'Huh. Someone's got to look after you. Where's Roberta?' She didn't want to mention her, but she had to clear the air, get things straight between them.

'This isn't her scene. She's not the mothering type.' Then the comment he'd made about her being a potential mother hit him and he had a pang of conscience. 'You really shouldn't be doing this, Andrea. People will talk. Roberta would skin me alive if she knew you were here. She's quite possessive.'

She gave him an old fashioned look under lowered eyelashes from the other side of the table and emptied her mouth before replying. 'Can't a girl do someone a favour? If she won't come and cook you a meal, she's not much use!'

He wasn't sure if he liked that remark, but didn't want to analyse it. He was beginning to warm up and feel less shattered. He pushed his chair back and reached for a bottle of red wine from the top of the cupboard. It wasn't very special, with a screw cap, but it would do. 'Drink?'

'Thank you. That would be nice.' It was the same as they'd had that night she'd had him get her orgasmic.

A full glass and then some later and he was even warmer. 'Thanks, Andrea. I suppose I needed that. Maybe I'd have just crashed out on my own. What time do you have to be back? I can do the washing up.'

'Not yet. I'll do it.'

'Then I'll dry.'

It didn't take long, and in standing beside her at the kitchen sink, her nearness was getting at him. She ducked from under the reaching arm, dried her hands and winked at him. 'Now, now! I'm not Roberta! I'll go and see what mess she left upstairs.'

Her light footsteps up the stairs, and then he heard her humming something as she moved about. A call, "Do you want me to deal with the laundry?"

He moved to the foot of the stairs. 'If you like, not my scene.'

A laugh came back at him. 'You been playing with her panties?'

That made him cross. 'Leave them!' It was all he had left of her, and he bounded up the stairs. The girl was holding them against herself.

'Bit larger than mine. Look.' Before he had a chance to do anything, she'd lifted her skirt hem and peeled her dress over her head. All she had left was a pink skimpy triangle and just enough bra to warrant the name. 'Bit sexier?'

His reaction was instinctive and commonsense nearly went out of the window. 'Last time you did this to me, Andrea, you messed me about. Don't do it. Put that dress back on. You're a virgin, you said. Just stay that way!' He made to leave the room and reached for Samantha's discarded bit of cotton, but Andrea easily avoided him, and in a trice she'd stepped into them and pulled the plain cotton over her pink thong.

'Fancy me now?'

He leant across the newly made bed to grab her, but she side stepped and he landed flat on his tummy, so he rolled to grasp a leg and then she was knees on top of him, tearing at him, the pants tore, his temper was up and with her own passions aroused with the inevitability of him taking her, sheer animal instinct took over.

It only took him minutes and she'd screamed with the sharp stab of pain, and then responded by nearly driving him into the mattress before clenching her thighs round him as

142

best she could. 'God! Why didn't I get you to do me before?'

The enormity of his actions hit him as the adrenalin ebbed away. What on earth had inspired him to take her, it was as good as rape, heaven help him. She didn't seem to care, her eyes were shining, her colour was up, and the dew drops of perspiration rolled between her breasts.

'Bloody bloody marvellous!'

'I hurt you.'

'A bit.' There was blood on the covers, just a smear, and a dampening.

'I'm sorry.'

'Don't be. I deserved it. One way of being de-flowered. Not bad. Better than rape on a bit of waste ground.' She was referring to her near brush with the yob.

'You don't mind?'

'Not in the least. I'd better not get pregnant though, had I? Might foul things up with Roberta for you. I wouldn't want to do that. Sorry. You know there's nothing else between us?'

'What do you mean?'

'I've no designs on you, Andrew. Just this.' She was still sitting on him, making him squirm. He was ticklish and she laughed, eased herself back and looked critically down. Reaching with one hand for the torn pieces of cotton and nylon, she used them and dropped them back onto his chest. 'Souvenir.'

'Did you intend this to happen?'

'No, I don't think so. Well, I don't know. Perhaps I did. I didn't know how you'd be. Do you mind if I said I felt sorry for you?'

'Strange way of feeling sorry, sacrificing your precious virginity.'

She laughed, a light girlish laugh. 'All in a good cause!'

'Now what?'

'Do you want me to stay the night? I will if you want. No obligation.'

'I don't know.' His mind was spinning.

'Then I will. I promise I'll be good. And I won't ever tell. Promise.'

So it was that they cleared up the rest of the debris, put the lights out downstairs, and she got into bed with him as though it was the most natural thing in the world, wrapping herself round him and feeling the comfort, just as he did. They slept, entwined, and in the morning he made love to her again, quietly and gently, and then she got up and showered and dressed and tidied up and kissed him and went away.

NINE

There had been no call from Samantha, at least, none he'd heard, but then other things had happened. Andrew's morning, having started so beautifully, became as uncertain as the weather, which had turned grey, threatening, and rather ominous. Had she arrived safely in London? Had she managed to catch her flight? Would she let him know when she arrived in Sierra Leone? He then asked himself, why should he care? But he did care, peculiarly, despite his savaging release of feelings on Available Andrea. With a cynical laugh at his own description of the girl, he felt he had to ring her.

'Andrew. You okay?'

'Hmmm-*mmm*. Rather. Still glowing, or at least I think I am. I can't see at the moment. You did nice things to me, Andrew, and I have *no* regrets. Can we . . . hang on a minute?' There was some muttered conversation in the background with her hand over the mouthpiece. 'Sorry. I'll have to go. Look, just let me know what you think. I won't get in the way, promise, and no obligations. Just a mutual need satisfied? Okay?' The phone went down.

He leant back in his office chair and pondered. What had he done to deserve having her on tap? The day might be grey outside, but this was almost too good to be true. The loss of Samantha was less impacting today, after last night's catharsis. Now he had to make his peace with Roberta.

'Roberta Smiley.'

'Andrew.'

'*Darling!*' Now he felt like a cad. 'Has she gone?'

'She's gone.'

'How do you feel? Lonely?'

'Sort of. When can I see you?'

'Now? We have to work out some logistics. Sooner the better. I've had some real positive vibes from some people about the I.D. weekends.'

'I.D.? Sounds a bit technical?'

A gurgling laugh and a sudden cough as she all but choked. 'Sorry, Andrew. My sense of humour. Interior Decorating. I. D. Got it? Instead of I.T.? Come on, hubby-to-be, come and earn your title. I'll get Mary to put the kettle on. It's coffee time.' Without waiting for any reply, she put the phone down.

As he slammed the door behind him, any thoughts of trying to reconcile his adventures with Andrea vanished, as if he was compartmentalising his life. Samantha had gone and now the family home was tainted with promiscuous gymnastics with another girl, which, on recollection, was more or less what Sam had hinted at; 'there's always Andrea, she'd move in like a shot' echoed in his brain. Well, maybe she should. He'd lease the house to her, she wanted out from under her parent's roof. Then he had a perfect excuse to visit. Was that being devious, or double-crossing?

No, he didn't think so. Andrea had firmly stated she'd no thoughts of any form of a relationship, just a need to satisfy her urges. He *loved* Roberta, and that was infinitely more than just sex, though that side was sublime. Andrea was merely a receptacle for his excessive masculinity, he told himself, whether that was an ego trip or a male fantasy. Whichever way, it would impact on Roberta's world, even provided there were no slip-ups. He blanched at the concept of Andrea falling pregnant; that would really mess up things for everyone. Roberta wanted children, which was fine, provided they were hers.

Roberta, his lovely Roberta, was waiting for him, standing on the Manor steps, hugging a cardigan around her shoulders against the threatening rain and cooler day, unlike the sunny welcome of previously. 'Come in, quick, so we can keep the place warm! Not a summer day, is it? Coffee?' She led the way into the kitchen, taking his kiss as the most natural thing in the world.

Mary looked up from her mixing bowl and smiled at him, pleased that Roberta had someone to care for apart from herself. 'Good Morning, Mr Andrew.' Just that, no reference to his separation.

With coffee mugs filled, Roberta edged him through into the sitting room, and catching his glance at the hearth rug, laughed, poked him in the midriff and he nearly spilt his coffee.

'Hey!'

'I saw you. Looking at the rug. Where it all began!'

'I thought it was on the roadside, you unconscious.'

'I prefer the rug. No, NO! Not this morning!' He'd put his coffee down and was advancing on her. 'Stay away! I've a broken wrist, remember! Sit down, behave. I want to talk to you.'

They discussed the whole of the Interior Design weekend course idea, and the conversion of the spare rooms to a Bed and Breakfast format, how it would impact on the way the Manor worked. Roberta saw Andrew in a different light, much more than just a figure man, but full of practical ideas and sensible suggestions. Mary came in with a new jug of coffee and a plate of chocolate biscuits and Roberta got her to sit down while she ran through the ideas.

'As this may change things quite a bit, Mary, I want to make sure you wouldn't mind. Mean a lot more work; maybe we'd have to get you some more help. What do you say?'

There was something so sort of dependably nice about Mary. Andrew's involvement with her as Roberta's mainstay hadn't been all that long, but he'd become attached to her dependability. She took it all in her stride without any apparent worries about the potential upset in her routines.

''T'will need some thinking about; but I dare says we can cope. There's a lovely little lass I knows who mebbe might like a bit job. She's not too bright, see, but along of me she'd be all right. Do 'er good.' Like mothering Roberta all over again.

If that was all it took, then we've got off lightly, thought

Roberta. 'Sure, Mary. When she's needed. We've got a fair amount of work to do in the house first, putting in the extra plumbing and so on, and we've got to get the old big barn converted into a studio cum workshop. That's something I wanted to do before . . . well, you know, but it never came to anything. In the meantime, Andrew's likely to move in with me, is that all right by you, - I mean, won't offend any sensibilities?' Too bad if it does, she thought, though she'd rather keep Mary sweet.

'If that's what you want, Miss Roberta. So long as he's domesticated. I could do with a hand with the chores sometimes, you knows!' She had a smile for him and a bit of a chuckle. If she'd been fifteen years younger . . .

Andrew grinned back at her. 'I have been known to do my bit.'

Roberta patted his hand, proprietarily. 'He's quite well trained, Mary. I'll keep him under control.'

He wasn't too sure about that; it sounded as though he was beginning to lose his independence to these two women, but just grinned at them. What else could he do? Mary rose from her chair and moved away. Her parting shot was welcoming. 'Nice to have a decent man about the house – I'll organise some lunch, shall I?'

Roberta wasted no time after clearing the air with Mary. 'Tonight, then, Andrew. You'll be sleeping with me. Fancy the idea?'

He nodded, not liking the memory of last night. Sleeping with Andrea had been fine at the time, but he hoped he wouldn't rue the day, sorry, night. At least here he'd be free of her temptations. 'I'll have to get some things together.'

They spent the rest of the day walking about the house and then the barn, discussing the practicalities, jotting down the ideas on paper, till long past teatime. Mary, as was her wont, had gone off home, leaving a suitable supper all prepared for them. She only stayed on when needed so the house was theirs.

'Go fetch your things, Andrew. Before we have supper. Please.' After the brilliant day working their way through the project, when the two of them realised they were working so well together without any excessive physical contact, the tone in her demand, said as they were about to go back into the house after another trip into the barn to check on a dimension they'd forgotten, was different.

'Sure, Roberta. You are all right with this, aren't you?' He had to make sure, and looking at her now, she seemed just a little fragile. Maybe it had been too long and stressful a day. He was looking up at her, she on the top step, he about to follow her.

She looked down on him. 'Just go now, Andrew. Don't be long.' Without waiting for a reply, she went into the house and closed the door on him. Strange, he thought, not like her. Oh well. He reversed his steps, climbed into the car and took off.

Back at his house the feeling of desolation hit him again, total silence, just nothing, No Samantha, not now, not later, not for – he couldn't bring himself to say or think, ever. Ages, that's it, ages. A month or two, a year. Trying hard to shut off the memories, he went to fetch a suitcase from the spare room and then moved into his bedroom. The room was redolent of Andrea's scent, and though she'd straightened the bedcovers for him, the recollection of their romp. Romp, just that. Taking her virginity, so what? It was her, not him. Girls will be girls. He filled the case with shirts and things, took hangers out of the built-in wardrobe, threw the jackets and so on over his arm, and beat a retreat. He dumped the lot into the car, then thought of the answer phone. That took him another twenty minutes, collecting all the messages. He'd have to do something about the phone. The house phone – he'd forgotten. Best see. There was a brief call from Samantha. 'Just to say the flight's going to be on time. Give my regards to Andrea.' Nothing more, no 'love', no nothing. He felt empty, drained.

The journey back to the Manor, just a mere ten minutes, seemed like an hour. He parked the car round the back this time, alongside Roberta's. His and hers. The back door was ajar, and he heard music coming from somewhere.

149

'Roberta! I'm back!' No reply, maybe she can't hear above the music. 'Roburrtar!'

He dumped the case in the passageway and piling his suits and jackets on top, went looking for her. Of course, the sitting room. Her choice of music was interesting, one of those pieces everyone likes, Rachmaninov. As he pushed open the door, the music swelled. She was curled up in her chair, legs under her, eyes closed, injured arm lying in her lap, absorbed in the music. He tiptoed across to her, gently leant over and kissed her forehead.

She opened her eyes, frowned ever so slightly and motioned him to a chair. Sitting back, looking at her, taking in the vision of her, he too found the music relaxing, soothing, and added to the redolence of the ambience of the old house. Another world, this, and a far cry from his place; it was if he'd crossed over some mysterious, mythical Tolkien divide. The final chords and silence. He waited for her to move.

'I love that piece, Andrew. It's so very, - soothing.' She unfolded her legs from under her, and sat up, smoothed her skirt down, looked very demure. 'I hope you didn't feel dismissed too abruptly, darling. Only it was best you did that before we got involved with our first evening at home. You don't mind?'

He shook his head.

'Good. Get everything you need? Pyjamas, toothbrush, pet teddy bear, that sort of thing?' She giggled. 'Not that I can see you wearing 'pyjams' somehow, any more than I do. Except when I'm ill, which isn't often, I'm glad to say. Would you nurse me if I was ill, Andrew?'

'Of course.'

She stared at him for a brief moment, as if to register the statement. 'Shall we eat? Mary's done one of those tray bake things, lovely prawn and haddock. It's a speciality of hers, only for special people. You're honoured. And another bottle of that Chablis we had? Then maybe an early night?' She giggled again. 'Am I seducing you, dearest Andrew?'

Why, oh why, had he succumbed to Andrea's wiles, when this lovely girl was his for the taking? 'Seduce away, R. I love you for it. Can I go and get myself sorted and changed?'

She stood up. 'I'll help you find homes for things. Do you mind?'

'Not at all.' It was like booking into a posh hotel, chambermaid and all. She'd already emptied two drawers in one of the chests and allowed him to cram his two suits and a couple of other hangers with jackets and trousers into her wardrobe. Putting them onto the same rail as some of her swishy dresses gave him a vicarious thrill, almost as if he'd undressed her.

'Right. I'll leave you to do what you want – I'm going to start the supper. Then it'll be my turn, and no, I shan't need your help, *thankyou*. Not this time.' With a flounce and a quick pick up and drop of her skirt, she left him, and he heard her skipping down stairs, whistling as she went, another trait he'd have to get used to, someone around who danced and sang, unlike poor Sam.

He chose one of the shirts he particularly liked, left it and a clean pair of trousers on the bed, stripped off and luxuriated in her shower. Then dressed, combed his hair and went down, through the marvellously evocative hallway, and back into the gleaming well lit kitchen. This was all too wonderful. She was peering at the dish in the top oven, bent over, and he playfully tapped her bottom.

'Sorry, couldn't resist you. Bathroom's free.'

'Pest. I can see I'm going to have to watch my back from now on. Not used to this. Love me?' She turned and he wrapped arms round a slim waist.

'I love you.' And thought he meant it, believed it, and vowed he'd try and steer clear of temptations elsewhere.

'Go and pour me a sherry. Small one, dry. Oh, and uncork the bottle. Man's job. I shan't be long.' She checked the oven temperature again, adjusted the control, frowned at it, grinned at him, and left the kitchen. Once more he heard the light run of dancing footsteps up the stairs and along the landing and his heart began to sing. He did as he was told, uncorked the bottle left in the fridge, put it back, had a peer at the dish in the glass doored oven, then went and found the sherry.

He wasn't a particular fan of dry sherry, instead mixed himself a small gin and bitter lemon. The drinks cabinet wasn't large, but comprehensively stocked and the recollection of the first dinner party with Roberta's solicitor girl and her husband came to mind. At least he didn't drown the gin like whatshisname had. Sipping his glass he wandered to the window and stood, looking out, liking the view far more than his own postage stamp lawn and borders.

'Monarch of all you survey?' She was back. Gorgeously. 'Told you it wouldn't take long, there's not much of it to put on.' And she gave him a twirl, the light blue flimsiness of the fabric – what it was he couldn't tell – rose like a mist round her thighs and showed her perfection. The dress above her waist was caught in two crossed pleated drifts across her breast, revealing the depth of her cleavage, where a silver brooch with a complicated design dangled. There wasn't much else to it, and obviously no bra. 'Like it?'

'You're a dream, R. It's stunning . . . ' A now familiar pull at his stomach muscles and a prickly feeling in his eye. 'You are a beautiful, beautiful girl.'

'That's all right then. It's worth the money?' She was playing with him.

'Whatever, Roberta, it was made for you. You're gorgeous. And just for my benefit?'

'You're right, Andrew, it was made for me. As my accountant, you'll have to see the bill sometime. Not tonight. And not just for your benefit, this, it's for us both. You to look at, me to love wearing. Now, supper?'

'Don't I get to kiss you?'

'Nope. Save it for later.' She retreated, and following her, found her one handedly shrugging on a pinafore. 'Don't want to mess this up, now do I.'

'How *did* you get into it?'

'Ah, that would be telling. You'll find out, when *you* take it off. Get the plates.'

With a strange admixture of style and circumstance, they ate at the small tables in the sitting room, like two delinquent guests at a Reception, unable to join the party. The Chablis was as he remembered, and the Mary's fishy tray-bake sublime, her pastry mouth wateringly crisp and yet soft. Roberta chattered gaily on about all her old school friends, some of her childhood exploits, and he got the impression she was nervous, especially as she kept asking if the meal was all right as well as keeping the glasses topped up. Once they'd cleared the entire dish, no mean feat, she jumped up and disappeared into the kitchen, to emerge with two dishes of home made ice cream.

'It won't go with the Chablis, darling. Empty your glass. No cheese tonight, sorry. Coffee though, if you want some.' She fluffed her skirts again as she sat down, and again he thought how ravishing she looked.

'You know, R, this is the best evening I've known for ages, if not ever. You, Mary's cooking, this,' – he took another spoonful of the raspberry ice-cream – 'the wine, the Manor. It's all like a fairy tale!'

He got a laugh as she wiped her mouth with the back of her hand. 'Sorry. Not ladylike. I hope it won't all disappear at midnight. You'd just be left with a slipper, and I can't see you wandering round the neighbourhood looking for a one-shoed Cinderella. You'd best keep hold of me.'

'Oh, I'll do that all right, never fear.'

And he did, the beautiful dress fell away from her on the release of just one catch at her waist, and there wasn't anything else. Waking up with her tucked into his arm was the most wonderful thing out, her long dark hair spread all over the pillow, her warmth so close and the subtlety of her scent. He couldn't help it, and loved her in the early morning light with a tenderness that even surprised him.

'Mmmmmm.' He didn't ask for anything more. Her deep breath and the snuggle back was enough.

It was the sound of Mary, clattering about in the kitchen downstairs that woke them next.

'Lord, is it that time already? Whatever will she think?' Roberta sat up, suddenly, and caught him with her plaster. She'd managed so far very well, keeping it out the way, but cursed it now. 'Bugger. We'd best get downstairs before she comes looking for us!' Totally naked, her frontage was too tempting, but she knocked his hand away. 'Out of bounds. Past the witching hour.' Then she relented slightly and kissed his forehead. 'Great night, Andrew. I think I even had goosy pimples in the right place. Try again sometime?'

As a prelude to getting up, he had to stretch, enjoying the space. A large bed made all the difference, especially with an attribute like her. 'At your service, mistress!'

Another giggle. 'Lovely service too. Now up, go on. Get out.' She pushed at him with the plastered arm, so there was no argument.

Life with Roberta was going to be fun.

Mary looked at them both as they entered the kitchen, and Roberta had snatched his hand to hold as she opened the door, so they emerged like two delinquents. 'Enjoy my fish pie, then?'

'It was lovely, Mary, as always. I'm afraid we finished the bottle, and there's not too much ice cream left.' Roberta lifted Andrew's hand. 'Look what I found in my bed this morning!'

Mary laughed, and Andrew hadn't heard her laugh quite like that, great guffaws of genuine mirth. 'Well, I never! Fancy that now! Did he behave himself, *Mistress* Roberta?' The emphasis on the 'Mistress' was just enough.

Roberta actually blushed. 'Oh, yes. He knows what a girl likes.'

'That's all right then. You'll be wanting breakfast?'

'Yes please, Mary.' Andrew had to get a word in, and started playing the women's game. 'After all, one can work up an appetite, even in bed.'

Roberta's blush deepened, and she nudged him. 'Behave! Bacon and egg?'

'All organised,' Mary smiled. 'You two go and enjoy the sunlight. Sitting room? Five minutes?'

Later in the day he and Roberta came to an arrangement over the conversion of the disused storeroom, a former Butler's pantry, into an office primarily for him, but where the new facet of her own business could also be controlled, and in the ongoing days he arranged the transfer of his business line, took one afternoon to empty the room in his house of all the business papers, disconnect the computer and associated printers and ferry them up to the Manor. Royal Mail were given re-direction instructions, but he didn't alter the home phone, not yet. All he had to do was remotely interrogate the answer machine every now and again.

The potential new side of her business, the courses at the Manor, reached the stage where contractors had been called in to give estimates, and they would be making a 'point of no return' decision any time once the quotes came back. All in all, it was quite exciting. He'd driven her into London twice to keep that side alive, if only on tick-over, but she mainly occupied herself learning something of his business, answering the phone, and dreaming.

Hence life at the Manor settled down to its new routine and he and Roberta grew increasingly fond of each other, day on day. It was well into the third week of their joint occupation of her bed she decided to remind him again that she hadn't needed to keep him at arms length for *those* days.

'What do you mean, R?' She was lying on his arm, and he tugged it out from under her, rubbing to reduce the pins and needles.

'You mean you've forgotten about us ladies having a week off a month?'

It hadn't crossed his mind, but then, with Samantha well over that particular hill it didn't feature.

'Oh. Errmm. You mean . . .'

'What do you think I mean?'

'You aren't . . .?'

'Pregnant? I may be. Subtle changes in lifestyle, dear Andrew. What do you think?'

'I don't know. Well, yes, I do. I suppose I shouldn't be surprised. Are you sure?'

'No, but with the marvels of modern science, it won't take long. Happy?'

He thought for a moment. Roberta, pregnant, by him. Her first child, what she'd always wanted. A somewhat mind-blowing situation, but then, as neither of them had ever expressed concern over contraception, and she was so, so lovable, it was going to happen. And she'd hinted as much . . . *you'll make me pregnant, she'd said that time. . .* Would she be all right, at her age? He wouldn't want her damaged in any way, for her sake as well as his own, maybe selfishly.

She poked him. 'You're too quiet. Aren't you pleased?' From her point of view it was a happily miraculous state of affairs; what she'd dreamed of ever since that first trip to London. The way they worked so well together, loved so well together and mostly managed the day-to-day living with scarce any hint of acrimony, she couldn't have wished for better. Dreams come true in a wonderful way, and his constant caring the best part.

He turned his head to look at her, loving the way her face was framed with the glorious mass of hair, and stroked a few wayward strands away from her forehead. She was so beautiful.

'If having a child by you is the way our loving becomes life, then I'll love our daughter – or son – because it's yours and mine and . . .'

It was all she wanted to hear, and as tears moistened her eyes, she whispered so so softly he could scarce hear. 'It's all I wanted. You, your caring, and our child. Bless you, Andrew, bless you, my darling.'

They stayed quiet and relaxed, absorbing the moment,

before she needed to move and ease her still immobile forearm. Beginning to stroke the small of his back with a free finger, she said, 'I think . . .' but that was all she managed before his kiss started them once more towards the edge of stirred senses and unreserved loving.

TEN

Her own doctor confirmed Roberta's maternal state two weeks later, the same day as she had her plaster removed. Her arm, luckily, had been reset without any misalignment, but she was shocked at the way in which the whole thing felt so weak and wobbly. When she queried it he laughed. 'You've been so used to the plaster's extra support your wrist doesn't believe it's got to do things for itself. It'll be back to normal in a couple of days. Just don't knock it; else you'll have a real bruise. Massage it well, and keep flexing the joint. It's fine, Roberta, really.' He was quite an old friend, her chap, and whereas he was extremely curious as to the whys and wherefores of her pregnancy, kept his questions to himself. She sensed his inquisitiveness, however.

'Andrew will be pleased about the confirmation, Mac. He and I are the best of pals. We're going to make the old Manor earn its keep, you know.' She watched his bushy grey eyebrows lift, as she knew they would. 'Bed n'Breakfast for budding Interior designers. Loads of lolly. All the bright young things will be flocking to the door.'

'Andrew?' He could ask her now.

'The best thing that's happened to me. Accountant; picked me up when I fell off that stupid horse my ex. left me. Perhaps he knew it would throw me off and possibly save him lots of money.' She reflected on that. 'Do you know, I think there's more in that than I thought? In which case, him throwing his car off an alpine road doesn't sound too bad a swop. Oh well.' She put it out of her mind. 'What next, Mac?'

'Usual things. Routine check-ups, antenatal courses, one or

two decisions eventually. We need to keep a close eye on your blood pressure, being the er, sorry, Roberta, age you are. Don't want any mishaps, do we?'

'No, *we don't!* Not after all the trouble I've gone to to get this far. I'll be a good girl, I promise. And Andrew's great.'

'Forgive me asking, Roberta, but will his name appear on a birth certificate?'

'Good Lord, yes. He's into this as much as I am.' She coloured up and her doctor Mac grinned.

'That's all right then. Just be sensible – and, oh, *do* watch that arm!'

Back at the Manor, Andrew was overseeing the first steps in the conversion of the bedrooms, wincing as floorboards were lifted, disliking the splintering sounds. Mary had driven Roberta into town, so he could concentrate. More and more time had been taken up by this side of things, and he was now, reluctantly, turning down some accountancy jobs he'd have been only to pleased to have had a couple of months ago, but in his heart of hearts, he found this far more satisfying. He'd offered Andrea the lease of the house, but she was still reviewing her options. She'd been very good about Roberta, he felt, and he didn't feel any animosity from her, quite the reverse. He knew he had one more hurdle, though, another meeting at the Brewery, and that was scheduled next week. The confirmation e-mail from Samantha had arrived, to the effect she was installed, had a nice bungalow and a couple of locals as servants, the system was up and nearly running, and she hoped he wasn't lonely. He fired one back at her, merely wishing her good luck, and hoping she was well. And that was it. He still hadn't heard from either June or Peter yet, wondering what was going to happen when they found him installed at the Manor. All in good time.

Roberta and Mary were back. 'Co-eee! We're home!'

He abandoned the two enthusiastic plumber types and found the girls in the kitchen with the kettle already on. Roberta flung her arms round his neck and slobbered. 'Yes, *Yes.* YES!!'

'Hey, steady on – your plaster's off?'

'Of course. All back to normal, well, once I've got used to it. Did you hear – it's YES.' She nearly shouted. 'I'm officially a pregnant mother-to-be! Oh, my clever, clever darling Andrew!'

Mary looked on at all this, smiling at the same time as shaking her head. Difficult to comprehend how the girl had changed so much in the last few months, and all because of that fall she had. She made a large pot of tea and poured two mugs Andrew could take back to the plumbers. Once he'd gone back upstairs, she risked her precious girl's good humour.

'My dear, I'm very happy for you both, but don't you have to see what complications this brings, with him being married and all?'

Roberta didn't want to know. 'He'll sort things, Mary, I know he will. Once Samantha is told, I'm sure she'll let him go. Now, what are we going to eat? I'm starving. Got to eat for two now, you know!'

Mary had to admit defeat and gave a motherly, knowing smile. She was just as good as any daughter should be, that one.

That evening, the two of them got round the dining room table and discussed the action plan. The Bed and Breakfast conversion was under way. The barn revamp would start next week, and now they had to start advertising. Roberta had decided she would move the London business back to the Manor, and she'd consider the conversion of the house into flats, so they could keep a *piéd-a-terre* in the City and let the other floors. That made good sense to Andrew, and they decided to seek advice from two or three London Estate Agents. She asked him about his house, and as he still hadn't had a reply from Andrea, wondered if he, too, shouldn't put it into the hands of an agent to let short term.

'Hope Samantha doesn't suddenly decide to come home, then.'

'Perhaps that will decide things one way or another.'

'I think Bump will do that, Andrew. Will you tell her?'

'Not yet.' He was a trifle alarmed at the prospect. 'All in good time.'

'But you *will* tell her?'

'Yes, I'll tell her.' He was more concerned about telling his own kids that they may have a currently illegitimate half brother or sister. 'I've never asked, R, about your folks. Your family. You've never said.'

She pulled a face. 'No. I'll tell you, one day. Not now.' She pushed her chair back. 'Do you know, it's nearly half past ten, and we haven't had anything to drink? I'm parched. What do you fancy?'

'You, in a word. Glass of red wine, and a nuzzle. Shall I be rude, and ask about . . .?'

'Shan't say. You find out!' It was a game they'd suddenly invented, or being correct, she'd invented, asking him to guess whether she was with or without underwear. Usually this resulted in a scuffle, or a chase round the room before he managed to either wrestle her to the ground or up-end her. With her arm previously in a plaster lump he'd had some nasty knocks, but the tide was now in his favour. She managed to get round the table and keep him guessing, then suddenly darted to the door, and laughingly made it to the hall before he grabbed the edge of her skirt. There was a rending sound, and she lost the best part of a whole wedge of fabric.

'Ah hah!' She was still decent.

'You lose!' Their rules meant she couldn't be touched till she was properly in bed . . . 'You owe me a new skirt. Go and get the wine. I'm upstairs.'

She'd divested her torn skirt and her top, when the phone rang. She yelled, at the top of her voice, 'Andrew – let me take it!' then reached over the bed and lifted the mobile off its pad.

'The Manor, Roberta speaking.'

The voice sounded crackly, a long way off. It sounded like 'Cirmannthar.' Roberta's light hearted mood vanished. 'Hello?' she replied, cautiously.

'Sit Cimantha. Gan u ear mee?'

'Just about. Speak clearly.' She enunciated her words slowly.

'Gan I speek to Andru?'

161

How did she know he was here? Should she acknowledge her, or pretend? The line hummed and crackled again. 'erberta?' The voice didn't seem distressed, particularly. Oh, Andrew, hurry up!

'Just a mom - ment.' She played for time, heard his footsteps, covered the mouthpiece. In answer to his quizzical lift of eyebrows, she mouthed 'Samantha – bad line. Wants to speak to you!' He pulled a face, then nodded. It had to happen. She handed the phone over.

'Samantha?'

'Fort I'de pass on con drat u lay shuns. Well dunn. No wurreees. Aisle ee mell. Lukkee gul. Givv er besss ishes. Tayk air. Bye.' The line hummed, uselessly; she'd rung off.

Andrew looked at Roberta, speechless, his mouth half open.

She had to laugh at him, looking so comical, despite the enormity of the circumstances.

'Your face!'

'Roberta, she *knows!* How the heck, way out there, and she *knows!* She said 'Best wishes, Lucky Girl, offered congratulations. Oh, *Roberta!'*

'Now what?'

'She said, I think, she'd e-mail. Who would go to the bother of letting her know? Bad line. She sounded drunk.'

'Probably was. Gets to you, I suspect, all that suffering, all that agony.'

'What do we do now?'

'We? Darling, she's *your* wife! I can't do anything, other than hatch our baby, which I fully intend to do to the best of my body's ability. Sorry, my love, but much as though I'd like to help, I can't. Wait for her e-mail. Can I get into bed, now?' She'd peeled off bra and pants while she talked and slid under the sheet. 'Coming?'

He'd left the wine downstairs, and couldn't face anything now; his appetite had been blunted, for everything. He lay beside her, staring at the ceiling, wondering. Something strange was going on, he was sure. Eventually, sleep overcame him. Roberta had already succumbed, out of sheer boredom and disappointment.

First thing he did after breakfast was look at his e-mails. Binning the usual plethora of rubbish, it left him with three. One from June, which was a routine 'how are you we're fine', and he wondered how much she'd been told; another from a former colleague asking about a technicality, and the one from Samantha. With some trepidation, he opened it.

'Life out here is a revelation, but I really feel wanted. No regrets about coming. Don't tell Andrea everything! Sorry I landed you with her. If everything's working with R, she's what you want and it all works out, let months go by, we'll discuss in good time.'

It was signed off as just 'Samantha'. So it was Andrea, via her mother. How close had those two women been? Would she have been told about that stupid, stupid mistake when Andrea . . . he paled at the thought. God, what a mess. So now what? Did he come clean with Roberta about his foolishness, or sweep it under the carpet and hope it never got mentioned?

Roberta came into the new office room and found him staring at the screen, elbows on the desk, head in his hands. It was too late to delete the message.

'Darling?' Concern in her voice. 'What's she say?' She leant over his shoulder and massaged his neck as she read the text. 'Andrea? That girl? *You told her!*' Her voice rose to a squeak. 'Why?' She backed away, and he swung round.

'Because I've been a bloody fool over her. I can't explain, and I don't know why. *I just don't know why!*' His repetition was croaky, his eyes pricked and he felt tears. He'd messed it all up, because, why, was she just too available, or was he gullible, or had his affair with Roberta been seemingly insecure at the time? 'Roberta. I need help. I'm scared of all this.'

She looked at him in disbelief. 'You! Scared? Andrew, for heaven's sake!' She pulled the other desk chair round and sat to face him, her anger at Andrea's involvement cooling somewhat in the face of his woebegone and tearful expression. 'Tell me. Just tell me, Andrew. I need to know, and then I'll decide where we go from here. Just one thing. I shall need a solemn promise from you, that you'll never let that girl *ever* come between us. Ever!' Her heart started thumping. He had become her life and soul, the father of her newly conceived child; she loved him, couldn't even consider not having him around now, but it was becoming a bad dream. She wasn't going round the same loop, was she? Michael – saw another girl's knickers, and off he went. Andrew – no, he wouldn't!

He just didn't know how to get himself out of the mess. Too bloody susceptible by far, that was his problem, which had landed him with Roberta and then Andrea before his feelings for Roberta had crystallised into this undeniable and profound love for her, yet he'd still let Andrea push his male ego about . . .

She sat and stared at him. Loved him, even in this very un-Andrew state; seeing him in a new and fragile condition, and her latent mothering instincts bubbled up.

'Tell me, Andrew. I won't be cross, I promise.' She thought of his situation and began to get something of an understanding, so added slowly and quietly, as if talking to herself, 'I'm not perfect myself, am I, showing you my knickers when I needed you? I suppose Andrea did the same?' Then with a wee bit of a cynical laugh, added, 'We girls!'

There was quiet between them, as their respective minds worked through the situation. She had to restart the dialogue.

'Darling. Look at me. Trust me. Tell me what happened, and then maybe we can move forward. I don't want to lose you, Andrew.'

'I'm not sure you really want to know. It's too messy. Maybe I'm too easy going, too susceptible.'

'You *have* to trust me. If you don't, then there'll always that black bear lurking in your mind. Get rid of it, Andrew. *Tell me!*'

Her eyes, those beautiful brown eyes with the amber glints, willing him to get it off his chest. He stumbled over the first few sentences, trying to explain to himself as much as her what went through his mind at the time. He ran through the Brewery meeting, how Andrea was attacked, how he'd felt lonely that evening, and how she simply wanted her own kicks, and then his narrative faded away.

'Go on. There's more, isn't there? You *have* slept with her?' It hurt her to ask, but then he'd lived with Samantha, as she had to tell herself. What's the difference? 'I want all the sordid details, Andrew. What colour knickers did she wear?' Making it sound light hearted, she began to be aware of her own feelings, imagining a scenario.

He was in suspense, hanging on a slim thread of chance above a pit of disaster. He could not believe this was happening to him, facing an inquisition about one affair from a lady with whom he was having another *affaire*, and he still married. Was it an *affaire*? No, it was more than that, a lot more than that.

'I slept with her, Roberta.' There, he'd said it, and she hadn't moved, merely twitched her skirt over her knees.

'And?'

'That's it. I shouldn't have. I should have kicked her out.'

'You mean this was at your place? When?'

'Weeks ago. While you still had your arm in plaster. The evening after Samantha left. I was shattered; she rang and then came round. I didn't invite her, she just came. Made me a meal, straightened the place up. Offered to sort the remnants of Sam's packing. Then one thing led to another, I got cross with her, started wrestling with her over something of Sam's, and it was her, Roberta. She virtually raped me. Then she offered to sleep with me, and I was just zombied, so I let her. I guess she was just bloody available. It was her first time, Roberta. I just wish it had never happened that way, 'cos she's actually a very nice girl, and if she hadn't been it would have been easy to tell her to get lost. That's it really. She hasn't fallen for me or me her.'

Roberta felt for him, knowing full well how he had responded to *her* advances. It wasn't supposed to happen like that, and he'd more than made up for it since, taking the initiative more often than not. But what to do with Andrea? 'I hope there's no complications, Andrew. If it wasn't premeditated, then I guess she was vulnerable?' Practicalities, now, to try and put the lid on incipient jealousy. 'You didn't say the colour?'

Did it matter? 'Oh. Pink, I think. Can't remember, other than there wasn't much of 'em. Why the question, does it make a difference? Yes, she would be *vulnerable,* as you put it. It's a mess, isn't it? I wish it hadn't been like that.'

He wasn't asking for forgiveness, but then, there wasn't really anything to forgive, if it had been the girl pushing herself along. He was as vulnerable as the next one, except that she had become proprietorial. He was *her* man, and she did not want to share him. He was *hers!*

'No, I don't suppose you do. I only wish I'd been thinking enough to be the one to do the comforting, Andrew, because that's all it was. What would you do if she tried again?'

'Tell her not to be so cheap, or something.'

'Hmmph. We'll invite her here, Andrew. See how she faces up to the challenge – and I'll be watching the body language. In the meantime, consider yourself lucky. You can stay!' She leant back on her chair and began to smile at the gamut of expressions crossing his face.

'I don't know I deserve you, Roberta, considering. Samantha might just have walked out.'

'She did.'

'Oh.' It was true, but not for that reason, was it? 'You don't think she knew about us, do you?'

'She obviously does now, though I'm not sure if we aren't over reacting. There's nothing specific about me being pregnant, is there?'

'Wee-ll, no, not really. I suppose the congratulations could be just a cynical way of recognising you and I have got together. I don't know if she'd be disappointed that I didn't go for Andrea as she hinted I should, she being the daughter of her best friend. I just don't know what's in her mind. Then she's suggesting that I don't tell Andrea everything. That was another weak moment, confiding in her that I was having an *affaire* with you, but I suppose it was to try and keep the lid on her own ideas. And now she's apologising about 'landing me with her'. Well, she hasn't 'landed me.' You have. Should I reply?'

Roberta thought. Andrew had told Andrea about their relationship; the girl had been the pushy one after the maybe forgivable 'come-on' he'd given her early on. So maybe it would simmer down. It *had* to, just had to. 'Tell her you're being well looked after, and hope she is too. Don't mention Andrea. Here, let me.' She moved to lean over him, typed away.

'*Glad to hear all is well,*' – she paused, thought some, stared at the screen, carried on – '*time passes very constructively. New business with R. working well. Should see positive results in nine months time.*' She giggled. 'What d'think?' Her hand moved the mouse pointer over the 'send' button.

'Bit obvious, R. Best put 'several' instead of 'nine'.'

'Okay, spoil sport.' She changed it, and clicked. It went, and the original message on the screen sat there. On impulse she move the cursor to delete, looked at him. He shrugged, and she clicked again.

'Right. Now that we've got things sorted, breakfast. Then a walk round this beautiful garden of ours, and back to work. Okay?' She gave him a kiss on his cheek and pushed herself away from the desk with her newly mended arm. 'Ouch! Oh, and think of some reason to get Andrea up here. I meant what I said. And another thing, you haven't said anymore about our week away, yet. You promised!'

'So I did. What with one thing and another we seem to have got sidetracked. We can't while this work is going on, can we?'

'True. But as soon as it's done. Then we can have a break before we start taking bookings, right? I want to go to Ireland. Never been, and I fancy the peace and quiet.'

'Suits me. We once went to Dublin on a weekend, ages ago. Samantha got drunk on Guinness.'

Roberta laughed. 'That must have been a sight. Don't fancy

Dublin, then. Let's get lost somewhere miles away. A cottage just for two?' A dreamy look came into her eyes; Andrew saw and treasured the look of her. He was a lucky, lucky man, and promised himself he'd be a lot more careful.

ELEVEN

Two weeks later, and they were on the ferry for Ireland. Such a lot had been packed into that fortnight, too, so they were both continually tired, and once or twice their tempers had been brought to flare-up point. On one occasion Roberta hadn't liked the way Andrew had spoken to Mary about the choice of meals, which made her very cross, and he in turn had castigated her over spending too much time in the garden. They even had a stand-up row in the kitchen another time when Mary had walked in on them, and she brought them to their senses in double quick time.

'Like a proper married couple, you two. I'd knock youse heads together for two pins. Stop it, the pair of you! Else I'll leave.' Roberta was shocked; Mary had never said that before. It just proved that they were settling down to each other's way of going about things; the initial passion between them had also stabilised, so there was less frolicking and more tenderness. Andrew had been forced to accept Roberta's denial of her comforts for a night or three after the Andrea sort out, understandably, but after that she was as loving as ever. Andrew cajoled Andrea into coming up for an evening shortly after the last project meeting at the Brewery, but he remembered how nervous she had been, and how much care she'd obviously taken with her appearance. Even Roberta had commented later that night after she'd gone, and that was way past midnight.

'I can understand how you fell for her, Andrew. She's a peach of a girl.' Then she had giggled, the sound he had come to know and love. 'Scared of me, I think. Don't think she'll drop her knickers for you again, somehow.' Andrew had been shocked, but then he too had laughed. Actually, their evening had been quite fun, and ultimately, when Andrea had relaxed after the meal and had a couple of glasses of red wine, her favourite, she'd said something about her home background that made Roberta cringe. 'It makes more sense to me, Andrew. As an only; and with a father who virtually ignored her, of course she was subconsciously looking for male – er, dominance – I suppose. If you hadn't, then someone else would have, and maybe less sympathetically.' She'd heard a bit more detail of that traumatic evening, so when Andrea openly admitted she'd been wrong, Roberta had reached over and patted a delectable knee. 'So long as you enjoyed it, that's the main thing.' Then she'd looked her partner straight in the eye and said, 'He's quite good, isn't he?' And Andrea had blushed as Andrew bit his lip. Her somewhat racy comments about Andrea's future activities were likely to be accurate after that evening. He had to admit, Roberta was a clever girl, bringing the whole thing into the open and not giving way to a swingeing attack on her, unlike her reaction the first time he'd inadvertently mentioned the girl's name.

* * *

She was curled up in a large armchair in the passenger lounge as the ferry ploughed on under the lightening sky. Sailing early had been her idea, but now she was fast asleep. Andrew couldn't keep his eyes off her, despite the messed-up hair and a tatty pair of slacks; she was looking vulnerable, younger than her years. Her growing pregnancy had rounded her features, given her less angular looks; a blooming appearance was the phrase. So far she'd given no trouble, the last check-up she'd had only three days ago hadn't thrown up any problem, not even with her blood pressure, and now there was a date. Mid January! What a time of year!

She woke with a sudden jerk. It looked very much as she'd forgotten where she was, then as realisation came with a shake of her hair and a follow up smooth down, he got a slight smile.

'Not quite the same as our cosy bed, Andrew. I've had some funny dreams. Are we anywhere near? I could do with a drink or something.'

He stretched, arms above his head, hands clasped, and stifled a yawn. 'I'll go see. Coffee? I'll ask.' Pulling himself off the settee couch thing, he peered out through the plate glass windows. 'There's a lighthouse over there – and what could be land.' The ship was as steady as a rock, he mused, if that wasn't a stupid comparison. At least it had been a smooth crossing, and quiet. Only a few people moved about, the rest of the passengers were like them, comatose. Quizzing the steward, the guy said 'about an hour', and took his time producing two overly milky coffees in foam plastic beakers.

'Yuugh!' Roberta took a sip and grimaced. 'Still, at least it's hot and wet. An hour, you say? Well, I'm going to find the ladies and see if I can freshen up. Don't want your new bride-to-be looking rough on her honeymoon?' He got a wink and an atypical Roberta style eyelash-lowered coy smile. He had to smile back at her, blew her a kiss. She swallowed another mouthful, put the beaker down and wandered off.

It had been tough going, organising the time away, but in the end Mary came up trumps and said she'd live in for the ten days or so, answer phones and look after the residual work. They'd found a holiday cottage down in West Cork, not far from the sea, tucked away, 'ideal for honeymoon' said the blurb on the web site, the pictures of the stone built single story place with the trees behind and the interior view seemed to fascinate Roberta, so they'd booked it on spec. Driving across Wales had been tedious, and he wasn't sure what driving on Irish roads would be like either. Better than flying to some over priced, over hot, over sexed resort and living on a sun bed all day, and he was relieved that Roberta hadn't any leanings in that direction, *au contraire,* she was an outdoor girl at heart and he was looking forward to taking her up into the hills.

'I'm back!' She'd come back round the lounge the other way and surprised him. Looking a lot perkier too; the change in her metabolism over the past week or two was making her glow. She leant over the back of the settee, presented him with proper 'good-morning' kiss, and then sniffed, wrinkling her nose. 'You need a wash, too, my man. I ain't having you in the car all day smelling like that. Go on, I'll look after the bags.'

Half an hour later, and they trooped back down to the car decks, obeying instructions, waited interminably for the stern doors to open, then joined the queue, rattled across the ramp, and they were in Ireland. Roberta was like a teenager, almost on the edge of her seat, swivelling her head around to try and see everything. 'I thought Ireland was a hilly place?'

'I think it is, but not until you get a fair bit west, or north. It's very agricultural, you know. So lots of meadow land and so on. Got the maps?'

She soon found Irish maps, like Irish roads, took some getting used to, and they'd taken a couple of wrong turns before she got the better hang of the philosophy. 'Not like England,' was a repeated comment, until Andrew got exasperated, and became forthright.

'R, – if you don't shut up about England I'll take you home!'

Her sideways glance was a picture. 'Sorry, darling. I don't want to be taken home. I just want you to take me where we can make love *all* day.'

'Bet you'd get bored if we did.'

'That, my dear boy, has got a degree of innuendo about it. I refrain from replying. Just so long as you keep me happy.'

'I'll try. Don't we turn off here?'

* * *

The first night was a stop in a bed and breakfast, a farmhouse down a dead end road, on the side of a hill, overlooking a tidal river; the lady running it typically welcoming Irish, oozing good-natured charm and hospitality. She took to Roberta straight away and mothered her, asked her all sorts of questions, and before long it was if they'd known each other for ages. It set the tone for the rest of their stay, absorbing the friendliness and the almost complete lack of interest in time. Tomorrow was quite soon enough for most of the Irish, it seemed.

As the journey westward progressed, Roberta's concept of Ireland was fulfilled, with the hills appearing as if from nowhere, the grass as green as green, the waterfalls full, and the hedges coming alive with colour. It rained a little during the day, but as they eventually reached their cottage, up a very winding, steep road only just wide enough for the car, the clouds broke just in time for the setting of the sun over the hill.

'It's magical, Andrew. Listen!'

'I can't hear anything?'

'Precisely! No traffic, no aircraft. No *people!*' A dog barked and the sound echoed round their valley. Roberta laughed.

'Shhh. You'll be heard miles away!'

'So what? I'm a happy, happy girl, all alone with just you.' She picked up her case, and carried it through to the only bedroom. 'Andrew!' Her exclamation sounded surprised.

'What?'

'Look at this!'

He followed her into the room. The large patio style windows opened straight onto decking; below that the lawns ran away down to a shrub covered bank, with trees beyond. The late evening sun could just be seen through the trees, glowing a streaky red.

'Isn't it just perfect? *And a* king sized bed!' She bounced onto the bed on her bottom, trampoline fashion, and tumbled backwards, feet in the air, rolled over and fell off the edge. 'I'm going to change. What about supper?'

'We've got to go shopping. No Mary here. What about the local pub?'

'Okay. Skirt or trousers?'

'You know me.'

She rummaged in her case, pulled out one of his favourites, the full-skirted blue cotton dress she'd worn the night she'd broken her wrist.

'This one?'

'You always look pretty in that. You'll need a sweater or cardigan though. My guess the evenings could be chilly.'

The pub was two miles down the road, the journey an adventure in itself. Quite busy, yet the very efficient girl took an order for a pie and chips, a lasagne and two pints of Guinness and still had them all on the table in minutes. They had nods and greetings from almost everyone, and Roberta was pleasantly surprised that hardly anyone eyed her up and down like they might have done in an English pub, sizing up her availability. Even the young men at the bar just smiled pleasantly at her and carried on with their conversation.

'Isn't it nice?' She was still looking everywhere; the bar, the décor, the people, through the window at the street outside.

"Don't let your meal get cold, R. What do you think to the Guinness?' He'd already downed a third of his, and munched away at his chips.

She sipped, and then took a bigger mouthful, leaving a frothy moustache on her face. Andrew laughed; she frowned at him, wiped her mouth and chuckled back. 'Cold. But nice, nicer than I'd thought. I don't think I'd have drunk this back home.'

'Part of the local colour. All we need is the music.'

'Music?'

He nodded at a blackboard. *'Music tonite'* *'Sean and the S'elves'*. Catching the waitress girl, he asked what time the music started. 'Anytime soon, now, when they get here,' the smiling reply.

'You want to stay?'

'If you like.'

Soon, in Irish terms, was an hour and half later. Three girls and a swarthy looking thin man in his early twenties fell out of a decrepit car, lugged in their musical instruments in cases, set themselves up in a corner and just started playing, with no ceremony, no introductions, merely a round of drinks on a tray. Soon the bar dwellers were singing away, the old chap by the fireplace dug out a harmonica and the publican brought his own *bodhran* out, so the music got louder and louder. Roberta, well into her second pint, had truly entered into the spirit of the evening. With flushed and animated face, she was a different girl, a million miles away from the suave socialite he'd seen back at that Manor dinner ages ago. Another couple in their thirties got up and started dancing, Irish fashion, soon joined by another older couple.

'I'd love to do that, Andrew!'

'What, Irish dancing? All that arms by the sides knees up and tap stuff?' He nodded at the group. The younger girl's skirt was twirling round her no-tights-on thighs and she was a pretty sight.

'Mmmm. Yes. Shall we try?'

'What, *here? Now?*' She couldn't be serious! But she was, and before he knew it, they were being clapped on the floor, and making a passable stab at it, though nowhere near as good as the others. The band gave up to reinforce its Guinness absorption and they collapsed back onto their chairs. The waitress girl, in passing, smiled at them again, and a woman from the adjacent table leant over to say, 'Well done, now.'

Roberta was radiant, but time was running on. 'Home, I think, Andrew. After all today's miles, I'm beginning to feel bushed.' All concern, Andrew helped her up; they bid the whole bar a 'good-night' and went.

Back in the bedroom, not bothering to draw curtains, she fell out of her clothes, tumbled into the middle of the bed and was fast asleep in minutes. Andrew, undressing more sedately, slid carefully alongside her, curled up to her shape, cupped a hand round a curvy bit, and he too fell asleep.

It was just after dawn when he woke. They hadn't moved as far as he was aware, but a sleepy head turned sideways towards him. 'Hi. What's time?'

'Seven, ish Sleep well?'

'Best nights sleep for ages. You?'

'Mmmm hmmm.' His hand caressed, and she turned

towards him, sought his kisses, and he could feel her toes running up his shin. So, what better way to start a day? His other hand slid downwards, and found.

Breakfast was basic, coffee and leftover buns from yesterday. There was a desperate need to go shopping, but it took an effort. She'd breakfasted in nothing but a towel and it kept slipping. Finally, Andrew reached for it, pulled, threw it onto the only settee in the room, and enjoyed the sight of her as part of breakfast.

'You're incorrigible.'

'I seem to remember you saying all you wanted was loving?'

'So I did. Oh well. I'd better get dressed before . . .'

'Before what?'

'Before I get cold.'

There was another rough and tumble, ending with them on the floor in a heap. He struggled up, picked her up and carrying her back into the bedroom, dropped her unceremoniously onto the bed and gazed down at her, she without a stitch on, and totally shameless.

'I love you, Roberta girl. Now get dressed.'

'Yes Master. I love you too, despite what you do to me.'

'I thought it was *because* I did what I do to you.'

'Oh, you pretentious thing, you!'

He tried to grab her again, but she rolled dexterously sideways. As he landed on the bed she escaped, picked up a pile of clothes and locked the bathroom door behind her. He grinned, loving the fun in their togetherness and got dressed himself.

* * *

The whole week followed much the same pattern; they explored the scenery during the day, spent the evenings mostly in the village pub on all but two nights when they were far too far away to return in sensible time. They made a number of

176

friends, one very artistic couple in particular, but loads of other acquaintances; and vowed they would have to return.

On the penultimate day, with a clear sky giving them the portent of another dry one, they took to the hill above the cottage, an unspoken challenge to reach the top, where rocky outcrops and swathes of heather showed above a wedge of woodland, and not a building in sight. With a bag of sandwiches, two bottles of water and an apple apiece, they set off in high spirits. Roberta felt she'd be too hot in trousers; reverted to a skirt and just hoped they wouldn't get into bracken or gorse, though Andrew shoved her jeans into his small rucksack just in case. It took them the best part of two hours to climb above the treeline and reach the point where good views expanded of the bays and glistening blue water to the south. Another half hour and they stopped to lunch on a convenient flat-topped rock. The country had now really opened up to them and was shimmering in the heat of mid-day. Roberta lay back, shielding her eyes against the sun.

'If I had known this was going to happen to me three months ago, I'd have never believed it. It's just so perfect. You, me having a baby, being here, having a partner in every sense of the word. Why didn't we meet each other to start with, Andrew, when we could have been spared all the mess?'

Andrew, propped on one arm, hand flat on the warm rock, legs stretched out, was gazing into the distance, heart full of the day, the girl at his side, the beauty around. She was his, to treasure, to love, to work with, sleep with, eat with, everything. The only sound was the skylark twittering way up above them and the constant buzz of myriads of insects. He turned towards her.

'I doubt we'd have felt the same about each other if we had, R. It's the second time round that makes the difference.'

'Whatever do you mean?' She half rolled onto her side so she could see him, looking up at his far-away eyes.

'That we're older and wiser; sadder as well perhaps. I love you because I see you as a complete person, body – lovely; mind – sharp; soul – delightful. And bloody intelligent and inquisitive and oh, interesting. Lots of things I now know matter that I didn't appreciate when I married Sam. She and I laughed and loved, but somehow we were still worlds apart. Strange, isn't it, that another person suddenly shows you what you really need to make yourself complete? You're all that, Roberta.' He touched a hand, stroked her fingers. 'Oh, yes, I know we have rows now and again, but we always *know* why, and can see where each other's going. That makes a difference. Another thing – you needed me, or someone like me, whereas Sam didn't *need* me. She got on well enough by herself. So did I. So we weren't interdependent, which I guess you and I are, to a large extent. Two pieces of a jigsaw puzzle that key together. Sam and I were the same piece in different colours.'

Roberta picked a stalk of grass and chewed on it, reflectively. 'What about me, then, Mr Psycho Analyser? What did I learn first time?'

'You had someone who didn't appreciate you, was only interested in himself, saw sex as a fundamental requirement and had no loyalties. You needed a status symbol, marriage was the thing to do, and everyone else did it. So the first available guy with the right connections got the job. Now, you need someone who *cares* for you, isn't too much bothered about himself, takes sex as a beautiful add-on, and is now fiercely loyal. And I mean it, Roberta.'

She thought about his statement, staring at the tremendous scenery rolled out in front of her, the distance and the immensity of the country's impact on her mind. True, Michael had no real feelings for her views, her ideas, or her wants. She'd gone along for the ride, with only her body as collateral, and he'd sure used that. The wonder was that she hadn't become pregnant by him with all the bonking he'd given her. Okay, so she used contraception now and again, but hadn't been all that diligent, and yet after only a few *wonderful* couplings with Andrew, here she was, preggers. As for loyalty, well, Andrew had hit the nail on the head. The only loyalty that other man had had in the end was – she laughed at her pun – was his end. And getting it up. Yuck! Andrew's last phrase echoed – '*I mean it, Roberta*'.

'Sounds like a mission statement, Andrew. Part of the employment contract. I think you're right. Still a shame that people get hurt in the process. I mean, Samantha, running out on you, and Michael killing himself chasing a different pair of knickers.'

'I don't think Samantha ran out on me, R. She needed another challenge, which wasn't me. She knew what I had, what I could do, it wasn't enough for her, and so she'd started drifting ages ago. I became a bit of flotsam on her tide. So I had a 'to let' sign on my face. 'Vacant Possession' – wife no longer in residence. I mean, she never reached for me, never tried to seduce me, I got kissed every other month; despite all my efforts, she just didn't respond. Lay there and took it like some horizontal punch bag. Is it any wonder I found Andrea irresistible- despite your best endeavours, R, at the time I was hungry for all the affection I could get? Not any more, though, girl. You're all I want or need. And Michael died happy. His adrenalin was running, and he probably had something in his trousers that interfered with the gear stick. Pity about the girl, though, bet she was disappointed. No orgasm that night.'

Roberta giggled. 'Andrew, you do have an odd sense of humour! Well, we've had some open-heart surgery up here, haven't we? You know, I think I love you, Mr Psychoanalyst. You're about right. What I have noticed is that you can love me without being randy. Just *nicely*. As though you love *me*, not just my body. Which gives a girl the shivers all down her spine and into other bits as well. I like the bit about a horizontal punch bag. Didn't I use that expression some time as well?'

'You may have, love. I got it from somewhere.'

Roberta sat up, smoothed her skirt down over her knees, and gazed over the miles stretched out below them. 'You know, I think I'm going to remember this day for the rest of my life. Let's get to the top.' She got up and offered him a hand. As she pulled him up, they closed together and just kissed, a motionless, all absorbing, kiss, a fusion of souls.

'I love you.'

'I love you, too.'

'Right then. Last one to the top cooks.'

It was about another five hundred feet up, mainly grass and dried peat hag. They scrambled and ran, ran and puffed, gasped and walked, and reached the top simultaneously. The ground was scored with runnels for water, some deep, some wide, all dry, and the grass beginning to scorch brown. The heat was almost over bearing. They collapsed onto the flat-topped grassy knoll that could have been the highest point, though the ground running along the ridge undulated. The view now went both ways, the miles disappearing into the blue shimmering haze above the valley green and browns below.

'Bloody marvellous.' He stood, hands on hips, half bent over, taking deep breaths.

'You don't need to swear, Andrew, but it is. I'm puffed. Any drink left?'

'A bit. Don't gulp; swish it round in your mouth. Here.' He passed her a bottle.

'How long will it take us to get back?'

'Not as long, but we do have to take care, a trip in one of these drain channels could break an ankle, and I don't fancy carrying you down.'

'Nor me you. Ten minutes?'

After a last longing look, they turned their back on the ridge and started on the route home. Making good progress, but with frequent little stops to survey the terrain and take breathers, they made it back to the wood. Along the side of the conifers the grass was long, lush and green, spongey but still dry, and in the shadow it felt chilly by comparison with the baking sun of the open ground.

''Scuse me a minute, Andrew, I need a pee.' She ducked into the wood and he turned his back on her. A minute, then a call, 'There's a sort of path, here, should we follow this?'

He turned round and saw her point. It seemed feasible, and anything to stay out of the sun. She led the way, humming to herself, as the path widened and narrowed, the trees opening out and then thickening up again. They seemed to be going sideways along the contour, until the path dipped steeply down and she was scrambling, one hand on the slope, the other balancing her sideways steps.

'Careful.'

'I'm all right.' Then the descent ended on a small grassy area, a clearing where the sun caught the gap in the trees. 'This is rather a nice spot.' She sat down on a fallen tree bole and waited for him to join her. 'Pity we didn't find this earlier, made a good place for a picnic.'

'Possibly. No view, though.' He put an arm round her. 'I think you're a great girl, R. I couldn't have done this with Sam. I've thoroughly enjoyed my day – our day.'

'Have you, darling? So have I. There's only one thing missing.'

'Hmmm?'

'Silly boy. I've a present for you. Open your hand and close your eyes.'

'Oh!' She'd given him her pants.

As they lay, entwined, their body warmth and the sun keeping their nakedness pleasant in the ever so slight breeze, she was purring, almost audibly, her inner girl thrilled with what he was able to bring out in her. She'd been good for him, too, she could tell in the way he moved within her. It had been heaven, in heaven. He was kissing her, her tingly bits and then her lips, and she was as relaxed as she'd ever been. Absolute Heaven.

She had to move. Her arm was – had – gone to sleep, and the pins and needles effect would kill her. And her bottom was being moulded to a twig, or a root or something, she couldn't tell, but it was becoming sore. Andrew was fast asleep, bless him, but then he'd been the energetic one, and she, for her sins, his cushion. There was a lot to be debated over al fresco connubial activities, but if the vote was going to be taken, interior springs had a distinct advantage. How was she going to wriggle out from under? Then there was that itchy feeling on her shoulder blades, which she was sure, was of animal rather than vegetable origin. At least it wasn't sand. She peered sideways. There was the heap of abandoned clothing, including, rather intrusively, her boots standing to attention on top of her folded skirt and jacket. His were lying on their side, just as he'd dropped them off in his haste to divest his trousers. She couldn't help herself, and giggled. She'd been the thinking one, after all, she'd started him off, but he couldn't stop once launched. She thought of Andrea, and giggled again. The girl only got what she deserved. Andrew woke up.

'Roberta? Oh, my darling, I'm sorry.' He raised himself on one elbow, grimacing at the pain of sharp grit digging into the bony bit. He wriggled back and sat on his haunches. Not a pretty sight, she thought, much better when there's some life there. Carefully, a limb at a time, she raised her knees. Lovely sight, he thought, looking at the tempting bushy bits, lying a bit flatter with the damp of mixed origin. She swung her knees together sideways and took temptation out of view. They sat staring at each other, momentarily, unsure of what to say.

'I think,' Roberta said, very carefully, contemplating her toes, 'That's the best sex I've ever had, and I shall have the scars to prove it. The thought of going home appals me, but we can't stay here for ever.' She rose to her feet and stretched. A bit of twig fell off her buttock and she brushed away to rid her self of the rest of the accretions. Andrew watched and marvelled. How controlled she could be, after being such an animal; that was the only word for her, with all the wanting and the taking and the ultimate electric jazz of her. She caught his glance and grinned. 'I know, I'm all female, I can't help it, that's how I was made. Same as you were, lover boy, ten out of ten for you. I just hope no-one's got us on video, or if they have, I want copyright.'

The trees were rustling in the growing breeze, as if in gentle applause. The grass where they had lain was distinctly flat, and she bet she had a chlorophyll coloured behind. She looked round, but the clearing was devoid of any sinister interlopers, apart from a cross magpie hopping from branch to branch. She looked up at the movement, and giggled again. 'You're only jealous because you can't do what we do,' she waved at it and was rewarded by a raucous squawk as it flapped away.

Andrew had collected his things and was decent again. She bent down, picked up her skirt, stepped into it, and then pulled her lightweight sweater over her head. Bugger the bra, she thought, I'm in the shower as soon as we get in. Her pants were in Andrew's pocket. The long socks made her feel less than sexy, and the boots, when laced up, even worse. 'Come on then, Mister. Let's go home.' She took a long look back at the clearing as they entered the trees. That had been something to add to the memory banks; even if she never had sex again, which was highly unlikely, it had been a day she wouldn't forget.

They went back to the pub that night, and sat quietly in the background, taking everything in; the banter, the *craik* as the locals called it, and the good nature of it all. Their particular friends – of a mere four days – came over and joined them. Ken and his girlfriend, wife, partner or whatever, Sheila, both extremely intelligent if very unorthodox people, who lived in timber shelters in the woods and made a living out of selling their art at local fairs. Their conversation was stimulating and their attitude to life a lesson in how to avoid stress. Roberta was listening to Sheila, Andrew Ken, and then somehow the conversation took an interesting slant, and Sheila was left talking.

She had no inhibitions. 'The best thing about living outdoors is making love. If you haven't experienced the feelings you get with the skies above and the grasses below, then you haven't lived.'

Ken was nodding. 'Beats this craze the youngsters have for making car springs rock.'

Sheila looked at him sideways. 'He knows, I suppose,' and she laughed, knowing full well he would never have done anything like that or ever would. 'What about you two?' Her dark eyes caught Roberta's.

She couldn't help it; she knew she'd blushed.

183

'Aha! Auld Ireland working its magic again? Am I right?'

It was up to her, Andrew wouldn't own up. 'Today; yes, you're right.'

Sheila reached across the table and shook her hand. 'You'll remember. Congratulations. I could say join the club, but there isn't one; it's far too precious for that. Andrew? Was she good?' Sheila's eyes were dancing, egging him on.

He couldn't believe he was discussing this. 'The best. This lady I love,' and was rewarded by Roberta's glance and the way her eyelids lowered.

Ken shook his hand. The pair got up, simultaneously, as though they were mind controlled. 'The best luck in the world to you both. And to the child you're carrying, Roberta. It will have all the love in the land. We'll see you again.'

'How did he know I was pregnant, Andrew? Lovely phrase – *all the love in the land* – beautiful people, weren't they?' They were back in bed for the last night. 'No, don't go in me tonight, Andrew. I want to remember this afternoon. Just cuddle me, love me but only that.'

He thought he understood, slipped a hand over her curves to hold her gently and she'd gone to sweet sleep in minutes. His last waking thought was a picture of her on the grass, eyes closed, in rapture.

TWELVE

Bang! Bang! Bang! What on earth? Andrew came to with a start and a thumping headache. Roberta stirred, but didn't wake. He eased out of bed so as not to disturb her, and slid trousers on, a sweater over the top, looked at his watch. It was only seven o'clock. Why had he had that extra glass of wine last night, and a rough one at that? Who on earth was making that racket? He padded down the stairs and barefoot across the hall, which always gave him a vicarious thrill. The thump on the door again; there was a bell, for God's sake. He slid the bolts back, turned the key.

One of those ubiquitous white vans sat on the gravel and a curly haired youngster with a clipboard stood on the top step. 'Sorry to be so early, guv, first delivery, got a full schedule. Couldn't come back this way. Sign here.' He pointed to a space with a stubby pencil. There were three boxes on the gravel. Andrew scribbled; the lad actually grinned and gave him a half salute, jumped back in and was gone with a spurt of gravel and a waft of blue diesel fumes. Andrew waved it away from his nose, picked up a surprisingly heavy box, dumped it in the hall, returned for the other two, and shut the door behind him. A sleepy towel-robed apparition stood at the top of the stairs.

'Wass all that racket, Andrew?'

'Delivery. Our publicity leaflets, by the look of it.' He slit open a box and pulled out some of the tri-folded leaflets.

'Oh, let me see!' Roberta came down the stairs, cautiously. She was not at her best first thing, and did not want to precipitate another retching session before breakfast; it was bad enough afterwards. Andrew handed one to her as he scanned his copy.

'Not bad. Not bad at all. Nice picture of the lady of the

185

Manor. I like the barn photo. Clear text. Yep. Should do the job. All we have to do is get them distributed.'

It had been the first thing they'd done after coming back from Ireland. It had taken much longer than they had thought, and the proofs had gone back and forward a time or two before they'd been satisfied, but now here they were, even if it was half seven on a Monday morning.

Roberta had been in a state of euphoria all the way home from their week away, despite her constant muttered comments about how crowded England seemed, and weren't the people rather surly in comparison to their Irish friends. Andrew didn't like the denser traffic, admittedly, nor the difference in the cost of fuel in the U.K. He began to wish they could move the whole operation into Ireland, but that was impossible.

Now they were into the last lap; the conversions done, the decorators (surprised to be working for a recognised name in the London Interior Design scene) finished, and Mary had had a whale of a time buying new linen and towels for the guest rooms, let alone choosing toiletries. She'd taken on the youngster she'd spoken of to help part-time in the kitchen, a slightly educationally sub-normal girl of sixteen who had a lovely manner even if you had to tell her four times how do to things. Once she'd got hold of the ideas, though, she was fine. Andrew just found it disconcerting when she'd stand in the kitchen, hands clasped, waiting to be told what to do next. Mary thought the world of her none the less, and he guessed she'd show her worth once the system was up and running.

He took Roberta by the hand, and led her back up stairs. 'Too early for you, my lass, have another hour. I'll shower, and then do a bit in the office before breakfast.' He enjoyed cosseting her, now four months gone, and she had a lovely incipient bulge. She initially had resented being pandered to, but was getting used to the attention. Every aspect of her condition had a bonus somewhere.

Sitting at the office desk, freshly showered, he tackled the e-mails. His own, once he'd got rid of the usual rubbish, he dealt with quite easily and was about to move to Roberta's when a new one arrived as he watched the screen. *Samantha.* There had been an intermittent exchange, even more pictures of her bungalow and the place where she worked. It hadn't seemed too bad, and she'd not asked about Roberta, or Andrea, come to that, so maybe she was too preoccupied.

'*Hi Andrew. Just to let you know Peter's coming out next week! June's upset you haven't contacted her, the ansaphone's full. Give her a call. Best wishes. PS How's your love life? Samantha.*'

Peter going out there! Well, he would if it was organised and basically free. As for June, he'd left a message on *her* answer machine and had no reply. He'd kept putting things off, he knew, and sooner or later they'd have to know. He stared at the screen and thought. Should he, or shouldn't he, take the plunge?

'Roberta!' He called, thinking he'd heard her footsteps.

'Yes, darling?' She pushed open the door. 'Anything?'

'E-mail from Sam. Look.'

She leant over him, as she usually did, with a hand running through his hair. 'How's your love life!' She snorted. 'She doesn't mention hers. Bet you there's someone. White girls aren't ten a penny out there, I'm sure.'

'I want to tell her about our baby.'

'Fine. She'll have to know sometime. So long as she doesn't come rushing home and drag you away. Not that I'd let her; drag you away I mean. What's this about June?'

'We seem to trading defunct answer phone messages. She doesn't seem to recognise she has parents, but she's okay. I'm not fussed.' He was typing as they talked.

'*Hi, Samantha. Thanks for yours. Hope you enjoy Peter's visit. I'll have another go at June, she didn't reply to my last call – went on her answer machine. Roberta's pregnant, our child due mid to late January. Does that answer your question? Regards. A.*'

'Yes?'

Roberta shrugged. 'Send it. She'll tell your kids. Save you the bother. I'm happy.'

'Really?'

'Of course, I've got you, our child, a business, a lovely house, what more do I need?'

'I love you.' The surprise of this situation never failed to move him.

'So you keep saying. Love you too. Now, can I do *my* e-mails?'

Andrew clicked on the 'send' button and the message vanished. He let Roberta slip into the warm chair, watched her wriggle her bottom to get comfortable and left her to concentrate. He walked out into the garden and sniffed the air. Another warm and sticky day ahead and the flowers were already scenting the borders. It was a lovely place to be, but he was aware of the pressures building and couldn't be sure what the future had in store. His house still sat empty, costing him money; he and Samantha still had to decide whether to divorce; Roberta's new venture would have to prove itself; his business was still expanding; and come the New Year, another dimension would emerge. That was something again, another facet, family life. The prospect of sleepless nights and nappy changing didn't appeal, but Roberta's happiness was paramount. And there she was, his lovely girl, coming across the grass to meet him, grinning all over her face.

'First bookings, darling! We've got some bookings!' She seized his hands and waltzed him around.

'Hey, steady on, you'll have us over!' Her enthusiasm got to him. 'Well done! When?'

'Second week in September. Four ladies. Suit you?'

'Great. Where did they come from?'

'That magazine – the one that rang about adverts? We - I – explained what we were doing to that pushy tele-sales girl? Well, it seems there's a bit of editorial and the e-mail contact. So who knows, we may have some more.'

'Well well well; have we started a bookings diary? We'd better, in case we take too many! Did we get a deposit?'

She frowned at him 'Always the practical one! A telephone number, an address, and a cheque in the post, Andrew, okay?

Now, you said you needed some office time? I'm going shopping with Mary at eleven.' She still had his hands and now pulled him close. 'It's going, darling, it's *going!*' As he bent to touch her lips, she added, 'Andrew, darling, just let's hope it all works.'

'It will. It has to. Let's hope nothing fouls things up for us.' He still had Samantha on his mind.

Later in the day, when the atmosphere had become really far too oppressive and they'd retreated to the courtyard garden to welcome the cool and the shade of the big canopy they'd recently bought, Roberta came up with another of her idealistic whims.

'We've not entertained anyone since you moved in, Andrew. It's time we did; showed the world what we're all about. I fancy a sort of open day, before I get too gi-normous. While the garden's still got some colour. It'll be a mixture of Gardens Open, showcasing the business, and who knows; maybe we'd even rake up some sponsorship. What'd say?'

Andrew pulled a face. He needed to think about this. Fine for Roberta, because she was effectively Lady of the Manor with social standing, for what it was worth, and her business would take the strain, but where was he in all this? A sort of interloper, some might even say gold-digger, or worse still, toy boy. He voiced the doubts he had about his involvement.

Roberta got cross. '*You*, Andrew, are my partner. You're my lover, the father of my child-to-be, my financial advisor, and the guy I wouldn't swop for Tom Cruise. So don't think you're only to be seen as some background figure that pops corks and answers phones. You're not. You're the other half of me, and I don't care who knows it.'

'But I'm still married to Samantha. I've got two kids – adult, sort of, kids – who you haven't met, nor they you, and I'm very obviously living with you, which I love, but it could backfire on us. Think of all those 'politically correct' types who have money to burn on new interior décor; you wouldn't want them walking away when they find out what sort of a girl is choosing their curtains, now would you?'

Roberta wrinkled her nose and sniffed. 'I still don't care. You and me, as they say, are an item. Strange expression that, 'item', sounds like something you bought in a supermarket.'

Andrew had to laugh at that. If she decided to go along with an open day there wasn't a lot he could do about it, she was the boss. If he were to be paraded as her 'partner', he'd live with it. Actually, heart of hearts job, he'd be proud to be seen as 'hers'.

'Okay, love. So long as it doesn't tire you out. Sooner rather than later, eh?'

She smiled at him. She knew she'd win, bless him. She'd put some things onto paper in the morning, then they'd have a meeting. They often had mini-meetings, always quite formal, but it helped to keep the business side apart from the domestic – and loving – side. Neither of them was quite so demanding of each other now a days, but, boy, when it happened, *it happened!* 'Fancy an early night then?' she asked, putting a hand on his knee. 'It's been a week.'

'You checking?'

She tapped her nose. 'I have a memory for these things. You wait. Let's go and eat, then I'd like to sit and read, play some music. Just a nice relaxing evening. A glass or two, then who knows?' She hitched her skirt up a fraction, watching his eyes, and laughed.

THIRTEEN

The idea of the open day had grown on them, another sort of challenge, as if they needed one, but then that's what made life so generally exciting, challenges. With all the conversion works now behind them and candidates for Roberta's first weekend course on 'How to Flatter your Home' all signed up, it seemed a natural. The garden was as near make-over perfect as it was likely to get for the time of year, albeit some of the flowers were going back; the Barn was all spick and span and redolent of new paint, and Roberta, well, she was blooming in the full flush of her pregnancy.

The grot of Andrew's past domestic life was fading; Samantha's only reaction to his announcement of Roberta's condition was a brief congratulatory one, and a veiled comment about 'getting things sorted when she came home', though no time scale was mentioned. Peter must have fallen on his feet out there; somehow he'd managed to wheedle his way into a job and a work permit, so that was that. June – now, different kettle of fish, that girl. When he'd finally got to speak to her, she'd ranted and raved about the 'sanctity of marriage' and how he was abusing his position, how he'd let her down and she'd never forgive him. She'd slammed the phone down on him and he hadn't heard from her since. Nothing he could do about that, given the circumstances; the only way she would come round was if her mother told her everything was fine and he was back under the marital roof. Fat chance. He let his mind drift away from that situation to find a few days later he'd almost forgotten the spat. If she needed him, she'd come running.

Andrea, dear Andrea, that other bit of sexy intrusion into his former boringly stable existence, hovered on the edge of his mind like a persistent decorative moth, fluttering her wings and showing her underskirts. Roberta tolerated her and her not infrequent visits to the Manor, ostensibly to keep the Brewery account running. Strange how she organised to visit him so he didn't have to go to the Brewery, but it suited him; the Brewery premises gave him the shivers.

'Darling?' Roberta was calling. His idle thoughts stopped in mid flow; looking back to the house he saw white bathrobe, uncombed hair and her smile through the window. 'Breakfast?'

'Coming!' These early morning forays round the garden were his source of inspiration, allowing precious time when the rationalisation of mind prepared for the immediacy of the day. And there was Mary, cycling up the drive; he waved at her. Discreetly, in something of a strange indefinable way, she had become the mother figure to him, let alone demonstrating her consistency to Roberta; an indispensable part of comfort in life at the Manor.

Roberta was mixing up her strange morning cocktail of fruit juices; experimentation had finalised a resultant concoction that gave her system the kick-start of the day. She'd named it 'Even Keel', something of a weird counterpoise of grammar and hearsay. Whatever, it worked. A proffered glass and a cautious tasting sip to signify solidarity with her mission. He wiped his mouth and swallowed the 'Yuk!' with the mouthful. Her smile told him she'd known about this manners and forbearance mixed in with his constancy of love. Watching her swallow the rest of glassful, her eyes fixed on his, amused at his grimace over the experienced sourness.

'It's not that bad! Better than heaving over the sink, my love.' The glass on the draining board, the routine of closed eyes and lifted chin for her kiss: 'Um ummmmm. Another day, wonder which bit is getting added? Like building a Lego model, 'cept she's live.'

'She?'

'Why not? You like girls. I'm making another one for you.'

Laughingly, he held her close, savouring the feel, warmth, smell of her. 'If it's a boy?'

'Then we try again, my son.' She pushed away from him, hearing Mary's footsteps. No hesitancy in adding, 'Whichever, still ours, and loved. Wet nappies and all!' She poked at him, and threw a 'Morning, Mary!' as she headed back upstairs to dress, nakedness under a loose bathrobe his – and hers - morning delight.

Over coffee and hot buttered toast they pored over the invite list, the nth time. Two hundred and twenty three people, or couples, or business names, down from near three hundred, pared, amplified, slimmed, reworked, but finalised, *today!* Misgivings, certainly, she was the one with tummy wobbles now despite it being her concept; his butterflies had long since flown.

'Are we sure?'

'Sure. Look, my love, it can only be good. No such thing . . .'

'. . . as bad publicity! Yeah, yeah. *You* post them!'

'Fine. Prayer mats, girl. Good weather or I quit. Two hundred in the barn after a teeming shower?'

'We said a marquee?'

'We did. So we did. Spoil the grass though.'

'Coconut matting?'

'And chairs, and tables, God, how the costs keep mounting!'

'Who's paying, then? Worthy Accounts?'

A cough. 'Ten percent added, Roberta the Smiley, unless I become an official Partner.'

She hated him poking fun at her name, deep internal voices telling her she'd rather be a Worthy Roberta than a Smiley one, but not while there was a Samantha still in possession of the legal title. 'Marry me, then.'

'Okay. Come on, then.' He pulled her out of her chair and catching a surprised hand, towed her out into the garden, into the sun and shadows of the space beneath the old beech. Still holding her hand, he kissed each finger, took off his gold signet ring, and slid it into place.

'I thee take for my unlawful weddable, beddable mistress. Forever and ever. This ring exchangeable for a nicer model when conditions allow. Best I can do, my lovely one.'

She had to giggle. 'Do you know, Andrew, you're much more livelier and funnier than you ever were? You were such a staid old thing when I first met you, and now look at you!' She twirled the ring loosely round her finger and kissed it. 'You mean me to wear this?'

'If you want to, kiddo. Symbolic. Just don't lose it, else I may not be able to swop it as promised.'

'Oh, dear, dear Andrew!' With arms around his neck and taking more kisses, another historic moment froze into their minds, and then it was her turn to drag him across the lawn. 'I'm hungry! Mary's toast will have to double up for a wedding breakfast. Then we'd better get some ordering done; get that marquee booked. Oh, yes, and I'll ask Marjorie to organise adding your name as an additional Director.'

Having these fun moments with Roberta made life so inspiring. The mundane hours till a late sandwich lunch, dealing with the accountancy business, his side of things, seemed so much easier. Andrew went back to his desk, humming to himself.

She disappeared into the Barn and concentrated on doing more work on her system of filing materials. Investing in a better computer was a decision she wasn't regretting one iota either, or that luxury of an all-singing all-dancing digital camera. By the time she'd finished and ready to re-join Andrew she too was singing. The new feeling that heavy-ish gold band had on her finger had made all the difference; shoving a bit of tissue under it to keep it in place. The only tug at her was the knowledge it had been a Samantha gift, but then so what, she'd inherited the mantle so why not the ring? And she'd had the *faux* honeymoon, that lovely week in Ireland, which would *have* to be repeated.

Mary's sandwiches were becoming a tradition, though the poor woman had to stretch her imagination day on day to ensure the variety. Roberta was sure Mary spied on the racks in the Supermarket to win ideas. She joined him in the kitchen, caught him sneaking more olives out of the bowl. 'Oi! Leave some for me! Mary, don't let him!'

'Stop fretting, Miss Roberta! Plenty more. Them's fresh tomatoes in there, and if you wants salad, I put a new bag of them mixed leaves in the fridge. The water jug's been there a while, should be cool.' Another Mary idea, that, and a good one. Gone were those wine-sipping lunches that only made her a) sleepy and b) looking for some t.l.c. that had gotten far too protracted and diminished the luxury of night times; after a rethink, they now had the healthy option. If the sun shone and it was warm, then out to the patio garden, if not, a retreat to the sitting room.

'Where?' Andrew had the plates on a tray.

'Out. I'll bring the jug.'

Feet up on the bench, slim ankles and light cotton skirt accentuating the fuller curves, she nestled into his shoulder, relaxing as the early afternoon quietened around them. Andrew reached for another sandwich, trying not to disturb the niceness of her warmth and weight. 'You're not eating. For two, you know?'

'Mmmm. Savouring the moment, my love. Thinking.' There was a comforting hand cupping her breast, whilst a munching sound was in her ear. 'Don't chomp!'

'Sorry. I'm hungry, and it's lunchtime.'

She struggled to sit up, swung her legs down, and lifted a sandwich off the plate. 'I do so love these moments, Andrew. I'm a very lucky girl. You, this place, baby Miss, *us.*' The waft of faint scent from the roses, the robin waiting expectantly and cheekily for the crumbs and the drift of small clouds across the summer blue sky, Andrew alongside her, it was all too, too marvellous. 'Will it work, my love?'

He watched her bite, small white teeth, those fulsome lips; the special amber flecked brown eyes and the glossy hair, the length of her neck merging into curves and mounds. She was the most precious person out. 'It'll work.' Unconsciously, a deep sign escaped him.

195

'Andrew?'

'Hmmm?'

'You sighed?'

'Did I? Sorry. Thinking.'

'Yes, it shows. I know you. What about?'

'You, how precious you are to me. What I'd do if anything went wrong. The kids, well, June particularly.' That girl was a potential problem with her straight-laced concepts, and he wasn't at all sure how to handle her.

His partner in crime, business and passion reached for another sandwich. 'Don't worry about it. She'll come round. And what goes wrong, we sort. Simple. What shall we call her?'

'Who? Oh, *her!*' He patted Roberta's swelling belly and looked around. 'Aubrietia. Begonia. Cineraria. You say.' Roberta cuffed his ear with her free hand. 'Ouch!'

'You horror! Just because we're in the garden! Just as well I didn't ask you indoors or what – Armchair, Banisters or Coalscuttle! Really, Andrew! I wondered about Bridget. Or Caroline. Though seeing as you mentioned it, Aubrietia sounds quite nice. First of – how many?'

Her dancing eyes were mocking him.

'Roberta, my darling girl, let's get you through this first, shall we? Aubrietia Bridget. Then she can be a flower *and* a saint. Unless it's Andy Barry. Ouch!'

* * *

The 'Open Day' publicity machine swung into action and the replies to the invites came in remarkably quickly. One or two 'no's' Roberta put down to snobbishness, but the majority were acceptances and they had quite a few phone calls saying how much folk had appreciated having the invite. Three of the 'flyers' of the half dozen she'd sent to her suppliers with suggestions they might like to contribute to the event to obtain some mention or display space came good as well, which lightened the financial side, to Andrew's delight, and one company she'd never dared to deal with because she thought them far too way up-market actually wrote to ask for space.

'Heavens!' When she'd read the letter, she showed it to Andrew. 'Who would have believed that a simple supplier of paint could spend that much – look.'

"if you could possibly consider letting us have a small space - say twelve by twelve – we would be able to offer you fifteen hundred pounds for the two days."

'*Two* days? Who said anything about *two* days?' Andrew was surprised.

'Their mistake. I'll phone them.' She waltzed off into the office and came back, ten minutes later, grinning all over her face. 'Same price. One day. But it is a marquee job. Problem is, they want to invite their own customers. Whatcha fink?'

'How many, for heavens sake?'

'I suppose we could ration them? But think of the money – and the extra footfall.'

'Yes, all over this delightfully unspoilt garden of ours – yours.'

'*Ours!* Only a day, Andrew, and we could fence this bit off?'

All the little snagging details were ironed out between times, as Roberta fitted in three new design contracts and Andrew took on two more long-term clients. Life was busy. The three weeks to the Open day sped by. On the Friday before Andrew garnered two of his friends from the Sports Club and got them to help with the fencing, the signing, the roping off of the car park in the adjoining field, and Roberta called in Mary's offer to provide additional ladies to 'do' flowers and the extra bits of cooking as she now wasn't able to do quite as much. The new girl, Hazel, had settled into the routines well enough, but she had her limitations. Marjorie, Roberta's solicitor friend, phoned to ask if she could help rather than just be a guest, which was nice, and given the job of stewarding in the Barn as back up. Her husband, dry old Martin, surprisingly said he didn't mind car park duties, and by the end of the day both Andrew and Roberta felt all was in place.

The paint company's marquee had arrived and been erected, very swish, and Andrew even had their cheque in his desk.

All they needed now was fine weather, and luckily the day came in bright and clear, with a sharp autumnal tang to it, even though it was only just September. Roberta fell out of bed, literally, and woke Andrew as she pulled ineffectually at the duvet to try and stop herself sliding completely onto the floor.

'Hey, girl? Are you okay?' He rolled over and peered at the scrumpled heap, trying to unravel itself from voluminous nightie and tangled duvet cover.

'Look at me! No, I'm not, give me a hand!'

Trying hard not to laugh, he climbed off the bed and walked round, found a hand, and helped to her feet, before applying a bit of tender loving to affected parts. 'Better?'

A mollified Roberta kissed him back. 'You shouldn't roll onto my side. I need more room than you. Try sleeping with a little girl *in* your tummy rather than on it!'

'Sorry. Shall we tie you in?'

'Hmmph.' She did a crab hop to the window with the duvet cover to stay warmer. 'At least it's fine. I'll shower; you go liven up the Aga. Mary's due in soon. Hazel will come with her. Sleep well?'

'Uh huh. I'll be happier when this is all over. Just make sure you don't overdo things today, R. And remember we've guests in on Sunday week!'

'Now am I likely to? With a two-day course to run? Go on, hop it, let me have some peace.'

The gentle sparring was now all part of the daily routine, for all the world as they had been together for years instead of a few months and it meant so much to him. Dressed and whistling cheerily to himself as he filled the kettle, lifted the cover off the hob, set out a couple of mugs, the natural every-day motions; able to smile a welcome as Mary and Hazel arrived.

'All set, then, Mr Andrew?'

'What will be, will be, Mary. At least the weather's on our side. Just hope we've everything organised and not left anything to chance.' He gave a special smile to Hazel and got a beaming one back. Evidently she had a soft spot for him, judging by the way he always got preferential treatment, in this case a quick offer of the biscuit tin. 'Thank you.' She knew his weaknesses, too.

Mary had her apron on and started on the sandwiches, pushing the butter tub at the girl.

'Come on now, lass; let's get these done afore Miss Roberta has her breakfast. Take her this, Mr Andrew.' She'd also mixed up the fruit juice, and Andrew retreated to find his love.

'Thanks, darling.' Roberta was out of the shower and combing her hair. 'I don't feel too bad this morning. P'raps the nausea bit's wearing off. They said it would. I even feel like a decent breakfast – no, don't say it.' The phrase 'eating for two' was getting a trifle over-used.

'Don't mind me in these, do you?' 'These' were a pair of well cut slacks, generous enough to wear without being too tight, but they did rather emphasise the bulge.

'If you're comfortable, dear, I've no worries. And if folks make some comment, they do. I've nothing to be concerned about.'

She got a salutary kiss on her neck and reached for his hand to stroke her cheek with it. 'Dear Andrew! Love you. Let's go make history!' Getting up from her stool in front of the mirror, she had to kiss him again before the two of them went down to breakfast.

The first comers were, happily, Marjorie and Martin followed by Mary's recruits from the village, then the Paint Company's sales people turned up and the day began to hum. First comers to the event were able to have coffee and biscuits in comfort, but it wasn't long before Martin had his work cut out to get cars parked sensibly, and the rush was on. Roberta took to her role as hostess with great aplomb, moving around the barn with its different little open rooms all set out as examples of what she could achieve, happy in knowing Andrew was greeting the guests as they came, and Mary was coping admirably with her retinue of girl helpers as well as showing the more interested the Manor's new Bed & Breakfast facilities. One person was missing, though, and Andrew was just a little surprised. Andrea. She did say she wouldn't have missed it, and she'd be happy to lend a hand, but she hadn't arrived.

Lunchtime, or at least, midday, came, and with it a bit of a lull. First comers had mostly left, only a handful still browsing, and Roberta took a chance to retreat back to the kitchen to coincide with her partner's need to snaffle some sandwiches.

'Going well, Andrew. I've taken four orders, and quite a few enquiries that could come good. Two for the course. What about you?' She was a happy girl, he could tell.

'One or two comments about my role from thems that knew me of old. A bit of a struggle trying to be nice to one couple Sam knew better than me, I think they gate crashed. Otherwise, no, seems to be going well, as you say. Don't know about the Paint chaps, apart from seeing their marquee quite full at times. And we've the afternoon yet.' He wasn't sure about mentioning Andrea, but Roberta read his mind.

'No Andrea?'

'Not seen her. She did say she was coming. Unlike her; p'raps I'll give her a call?'

'Do, darling. Extra pair of hands and all that. Look, I'd best get back. Mary, have we still enough supplies?'

Mary could just nod, with a full mouth from her lunch. Hazel, too, was quietly munching away at her lunch on a plate, sitting perched high up on a stool. Andrew glanced at her and had to look away. That girl wasn't as modest as she should be. Roberta noticed too, and nudged him, saying, *sotto voce*, 'Just as well it's you and not the ex. He'd be riveted. Let me know about the other girl.' She skipped away, and Andrew followed more sedately, dragging out his mobile.

Andrea's home phone was engaged, according to the

message. He waited for the beep, and then added 'Missing you, Andrea, what's up? Call me,' to the tape. Snapping the phone shut, he went back into the fray. It was half way through the afternoon, almost at their busiest, when the mobile chirped in his pocket. Retreating to the shade of the Manor's mellow stone wall, he took the call.

'Andrew, it's Andrea. I'm sorry I didn't get to ring earlier, only there's been a bit of a flap on. Can't explain now, but it's the Brewery. I'll get up to you within the next half hour, with a bit of luck. Everything going well?' She sounded upset, a strain in her voice.

'Yes, going like a train. *Loads* of people. Miss you!'

'Thanks, Andrew, I know I've let you down, but couldn't be helped. See you soon.'

Then there was another set of people he knew. Oh well, back into explanation mode again. He strolled across to meet them, smiling, greeting, accepting their congratulations before sending them off towards the barn. What was the problem with the Brewery then, that involved Andrea at a weekend? The outfit seemed to be climbing out of its doldrums now the tenants were able to see more clearly how their profitability was improving with increased gallonage. He pulled a face. Another car; when would it stop – poor Roberta will be dead tired tonight! Then he recognised that particular car and his tummy gave a jolt, he couldn't believe it, June! His *daughter!* Oh Lord! What on earth is she doing here? She never rang? She hadn't had an invite, despite Roberta's suggestion, unless the devious girl had posted one anyway when he wasn't looking. Well, he had a minute or two while she - they - he couldn't tell if William was with her - parked up. He had to alert Roberta, and walked swiftly over to the Barn. Roberta was in full swing with a delightful pair of youngsters, not sure if they were a couple or brother and sister.

She saw him, and broke off. 'Darling! These two are doing a restoration job on that old Rectory in Barfield. Karen and er – Chris, meet Andrew, my partner. I hope we'll be able to offer some help?'

The spokesperson was Karen, the tall one with the flowing blonde hair and a dimpled smile. 'I think we've fallen on our feet, here, with such a *wonderful* design team on our doorstep! Chris and I will be over here *far* too often! I think this is *fabulous!*' She certainly knew how to turn on the charm. It still wasn't clear which role the Chris was playing, but this was no time to find out.

'Nice to meet you both, it'll be good to have a challenge close to home. Roberta, can I have a word?' He drew her to one side, and hissed in her ear, '*it's June! She's here – and Andrea's had some problems with the Brewery, but she's on her way, hopefully. Help!!*' That startled her, judging from the change in expression.

'*June?* How come? What's she here for?' Roberta obviously hadn't invited her, then.

'No idea, R, but stand by for fireworks. Maybe she saw an advert or that article in the county freebee mag. I'll have to go, darling. Wish me luck.' Roberta gave him a hand squeeze as he wheeled round, offering the young couple a wave as he went out of the Barn's door. June was coming across the grass, alone. Despite her earlier voiced strong disapproval over his liaison with Roberta, she seemed to be smiling, and he couldn't help but admire her figure, the 'shoulders back' stance and the well-coiffured hairstyle. He had to be proud of her and enjoy his daughter's presence, the bob of her hair and the swing in her step.

'Hi, dad. Thought I'd surprise you. Don't mind?'

'Why should I mind, June, dear? Lovely to see my daughter after so long, and looking so pretty! William?' He gave a chaste kiss on both cheeks, continental fashion.

'Busy, dad, so I took the opportunity. It's quite a drive, though.' She looked around, took in the expanse of manicured gardens, the size of the Manor, and the evident buzz of the place with its visitors. 'You *living* here, now? Lovely setting. Do I get to meet the cause of all the trouble?' Her smile was converted to more of a grin. 'Sorry, dad. But I've still got to fully come to terms with all this. Mum's told me she doesn't really mind, 'cos she says both of you needed a change. It's just, so, unreal or something. Happens to others but not to your *own* parents. Makes me feel rather vulnerable, in case William gets smitten elsewhere.' The grin disappeared and he could see a worried girl underneath, the openness of her.

Taking her hand, he led her off towards the Manor's front door, avoiding the issue for the moment. 'Come and meet Mary, June. She's our mother hen, but don't tell her that. I'll get Roberta in shortly. You'll stay?'

'Stay, dad?'

'Yes, stay. As in Bed and Breakfast. You surely don't want to drive all the way back south this evening? Then we can have dinner together, and catch up. It's been too long, June. Far too long, and it's my fault. I'm sorry.' Now she was here, it felt great.

Her hand tightened in his and she gave him a sideways glance. 'You sound different, dad. Not like you to apologise?'

'Thank Roberta, June. I do hope you'll like her. Would William mind if you stayed? You can ring him?' He stood back and let her go through into the entrance hall, hoping the effect on her would be as it was for him. He wasn't disappointed.

'Dad! You live *here!* It's beautiful!' She was looking around, poised on her high heels, taking in the redolence that was the old-world charm of the building. 'And I can *stay?*'

'Of course. We've no one in tonight. Brought anything with you?'

A coy smile. 'Well, I did think I might have found a hotel or something, and William's not expecting me back until late tomorrow. But I wasn't going to presume, really. Sure Roberta won't mind?'

'Mind? My dear girl, she'll be delighted. She's always talked about wanting to meet you – and Peter – though if he came here we may have difficulty in prising him loose again.' That comment brought out a chuckle from June, she knew Peter as of old. 'Come through to the kitchen. Mary may still be busy, but I'm sure we can scrounge a cup of tea. And you'll meet Hazel, she's a wee bit E.S.N but otherwise a charming girl. Works hard.' Pushing open the door, he led the way down the corridor into the kitchen. Mary wasn't there, but Hazel pointed to the back door. She must be refreshing the buffet table in the Barn.

'Hazel – this is June, my only daughter. Can you get us a couple of mugs of tea?' The girl smiled, as she always did, and carefully got the mugs down, added the milk, took the ready pot from the Aga and filled the mugs almost to overflowing. She rarely spoke unless necessary – so the smile had to say it all.

'Thank you, Hazel.' June took her mug and perched on a stool, as her father took his and leant back on the work surface behind him. Hazel went back to her slow buttering of the next batch of scones. 'You won't be missed, dad?'

'I think the rush is over, dear. It's Roberta's thing, but yes, it has been a bit hectic. Gone well. She's a happy girl.'

June considered her words carefully. Meeting her father again after nearly six months, and noticing the change in him, less haggard, brighter somehow, evidently the new scenario was to his benefit. Her mother, way out in Africa, was busy, and didn't seem anxious to get home. Peter couldn't really care less. So she had to accept the situation, despite her previously strongly held – and voiced – views on the sanctity of marriage. If it wasn't working, then change was inevitable. 'Are you happy, dad? No regrets?'

Her eyes – Samantha's eyes – were holding his. Hazel had her head down. 'No regrets, June. What we had was fine, I've got memories that won't fade, but the old order changeth. We had what we had. Now we're doing our own thing, it won't diminish what we've felt before. If ultimately the wheel turns full circle, it does, but I've no regrets. No, none.'

The back door got pushed open and Roberta was there, with Mary close behind, arms full of derelict tea things. 'Did I hear something about no regrets? June! Lovely to see you; let me dump this lot.' Roberta slid her tray onto the draining board and turned back to the girl. 'I won't say just like your father, 'cos your not. Damn sight prettier. I'm so glad you felt you could come.' She held out a hand, and as June took it, pulled the girl towards her and gave a cheek-to-cheek kiss. 'Well now. Mary – this is Andrew's daughter, June.'

Mary kept an impassive face. This was a strange thing. 'Nice to meet you, er, June. I see Hazel's managed the tea? How about a scone or three? Reckon we're over the rush now. You can rest them, Hazel. Shan't need no more.'

June hadn't imagined Roberta quite like she was – she'd thought more of a slinky go-getting type with shorty skirt and plenty of bust, but in the flesh, well, different. Nice, a wholesome sort of person, not flaunting but still nice. A bit Italian, or some Spanish, somewhere, with that oval face and dark hair, darker than her own. And bulging somewhat, so it was true. 'Dad's said I could stay. I hope he's not committing you . . .'

Roberta grinned at her Andrew. 'He's okay. I'd be cross if you didn't stay. Mary – we've a room made up?' Mary rolled her eyes. As if. But an extra for dinner tonight, it seems. Peel some more potatoes then, another few slices of that beef out the fridge. Not a problem.

Roberta's smile broadened. 'That's settled. I'd best make sure things wind down out there. Andrew?'

'Sure. June, can you get your things in from the car, and then Mary'll show you a room. Dinner at about seven? Just have a mooch around, while we're putting things back to rights?'

Quiet had descended. The last car had gone, the Paint people's marquee soon down and removed, Andrew's mates from the Sports Club demolished the temporary fences, took down the notices, and so, apart from some worn patches of grass, it was back to normal. The Open Day was over, done and dusted. Half past six, and the evening light was dimming down the garden. Roberta slipped her arm through Andrew's and squeezed.

'Tired?'

'Sort of. Good day, though, worked well. Let's just hope it produces results.'

'Oh, it's done that, dear. Probably more than enough work now, let alone the live-in courses. Maybe we've overcooked things. Have to take on some help. Which reminds me – Andrea – she hasn't turned up, has she? You spoke to her?'

Andrew felt a twitch of concern. She *had* said she'd be up. Unlike her not to let him know if she couldn't meet her promises. 'P'raps I'd better ring her again?'

'Yes, do. I'll go and get myself through the shower and changed.' She twisted her lip in reflection. 'Invite her for dinner, love, if you want to. The more the merrier. June will know of her?'

'Should think so, dear. Sure?' He got another squeeze and a nod. 'Okay. Don't be too long up there, 'cos I feel a bit grubby myself – and no, it's not the evening for a joint effort!' They both laughed and Roberta pulled away from him and skipped – yes, skipped, back into the house.

Pulling his mobile out, he rang the missing Andrea.

'I know, Andrew,' her voice sounded tearful, 'I'm so sorry to have missed things. I'm back at home now. You'll never guess . . .' The pause was too significant and he sensed she was emotionally speechless.

'Andrea, come here. Come and have dinner with us. June's here – my daughter? Then you can tell us what's happened. See you as soon as you like?'

There was only the sound of her breathing, a muffled 'Yes, I'd like that,' before the phone went dead. He shook his head. What on earth was wrong?

FOURTEEN

When Andrea's car finally scrunched up the drive, it was gone half past seven. They'd held dinner back, much to Mary's annoyance, but Roberta was as concerned about the girl as Andrew. He heard the noise, went to meet her down the steps and she fell out of the car and straight into his arms. Though she must have made a bit of effort to dress up, her face, and her eyes, showed her fraught and distressed. All he could do was hold her and feel the sobs coming. She buried her head in the curl of his arm and they stood together until she moved.

'I'm sorry.' Her tearful eyes found his concern.

'For what, Andrea? Coming here so I can offer you some support, or whatever? Come on in, girl.' He kept an arm round her shoulder, shepherding her up the steps, holding the door and letting her go on through.

Roberta was there, waiting, took over, and sat her down on one of those tapestry chairs. 'Tell us, Andrea. What's the matter?'

'The Brewery – we've had the Receivers in and Mr Howard's had a heart attack. I've had an *awful* day!'

Roberta looked at Andrew, appalled, held her hand to her mouth. Poor girl! She'd obviously taken it very, very hard. However, this was no place to carry on any form of interrogation. 'Come on through to the sitting room; oh, what a shame, how is . . . no, just let's get you in here.'

Ensconced in a fireside chair, with June as an unwitting observer to the telling, Andrea relived her day. A phone call from Barry, the Finance guy, could she come in, there'd been a problem, and once there, confronted by these two blokes, and the explanation that the Brewery's suppliers, nearly all of them, hadn't been paid because the Bank had queried the accounts, and somehow it had turned out that a lot of the incoming monies had been diverted. Diverted?' Andrew was shocked and not just a little alarmed. Mr Howard had been called in, and when questioned, had had a heart attack. He was in hospital, but the prognosis wasn't good. Andrea had borne the brunt of the enquiries, but couldn't be faulted. The Office administrator woman, Ida Rollason, was away on leave, but Andrea was sure she and Mr Howard had cooked up things between them. And now it looked as if she was out of a job. It was too much, all too much. She was crying again, great floods of tears. Roberta stayed Andrew's movement, and shook her head at him. Sitting on the arm of Andrea's chair instead, and putting her arm round the girl's shoulders, she just let her cry.

Thoughts that ran in quick succession through Andrew's mind; this girl, this only child, still living at home, devoted to her job, pretty, crazy ideas about her sex, he'd *loved* her, she'd nearly wrecked his relationship with Roberta, her mother one of his wife's best friends, nearly raped that time, and here she was, being cosseted by the woman he loved beyond belief, with his *daughter* looking on? Surreal.

Mary brought the tableau back to reality. 'Dinner?' She'd quietly eased into the room, sized up the situation. There'd been rumours, but not in her mind to air them. Andrea, now she was a pretty kettle of fish, and an odd piece of any jigsaw. 'It won't hold much longer, Miss Roberta.'

'You're right. You'll be better with something inside you. Let's eat.' Easing herself off the chair, she gave Andrea a lift and the girl rose, brushed her skirt down, wiped her eyes on the back of her hand and sniffed.

'Sorry,' she said, ineffectually. 'I haven't much appetite.'

'Understandable. However, we might tempt you. Andrew?' Roberta motioned with her head. June was standing now, quietly waiting to see how she'd fit in to this, wondering about her father, how he'd got so involved. Different, she thought again, how different, and more purposeful, more alert, more *with it*. Roberta had done this? Some lady! His face was crinkling with that lovely smile of his and she took his proffered hand. Ashamed, now, she was, about the selfish feelings engendered when she'd first heard about all this. Her mother seemed to be happier in this adventurous job she'd got, and now her Dad was full of life. The emotion of being with him, feeling his renewed love for her in the squeeze of his fingers, meant she found herself on the brink of tears as well, and that would never do, not while this poor Andrea girl was so traumatised. She'd love to help somehow, but hadn't a clue how.

Roberta had taken Andrea through to the dining room, and in that brief moment alone she could whisper, 'Sorry, dad. She's nice. Glad for you,' and felt her stomach contract as his renewed smile and squeeze dug at her emotions again.

Mary had done some lovely thin sliced beef in a gorgeous sauce; there were beautifully cooked runner beans and duchesse potatoes, simplistic but rewarding. Andrea picked at hers, then as the glass of burgundy began to help ease the tensions in her, started to empty her plate. June saw her visibly relaxing, and wondered anew at the new version of her father, gently bringing the girl back to life with smiles and well-chosen remarks. Roberta didn't ignore her either, between the two of them Andrea's stressful appearance diminished and the light came back to her eyes.

'June?' She nearly jumped, lost in a reverie of re-vamping her thoughts.

'Sorry.' This seemed to be the word for everyone tonight and she nearly laughed, but swallowed and smiled up at Roberta.

'How long can you stay? I know we've got you for tonight, but it would be lovely if you could stay a while longer, so we could get to know each other better?'

She blinked. Stay? A moment's thought. William? Well, he'd cope, be good for him. The job, well, she was on leave anyway which is why she'd decided to make the journey; in her heart of hearts she'd needed to do this thing. Why not? Mind you, I've only got one spare pair of pants, and that - oh, to hell with it!

'If you're sure . . . I'd love to stay another day or two. Yes, it'll be great. Thank *you.*' Her father was obviously pleased at the idea, too. Yes, and the tight grief at his abandonment of her mum or their drift apart had ebbed away.

Roberta inwardly heaved a sigh of relief. The hidden stumbling block of Andrew's distant daughter was going to be a thing of the past. She liked this girl, with her Andrew characteristics and the firmness about her softened by some of what could be Samantha's qualities. And Andrew would be so much more relaxed as well. Great!

'Right. Andrea – you'll stay the night?' In for a penny – and something of what Andrew had mentioned a lot earlier on about this now unhappy girl came back to mind. 'Then we can see what tomorrow brings?'

Andrea looked up. She'd not dreamt of this as an option; to be truthful she had dreaded going back home to face the ongoing inquisition from her parents. 'I've no things.'

'Then it's a yes. Ring your folks, now, while we clear the plates. There's a lovely pud. Mary?'

Andrew's heart was singing. Roberta, his darling girl, a happy girl; June, a daughter restored to mutual favour; and Andrea, his unsought but welcomed, possessed, revelation; three lovely ladies, and all under one roof. What more could a man want? Though technically it was still summer, the evenings drew cold, and Mary, bless her, had lit the sitting room fire while they'd lapped up another of those speciality desserts of hers, apricot soufflé and chocolate home made ice-cream. Seemed a shame to spoil it with coffee, but liqueurs were the thing. With curtains drawn, the logs crackling, it was heaven. Roberta'd put a disc on, and gentle Elgar flowed through the room. Andrea's eyes were closed and she seemed asleep. June, with recollections of an unhappy William on the telephone moments before the dessert, taking her turn after Andrea, was still in pensive mode. Her father seemed blissful, eyes on Roberta. She, too, was relaxing with her eyes shut, but must have sensed her look and caught the glance as she opened them. June received that that warm smile, and a wink. Her father's head was falling; he was dozing. She grinned back; her dad was okay with this new girl in his life. A child, though? How would he feel – how would she feel, with a step sister or brother so much younger? And she had yet to conceive? Maybe it would encourage William, if there was a new baby about. He wasn't all that ardent, sadly.

Anthea woke up. 'Sorr . . . ' No, that wouldn't do. 'I shouldn't have dozed. Maybe . . .'

Roberta got up, carefully. Her head was a trifle muzzy after two glasses of burgundy, a Cointreau and a day dealing with people, not good for little Miss unborn. 'You're right. Bed, everyone. Andruuuuw - Bedtime.' He jumped and Roberta chuckled at him. 'All us girls about, and you fell *asleep!* Shame on you. Andrea, June – would you mind sharing the twin room? You don't have to, but . . .' The two girls looked each other and sensed no objections either way.

'Sure, why not?' June was the first invitee, she was okay with Andrea, and that girl might be better off with a companion to stop, or at least diminish, her brooding.

The twin room was at the end of the wing corridor, a largish room that echoed the size of the master bedroom, but decorated in true Roberta style, pink and beige, warm and comforting. June had her bag and a nightie, long flowing thing in blue cotton. Andrea had nothing, but didn't care. She stripped off and merely fell into bed as she was, asleep in minutes. At the other side of the house, Roberta was brushing out hair in front of the mirror, Andrew already in bed and reading. The Manor was quiet.

'I think,' Roberta said, quietly, 'I'm the luckiest girl alive.' She put her brush down, swung her hair so it bounced, and slid in alongside him, pushing his book away and offering her face to be kissed. 'Just one small thing.' She twisted his signet ring on her engagement finger, and wished. 'Did June notice, do you think?'

'Probably not. Else she'd have said. I'm a lot happier now she's come round.'

'You said she would, darling. You know your daughter, don't you?'

'I love her, Roberta, always have. Despite her rather strict views, but those seem to have softened rather, I'm glad to say.'

She snuggled down alongside him, moulding herself as best she could. 'Ouch!'

'What?'

'It's a bit early for Bulge to start kicking me, but I'm sure she did. Too much wine. Oh well. What are we going to do about Andrea?'

'Do we have to do anything?'

'You know we do. She's your protégé, isn't she? In more ways than it's right for me to know about, but I'm glad I do. How's this going to affect you, Andrew?'

He considered. It really was a bit late in the day to think about the Brewery, but it would impact on his side of things, no doubt about that. As for the girl, he'd had this weird idea when they first met she'd be a good person to employ, self-indulgently and pre-Roberta, for he'd fancied having a decorative and willing girl within reach. Then the relationship with this lovely lady in this bed with him had deepened beyond belief, and after the precipitate disaster when Andrea had helped him clear Sam's things. . . should they consider offering her a job here? Or would she be too much a temptation? She'd come up often enough and he liked seeing her, but constantly?

'Shall we give her a job? We talked about getting help in now the project's taking off?'

Roberta withdrew her arm and clasped her hands behind her head to stare at the ceiling.

Should she, would she, will she, won't she? 'Oh, *knickers!*'

'Pardon?'

'Leave it, dear. Go to sleep. We'll discuss it in the morning. Turn the light off. Night night.'

* * *

June came alive suddenly. She'd heard a noise, and with it the realisation she wasn't in her own bed, no comatose William snuffling away pretending to be asleep when she darned well knew he wasn't, so what, then? It must have been the loo, and not hers, no gurgles and sploshes. The Manor! Of course, and Andrea – her bed covers thrown back; then the girl was in the bathroom. She sat up, stretched, put tentative toes down to the comforting softness of a really nice carpet, and stood up, stretched again. Daylight, so must be sevenish. Her watch, strap flat on the bedside cupboard thing, told her different. Eight, gone. No wonder she felt a hollow tum. The bathroom door bolt slid back and a naked Andrea emerged, towelling her hair. So she must have had a shower?

'Morning, June! Apologies if I woke you, but breakfast beckons. All yours.'

'Good morning. I must have slept like a log. Lovely comfortable bed. How're you feeling after a shower?'

'Heaps better. Rested. Bit of a clearer head too. You're very like your father.'

'Thanks. A compliment! Roberta said I was prettier. You don't look too bad yourself, Andrea. I envy your boobs.' True, there must be all of a thirty-four C there, whereas she just managed a 32 B. Dad would love to get an eyeful of those, she thought, not knowing that her father had had the kissing of the aforesaid boobs, let alone the feeling. The eyes wandered down, and Andrea seemed not to care. She towelled away, a leg at a time on the bed to dry her toes, and June had the full view. She felt suddenly uncomfortable, abruptly turned, snatched up her toilet bag and disappeared into the bathroom. Andrea heard the shower go on; she'd seen June look. Little did she know!

Mary thought she might as well have spent the night at the Manor, in the little room at the back that Roberta was happy for her to use, given she'd left late and was back again so early. Those girls would welcome a good breakfast, I'll warrant, she thought, and set about putting a dozen bacon rashers on a tray into the oven. Roberta was whistling away somewhere, so Mr Andrew must be about. The kettle was steaming, and she moved it away from the hot ring for a minute before making the coffee. That'll bring 'em in. Nothing like the smell of fresh coffee of a morning let alone the bacon.

'Morning, Mary! Thanks for last night. Sorry we were so late. That poor girl, dealing with all that trauma. Hope she's better this morning. Nice to have a house full. Andrew's in the office, he's a bit bothered about that Brewery thing, being sort of involved. Shame, isn't it?' She prattled on. 'Good to have Andrew's June here, too. Nice girl. She'll be staying at least another night. Don't change the beds; maybe Andrea might want to stay on as well. Hazel having the day off? She did well yesterday; good kid that. You look after her well. Shall I do that?' She took the coffee percolator from the shelf, letting Mary concentrate on the breakfast pan.

When Andrew emerged, looking pensive, she raised her eyebrows at him. 'Well?'

'Nothing there that I could have seen, R. All I was doing was watching the returns. I didn't see the Bank account entries. I'm just wondering if there weren't another set of figures done, and the difference disappeared; that might account for the dissatisfaction from the tenants, and even why they called an outsider in, to provide a smoke screen. I don't thing there's anything to worry about, but I shall have to raise it with the Receivers. I wonder who they are? Maybe Andrea will know. She not down? What about June?'

'Neither, darling. Want some coffee?' She poured a mugful, added his spoonful of sugar. She'd stay on her fruit juice, didn't fancy Bump getting hyper on caffeine, hoping she hadn't a baby hangover. 'I'll catch up on yesterday's contacts, Andrew. Maybe later we'll go through them? See what June wants to do.'

He sat down, took a piece of toast. 'I'll wait till the girls appear, Mary, before you serve up. We'd better have a sit-down lunch. That a problem?' Mary didn't need him to suggest these things, she was already organised, and scowled at him. 'Sorree!' Then he added, 'You're a Brick! and she laughed.

Once the two girls appeared, a delight on the eye, they had

a conventional breakfast, and Andrew basked in the pleasure of the company of the three women in his life. June said she wanted to walk around the estate, if that was all right, and Andrea suggested she and Andrew went over the possible ways in which the Brewery could survive. He didn't really want to, but it was nevertheless a sensible suggestion. They'd take the books and papers into the sitting room, to leave the office free for Roberta.

Once closeted in the sitting room with the girl, he found his thoughts were not entirely focused. His heart wasn't in it, more with June, Roberta's successful day, and how they could move forward. Andrea herself was a distraction, too. She kept getting too close, her forearm touching his and giving him goose pimples, the fresh clean scent of her and the fulsome figure. And he knew her. Could they realistically offer her a job here, with the dangers of her feminity?

'Andrew! Concentrate! You haven't heard a word. I said, Barry took the spreadsheets away, and we *never* knew if the income figures tallied with the gallonage. Only the projections. The tenants wouldn't see our projections; they'd only report the gallonage and wait for the cheque. If they didn't get what they thought they should, no wonder they complained. Then Howard might have had Barry pay them more, and starve the creditors. He probably did that on a seesaw basis for months, and then someone rumbled it? It only needs one.'

'You may well be right. If that is the case, then the Receivers will soon find it. Does the Brewery have a future? We know Howard was supposedly fighting off some takeover feelers. Might not be a bad thing, at least it'll keep the employment going. Do you want to stay on?'

Shaking her head, Andrea looked at him straight in the face. 'I'd rather work for you.'

'Me – or Roberta?'

'Either, both, whatever. It's a lovely place to work in. You need someone, don't you? I'm sorry I missed yesterday. In all ways.' Leaving the table, she crossed to the window and looked out over the lawns, at the clouds, rather dull and menacing now, and the block of the Barn away to the right. Of course, she knew she was a temptation, and he'd been too easy to seduce, not that she'd really set out to achieve more than an enjoyable flirtation; what had happened was a natural sort of human response thing, the danger was it *could* happen again. Turning round, she put her hands behind her, onto the window seat and heaved herself up. Legs swinging, hands under her bottom, she looked at him. 'I know. You'll always think of me as a temptress. Too accessible. Too fond of you, which I am. If I promise to wear trousers all the time, and cut my hair short, and not wear scent or make-up, will that help?'

That caused him to crease up. 'Andrea, if any potential female employee offered anti-attraction devices at interview, I don't think she'd stand much chance. We may be looking for a receptionist as well as an administrator, so looks would have to have some bearing on it. I certainly wouldn't be looking for an ex-prison warder type. No, I should think Roberta would have you off the premises sharpish if she felt we were straying off the straight and narrow. I won't deny you may figure in our business plan, my girl, but let's get the Brewery sorted first. Okay?'

'Well. Yeah.' She grinned, he was perfectly right. 'So I may stand a chance?'

'Subject to management approval, yes.'

The leg swinging stopped and she jumped down. 'In that case, I'm a happy girl. I just envy Roberta.' She saw him frown. 'Okay, okay. But I'm not going to ignore you, Andrew. I can't.'

'Just keep the girly feelings under control, Andrea Chaney. Someone else will show up eventually. Shall we go and get some lunch?'

With some trepidation, June had gone out for her walk. She needed the space, the time to think, and she was afraid of her thoughts. The flying visit had sort of got a bit out of hand; all she'd started off with was the concept of filling in the hole she'd dug between her and her dad, now it was taking on a mysterious new dimension. As a relatively newly married girl,

216

she knew she hadn't got much of a clue about what it was like twenty years down the line, seeing the same face every morning, feeling the same hand grope round your sexy bits, feeling – well, yes, we won't go into that, she told herself, pulling a face. The same sort of meals, the same daily chat. Even the same snog. Was she really going to manage to survive twenty years or more of William and his ways, his ever-present pash for buying the next big thing in computers and the hours of time spent poring over the laptop in front of the tele when she wanted to watch Neighbours? How had her dad survived so long? Her mum, she'd always known, was tireless in her pursuit of bargains, selling things, persuading folk she was the only person capable of organising a luncheon for thirty at a fiver a head and ignoring her dad most of the time. So perhaps it was no wonder he'd taken to the lovely Roberta. Yes, she *was* lovely! That oval face, the dark hair, the lively eyes, the good figure and the ever-present laughter. So okay, she hadn't the size on her that Andrea had, but she'd a nice shape. And she evidently adored dad; you could see it in those amber glints.

She'd come to the end of the Manor's entrance road. Which way? Back, or through the fields, up the slope towards the trees maybe, or on into the village? The cloud cover was giving the day an ominous feel, in tune with her mood. She walked on, down the road.

What was mum going to do, stay in Sierra Leone, come home after her stint and then go someplace else, come home for good, try and patch up things with dad or get divorced? Roberta was expecting dad's child, so that sort of meant a divorce anyway, didn't it? She couldn't see him going back to mum somehow, not with the lively life he'd got at the Manor, and anyway, it was a super place to live. Little tweaks of jealousy crept in. Lucky Roberta, lucky dad. What had happened before dad? She'd not asked, unsure of her ground. Where did Andrea fit in to this? She was pleasant, sure, and drop-dead gorgeous in the figure/looks department, and if she wasn't mistaken, there'd been a flicker of something between her and dad as well? Was the old man getting randy in his old age? Old age! Not yet fifty! He'd obviously clicked with Roberta, and quite soon after they'd met, by her reckoning. Who'd made the running? Dad? More like Roberta, she was sure dad wasn't a go-get-'em sort then. He might be now.

She'd covered some distance and the Manor entrance lane was out of sight. A few spots of rain and she'd not got her coat. Stupid girl! Abruptly, she turned, and started marching back.

What would Peter think to all this, out with mum, and doing things for her to earn his keep? P'raps that was no bad thing, maybe he'd stop with her. He wouldn't care much about dad's fling with Roberta. No, flings not the word, craze? No, more than that. Infatuation? Probably more than that, too. Uh, more spots of rain; hope it won't get worse. William. Poor William! He just hadn't got to worry about her being away for another day or two, do him good! With a jolt she realised it was the first time she'd been away on her own since they'd been married. Hope he managed to eat, that she wouldn't have a panic phone call asking her where the baked beans were, or that she'd have a mountain of washing up to do when she did get back. Damn this rain! She started to hurry her pace.

Andrew looked out of the sitting room window. Lunchtime and no sign of June. She'd been gone some time and it was turning into a steady downpour. He hoped she'd got a coat.

'Andrea – did June have a coat?'

The girl was sweeping up the papers prior to shoving them back into the file. 'Not sure. Doubt it; the sun was still shining when she left, if you remember.' She joined Andrew at the window, and put her hand in his. 'We don't know where she went, either.' As he turned towards her, she took a deep breath. 'I want to work here, Andrew. With you. I'll be a good girl, I promise.'

How could he not yield to the temptation represented by those slightly parted lips and eyes that searched his? The girl he'd made a woman, seen her, and she'd made his pulse race? He brought her hand to his lips. 'Sure?'

She had to chuckle. 'I can but try. Maybe we shouldn't be alone together. Roberta . . .'

'Yes?' The sitting room door had opened, quietly, and there she was. Andrew dropped the hand. 'I saw you, mister! Leave the girl alone.' She was laughing. She knew, of course, but remained totally confident, and anyway, so what if Andrew did kiss the girl? 'Come on, you two. Stop flirting and come and have lunch. Where's June?'

'Still out and likely without a coat; mebbe I should go down the road with the car and see if I can find her?'

'Might be as well, Andrew. We'll wait till you get back.' She took Andrea off to the kitchen as Andrew picked the car keys off the small table and headed out to where his car was parked, not quite getting soaked in the short distance.

He found her, only a mile away, head down, walking briskly towards him, with a lift of head and a big smile to appreciate that he'd come for her. Dropping into the front passenger seat, shaking her hair free of rain, brushing the damp away from her front, touched his knee with a hand.

'Thanks, dad, thoughtful as ever. Stupid, going out without a coat.'

He grinned back at her before driving on a short distance to get to the next gateway and reverse in order to turn round. His arm went across the back of her seat to give support as he looked back to see the car into the gateway, then he stopped. 'You okay? I mean, with what's going on?' Being out in the car with her was the opportunity to talk. 'What do you think to Roberta now you've seen her?'

'She's lovely, dad. What more can I say?' Staring straight out of the windscreen, across the road where the rain was bouncing splashes off the growing puddles and across the fields where the trees lined the dark grey sky; she saw her mum in her mind's eye, dealing with naked brown skinny children with pot bellies, the heat, the flies, the battle with bureaucracy for meagre supplies. 'You wouldn't have gone with her. She knew what you were like. Inevitable, I guess, something would have happened. If it wasn't a Roberta, it may have been an Andrea. Whoever.' She didn't notice his instinctive little jerk of surprise at the mention of Andrea.

'Roberta fell into my life, June. It wasn't premeditated. And it happened before your mother's announcement of what she wanted to do. My weakness you know, as you said; thoughtful, more caring, actually.' He related how the horse had thrown Roberta in this very lane and it had all gone on from there. June's interjection, the gasp when he explained why Roberta had cried for support when her ex-husband was killed showed him she understood, and he was minded to let his arm drop onto her shoulders. 'I couldn't have just ignored her, June. She needed someone, she chose me, I responded because it felt right. It just went on from there, and now I love her. We're having a baby, June. A sort of unofficial step-sister for you.'

'I know.' How did he expect her react? Full of joy? Cross? Neither, really, not entirely sure though. 'Roberta's first?'

'Yes. What she's always wanted, but not with first husband, it seems. I know, she's older but it seems to be going fine.' Would June say about her and William? 'Are you . . .?'

'No.' Her reply was abrupt. 'Early days, dad. William's not all that bothered.'

'Don't *you* want children, June?'

She sat quiet, still staring at the rain. She wasn't sure; her tummy gave her queer signals she couldn't interpret. 'Time we went, dad. It's lunchtime.'

Withdrawing his arm, he restarted the car and drove back up the lane. Sore point, then, children. He wouldn't mention it again.

There was a phone call early afternoon. The rain had eased, June had gone across to the Barn with Roberta to see more of her set-up; Andrea had been persuaded to spend time sorting through some of the remaining old papers left from the clear-out upstairs that neither Roberta nor Andrew had inclination to deal with, and Andrew was in the office, minded to get on with outstanding Accountancy client's accounts. Picking up the phone and tucking it under his chin as he pushed a file back onto the shelf, he gave the usual reply. 'The Manor.'

'Mr Hailsworthy?'

'Speaking. How can I help?'

'Smythe and Richards. Alan Richards. We're dealing with the Brewery. We'd very much like to talk to you about your involvement? Say tomorrow morning, eleven o'clock? And I believe you have Miss Chaney with you? We'll need to have some further discussions with her.'

This he could do without. Automatically his back had gone up; he wasn't having any tuppenny ha'penny auditor guy telling him when he could turn up. 'I'm sorry. Tomorrow morning is *not* convenient. I could come over later in the afternoon, around three? I can only spare an hour, though.' Then he tried to ease things a bit. 'I'll see if Miss Chaney can come with me. She's very upset at all this. Have you heard how Mr Howard is? I understand he collapsed at the news of the . . .' The what? Collapse of his empire? Realisation his fiddle had been discovered? Threat of legal proceedings, angry shareholders?

No alteration in tone from this Richards bloke. 'All right, Mr Hailsworthy. Three o'clock tomorrow. I can't comment on Mr Howard's condition. Thank you, look forward to seeing you. Goodbye.' And that was it, not a lot of human understanding there. A business, an employer of local people, shareholders, tenants; now just figures on paper and a commission taken out of whatever resources could be salvaged. Not his scene. Loss of business for him, though, just when he thought it was going to get somewhere; just as well he'd got Roberta and the new Interior Design Company to take his mind and time.

The rain changed to a steady drizzle, a wetting, dismal afternoon, so no prospect of a bright happy tea party in the rose garden today, but mugs in the kitchen and chunks of Mary's fruit cake instead. They all foregathered, like having a briefing session. Roberta was in ebullient mood, and happy with getting to know Andrew's June, whereas Andrea wasn't at all pleased with Andrew's revelations about the Smythe and Richards telephone call.

'Not much I can do about it, I suppose technically I'm still an employee and being paid, for how much longer, heaven knows. At least we'll give each other moral support. You don't think it'll rebound on us at all?' The worried look didn't sit well on her, lines on her forehead where lines shouldn't be.

Andrew hadn't managed to discuss the possibilities of giving her a position with the new regime with Roberta, not yet, though he could see the speculative glance his partner gave her. 'Shouldn't think so. What I did, and the help you gave me, couldn't be construed as anything other than what it was. A financial exercise to encourage tenants' sales. Nothing quite like the creative accounting that Howard seemed to be into. The guy on the phone wouldn't be drawn over his condition, other than sounding unconcerned.' Andrew shivered. 'That's one aspect of accountancy I would *not* like to be in.'

Roberta threw in her contribution. 'I think it's all a ploy, part of the big company's take-over tactics. You know, grab an opportunity, exploit it, make it sound worse than it is, and then when everyone takes fright, the business value drops, cheaper all round. They win, you lose, tough. That's business. Sad, though. Look on the bright side, Andrea. One door shuts, another opens. Who knows what might happen? Anyway, I'm going to close up. June's getting interested, aren't you, dear?'

Oh ho! June's a dear? Well, so much the better. Andrew heaved himself off his stool. 'Going to spend William's money, June? Get Roberta to plan you a makeover? Cost you!'

His grin told her he was joking and happy, and she was getting to enjoy her stay. Such a change to have folks around her who laughed and were light hearted. William was so serious. Her father was now looking thoughtful.

'R, what you said, about the Brewery. You may be right. More to this than meets the eye. Thanks, darling, that was an inspiration.'

She grinned, curtsied, 'Thank you, kind Sir, glad I'm of some use. Now – we'll all need to do something useful till dinner. Any ideas?'

* * *

June felt she had to get home. She'd been away two days; it was going to take her another to get home and sort herself out, much as though she would have been happy to stay put a while longer. After breakfast the following morning she slid her things into the holdall and said her goodbyes. Roberta kissed her, gave her a squeezey hug and said 'come back soon', Andrea also gave her a cheek-to-cheek kiss, wished her 'all the best', as if she was going for a job or something, but it was her dad who saw her to her car. Suddenly she found herself in tears, and buried in his sweater, his hands clasping her shoulders. 'Dad, I'm so sorry,' she mumbled into his chest, 'I should have known you were only a softy over the girl. She's so nice, and pretty, and fun. She's so lucky to have you. Can I come again?'

Andrew tilted his daughter's tear streaked face up to his, felt the prick of his own emotion in tear form with the relief that she at least was on his side. 'Of course, June dear, of course. Any time, and the sooner the better. Bring William if you want, but give us a call first?' He held her at arms length and searched her face. 'What will you tell your mother?' He saw her incipient grin.

'That you're happy and contented? Well looked after, and she'd not to worry? It's true, dad, isn't it?'

'It is. I'm very fortunate, daughter mine, in finding someone like her. No disrespects to your mother, but times have changed.'

'I realise that now, dad. I'm glad I came.'

'So am I. Now drive safely, give us a call when you get back. Give my regards to William.'

When her little car was nothing but a distant diminished rumble of exhaust, he went back indoors, pleased she'd been but saddened by her going and the lopsidedness of their relationship. Now he had to wait and see what Samantha would say once June had reported her visit. Back to the desk; at least he wasn't bored.

After lunch he gathered his Brewery papers together and tried to get mentally prepared for whatever might arise. Andrea

223

and he both got a kiss apiece from Roberta as they left, who felt for Andrew's protégé; being in a potential 'no job' position wasn't fun by any means. Andrew, she knew, also felt professionally slighted by this; she just hoped no brickbats would come his way. She didn't like him having dour moments.

Andrea followed him in her car to her home, so she could get changed, not least to attempt to bolster up confidence by being in her best 'office suit'; left her car there as she didn't want to feel pressurised to stay and this was as good a way as any to minimise the chance. The Brewery yard seemed unusually quiet, despite there being no cessation of production until matters had been resolved or until stocks of grain had run out; the morbidity of potential closure hung over the place. As they got out of his car, Andrea shuddered and wrapt her arms round her suit jacket, hugging the thing close to her. So much had changed in the six months she'd known Andrew, her job, her life, her emotive state; it was all akin to a bad dream, apart from Andrew. If she hadn't had him to support her in all this she'd have turned into a bitter and love starved creature.

'I'm not looking forward to this. And I used to think it was so wonderful, the buzz of the place, the great feeling I had when the figures came in, the chat from the blokes, even Barry could get flirty at times. And now – look at it, the place has lost its spirit. You can tell.' She fell silent as they walked side by side up the steps, not daring to hold hands, though Andrew sensed she'd have liked to.

'If Howard was at the back of all this, he's got a lot to answer for. And to think he was telling us about resisting a take-over! Maybe Roberta's right. Perhaps it was all a ploy and he'd been offered a backhander from the big boys. Who knows? He might not live to profit.' His reply was in a hushed voice; her steps were three to his two, her heels clattering on the terrazzo floor of the office block as they approached Barry's office. Briefly, his arm went round her, feeling the slimness of her waist, the vulnerability of her; she was only a youngster. He could give her near twenty years, and yet he'd been the de-flowering of her. A coldly exciting yet numbing sensation flicked through his mind once more; the awareness of the opening of that channel of contact between them had left a scary intimation of incompleteness. The slight turn of her head and the fleeting softening of her eyes towards him jolted his conscience. He withdrew his arm as they got to the door, but that moment of contact had redefined their relationship.

The two men from the Receivers in the office looked up as they entered; the one was behind Barry's desk, the other sifting through the stack of papers on a side table. The man behind the desk stood up and offered a hand across the mess of documents. 'Alan Richards. Thank you for coming, and bringing Miss Chaney. I'm sorry that we had to ask you to come in but we have to explore all aspects. Miss Chaney, would you go with Mr Patterson. He'd like your help to understand the procedures you adopted.' No please then, just an instruction. She was a mere employee. 'Then you can take indefinite leave, as the other office staff have. We'll let you know the outcome.'

'What about Mr Howard? How is he?'

'We heard yesterday that he was holding his own. Very unfortunate that this should happen. Roger?'

The other man, a younger man with sandy hair and a receding chin, moved his checked pile onto the floor and went to the door, standing to hold it open for Andrea. 'I'll wait for you by the car, Mr Hailsworthy,' she said, not looking at him. 'Or you'll wait for me?'

'Of course.'

She went, and Patterson closed the door behind them. Her steps faded down the corridor and Andrew was left with this Alan Richards.

Forty minutes later it seemed Richards was satisfied. Andrew managed to keep calm and focused, despite his gut feeling of unease about the whole affair. At least there had been no sense of accusation of any false accounting directed towards his involvement, and his interpretation – Roberta's intuition – was confirmed when Richards closed the file in front of him, leant back, stretching his arms behind his head and cracking his knuckles, before flexing his shoulders and standing up once more. 'Thank you, Mr Hailsworthy. Or may I call you Andrew? The light's beginning to dawn. Have you guessed how all this happened?'

So now it was 'Andrew', was he no longer on the side of the ungodly? 'Two sets of figures. Somewhere there's a little black book?'

Richards laughed and the veneer of impartiality slipped, less tax inspector attitude, more fellow figure cruncher. 'Dark green, actually. In Howard's desk drawer. His er, health problem allowed us to find it. Unfortunate for him, fortunate for us. Sad, really, but there we go. We shall have to present our findings to the C.P.S., but it does seem the Brewery's more profitable than we could have assumed from the official figures. We can't really discuss this in any greater depth at present, you understand, but if you're interested . . . ' The option hung in the air between them.

Andrew rose, pushed his chair back to the desk. He had to keep his distance, unsure of how Andrea was faring. 'I was a smoke screen? Yes, of course I'd like to know the outcome. I still have a client responsibility here until I've something in writing. Then there's an account that I shall have to present. The future?'

'Uncertain. Not up to me, but my instinct is that we'll have to act on the basis of the 'official' figures, which means a sale of assets to cover paper debts. Including yours. I'll get our office to write, formally ending the contract. Sorry.'

Andrew shrugged. What else could he do, smile happily? 'Miss Chaney and the other girls?'

'Not required. They'll technically be entitled to statutory redundancy pay once things clarify. Mrs Roberts will probably be kept on if she can prove no inside knowledge of Howard's actions. Howard was keeping those three girls for no good reason, you know. There's no justification, especially with another guy on board.'

'Barry?'

'Yes, Barry. If he stays he'll do the work. We'll see. Thanks for your time.'

Andrea was waiting, leaning with her back to the passenger door. Her eyes caught his and an infinitesimal lift of eyebrows and a ghost of a smile showed she had survived. The car unlocked and she slid into the seat beside him, skirt above her knees and no attempt to tug it down. 'Home, Andrea? Or do you want to stay on at the Manor?'

'I'd best go home, Andrew. You don't want me cluttering the place. Or do you?'

Staring through the windscreen, avoiding the magnet of her bare knees alongside him, he held his feelings in check and ignored the pointed query. 'What will you do?' he asked.

A shrug of shoulders, then she straightened her skirt and the bare knees all but disappeared. 'Not sure. Ask the Supermarket if they need another checkout girl. At least I've experience with figures.'

'Hmmph. Don't do anything too hastily. You want to go home then?'

She nodded. He put the car into gear, and drove out of the yard. She didn't look back.

He dropped her off outside her gate; she swung those legs out with another brief glimpse of thigh, leant back in to offer a kiss, and was gone, swaying skirt and lovely legs walking out of his day.

FIFTEEN

Two weeks went by, in a blur of concerted effort to maximise on the opportunities emerging from the Open day and the responses to their advertisements, the flyers and some more complimentary editorial in the classier home-style magazines. The first residential weekend Course came and went, not quite the unqualified success because neither Roberta nor Mary had anticipated the vagaries of vegetarians – especially one who didn't fancy eggs or cheese, and some hasty re-scrambling of the menu was done at the last minute, and then the problem of allergies to feather pillows. 'All part of the learning curve!' as Andrew cheerfully said, concentrating on getting the administration side streamlined. He was working nearly flat out, handling the office side while Roberta hosted an increasing number of visitors and still did house calls within reach of the Manor. There were times when she yearned for the buzz of the London life, the chance of going to a show, visiting her favourite eating places, so much so she badgered Andrew into agreeing they should take a couple of days away before she got past, as she put it 'the point of no return'.

'No return, darling? You crossed that line when you invited me to share a rug with you!'

She thumped him, playfully, and he nearly fell off the office chair. 'You know what I mean! Listen, sweetheart, it's time we came to a decision about taking on help. You'll need to get to grips with the Barn, learn to talk to clients meaningfully, so you can take over when I'm flat on my back. And I shan't want to do clients home visits before too long. So where are we with this?'

'Do you want us to advertise? Or do we take the line of

least resistance?' He got thumped again. 'Ouch! You'll have the Social after you, knocking me about.'

She laughed. 'In your dreams! You're no kid. I take it that Andrea's your least resistible line? We haven't seen anything of her for a fortnight, is she surviving, d'you think?'

'Expect so, hope so. What should we do then, R? You say. She may not want to come, there's bound to be some er, undertones? Is that how you'd phrase things?'

Roberta pushed the swivel chair round so she could sit on his knees, holding herself with an arm round his shoulders. She put the other hand under his chin, looked at him, eyes narrowed. 'I know you. You'd be putty in her hands if she cried at you, but I also know something of what *we've* got going, Andrew, and my reading of things are that you'll love having her sexy figure about but you won't want to dabble. Feast your eyes, fantasise your dreams, but keep out of her knickers, eh, boy? If I have a cast iron guarantee, then you can have her – whoops, I didn't say that. *Employ* her, if you think she'll stand up to the strain. Unless you want to her to compete with other beauties, I'm sure you'd love to interview other girls?'

He wriggled. She was no mean weight now-a-days, and much as though it was nice to hold her, his legs were going to sleep. 'You'll have to move, dear. Sorry.' She slid to the floor and smoothed her bulging skirt as he reassured her; 'I shall be the soul of discretion, R.'

'Hmmm, I wonder. Let's go have coffee. Tell you what, let's ask Mary, see what she says. Independent opinion?'

'Andrea?' Mary glanced at Andrew, with his impassive face. 'She's decorative. Nice manner. Can't speak on her abilities, now, but the Brewery wouldn't ha' kept her else. See how she copes then, give the lass a trial, can't do no 'arm. Better the deil you ken, ay. High times you took matters a deal easier, Miss Roberta.'

'*I'll* phone her, Andrew. Will she be at home, d'think?'

'Roberta darling, I'm not her keeper. Ring and find out. If she is, she is. If not, leave a message. Simple.' He wasn't one for trying to imagine people's whereabouts or homely habits.

Roberta went into the office and shut the door. The girl was at home. 'Andrea? It's Roberta, from the Manor. Hi! . . . yes, I'm fine, thanks, if a bit out of proportion, you know, 36, 48, 38! How's the Brewery? . . . No, Andrew's not heard. . . . Oh dear. You've had your notice? Hmmm. We'd like you to come and see us, Andrea. Could you come up this afternoon, have tea? Oh yes, we're very civilised. Cucumber sandwiches? . . . ha. ha! I'll tell Mary. See you later then. Thanks, bye.' Before she went back to Andrew she sat and reflected, was this a good idea? Well, she'd soon know, and one way of defining the boundaries. Bump kicked her, as if to make her ideas felt; trouble was she couldn't interpret whether it was agreement or not. Only three months to go.

Andrea's car was coming up the drive. Andrew wasn't exactly hovering, rather keeping an eye, or an ear, and he was soon on the steps. When she climbed out of the car, it was a different hairdo, shorter, he'd say cropped round her ears, though less to his taste, he could tell it was well done and made her looking a lot more mature, as did her trouser suit. He wasn't sure if he liked the new styling.

'Lovely to see you again, Andrea. You're prompt.'

'Don't want to be late for my interview. Do you like my change of image? I said I'd cut my hair and wear trousers, and I'm a girl who does as she says. I left the horn rim specs at home.'

He laughed, caught her arm and walked her into the hall. 'It's just nice to have you here again. Who said it was an interview? Merely an opportunity to discuss mutual benefits. We're in here.' He escorted her into the sitting room.

Roberta rose from her chair, held out a hand, then pulling the girl closer, gave her a less formal welcome, a kiss on both cheeks, but didn't make any observation on her presentation. 'Thanks for coming, lovely to see you again. Sorry to hear about Mr Howard. So it's a change of ownership, then? Do have a seat.'

Andrea neatly tucked herself onto the settee and Andrew stood by the window. Now he was even less sure that he liked the new hairstyle; he much preferred the longer bouncier hair, and the way it had waved around her face before. This was far too austere, less feminine, but that's what she said she'd do, certainly. Trousers didn't sit well on her hips either. Give him a skirt and a flash of thigh any day. Girls should have curves, not straight lines.

'At least he didn't have to stand trial for embezzlement. Quietly hushed up. You know who's going to have our brands now? Those acquisitive people from Suffolk. Better than the big boys from up north I guess, but it remains to be seen whether the site stays in production. Rumour has it they'll sell, as we're too small. Turn it into yet another supermarket instead. Ironic, really. I said I'd end up as a till girl, didn't I, Andrew?'

'We can do better than that, Andrea. Tell us what you think you could do for us here. You know what we're on about and something of what we have in mind for the future. Explain how you could fit into the outfit. Go on, feel free.'

I knew it would be like a proper interview, I knew it. They aren't going to simply give me a job because I've become friends with Andrew, or because I lost my virginity to him. I know he still fancies me, I can see it when he looks at me, the way we brush together. I know I'd let him; I want him to really make me tingle and buzz. Roberta would kill me. She'd kick him out too. I promised I'd be good, but it's going to be damned hard. Bet he hates my hair. Don't like it much either. If I get the job I'll let it grow again, and I'll wear some sexy clothes. Make me feel good about myself, even if I don't get turned on. What shall I tell them?

She sat there in a brown study, as though she was alone in the room. In a trance?

'Andrea?' Roberta leaned forward. 'Surely you've got some ideas?'

'Oh yes, sorry.' She began to feel a flush of colour. - *Concentrate, girl, this is important* - 'I was thinking. - *True, but not about the job* - Andrew mentioned something about a receptionist. I could ensure that all telephone calls were directed to the right person, or filter them out if I had guidelines, give information, arrange to send out brochures. I could meet visitors, show them round and explain what we – you - can do. Then in the office, I could certainly do all the day-to-day accounts, send out invoices, check payments, deal with supplier's accounts, do the filing, all that you would expect of a sort of Girl Friday. - *Clad in just a loincloth and another strip of cloth round my boobs, no shoes. Don't be silly, Andrea!* - Anything, really. - *Keep the boss man happy!* Oh, I know - I've not had experience of child care, but I could maybe baby sit if you were dealing with client's visits.' She tailed off, feeling Andrew's gaze coming at her sideways and Roberta having that little smile that made her look so lovely . . .

Andrew hoisted himself off the window seat, having sat while he wondered what was going on in that pretty head. 'I've no worries about your office skills, Andrea, and I'm sure you'd do a better job than either of us, once you knew what system we run. You'd need to be very sure about who you gave the 'filter' treatment to; we wouldn't want to lose a future client because they'd been given the brush off. Roberta?' This was passing the buck, but he wanted her to decide.

'What about weekends? Are you flexible?'

Flexible – I'd touch my toes for him any day - 'Provided I had reasonable notice, I guess. We had a sort of flexitime arrangement at the Brewery, not that anyone checked up. I used to keep an eye on the other two girls – it worked fine. I've no hang ups over just working set hours.' - *I'd even work nights.*

'Are you interested in design? What sort of magazine do you read? Done any home decorating?' Roberta was getting into the swing of this, despite it being a new experience. She'd had no say in the appointment of the last girl who worked here – for the late unlamented Michael – perhaps if she had he'd still be here. The nagging thought of seeing all that happen again with Andrew worried her; she wasn't one hundred percent sure of him, and she'd no idea of how she'd really feel if things went wrong. Okay, so they'd had a fling, but so had she; people in glass houses etc, but now she was carrying their child it was different. *He was hers – and he'd promised to marry her!* That should be a strong enough bond.

'I don't take any magazines regularly, just buy what I fancy at the time, *Ideal Home, House Beautiful, Home Style,* that sort of thing.' - *Maybe 'Marie Clare', 'Red' and similar every now and again, but she won't want to know that.* - 'I know what I like, and I like this,' she waved around the room, 'and what you've done in the Barn. I'd love to see what else you've done, if I get a chance. Oh, and I have wallpapered the downstairs loo at home.'

That set them all giggling. 'Don't worry, Andrea, we're not into actually *doing* the work, just specifying – and organising and supervising if required. I guess you wouldn't mind chasing contractor's blokes around?'

Maybe, depends. – 'Whatever is needed; you asked me if I was flexible. Anything, I don't mind.' - *Keeping the boss happy and smiling?*

'What did you do at school, and college?' Andrew took up the questioning again.

Oh Lor! - 'Seven passes in GCSE, usual things. Then I did a couple of years night classes on Business Administration, but I'd started as an office junior at the Brewery. They just moved me up a notch each time there was a vacancy. P'raps it was easier than getting someone they didn't know.' - *At least I didn't have to sit on Howard's knee, or Barry's, come to that.*

The same old thing, line of least resistance, Andrew thought, not that he had a quarrel with that concept as he'd seen it work well enough in most firms. Better the devil you knew and all that, as Mary had said. Which is precisely what they were doing here. Some devil, too.

'I'll get Mary to bring in the tea. Won't be a minute. Andrew?' Roberta stood up, and winced as Bump moved with her. As she left the room, Andrew moved to follow her; obviously she wanted to have words out of earshot. He smiled at the girl, got an uneasy grin in return.

'Well?' As Mary finalised the tray, Roberta, massaging her swelling tummy, asked him.

'Trying to be objective about her, she's got experience of an office, she's pleasant, she obviously sees us as 'nice people', she's the right age and I'm sure she'll present the right image. Whether she'll find it challenging enough, I don't know. But we need someone, and soon.' Andrew caressed her bulge. 'I'm happy, if you are?'

Mary picked up the tray and indicated with her head he should bring the teapot. 'Could do worse, Miss Roberta, if you pardon me for saying. The poor girl needs something to get her teeth into now the Brewery's closing.'

'Okay. We'll give it a whirl. What to we pay her, Andrew?'

He shook his head quickly. He'd discuss that out of Mary's hearing, but he knew they couldn't afford to be too generous. 'Let's give her three months trial, R, and we'll work out figures if she accepts, eh?'

Conversation over tea and small cakes hinged on matters other than the possible job, with Roberta gently steering round things like hobbies, recreational interests, holidays, before coming back to ambition. 'How do you see yourself in, say three years time, Andrea? You surely wouldn't want to stay here permanently – because there's no promotional ladder.'

Whoops! Trickeeee! - 'I think having a satisfying job and being happy doing it is more important than chasing promotion for the sake of it – provided that one's income is adequate. Maybe I'm old fashioned in thinking that a girl's ultimate endeavour should be a solid relationship with the 'man of her dreams' and being concerned with a family if that's on the cards. So maybe in three years I may have found a partner and a chance to make a home of my own. However, if the right opportunity came along where I could do a more responsible job, then I certainly wouldn't turn it down.' - *The man of my dreams is too close for comfort and do I feel a little perspiration?*

'Well said.' Andrew wasn't to know how he was affecting the girl's bodily responses. 'Would you come to us for three months – probationary, so we can both see how things work out?'

Neither of them had realised the three months end could coincide with Roberta's date, but Andrea had. 'Won't you need me while you're becoming a mum?' - *Bet Andrew will feel the loss of her um, services* – 'I mean, you'll need some maternity cover?'

Andrew looked at Roberta. The impact of Andrea's remark on the situation hit him. He'd be running the show, coping with a girl giving birth, dealing with his own side of things and goodness knows what complications might arise with Sam. Roberta met his gaze with those steady trusting eyes of hers. Well, Andrea would just have to understand it was going to be tough.

'True. Probationary period extended to six months? And we'll review your salary after the three. We can't afford to pay you the same as the Brewery, you know.' He named a figure. 'And free meals. If you travel for us, you'll get an appropriate mileage allowance.'

'And a dress allowance as well, Andrea. We want you to look the part. Trousers, by the way, are only for when you get ladder jobs.' Roberta didn't much care for imitation men.

Andrew saw her out. 'Can you start Monday?' He offered her his hand, keeping himself aloof. She took it, he felt the coolness and the gentle squeeze, accepted her slight smile and watched her close both eyes briefly. Then she nodded, once, slipped into her little car, gave him a wave, and drove away.

'Ill wind, Andrew. Would she have come our way if the Brewery hadn't collapsed, d'you think?'

Remembering his flashes of intuitive imagination at the peak times of his previous mix-ups with the girl in question, he thought it could have been something of a high probability, but he daren't say. 'Depends. If we'd advertised and so on, she may have given it a go. Are *you* happy with it, R?'

'Think so. I'm not going back over old ground, Andrew, for the sake of it, but so long as she just does what we ask and doesn't step over the traces, fine. I like her, I know you do, she'll be a good face to our clients, and we desperately need someone. Anyway, academic. We've given her the job. Any good at writing Contracts of Employment?'

He hadn't really thought about that side of the idea, but

Roberta was right. They had to do things properly. 'I'll have words, R. There are a few people I know who'll help get things sorted correctly. Now, what about this evening?' Was she listening? 'Roberta?'

Roberta eased up from her chair. He'd promised to take her out and here she was, wrapped in her own thoughts. She'd go and get showered and changed first. 'Sorry, darling. Shan't be a moment.'

As she left the room, he collapsed back into a chair, sprawled his legs out, tipped it back and stared at the plasterwork. Images of the girl wavered into his mind and eddied around, and then as he heard the shower start to run, were replaced by firmer pictures of Roberta. The girl who had taken over his life, and in this room. In a fit of sudden decision, he crashed the chair back on its legs, stood up, and with a fleeting glance at the fireplace where it all started, just to remind himself he wasn't dreaming, marched upstairs. No, he wouldn't be tempted by young Andrea. He still had to unravel his life from Samantha's, which may not be an easy task, more on the emotional side than the practical, and he needed no distractions. Yet, and he knew he wouldn't back away from it, that girl still needed someone to lean on, until she found a guy with the right specification. Difficult. He flung his clothes off and excavated his lovely mum-to-be out of the bathroom.

'My turn! You'll dissolve if you stay much longer. That's a lovely bump, darling.'

She beamed at him, all steamy and sopping. She was as proud of her maternal state as she'd been of her maiden figure. She only hoped everything would go back into place, at least she'd have a damned good try to ensure it did.

'Not long now.' She caught the towel he tossed over to her and started drying her hair. 'Best get that nursery sorted. I know, you don't want to do everything, but we've got to be practical. Can I get you to plan things tomorrow?'

They'd decided to turn the old paper store at the end of the corridor into a nursery; it was just big enough and certainly in the right place. She knew Andrew had some superstitions about having cots and blankets and so on organised before a birth, just in case there was a problem, but she had no reservations. And with her sex-determining scan ahead of her this week, at least she could then start her décor scheme. With his eyes and mouth closed against the water flow, all he could do was nod. What else?

The next morning there was an e-mail from Samantha.

Coming home next week, six months is up, I've leave due. How's our house? Hope Roberta's well, we'll need to discuss matters. Best regards, S.

Roberta saw his face change, and felt for him. 'Darling?' She often watched over his shoulder as he dealt with the in-box, and now she wrapped her arms round his neck, and nuzzled at him. 'It'll be all right. She had to come back sooner or later.' One hand came off the keyboard, and clasped hers, and his head tilted to allow her more access. It was a lovely thing, this loving gesture of hers, and sent shivers down his spine. She felt him draw breath, and then heard the sigh.

"S'pose so. It's just, well; I suppose I've been ignoring it, pretending it would never happen. Wonder if June knows. I'll have to spend a bit of time at the house, getting it back to rights. Oh, *Roberta!*'

'I know, darling, I know. At least it's before B-day.'

'True.'

'Ring June.'

'I'd better get on top of the rest of these.' The e-mails were becoming more relevant now, and since they'd re-organised the computer system with broadband and new software, it was a lot easier.

'I'll do them. You go into the house and ring June. Go on. You'll feel better. What do you want to say to Sam?'

'Oh, I don't know. 'It'll be good to see you, house okay, everything's fine?' Whatever. Thanks, R. I shan't be long.' He left her to it and she settled herself carefully on the chair, sitting bolt upright to avoid crumpling her protruding tummy.

'Andrew and I are fine, baby's kicking well, thanks. A will sort

house, no worries. Have a good flight. Let us know if we need to fetch you from anywhere, at least an e.t.a. Be good to see you. Regards, R.' Before she sent it, she stared long and hard at the blue screen, wondering. Would it *really* work out okay? Samantha couldn't force him back to her, not now. She'd have a word with Marjorie, sound her out about the complications of a divorce, and pulled a face. *Two* divorces she'd had to cope with. As an afterthought, she added another line. *'Andrea starting work with us as Office Manager next week. Brewery went bust, if you hadn't heard.'* She moved the cursor to 'Send' and clicked. A brief hesitation and the message went. Oh well, too late now. She filed the message under 'Personal', and read the next one. Oh goody, confirmation that the Evan's had accepted her quote.

Andrew found June at home. 'How's things? . . . Good, and William? . . . Oh, right. . . Yes, we're okay. Roberta goes for a scan again this week; we'll have the sex then, all being well. . . . Yes, I know, but Roberta wants to do her thing on the Nursery, and it's easier for colour schemes . . . yes, I know, but . . . no, I don't like yellow either. Preference? . . . Roberta wants a girl . . . no, I'm happy with that. Look, the reason I rang. Your Mum's coming home. You knew? . . . Thought you might. I'm going to sort the house out. . . . Live *with you?* . . . You haven't the room, don't be silly. . . . Further away, well yes, but . . . What about William? . . well, I'll have to leave it with you. Be nice to see you again soon, June. Loved it the other week. You can come and stay any time, you know that . . . yes, I'll tell her. Thanks, June. Love you. Bye'

Roberta pushed the chair back and stood up, carefully, easing her waist, what there was of it, with a hand, massaging her back and mulling over what hadn't been a bad morning; two positive orders and another three enquiries. She was relieved that they'd decided to put the courses on hold until after she was back to normal, though undoubtedly it was a shame all the work on those conversions was going to lie dormant. It would be such a relief to pass on this routine stuff to Andrea next week. She'd never call it a chore, but some days it did seem such a waste of time. Why didn't people use the phone and talk to us? All this time spent typing what you can say in half the time, and you get the inflexions of tone. Still, if it brought results, they'd put up with it, though some days she wished computers had never been invented, at least not to talk to each other. Drawing pictures of rooms and playing with colours on screen was quite fun, though she couldn't dispense with samples, and actually *feeling* a room, some how. Ah, he's back, and at least the frown seemed to have gone from his eyes. 'Andrew! How is she?' It felt so much better now he'd made his peace with June.

'Okay. She thought she'd offer to have Samantha stay with her. Said it might be better to have her that much further away. It's only for a week, because it seems she's going on some training course up in Sheffield, and then flies back to commission another new Centre. Peter's still out there and doing quite well, apparently. Wonder why he doesn't e-mail us?'

'Probably doesn't think it necessary. Has June got the space, and what does her William say to all this, I wonder?'

'She says the spare room is all up and running, and William doesn't mind. I'm not sure I believe her, but then, it seems he's got his head in some website all evening. She's going to put it to Sam tonight, and let me know. I will have to do something about the house soon, though. Won't I?'

It was a thorny subject. Roberta shied away from it now every time it was mentioned, almost as though it was a get-out clause in her mental arrangement with him and she had somewhere she could send him if it all went pear shaped. He'd far rather be shot of the place; too many shabby memories, and not just of life with Sam either.

'Once Sam's been and gone, Andrew. Once we know how her mind's working, eh?'

Roberta got Mary to run her to the hospital for her scan in Andrews's car, much more space than in the MGF that Mary didn't much like driving anyway, and that allowed her to go off and do some shopping whilst she was being looked at. Lying on the couch with that gadget running over her bump gave her the most strange sensation, watching her insides appearing on the odd blue screen all strangely wobbly, spookily even, and stretching her imagination as the girl explained there it was, her own little miniature new being, all cocooned and cosy.

'It's a girl, isn't it?'

The smile gave the game away; her consultant girl, Annabel, was really much less medical and more human when she smiled. 'Are you guessing, Roberta, or this intuition? Or shall I keep you in suspense? Look," as she moved the probe again, 'any better?'

'It all looks far too blurry for me. Please, tell me.'

With a more knowing smile, Annabel nodded. 'That one's a girl. I'm not sure about the other.'

'*The other!*' Roberta squeaked, and tried to half rise to peer better at the screen. 'Twins?' *Oh Lord! Whatever will Andrew say!* Are you sure, I mean, this thing doesn't show echoes or anything?'

'You'd be surprised at the comments I get when this happens. To be fair, we did have an inkling last time you came in, but now I'm sure. Twins. Certainly one girl, and more often than not the second is the same. Can't quite see, but it's probable. They look fine, Roberta. Two for the price of one, as they say. Lucky girl.'

Getting off the couch was the easy bit; standing up with this momentous conscious concern for *two* little people living in her tum was stretching her nerves. How she was going to look after these lovely embryonic little girls for another couple of months was mind blowingly problematical. In something of a trance she submitted to all the other tests, learning with some crumbs of comfort that her body was doing all the right things. Even blood pressure was within bounds, surprisingly after the shock she'd had, as Annabel admitted. 'Go home, Roberta, and enjoy yourself. Make the most of the time. Don't worry, we'll look after you.'

Andrew spent the afternoon in the office, concentrating on keeping his accountancy business alive, not that his heart was really in it to the same extent, not now all the colour and jazz of

240

Roberta's world had swept him along; a totally different type of client, not at all stuffy, or worried as so many of his clients tended to be, which, of course, was why they employed him in the first place. It was quiet, just the faint hum of the hard drive below the desk, the subdued rustle from the big trees out there in the late autumnal garden. He closed the file on the builder's account and leant back in the chair. She'd be in the hospital now, the new love of his life, getting the low-down. The nursery was waiting to be finished. Waiting, that was all. What a year! This time last year it had been touch and go, getting enough money in to ensure a decent Christmas, pandering to *her* needs. Where would she be this Christmas? Back in Africa, doling out presents to the little African orphans, cooking something of a special lunch to recognise the date in the calendar, being all things to all men, as the phrase has it. He pulled a face, a wry grin, wondering if she *had* anything going with anyone. Did he care? Well, sort of, but he couldn't define his feelings properly, not while Roberta was so uppermost in his mind.

Getting up from the desk, crossing to the window, to look out across the expanse of neat lawn and the barn and stables beyond, it was hard to imagine just how that simple action of going to help a person in trouble had brought him to all this. A simple act of care, of loving – *that simple?* And there they were, a mother and father to be, both in a newly discovered world, but for all that world, as if they'd been together since – whenever. Would it last, or was this a beautiful dream that could dissolve and wisp away like the mists in the morning? The last of the dahlias up against the wall were virtually the only remaining colours, soon the frost would cut them back and he imagined the crisp white that would sparkle over the grass, the delicate tracery of dew laden spider's webs, the steely freshness of the air and the echo of the village church bells on the Sunday morning. All so *English*, so *traditional*. He imagined the joy they'd have in taking their child to the church for a christening, so much part of the essentials of creating a *proper* family life.

Then the idyll shattered. How could they have a christening if they hadn't got a surname legalised? Or did it matter? Oh, *God!*

What was he going to do? What were *they*, he and Sam, going to do? Their life together, all twenty odd years of it, seemed like a completely different box, all packed up and stored away with a date, like his accounts files 'destroy after April the year dot', only this was a box he'd *never* destroy, no, all far far too precious. Precious? Yes, precious. It was their childhood style dreams, their holidays and their struggle and fun in building a home, and June, that happy child, and Peter, the struggle they'd had with him, and the first new car and the time she'd seduced him in the sand dunes, and then that party, going to the school fete, helping her choose her new frocks, seeing her in the candlelight across the table in that lovely restaurant, and loving her . . .

Could he really close the flaps on that box? He walked out of the office, closed the door behind himself.

* * *

The car turned into the yard behind the house, the rasp of the gravel the familiar sound. She patted Mary's arm. 'Thanks. Stay for tea?'

Mary nodded. She'd have to get the shopping out first. 'You going to tell Mr Andrew then?' Roberta couldn't resist letting Mary into the secret on the way home, and Mary had nearly cannoned into the car in front at the stopping of the queue at the lights. She'd taken it in her stride, though, giving her charge a sideways glance at the same time as offering congratulations, repeating the Annabel girl's comment about two for the price of . . . yes, yes, Roberta'd replied, I know. 'D'you think he'll be pleased, or shocked?'

She got an old fashioned look. 'Pleased, if his ego's got anything to do with it. Once he's overcome the surprise, like. Go on in with you, I'll put the kettle on.'

She couldn't find him. The office was all shut up, though the computer was still running. She called. 'Andruuuuw?' Silence. He wouldn't be upstairs, and she didn't think he'd be in the Barn. Must be outside, strange, he'd hear the car come back, and usually came to find her. While she'd still got her coat on, she wandered back into the chill of the garden, where daylight was ebbing away towards the oncoming dusk. 'Andruuuuw? Daarling?' There was no reply. She walked round into the rose garden, where they'd had so much fun and laughter in the summer days, where she'd egged him on to chase her back up to bed, where he'd been so ardent for her. Then across to where he'd mock-proposed to her, and she still wore his ring. *'Andrew?'* The first nag at her mind, *where had he gone?* She'd come to expect him telling her what he was doing, the same as she told him. It was part of *them.* He wasn't there, and she was bursting to tell him the news. Back to Mary, and the worried look with her.

'What's amiss, Roberta?'

'I can't find him. He never said he'd be out; he was watching the shop and doing his own work. He'd not go out, surely, not without leaving a note?'

'Try his phone, lass.'

'Oh, yes, *of course!* Silly me.' It rang, and rang, and the voice box message came on. Now she was getting worried, and Mary sensed the fretfulness.

'Mebbe gone for a walk. Check the coats, then.' His walking jacket was still there, and his stout shoes, and his stick. He hadn't taken to the fields then.

She sat down on a stool, legs straddled to ease her bump, eyes wide and troubled. 'Mary! *Oh, Mary!'*

'Hey, lass, don't take on. Nought to worry yoursen, not . . .' The word 'yet' couldn't come out. Then she had an inspiration. 'Bide awhile, sup your tea. I'll not be a moment.'

The other car had gone. Why hadn't she seen the space in the garage? Something told her he'd gone to his house, 'cos his wife was due back, wasn't she? Cautiously, she went into the office, closed the door behind her, and used the office phone so the house line wouldn't tinkle. His house phone, in the end, been left on, and mebbe, just mebbe, if he was there, he'd answer rather than leave it to the machine.

She counted the rings, four, five, six, before the first phrase.

'Hello, I'm sorry there's no . . .' and then it was interrupted. 'Andrew Hailsworthy, can I help you?'

'Aye, you can, Mr Andrew. You've a distraught girl here and not a bleep to tell her where you are. I'll not mince words, lad, just get yoursen back to her and quick.' She put the phone down and quietly eased herself into the kitchen. Roberta had moved into the easy chair in the corner and was hugging the cushion over her tummy. Her eyes were bright with new tears, as she looked up.

'Just keep yoursen patient, lass. He'll be here. Don't fret.'

'Mary?'

'Gone back to the house, lass. Take things canny; with that wife of his about to come home he's bound to be a bit off balance, like.' All this was another positive sign of the depth of her Roberta's feelings about the man, not that she'd been too unsure over the past months, but it was the first time she'd noticed how deeply affected Roberta had become when he wasn't around and she'd not been told where he was. Getting dependant on him, that was for sure. Lord help us if ought goes wrong between them, she thought. 'Go get yourself changed, love, make yourself pretty for him, then you've a surprise for him?'

'You're sure that's where he is?'

'Aye, lass. We should have thought earlier. Car's gone, so I phoned.' She grinned, and saw the flooding relief back on her girl's face. 'Go on with you!'

He'd been caught off balance with Mary's call, still in the depths of self-interrogation over where he was in all this; the precipitate journey back to the old house an unwitting test of his loyalties.

It was cold, damp, had a musty smell to the place, and not much of a pull to the heart in him until he'd gone upstairs, and re-visited the memory banks of loving and loving. How he'd nestled into the softness of her and felt at peace, even when they'd started to drift apart in character if not in human need. Different, spontaneously different, the involvement with Roberta, and that frenetic entanglement with Andrea; at least Roberta had never lain on this bed, and it sort of shocked him to realise she'd never actually ever been here. Everything had been neatly folded and put away in the cupboards; the mattress was bare, nothing to suggest the warmth and heat of those nights. Why had he come? No surety in his thoughts, no positive drive forward, just a urge to get some momentum channelled back into those odd ideas that he was still doing the right thing, unstitching the past two decades in preparation for the next, but this wasn't helping, mooching about here. June was right, this was no place for Samantha to come back to; it would be totally unfair and rather mean to expect her to stay in this mausoleum. Rather surprisingly, the fleeting idea she'd stay at the Manor crossed his mind; then the phone rang and the echo of the ring through the hall below startled him. Before he could get back down stairs the message had started to play, but he picked it up none the less, curious to see who would be trying to reach the number after all this time. He should have had it disconnected before now, but out of sight, or hearing rather, and very out of mind.

'Andrew Hailsworthy, can I help you?' An automatic response, that, then Mary's voice!

His heart lurched, he'd not left a note, and she was due back from the hospital; this return to introverted thinking had switched him into a stupidly dim attitude. Damnation! Roberta was distraught? Mary was right, he'd been less than caring this once, and that wasn't good, not for him, nor her. Not much use to his absent wife either. Drawing curtains, shutting doors, locking the back door and retreating to the car, and sorry, folks, you're still without neighbours – he almost waved at the twitchy curtains next door. Best get someone in to look after the garden; it had really gone downhill since the last time he'd been, whenever that was.

He put the car straight back into the garage, it wouldn't do to leave Roberta's pride and joy outside. He was surprised she hadn't noticed it gone. With some trepidation, he pushed open the kitchen door and got lifted eyebrows from Mary, no Roberta.

'You'd best make your peace with her, Mr Andrew. She was a

mite upset at you not being around when we got back. Doesn't do, not when she's in the state she is. You take care of her, d'hear? She'll be in the sitting room. I'll fetch you some tea in.'

She was sitting by the fire, exactly as she had been all those months ago, except there was a different profile. It was even the same skirt, Lord help us, and how could he not forget? It was the one with the stretchy waistband, so easy to slip around. Those eyes, wide and bright, followed him in and as he crossed the room towards her, not a word was said. He knelt down and reached to kiss her, but she moved her head away, though she did reach for his hand, sort of pushed him down.

'Andrew. Why?'

He nestled into her skirt, felt the warmth of her thigh, and laid his head on her knee. This was right, this was her, and the anxiety of the afternoon began to fade. He shook his head, unsure, and his eyes pricked. Deep psychological stirrings of a boyhood, crouching at his mother's knee, looking for comfort, security, the need for a feeling of being loved, and as her hand ruffled through his hair, the tears came. Oh God! What had he done?

She couldn't understand. What had upset him to behave like this? And she had all the delights of her surprise in her, bottled up, just waiting to trickle her momentous news out to him, the waiting for the anticipated dawning of his astonishment and how he'd have kissed her and . . . but this? 'Darling? Andrew, darling? I'm sorry, but I didn't realise you were going to go to the house, or I'd never . . .' He was shaking his head under her hand.

Being all emotional like this, it was stupid, childish, and not doing any good, she wouldn't understand and yet he couldn't explain, could he? 'Love me?'

He felt her hand stop its gently movement around his scalp, and then down to rest on his cheek, her fingers stroking runs of tears away, pressing his head closer to the warmth of her thigh.

'What's wrong, my darling? Is it Sam?' A sharp icicle of doubt stabbed in her head. This man of hers suddenly vulnerable to the pull of his former existence, that's why he went to the house? Mary had been right. And he'd woken the ghosts and brought them back with him, and she couldn't *love* love him, not in her condition, to make things right, but he was *here,* and asked her if she loved him. How could she not? Everything to her, he was everything; and what to do, 'cos their whole relationship was based on her need for him and not his need for her, *or was it?* Now she was feeling, seeing, his head nod. The tiny stab again, and the grey molecule of doubt multiplied like the cells in her babies' bodies. 'Andrew, darling, I *love you!*' She couldn't help it, it was true, true, *true,* and her world was so much part of him now, nothing, *nothing,* must happen to change things, not now. But it could, she knew. She felt him stir against her.

'I'm just not sure how to cope, R. Sam's coming home; the house is a wreck and she'll hate it. She won't want to stay with June 'cos she won't be in charge, and William's not her favourite person. I just don't know what to do.'

She took a deep breath. 'Perhaps you'd best go back there, Andrew, sort it out, while you've time. Then maybe things will fall into place. But I've something to tell you.' The mental picture she'd conjured up of the telling was lying in shattered shards of sad despair around her, and the rising fog of that misery eddying around had dulled the brightness of her day. 'It's twins.'

SIXTEEN

He'd gone. The truism of what needed to be done had cleared the doubt, and he'd gone. She cried, quietly, persistently, till her eyes were sore and red and the heaviness of her belly pressed hard onto her, achingly. Mary, her indomitable rock of absolute certainty, had been understanding and as tolerant as ever, with few words but valued. 'Had to be, love. He'll be back. She'll know. They have to work it out.'

Her bed was empty, cold, and huge. She could only lie on her back, and sleep wouldn't come, thinking of him in that house, all alone, waiting for an absentee wife to return. Despite the warm milky drink and the single aspirin her mind would not rest and she had a dull headache. For the first time since Samantha had left she was alone, no comfortable arms, no light touch across her breasts, no firm warmth against her thighs, and she ached. Her revelation over the twins had been a damp squib, no elation, no radiant beaming smile, but a mild acceptance, albeit with a reach and a squeeze of a hand, a single 'well done.' Mary's arrival with the tea tray had been a sort of uncomfortable pause in the silent drama of their working out of his disordered perspective. Then he'd taken the little holdall and pushed some clothes into it, removed the essentials from the bathroom, held her close for an all too short embrace, kissed her forehead, and gone.

He'd be back, after the weekend. Andrea was starting on Monday. The world didn't freeze and let them stop, it revolved, and their lives spun round with the every-day momentum they themselves had generated. She couldn't just say 'stop' and go back to being a motiveless divorcee.

He'd loved her, more correctly, she'd seduced him and he'd

248

loved her back, she'd accepted him and his foibles, risked the wrath and the sweep of the tides of his life, being sullied with the flotsam, jetsam of whatever floated about and pushed and pulled at him. She'd got away with it for six months or so, and the only contact with his former life had been June's arrival at their Open day. She'd been okay, and that had been one hurdle.

The milky drink had reached her bladder and the pressure was too much; she swung her legs carefully out and made her slow steady trip to the loo. In the bathroom some remainder of Andrew's things were evident, accentuating his absence, and fresh tears rolled. The mirror did her no favours either; that blotched mess with scruffy hair wasn't the Roberta she'd kept looking good for him.

Back in bed, trying unsuccessfully to rest on her side, she made a determined effort to think positively, to the time ahead when she'd be relieved of her body's obligation to build these little people, their journey to life would cause her pain, she knew and accepted; then her sleepless nights would be coping with their independent demands rather than fretting over Andrew's relationship problems. That put a different slant on things in her mind, slowing down her emotions sufficiently to accept the inevitability of it all; her children would be born, come what may, Andrew *was* the father, no two ways about that, and he was a legal partner in the business, so what had changed? His awareness of his obligations, which was only right? He was still the caring man she'd fallen for, and she reasoned, would have not been the man she knew if he'd abandoned Samantha at this crucial stage; she'd have been devastated if he'd ignored her in the same way. Her racing thoughts slowed, and totally drained and exhausted from the trauma of the day, finally she fell asleep.

Andrew, his thoughts switched into occupational therapy mode, got on with re-commissioning the house. He rang June, and told her what he'd done, i.e. returned to the marital abode, albeit temporarily, that her mother should be told, and would she possibly consider coming over to give him a hand tomorrow? How long had they got; did she know which flight she'd be on? Tuesday? June sounded both relieved and surprised. Yes, she'd come, be over by mid-day tomorrow, could she stop over? He was happy with that, actually smiled to himself, and pleased that he'd have his daughter back under his roof – *his* roof – for a night, possibly two. That would be nice, just the two of them.

The bedroom still smelt musty, but it was too cold to open windows; the heating would dry out the place soon enough and he was glad there was still some oil left in the tank. He'd have a meal in the pub, then an early night, ready for an onslaught on cleaning and so on tomorrow.

The guys he knew in the pub were surprised to see him; it had been some while since he'd last been. A certain amount of leg pulling about being chucked out all of which he had to take in good part. They weren't to know how different it all was, that Roberta had been strong in resolution that he should do the right thing, giving up some of her happiness so Samantha should have at least a proper welcome home. Really, she was a wonderful woman, his Roberta. And twins! *Two* little people, and his and hers! Something to look forward to. He sent mental 'goodnight's' to her, steeling himself to the lonely night ahead.

Once into the cold comfort of the empty double bed, inevitably his mind flicked back to the last time he'd slept here, with Andrea in his arms. The memory was both sweet and sour, but no way was he going to let her know he was here and here alone, or she'd be round here like a shot; he'd no illusions about that. She'd been too free with her body language at that interview, and there were interesting times ahead. Monday, she starts on Monday, and it would be like going back to the office. Could he handle it? He'd have to. Be objective about it. Gradually the bed warmed up, and he slept.

Saturday for Roberta was an awakening in a sweat, wondering why she hadn't had a 'good morning' kiss, and then having that sinking feeling knowing she'd be on her own all weekend. For Andrew it was a grey, dull and gradual appreciation of the pathetic breakfast he'd have and the start of a mind numbing round of chores. True, the bright spot was June's impending arrival, well, lunchtime by the time she'd get here. For his neighbours, it was a high curiosity day, because the car had stayed on the drive overnight for the first time in six months.

After his mere toast and ersatz coffee breakfast, he did a site survey, and started a mental list. Groceries, he'd need to eat. Cleaning materials, no, enough under the stairs and in the cupboard by the sink. Oil tank, sufficient for a month or two, so that's not a problem. Garden, that would take all day to get rid of weeds and maybe, just maybe, cut the grass if it stayed dry. The guest room, June would sort her own things, but he'd turn the mattress over. Covers off the three-piece suite, shake them outside. Then vacuum throughout, dust, if the day warmed up, then he'd open the windows. Best get started.

At half past ten he'd got the covers out on the line and the vacuum cleaner going in the lounge. He didn't hear the car, nor the knock, and he hadn't realised that the batteries in the door chimes had long since gone extinct, so it wasn't until a voice he recognised near shouted in his ear 'Andrew!' making him jump, that told him he'd got a visitor.

'Andrea! You made me jump!'

She put out an elegant foot and trod on the vacuum cleaner's switch. The high-pitched whine died, and there she was, all bright and beautiful, with a padded jacket over cashmere sweater and a body shaped pair of jeans. 'Sorry, but the bell doesn't work and you didn't hear me knock. What's all this then? Roberta thrown you out?'

'No. Samantha's coming home. Tomorrow. Back to square one, Andrea. No, not entirely true. Roberta's having twins. I just don't know where I am. Sorry. What brings you here anyway?' She was a nice thing to see on this grey morning, but why?

'Just passing, saw the car. Can I stop for coffee?'

On consideration, that wasn't a bad idea. Elevenses. 'Only got instant, Andrea, and still have to get the supplies in. Got to go shopping again, I'm afraid. Bit out of practice, with Mary doing it all. Spoilt!' He stretched, and rubbed his back. Vacuuming carpets wasn't his thing.

She laughed, and he loved the sparkle in her eyes. Her jacket came off, and the cashmere was clinging to the shape of her, that faint trace of her scent heady. *Roberta, Roberta, Roberta!* His mind was in conflict with his obligations, his allegiances and the nearness of this female.

She knew, she could see it in his eyes, and the way he'd looked at her, top to toe. What was wrong with that? Roberta wouldn't begrudge him; after all, she wasn't available at present, now was she?

'Are you living here then?'

'Until Samantha gets back and we get things sorted. Just a week.'

'Ah.'

'What's that supposed to mean?'

'On your own?'

'At the moment. June'll be here soon. She'll stay over.'

'Ah. Well, shall I put the kettle on?' *Damnation! I might have had a chance of a cuddle!* 'How long will she be?'

Andrew looked at the clock, checked his watch. 'Could be anytime, I guess. Depends when she left home.' His eyes caught hers, and she flushed. 'You're looking pretty this morning. I don't normally like jeans, but your's fit well.'

'Compliments, compliments. Thanks. You don't care for the hair-do though?'

'Not really. Let it grow, Andrea. I preferred it the way it was.'

'I promised I would be less tantalising, remember? Thank you for the chance at the job, Andrew. You won't regret it.'

'Hope not. We'll have a struggle though.'

'Struggle?' The wee bit of a frown put a couple of lines on her forehead. 'What do you mean?'

'You and me. Tempting.'

'Tempt away, Andrew.' They were so close, and she closed her eyes.

All she got was a chaste kiss. He didn't even put his arms round her. He could have asked her to go upstairs and she'd have gone, but he hadn't. Probably just as well, if June was coming.

'Did you say you'd put the kettle on?'

Back to reality, then. 'I did.' As she filled the kettle, her mind spun round the illogicality of her actions. Why on earth did this man bring out the schoolgirl crush in her? Stupid! But then, he'd admitted she was tempting, so it still wasn't the one way, even now. With the switch down, the wretched thing began to sing and she went back to him, just as he was about to resume vacuuming.

'Sugar and milk?'

'No milk. Sorry.'

'I'll nip down the road, Andrew. Anything else?'

'There's a list on the table. Are you sure?'

'Sure. Won't be long.' Picking up the puffa jacket, she shrugged it back on. 'Glad to be of help.'

No sooner had she gone then June arrived, her greeting quite matter of fact, her description of her journey atypical. 'Glad to be here. Ready for a coffee. Good to see you again, dad. You okay?' There was more meaning in her simple question than just that; 'you okay with being here and not with Roberta' is what she meant. Admiration for her father in all this, far more than she'd expected, she hoped her mum appreciated what he was doing.

'I'm okay.' The tone of his voice was flat. He was here, he'd effectively given a cold shoulder to Andrea and the only colour in the day was June. 'I'm grateful, June. Really, really grateful. How's William?'

'Don't go on about William, dad. He's just Williaming. Staring at the bloody screen all day, gives me the heebie jeebies. Quite glad to get away with a good excuse, actually. How's Roberta?'

'Twins, in a word. The hospital is pleased with her, but this isn't helping. She told me I should do this, you know. Look after Sam – your mother – sort the house, be here. Is she right?'

'Dad, it isn't up to me. You have to make the choice. I don't know. If William had walked out on me, not that he would, I might have ranted and raved, but at the end of the day, it's no marriage if you don't like each other's company, is it? It's got to be fun, and happiness, and all that; it's not just sex – is it?'

Andrew slumped down into one of the easy chairs. 'Companionship?'

June snorted. 'Companionship? Sounds a bit like the old folk's home, dad. Knitting socks and watching TV, drinking endless cups of tea and going for a walk on the prom. You're not that old and neither's mum. Look, dad, if you and mum have drifted apart, then there's no fun for either of you, is there? If she's happy organising the troops to look after little brown kids, then you should be happy for her, like she should be happy for you if you've got a new business and a new family to look after. At least Roberta's – *twins?*' It suddenly dawned on her what he'd said. 'Twins – two for . . .'

'Yes,' Andrew interrupted, with a sarcastic flavour to his voice, 'for the price of one, how many times have we heard that lately. I just hope she can handle it. It makes me a bit nervous, scared even, for her. I wouldn't want to think she would be damaged in any way – for her sake, June.'

'Dad, women through the ages have handled triplets let alone twins. Don't worry; she'll be fine, I'm sure. What does she think?'

'Don't really know – not about the twins thing. Having *a* child is what she'd dreamt about, she just wants children of her own, and well, two at once might just be what she needs. I'm torn, June, between what I see as my obligations, your mother and Roberta. I still love her, you know, and we've had great times in the past. To chuck all that away . . .'

'You're not throwing it away, dad. Memories are fine, but you can't survive on them. Mum will feel the same, I'm sure, but it doesn't mean you're shackled to each other. The legal thing is all that stops you doing what you want. When somebody else is involved you have to do the best for both. Right now, Roberta needs you, mum doesn't. She's happy where she is, and doing what she does best. As are you.

Provided you two don't fight over who has what, then go ahead. Have a divorce. Doesn't stop you being *friends* – or even going to bed with each other if you want to. No law against it. You can't *marry* Roberta if you don't divorce, dad, and what names are the twins going to carry?'

'What are you saying, June? That I *should* divorce your mum? You don't mind?'

June shook her head. 'No, dad, I don't *mind*; it's a shame you two haven't the same spark as you obviously did have, and it would be great if you still had, for all of us, but what's done is done. I've seen you with Roberta and you're heaps happier and much more my dad. I love you, I want you to be happy; if that's with Roberta, then go for it. If mum was going to be happier with you she'd not have gone off to Sierra Leone, and to go back after her six-month stint proves it. She could have opted out, you know, but she hasn't. Okay? Now, how about some coffee?'

'Andrea's gone for milk and things. She'll be back in a mo.'

'*Andrea*? What's she doing here? Dad?' June's voice rose a notch. 'You haven't got involved with *her*, have you?'

'No, *no*,' the reply was too snap and instantaneous for June. 'She saw the car and called in. She's starting with us at the Manor on Monday as office Manager, well sort of administrator, so we can concentrate more on the clients and the business than doing paperwork – she'll answer phones and so on, and anyway, with Roberta's hatching imminent . . .' he tailed off, seeing the narrowed eyes and pursed lips. 'What's the matter, you think I've designs on *her*?'

'Hmm. She's very pretty, and rather sexy. I know, dad, I've seen her. *And* she looks at you. She's dangerous, dad. She'd eat you for breakfast, and then what would Roberta do?'

He would have defended her, but the car was back, pulled in behind June's on the kerb. He got up from the chair, padded into the kitchen and re-juvenated the kettle. Andrea was all smiles at June, offered her a cheek-to-cheek kiss before dumping the Supermarket bags on the table. 'All here, Andrew, and a bit more, 'cos your list was a bit basic. Twenty-four pounds and fifty-three pence.' She pulled out the milk container and the sugar bag. 'Nice to see you again, June, tea or coffee?'

'I'll do it, Andrea, thanks. Good of you to pop by and do the shopping. I gather you're starting full time at the Manor on Monday?'

'All being well. I won't stop, Andrew, pay me on Monday. See you then. 'Bye, June, Andrew.' She knew when she wasn't wanted; June was in charge. All rather disappointing, but there wasn't any point in staying around.

* * *

The weekend passed quietly, Andrew and June worked hard on cleaning through, inbetween stints in the garden; they went out for a meal and a trip to the cinema on the Saturday evening and Andrew's spirits lifted somewhat in the delight of the company of his daughter. He spoke on the phone to Roberta at each end of the day, with mixed feelings. She was only 'up the road', but somehow neither of them felt inclined to offer persuasion to make the trip. Of Andrea there was no sign, and he was sure she'd taken the hump at the polite and quite correct 'brush-off' from June.

Roberta had handled the e-mails, and when she rang on Sunday evening, she was able to confirm Samantha's arrival on Tuesday morning, and please would someone meet her? Sam's own little car had been sitting forlornly in the garage all this time, Andrew had been minded to check it out and was pleasantly surprised to find it started first go. He ran it round the block, avoiding the country road that would take him up to the Manor. So Tuesday, lunchtime-ish.

Just Monday. Back to the office, after breakfast, to be there by eight thirty, and Andrew quizzed his daughter. 'You want to come with me, or what?'

June laughed. 'Or what? No, dad, I'll come with you. Keep an eye; make sure Andrea stays in line. I'm sure I can do something useful, even it's just dusting the furniture.'

'Mary won't take kindly to the presumption there's dusting

to be done, June. I'm sure Roberta will come up with something. All set?'

Prompt on nine o'clock Andrea's car crunched up the gravel drive. She'd combed out her set and got her curls to float again, had a smart little jacket and skirt to match, just above the knees. Much better, he thought, as he welcomed her into the office. She did get a welcome kiss too, 'cos no one else was looking. June was in the Barn with Roberta, being given instructions on how to sort and catalogue new batches of fabric samples.

'How's home, Andrew?'

'Okay. Not quite the same as living here, as you'd imagine, but it's a lot better with June around. Sorry if you felt redundant the other day. Good to have you here, hope you'll be happy with us.'

'I'm sure I will be, happy I mean, though maybe it'll be a bit strange at first. What do you want me to do?'

Andrew ran through the list he and Roberta had concocted; he showed her the system they'd adopted, how to access the programmes on the computer and the way they dealt with incoming mail. 'Okay? Any questions?'

'Lunch?'

'On the house. Kitchen table, between half twelve and two, according to how Mary's placed. We normally call it a day around four, four thirty. Leave you to find your way around; I'll be in the Barn. Give me a buzz if you need us – push that button on the phone – there's another one both in the Barn and the kitchen. Okay?'

She took off her jacket and the shape of her beneath her crisp white buttoned-front blouse was nice. A glimpse of the lace edging to her bra through the rise of the fabric; a trace of her scent. Settling herself into the chair, her skirt rode well clear of her knees; she looked up and caught his glance. 'Sorry, Andrew. You'd rather I wore trousers?'

'No. *No!* You're a girl, and I like having decorative girls around. Let's just enjoy the rapport, shall we?'

She hitched her skirt a wee bit higher, but he'd turned away, grinning.

At the end of the day they foregathered in the kitchen for afternoon tea and buns, as was the normality of the routine. Outside the winter's day had all but given way to the steely taste of a potentially frosty night making the contrasting warmth and brightness of the room all the more welcoming. June's day in the Barn had been a pleasant one, and useful; Andrea's day absorbing for her; Andrew hadn't done a great deal other than take two calls and chat to a visiting couple; Roberta, quietly sketching away at some design work, had been reasonably happy in seeing how her little empire was ticking along. Six months age she'd not have dreamed it was going to turn out like this, her heart was quite full of it all, and Andrew's return after two days away a lovely bonus.

She plucked up courage as Mary started pouring out. 'Do you really need to go back to your place tonight, Andrew? June can stay as well, you know, you don't have to be martyrs. Mary's got a nice dinner organised. And Andrea – you're welcome to stay for dinner as well, if you'd like?' Her request was more like a plea. She didn't want him to go; three nights alone were too many. It was nearing the end of the month and Christmas was coming. She'd want him around and they would have a party; she'd just decided.

Andrew sipped at his mug, looked at June. She nodded. After all their work it had been good to have a break and dinner and a bed here would be fabulous. 'We'll stay. So long as we're at the house when Sam gets back.'

'Thanks for the invite, Roberta, but I don't want to intrude. I'm an employee now.' Andrea's reply was polite and correct.

'Nonsense. We'd think you standoffish if you went. Stay, girl, you won't get asked every day.'

Mary didn't show any surprise. Almost a forgone conclusion, knowing her Roberta. She was just glad she'd bought enough supplies. 'Well now, seeing as that's decided, I'd like some help with the veges, any volunteers now? The rest of you can get out of the way. Seven o'clock?'

Andrew sent June home for her things, and while Andrea stayed put in the kitchen to don one of Mary's aprons and look very 'Coronation Street' as a result, Roberta and he disappeared into the sitting room. It was the first time they'd been alone all day, and he took her in his arms.

'I've missed you.' He kissed the top of her head, rubbed her shoulder blades, felt the pressure of her womb against him. 'How's our family?'

'Missing you too. Seemed like a week, a month, Andrew, you not being here. Done all you needed to do?'

They'd already gone all through what he and June had done in the house on the phone, but she was looking for some assurance that he didn't need to return.

'Place is all spick and span. You'll just have to bear with me, R, tomorrow; I shall have to play it by ear. I won't say I'm desperately happy about the prospect, somehow, but it has to happen. I'm just glad June's here to soften the edges. Thanks for inviting her; I'm happier about staying tonight. Goodness knows about tomorrow.'

'I think you'll best be firm and positive, Andrew. Simply come back here, leave June with Sam. If you want to, that is?' Her eyes had a sort of scared look in them.

It was another turning point, this, and he knew it. All this time with her had dulled the pain of the strange life he'd drifted into as the cracks in his and Samantha's marriage had appeared, deepened and widened and given way to the apathy that had been the breeding ground for his infidelity and hunger for taking advantage of whatever feminity had been available. Roberta had been the perfect foil for his needs, he'd taken what was on offer, then desire had been replaced with devotion, lust for a caring love; oh, yes, he loved her. Andrea had been a too-available second option, and who knows what would have happened if he'd met her first. And now Roberta was getting some of this feeling of unease that would not be good for either of them.

'I do, want to come back, that is. Of course I do. But you will have to understand that I'm a bit unsure what the outcome is going to be, R.' Her head was nestling into his chest and he was running his fingers round her shoulders, feeling the warmth of her against him, and trying hard to believe it was all going to be smooth running when he and Samantha started talking about their respective futures, though in his heart was that numbing concept of potential disaster.

SEVENTEEN

It had to be. There was no way it couldn't happen, short of a plane crash or something equally disastrous, unless he decided to abandon everything and just let her deride his indiscretions to take him back on board. That would mean destroying Roberta's life and his own happiness let alone the nonsense that would ensue from the change in relationships with June, with Andrea, even Mary, and all the flack he'd get from clients and friends; he'd never be able to be his own man ever again.

Roberta stirred, flung an arm over him, and awoke to smile happily. She'd got him back in her bed. 'Darling – sleep well?'

'Much nicer than on my own, that's true, though not the most mentally restful of nights to be honest. How's you?'

'Apart from learning to sleep on my back without rolling around which you already know about, fine. Let's get up, darling. We've guests on board, and Mary's always anxious. Young Hazel's coming back today as well. Race you to the bathroom?'

Breakfast with the roomful of girls was lovely, pushed the day's prospects away into the back recess of his mind until the last dregs of coffee had been poured and the final croissant no more than crumbs on a plate. June caught his eye, reminding him of the time, and the sharp painful thought of today's reality became palpable and crushing, which was at once both strange and unbelievable. How was it that he could feel this way when his *wife* was coming home after six months away? He should be glad, excited, happy and rushing to meet her instead of wishing it was a day that wouldn't happen, bit like knowing you had a hospital appointment that you'd put off for months but had to accept was a necessity if you wanted to go on living. And this was an operation with no anaesthetic and no prognosis with all the risks of blood clots and infections and God knows what else.

He got a careful hug and a kiss from Roberta, a thoughtful wave from Andrea and a meaningful 'Good Luck' from Mary before he ducked into the car alongside his daughter.

They drove straight to Stanstead. It was a terrible journey, lousy grey weather, intermittent rain, appalling traffic snarl-ups on the motorway and Andrew blessed the surreal calmness of his daughter's driving. Even in the passenger seat he could feel his nerves tensioned to snapping point. The car parking problems seemed a lot worse and he debated on how anyone in their right mind would ever wish to fly when the prelude was such a nightmare and his gut pulled as he recognised his memory's twist of Samantha's eternal phrase *'it's a nightmare'*.

June took his hand as they walked down interminable corridors for what seemed miles; she squeezed gently and gave a sideways smile. 'I know, dad. Don't say it. Just be grateful you don't live near the place.' The plane was late. *'Delayed departure, e.t.a. 11.30.'* Fretting time away in the crowded arrivals lounge might be slightly less disastrous than the departure lounge, but neither helped the blood pressure. Stress disorders? There should be a clinic on site to diagnose potential heart problems caused by such anti-humanistic nausea. Three plastic cups of ghastly coffee later and the tannoy gave the flight number they needed, by now his mind was numb to the half hour it took to spew out the passengers.

'There she is, dad. Look, in the red coat.' June was waving, jumping up and down, and Samantha saw them.

She was slim. She'd gone away all lumpish and shoulder rounded, a walking disaster of a woman; but this girl was erect, smiling, bronzed, and looking so smart. This couldn't be the Samantha he'd known and got so bored with, this confident woman walking across the concourse?

Her smiling eyes gave the impression of amusement and with the twitch of her lips a laugh. 'Andrew! And June! Lovely to be back! Here, darling, just this case.' He took the holdall and she brushed her lips across his cheek, put her arm round June and gave her a hug. 'You look well, both of you! Life at the Manor suiting you?' Without waiting for a reply she added, 'Lousy flight, all bumps and clouds. Looking forward to some peace and quiet. Can we get home before dark?' At the car she waited while he opened the rear door, and slid in, looking up at him. 'Come and sit with me, darling. I know June's a good driver, so she won't mind.'

She'd held his hand most of the way home, and sat quiet; he could have sworn she'd dozed which was more than he could, even though the weather had eased a bit and the traffic less intense. It took them just under the hour and a half, which wasn't bad going. Once in the house, she took her coat off and stretched, looking around her as if she'd never seen the place before. 'Hmmm,' she said, 'boring sort of a place, isn't it? Not surprised you high-tailed it to the Manor, Andrew. Clean and tidy though. Did you spring-clean the place, or was it June?' She turned to her daughter who was filling the kettle. 'Has William let you off the hook, daughter dear?'

'He's learning, Mum. Dad and I cleaned the place together. We've lived here a couple of days, but Dad's sleeping at the Manor. I'll stay here if you like.'

Samantha's eyebrows rose a notch. 'Well, I'm not staying here on my own, no way. Don't you want to give me a matrimonial welcome back, Andrew? June won't mind, I'm sure – if the Manor's all that organised she could stay there and *you'll stay* with me. It's only a few days before I've got to disappear on this course. Make the most of it?' She sat on the old stool and crossed elegant legs, the plain woollen skirt clinging to slimmer thighs.

The meaning was clear. Those eyes were thoughtful and she seemed brisker, more definite in her voice, a positiveness about her that together with her slimmer figure gave her an allure that echoed the girl he'd known and loved some twenty years back. She sipped at her teacup and pulled a face, reached for the sugar bowl. 'Not quite the same as abroad. June, dear,

I'm starving. Have we anything in the cake line? No such luxuries out there.'

There wasn't. June apologised, looked at her father, saw the way the wind was blowing, stated she wouldn't be long and went, the unspoken assumption she'd 'nip down to the shop'. It was *not* the way it should be for a homecoming but neither of them had worked through the plan as thoroughly as they should.

Samantha kept her eyes on her husband and took in the changes. She knew she'd lost weight, the work she did and the diet available plus the better feel she had in what she was now all about had wrought wonders to the point where all her old clothes had had to go. The Andrew she'd known was different too. Gone were those dull expressions and dreary eyes, he seemed more alert and perhaps springy was the word, though there was underlying tension and maybe *unease?* Yes, that was it, an uneasiness. Not surprising, given he'd slept with another woman and given her a child to boot. During the last few months she'd come to terms with that, based on her awakening realisation of how dreadfully she'd slumped into an amorphous lump. No proper male would have responded sexily to that old woman, anymore than she'd have delighted in giving herself to a boring old stick-in-the-mud house-husband with no imagination other than what was instinctive – you know, the flat on your back routine. She was hungry now, with a sharper mind and a coiled spring reflex to guard against those African blues. True, she'd experimented with a couple of the medics and they'd laughed their way through a few nights with no long term damage to either body or soul. How times had changed! There was the challenge then, sitting opposite her, and she'd give him a run for his money before she let him go. Oh, yes, she'd let him go, 'cos life was for living and she was not going to go back to being a *haus frau,* no way! Poor Roberta, she'd have a worrying time for a few days but if she really loved this Andrew of hers she'd come through it. But June would have to disappear. She couldn't play around with a daughter listening.

Andrew watched his wife, saw a new Samantha, a woman

264

with an indefinable aura of positive feminity he'd not known her to have for ages. Once maybe, he'd known her like this – if she hadn't slowly moved into that dumpling-like careless persona that had bored him rigid he might never have gone for a life-changing walk and picked up a love demanding Roberta. If! But she had, and he had, and life would never be the same.

'How's Andrea?'

He nearly jumped, lost in his reverie. That girl? 'All right, I suppose. She's working for us at the Manor now the Brewery's gone bust. An asset.'

'So you said – in your e mail. Lovely girl. Roberta like her?'

He nodded, conscious that the ground could become unstable at any time. He must be careful not to allow his thoughts betray the secret the upstairs bedroom had seen, nor, come to that, the lounge settee where he'd cuddled – explored - the nakedness of her. 'We'll need all the support once Roberta has the babies.' There was no point in skirting round the obvious.

'Ah, yes. The baby. *Babies?* Twins? Good Lord. Poor girl.' Samantha was startled, Andrew could see and wondered what else would be said. 'Enjoyed her, did you?' That was a bit coarse, he thought, and frowned. Samantha laughed. 'Sorry, but I might even be jealous. How about Andrea?'

This was getting a bit too close to home. He stood up. 'Samantha. What's happened is of no significance, is it? You and I, it isn't going to be the same. It can't be. What needs to be done needs to be done. One or other of us is going to have to organise a divorce. It's best if you stay here and I stay at the Manor. We can't sleep under the same roof if we're going down that route.'

This wasn't quite what he had in mind to say, but somehow it was happening, just hours after she'd got back. June, where are you, girl?

'Well, I haven't said what I'm going to do yet, Andrew. But I'm starving, and if June isn't back with something you and I are going out to eat. In fact, we'll all three go, once she's back. I'll pay. I'm going to see if the shower's alive – you have got hot water, haven't you?'

He had. She uncurled herself off the stool, picked up her

bag and brushed past him, waltzing fingers through his hair as she went, in a coquettish way, her skirt swinging as she left the room. He went outside to stand in the damp coolness of the early evening watching the streetlights spring to life. Where was June? She couldn't have taken all this while, surely. As he thought, his daughter's footsteps echoed along the pavement and he went to meet her. 'You've been a while?'

'Sorry, dad. Thought it best, give mum a chance to say whatever she needed to say. She's a lot slimmer, isn't she? I've spoken with Roberta on the phone, explained that mum's a lot more determined and so on, but not to worry. No,' she put a hand on his arm, as he was about to protest, 'I think it's going to be all right, dad. She's changed, and probably doesn't want to renew the old life; what was it she said, 'boring sort of a place', and she's only going to be here a few days. Live with it, dad, do whatever it takes. I'm going back to the Manor now; Andrea will pick me up in half an hour. Roberta's okay, but talk to her later?'

So at least he had the car. These females seem to have taken over and he was a pawn in the game. Back in the house, the shower was still running. June put the bread and cakes away, drunk a cold cup of tea, and as she was about to resume her coat, her mother came back down the stairs, in a pale blue sheer dress of some satiny material that clung, a ethnic style necklace and her hair clipped back with a similar comb. Whatever else she had in the holdall, this couldn't have taken up much room. He hadn't seen her look so sexy for years, and said so. He got a lift of eyebrows and a smile. June gaped. Her mother, looking like this?

'Right, where do we go? June?'

'I'm not staying, mum. Andrea's picking me up; we're going back to the Manor. You and dad are on your own, but Roberta wants you to have dinner with her tomorrow. And I'm not to take 'no' for an answer.'

Andrew took his wife back to the same pub where he and Roberta had met, those months ago. It hadn't changed much, but the restaurant was still as good despite the tat. He grinned at the way she wrinkled her nose as she always did when not impressed, but they enjoyed the meal, steering clear of all controversial topics and largely discussing her role with the Charity. It was an eye-opener, and he realised how deeply she was now committed to her work. 'How long will you stay out there, Sam?'

'They won't let me stay much longer than a year. Eighteen months maximum, then back for three. I may go out to South America but there's Indonesia to think about. I don't know. Peter will come back soon I should think, though he wants to get a permanent job with us now and that means doing a couple of training courses.'

Andrew laughed. Peter was a professional student so that wouldn't faze him. He'd seen the way Sam had spoken about what she'd been doing, the fervency and obvious dedication in her, and had been impressed. No more local market stalls, church teas, meals on wheels. This was big time. If that was the way it was, then so be it.

Once back to the house, she merely said, 'put the lights out, Andrew' and waited until he'd locked the doors, then took his hand as they went upstairs.

She slid out of her clothes and he watched her, looked at the lean tautness of her and marvelled. Just six months; such a different woman and she went on to prove how physically different and hungry she could possibly be.

Twice that night he'd woken, wondering wherever he was and which woman was in his bed until reality kicked him back to the startled awareness of her and he hadn't been able to help himself, a straying hand to explore contours that came alive under his touch and demanded such satisfaction as kept muscles and instinctive reactions going to desperation point. Absence, as the phrase had it, repeated in his head like a silly poem, made the heart beat faster, as this demonic demander rolled back to her place along side him. Even then, a hand found his and pulled it over to cover the heat and damp of her, not letting the mood change to relaxing glow but more toward a tempting revival. The whisper of shadow grey dawn wasn't going to change things either, not until she'd shown him yet another side to her. When at long last she'd dropped back to sleep he managed to drift off as well and it was the phone that woke him next, a muzzy head and an aching back giving him gip as he leant to catch a blurred glance at the time. Eleven! God almighty! With extreme care he slid from under a crumpled duvet that he was sure had gone round three times and attempted to stand up. His back! What had she done to him?

Downstairs and shiveringly aware he'd got nothing betwixt him and stark reality, a second before the thing cut into answer mode, he caught it hopefully before the ring woke Samantha. 'Andrew,' he answered. Pray it wasn't Roberta. It was.

'Darling? How's it?'

Was 'it' Samantha, the day, the night – oh, bloody hell – or what? 'Roberta, dearest girl. Can you imagine? She's totally, totally changed. I've had one hell of a night with her and I feel a wreck. Are you okay?' Waiting for her reaction and the time span spun into infinity. Would she explode into wrath or what?

A chuckle! *Laughing at him?* 'Oh, my darling! Making up for lost time, is she? So long as she doesn't get at your *proper* affections? Still *love* me?'

'More, more than ever. There's two sides to all this, R, and despite my shattered state, I think last night was a revelation. Best not discuss now, I think there's noises off. As soon as I can I'll get back to you, but please, don't hold all this against me?' Worrying, that's what it must be, for both her *and* him.

Another little laugh, thank heavens. 'No way, my darling. Not with the twins, no getting away. So long as she doesn't wreck you. Sore, are we? You wait.'

The phone went dead and he relaxed. Not out of the wood yet, not until Samantha had confirmed her intentions. The shower started which allowed him to creep upstairs again and grab some clothes. He daren't risk sharing the bathroom with her.

She was back into her yesterday dress and had washed her hair. A smoochy kiss and a press of her body against him, 'not showering? Hmmm, go on, get cleaned up. I'll just make a few calls then toast and coffee? What's your idea of the day, back to the Manor?'

'Ideally. I'm still a working man, whatever you think. We'll lunch up there. Unless . . .'

'No, that's fine. Whatever you want, I'm easy. Didn't June say we had a dinner invite?'

'We have. You don't have anything in mind?'

'Shopping, really; I need to top up my wardrobe, 'cos out there it's mail order or nothing. Then I suppose we ought to see a solicitor, though you could just forget all this Manor nonsense and come back out with me – you'd love it and I'm sure we could find you something useful to do. Even an accountant can do something else. You haven't lost your way around, ahem, the bits that need attention.' Her laugh was a sort of trill and somehow didn't sound quite right for her. Had all the stress she'd undoubtedly experienced unhinged parts of her mind?

Ignoring her comment, he left her alone in the kitchen with the phone and did as he was told. The shower was still steamy and scented and the scent wasn't Roberta's.

Roberta had been ahead of him, thinking and planning to make sure Samantha couldn't lose any time. Marjorie had been summoned, and when Samantha came up the front steps with Andrew, Roberta greeted them both like long lost friends. 'Lovely to see you, Samantha; my, you are looking well. Africa must suit you! Andrew, there's a pile of post in the office. I'll take Sam into the sitting room for pre-lunch drinks; Marjorie's here and it might be good to run through things with her? Mary's got lunch well under way; shall we say half an hour? Through here, Sam.'

She had no choice. Roberta's solicitor girl Marjorie was quite brisk and business like in 'running through' the procedure. Roberta smiled at her all the time, giving no opportunity for her to really bitch about the way she'd lost her husband to her. Gradually it dawned on her that Roberta had schemed all this, that Andrew *hadn't* been the instigator, despite his fondness for rescuing distressed damsels; it had been this girl all along; that all she'd wanted was a walking sperm donor and one who was pleasant and malleable and without a strong minded wife who'd cut up rough about seeing him pinched by another woman. She went quiet and thought about all this.

True, Roberta was pregnant, and huge with it, no mistaking the evidence. True, Andrew evidently cared very much for her. True, she'd been a bit of a cow. But, and a big, big 'but', she'd changed and she'd proved to herself he'd liked the change, oh yes, last night confirmed all that; so why lose him?

'I don't know that I really want to go through all this, you know. I think I need some time to consider. Maybe I don't want a divorce after all. Maybe Andrew might want to stay with me. I don't mind him giving you babies, Roberta; after all, it's only IVF without the nausea, isn't it? Doing things the *natural* way! Isn't that all you really wanted?' She swallowed her desire to talk real dirty and say far more basic things like 'fucked' and so on. Abroad there was no polite way of dealing with natural desires, it just happened and the kids her Charity had to deal with were the end product of unbridled procreative bonking. What Roberta had done was open her legs to someone willing to accept the invite. Her husband. She watched the girl's confidence wilt and the smile drifted away. The Marjorie girl sat down and waited.

Roberta couldn't believe this. Samantha was not the same woman, the one who had driven Andrew away, had virtually told him to 'play away', thrust him into Andrea's waiting arms, or so she'd thought. She moved across to the fireplace and stood looking down on the rug where she'd seduced this woman's husband. Seduced. Yes, she had. He'd never have taken advantage of her if she hadn't. She swallowed, and felt sick. The babies moved inside her, as if to say, yes, we're still here, and she knew she'd have to fight, fight hard to keep him. She *loved* him, dammit, and he loved her, having proved it in all his actions, his expressed physical and mental care for her. This woman didn't deserve him, making his life a misery for so long then running off and leaving him. Now just because she'd made a life for him, no, three lives now, and she'd found out that he was very good at stimulating the bits that made her feel good – bloody marvellous in fact – that other woman wanted to hang on to him. *No way!*

'Excuse me.' She had to get out, get some air, hear what he had to say. Mary saw her fly past on the way to the office and began to worry. The lunch was all but ready so it would be unlike her mistress not to have stopped to check. She waited a moment before following.

For Andrew the return to the peace and quiet of the Manor office was a benison, a calm to ease his soul after the mania of the past twelve hours or so. He'd been stupid to assume he could simplistically welcome Sam back to the house, give her a simple kiss and leave her to wallow in the emptiness of the place. He'd wished he could talk to June but she'd gone off somewhere with Andrea. He'd dealt with the mail she had left, run through the outstanding e-mails and was trying to get to grips with some of the Accountancy side of the business. The door flung open, and Roberta stood there, his Roberta, with tears coming and a hangdog look on her. 'Darling?'

'Sam, she's not going to let go! Tell me; tell me Andrew, you still love me?' Despite her bump, she flung her arms round him and squeezed. 'You won't go back to her?' The tears were flowing, running down and wetting his shirt. This was awful.

'Hey, hey, Roberta, whatever has she said? Come and sit down.' He let her collapse into his chair and stood over her, fishing for his handkerchief. 'Has Marjorie been rushing her fences? There's nothing she said to make me think it wasn't going to happen – in fact she mentioned seeing a solicitor herself this morning, so you getting Marjorie here pre-empted things. I'd better talk to her. Where is she?'

Roberta shook her head as if to say it wouldn't work, but at least it sounded as if there was still a chance. 'You still love *me*?'

'I still love you. Nothing's changed, R, except I was too

susceptible to feminity last night. What comes of being too soft-hearted, or too fond of making love to nice women? I do have to admit Sam's a lot better than when she went, and she's learnt a few tricks. All that aside, *living* with you is a whole heap better and with a family – oh, no, Roberta, I'm not swopping back. So there; you've got me and I've got you and the twins, embryonic though they may be. Marjorie'll come up with a means of sorting it out, never fret. Stay here a mo and I'll see what's to be done.'

Just as he was about to leave the office, Mary stepped inside the door. She'd had to hear what was said, though it wasn't in her nature but Roberta's happiness was on the line. There was a determined expression on her face. 'I have an idea, Miss Roberta, if Mr Andrew'll go along with it, though young Andrea might object.' She closed the door firmly behind her and faced them both. 'I knows that Mr Andrew has had more than a passing interest in Miss Andrea, d'you see.' She paused to see what effect that statement would have and watched with slight amusement, as he turned pink. 'I also knows he's an easy target for these adventurous young ladies, Miss Roberta, because you and I knows what we knows. So it's not surprising. I also knows that you mean more to him than most, aren't I right, Mr Andrew?' She watched him nod. 'Maybe your wife might be more open to the idea of going her own way if you uses Andrea as an excuse, if you get's my meaning. I'll say no more other than lunch is ready, if you've the stomach for it.' With that she opened the door again and quietly paddled away.

Roberta looked at Andrew. 'See where this has landed you?' She could see the funny side of things now, and at the same time felt rather sorry for him. Three ladies, all pulling him in different directions, and he just wanting a straight forward path to tread, along the same old contour line. She wanted him up hill, Sam wanted him back down, and maybe only Andrea was the one to show the way straight along that contour line. And she had the right shape for him, bless her boobs. 'Better marry Andrea then, so neither of us gets you.'

'Don't be silly, Roberta. She's not in the frame, never has been.' A moment's reflection, a remembrance of girly delights and something of the shame of letting Roberta down. 'How about telling Sam about how I spoilt Andrea's virginity like Mary said? Would that stop this change of heart?' The passion rush of that episode still clear and sparkling in his mind, the manner in which the girl had let go her inhibitions to take what was inevitably coming her way sooner of later; though now he was not at all sure it had been anything but disastrous given she was now in such close proximity. Still, if that episode was a key to Sam relinquishing her rights then some benefit might accrue. What would Andrea's reaction be if her sordid little de-flowering were made public? This was a mess; a squalid tawdry mess and it diminished the bright, colourful, happy feelings building between him and Roberta. He wanted shot of the whole performance, and deeply regretted giving way to base instincts last night. He should have cut and run, put himself out of reach rather than have been sort of sorry and sympathetic. Too late now.

'Andrew?' Roberta broke his train of disjointed thoughts. 'Mary's said she's got lunch ready. What do you want to do?'

'Take it as it comes, I guess. I'd better talk to Andrea as soon as they get back. And Marjorie when I can get her on her own. You still want to go on with all this?'

'God, yes. I wouldn't back down now, come what may. It'll be worth it in the end. I suppose.' Her voice dipped and went reflective, asking a repetitive question, 'you still want me – and the twins?'

'As ever, R. Love you. Let's go eat.'

Samantha gave the impression that all was well, chattered gaily on about everything except what was simmering along in all their minds, whilst Marjorie kept her own counsel and Roberta was pleasantness incorporated. Andrew withdrew into a shell, until the girls came back mid-way, conversation getting far more animated as Samantha quizzed Andrea on the breakdown of the Brewery's credibility.

Before long Andrea gave him a perfect opportunity.

'Andrew's been so good to me, Samantha. Shown me what I've been missing, cloistered away in that office. Really opened my eyes to what life is all about, in every way.' Her eyes flashed a glance at him, the meaning clear. *You took me and I loved it, why don't you take advantage of what I can offer?*

Samantha narrowed her eyes, glanced round at her husband. She recalled her comments about this girl, and wondered if. . .

He nodded and added his two pennyworth. 'She and I did rather get carried away – she helped me sort out the wardrobe after you'd gone, Sam, and we had a bit of a tussle that ended up somewhat, well . . .' he tailed off and left them to imagine the end result.

Roberta added her weight. 'Of course, we had a row over it, and he confessed but I've forgiven him. I mean, it was just the same as when we two first got involved. Poor man, he seems to have all us girls flashing our knickers at him. Better Andrea had *him* introduce her to womanhood than some scruffy guy in the back of a car, eh?'

Andrea had gone relatively pink, and stared at the tablecloth. Her innuendo had been taken far further than she'd imagined, to the point where she really did feel embarrassed and rather too warm. For a lunchtime confessional it was as good as reality TV.

Samantha's resultant scathing look at Andrew said it all. Roberta she knew about. Andrea she'd dangled in front of him as a bit of a laugh; she'd never expected him to take up her suggestions, but there didn't seem any doubt he had. Ignoring Marjorie's presence she asked the question. 'You *slept* with that girl? Despite this relationship with Roberta? Who else, Andrew, who *else?*'

He shrugged. 'It just happened, Sam. Who knows how one responds when it's there and being offered. Like last night.'

She could stomach Roberta. She might have lived with his bedding Andrea if there hadn't been a Roberta, because there couldn't be much common ground otherwise, but taking them *both?* She wouldn't be able to trust him, not now. The new girl in her wouldn't allow a storming out scene; that would have been all too childish. The shrug and the slight smile did what was intended, a de-fuse and 'let's move on' shift. Silence around the table, embarrassingly long, like a four cars on a roundabout each waiting for another to move and if it hadn't been for Mary bringing in a potful of coffee goodness knows how long it would have lasted. There was a certain common denominator here, and she didn't regard herself as being the lowest.

Roberta moved her chair back and carefully stood up, rubbing her back. 'Excuse me. I have a rest after lunch. Marjorie, thanks for coming. We'll be in touch. Andrea, dear there's a couple coming at three and it would be nice if you could meet them, take them through the Barn? Andrew, if you've a minute. June, I'm sure you'd like to show your mother round. Tea at four?'

At her organising best; and Andrew's instant recall of that first dinner party when she'd marshalled folk in exactly the same tone and managed to get him on his own to tell him he'd impressed her. Or something. Marjorie collected her bag and said her goodbyes, allowing Andrea to escape on the pretext of showing her out. Andrew stood up as Samantha rose, and she ignored him. June took her mother's arm and they left the room.

Roberta sighed. 'Nasty. Poor Andrea. I don't think she knew which way to turn, having her little romp aired in quite that way. Didn't do much for you either, did it, Andrew? Sordid. Are we going to survive?' Taking his arm, she steered him to the door. 'Come upstairs with me, darling.'

In the quiet comfort and warmth of the bedroom, she peeled off her clothes, welcomed his help with her bra, and stood before the cheval mirror. 'Not exactly a ravishing sight, eh, lover? It's gonna be a while afore I's sexy agen. Sure you can last that long?'

Loaded question, he thought. 'After today, my darling, I daren't look anywhere near another pair of legs.' She turned round slowly and his eyes took all of her in, the protruding belly, the swelling veined breasts, her still sexy looking bushy mound, those lovely thighs and well-proportioned legs. 'Except yours. Maternal or not, R, you're a good-looking woman, and I love you. We'll survive.' He'd answered her question, and moved to kiss her, lips, breasts, and tummy, and then ever so gently, stroked and kissed the intimacy of her.

Roberta closed her eyes and let the magic of the moment flow, easing the tenseness and the stress of the day. She felt his soft stroke of hands down her inner thighs and felt her children move. 'Mmmm. Mmmm. Sorry I can't, darling. Really, I am.'

There would have been a way she could have helped, but now was not the time. She moved to sit on the bed edge, and as she lay back he lifted her legs up, smoothed the cover over her. 'Shall I stay?'

'Please. Hold me?'

Slipping his shoes and jacket off, he folded himself down alongside her, put an arm over the mounded cover of her breasts, dimmed the lights and closed his eyes. The low residual sun of the afternoon had faded and the early twilight was already easing into winter gloom. Her breathing slowed and deepened, the rhythmic rise and fall of her chest gave him the consolation of her closeness and he drifted into a doze. This woman he'd love forever.

Samantha and daughter June walked through the Barn, taking in the room settings so lovingly constructed by Roberta. June knew she should not take sides and kept her own counsel. If her mother wanted to play her own games, then she'd stay aloof. The whole day remained a total strangeness, unreal and unexplainably weird with no sense in anything that had happened. Her father had patently had a steamy night with her mum; then Roberta had organised Marjorie to talk divorces and suddenly the ploy had blown up in her face, consequentially poor Andrea had had her knickers – or lack of them - aired in public, her mum had gone awfully quiet and dad had disappeared, presumably up with Roberta. So what was going to happen next? In the nicest display space her mother stopped to finger the fabric draped as curtain suggestions.

'I have to hand it to the woman, she knows her stuff. I never was much good at this sort of thing.' Samantha's expression seemed very reflective, introverted. 'I'm sorry, June.'

'Why, mum? I've no complaints. You've always been a good mum and we had good times.' The two women stood in contemplative silence for a couple of minutes before June summoned courage. 'You'll have to let dad go, mum. He's been so different, and it's not your fault that Roberta is who she is. None of us stay the same forever; look at William and me. And we're not rampaging around swearing at each other, are we? It's all very civilised and honest; dad's owned up to what's happened, *you* decided to go off abroad. I was upset first off, but now I've seen how good he is to Roberta and how much she loves him, I reckon it's come out okay.'

'Except I've lost a husband.'

'Oh, mum! You've been drifting away from him for ages! He didn't look for other women, you know that. Both Roberta and Andrea found him, and 'cos you weren't, er, *loving* him, they filled the gap. So you've only got yourself to blame. Sorry, mum, but it's true.'

Samantha walked away and looked at the next bay, unseeing. Her daughter was stating what she knew in her heart of hearts was true. Obviously Andrew had talked things over with her. If only she'd realised. Last night was still a lovely memory; was that all it was going to be, a memory? June caught up and slipped an arm round her, laid a head on her shoulder. Samantha instinctively cuddled her. 'So I'm on my own then?'

'Mum, we're all still friends. I love you, dad still loves you but he's *in love* with Roberta. Andrea was simply giving way to her needs and fulfilling feminine urges and they both know that, they're not stupid, though now she's found out what it's all about she'll keep coming back for more, I know her, but I don't think dad wants to compromise his position with Roberta. I'm a bit surprised about last night really. Can't have been easy for anyone.' She broke away and ran fingers through her hair. 'Find a new man, mum. Someone who's got no ties.

277

Dad won't mind, and anyway, you'll divorce him, won't you?'

Samantha reflected. Her daughter was older than her years and surprisingly forthright. So there wasn't really any choice, or to alter a phrase, she'd climbed out of the bed, not made it to lie on. 'Okay, June. I'll agree to divorce him if you're sure we'll stay friends. Will you stay with me tonight?'

'Of course, Mum. It'll work out, you'll see.'

The planned dinner party went surprisingly well. Roberta, after a couple of hours sleep, woke up quite perky; Andrew felt much more relaxed in the knowledge that all possible difficulties had been aired between them, June played a good role as listener and Andrea, amazingly, kept herself well in check. By the end of the evening with not a little alcohol to smooth out the small irksome comments it was if they'd been all very good friends for years. When Samantha and June put coats on to go home and Andrea was hitching a lift because she really couldn't drive, Roberta was surprised to have a cheek-to-cheek kiss from her rival. 'Look after him, Roberta. I'm just so sorry that I didn't appreciate him, even after all these years. I'll talk to Marjorie. 'Bye'

Andrew had a call from June first thing the following morning. 'She's gone, dad. Took a taxi straight after breakfast. Told me to tell you she still loves you; that she's sorry she didn't understand. I'd best get back to William. I'll call you when I get home. 'Bye, dad. Look after the new mum. Luv you.'

She'd put the phone down without giving him a chance to reply. Suddenly his life seemed truncated as if he'd been left marooned. On an island with no boats. He'd burnt them, well and truly. He took Roberta some breakfast up to their room and told her.

'Oh, darling. I'm sorry for you; it must seem dreadful. You've still got me. I won't let you down, promise. And the kids. It won't be long.' She patted her bulge. 'Only three weeks or so.'

Andrew sat on the bed edge. 'Shall I help you up? Andrea'll be here shortly.' He tried to speak light heartedly to allay his strange nausea, a sort of inner panic attack. Something wasn't connecting, his brain didn't really want to know and for two pins he'd curl up back on the bed and go back to sleep. Bereft of reason by Sam's caving in and running out of his life.

'Darling man. You go and start the work-a-day, I'll manage, take my time.'

He found Andrea already behind the desk though he'd not heard her come in. 'How do you feel this morning, Andrea? After last night?' It was a try, an attempt to regain normality.

'Fine, thanks, Andrew. Nothing like a good glass of cold milk to soften the hangover. How's Roberta?'

'Still a-bed. Bit over wrought after yesterday. So am I, come to that. Sorry about revealing our, um, workouts.' The recall vivid in his brain, standing behind her the temptation was too great. Of their own volition his hands reached up and rested briefly on her shoulders, fingers massaging lightly. Her head moved sideways and down, hair brushing the back of one hand. Her eyes did not leave the screen and she kept typing until those fingers strayed, round and down, beneath the crinkly fabric of her blouse, curling under the satin straps of her bra.

Abruptly, one hand left the keys and captured his just as it reached the swell of her breast.

'No! Andrew, don't. Please,' and hunched forward, enough to cause him to withdraw.

'Sorry.'

'I can't pretend about my wants, Andrew, but I'm trying to control them and this isn't easy.'

Not for me either, he thought. Not now. 'Sorry,' he said again. *Not really, but what else could he say? That he wanted her, not for any other reason that he'd had her, known her in the biblical sense and she was there and available, short skirt and knees showing and those stiff buttons under that pink blouse were evident and taut.*

She swung the chair round to face him, took in the situation. 'That desperate at this time in the morning?' *Her body was responding, damn it. It was all too bloody inevitable, would have had to happen sooner or later. She bent down, as if to retrieve the pen that had rolled off the desk. . . .*

Closing his eyes to her didn't help; her scent too powerful by far, and all sense vanished.

Too quick, too weird, dramatic perhaps, full of tension, risk. Ultimately she eased up, turned back to him and offered a wry grin.

All the lustful passion drained out of him and with it his confidence. He'd messed up again, instincts and passion ruled body instead of mind. Samantha had upskittled his brain. How could he face his Roberta if he'd reneged on all he'd promised? Stupid, stupid, stupid. Damn the girl. Abruptly he spun round and left her.

She shrugged, returned to the screen, feeling, well, unsure of what she was feeling. Used. Sad, maybe. Undervalued? But he had wanted her, needed her. Some satisfaction in that if not in any other way. She thought she understood and that was some comfort. She pushed it out of her mind and got on with the day's work.

EIGHTEEN

Samantha had flown back without seeing him again. Somehow he couldn't get her out of his mind; what with the change in her and the unchallenged acceptance of the divorce particulars Marjorie had filed, it challenged his perception of the way forward. Boats had been burnt. And Andrea had patently avoided any repetition of that morning's stupid encounter last week largely by ensuring she didn't stay alone with him. A weak moment, that. Happily he'd managed to nail his conscience down for Roberta's sake, vowing not to give in to temptation ever again but fully aware he'd given Andrea far too much in the way of a hold on him. That girl was dangerous even if she didn't take advantage, not that she had offered any real change in her demeanour. It was if the incident had never happened. As the days went by ultimately the tension eased between them and normality returned.

Roberta's birthing day was drawing ever closer. With Christmas looming, the days were full of customers all wanting room re-fits before the Day so they could show off to their friends and it seemed the entire world knew how good they were. Busy, busy, *busy*. He hadn't been able or desirous of taking on any new accountancy clients and even struggled to keep those he had. Luckily Andrea was proving her worth and they promised her a pay rise in the New Year. It was as if the Brewery had never existed.

'Darling?' Brushing her hair was ever a lovely morning ritual prior to those comfortable Mary breakfasts. In the mirror the face looking at him in reverse had all the hallmarks of flushed maternalism but still the girl he'd come to love.

'Mmmm?' He took the comb out of his mouth hold. 'You okay?'

'Uh huh. As okay as a balloon on legs. You seem particularly introvert this morning. Sam still getting at you?'

So perceptive, his Roberta. 'I do think about what she's doing, where she is. Can't help it. Just glad Peter's still out there. Sorry, R, but we did live together for a long time.'

'Don't be sorry, my darling. It's – she's – part of you, what you are. Caring. Remember caring? Since she came here I know it's been difficult and forced decisions on you. I'm just so damned lucky you're still here, and don't think I don't know. I love you, Andrew.' Twisting round in her cumbersome way, she held up a face to be kissed, and wrapped arms round his legs. 'You mean so much to me, I couldn't live without you.'

The tender kiss answered the appeal in eyes moistened with welling tears. 'Hey, hey, darling, isn't this too early in the day for tears? I'm not going anywhere. Certainly not out to Africa. I just hope she's not at risk.' He helped Roberta to her feet and into her clothes. Dressing her was as much a part of expressing his love as any. She grasped his hand and held on as they went down to breakfast.

She took a day off from the business and started organising the decoration of the Manor's hall for Christmas. Earlier in the week they'd had an eight-foot tree delivered and Andrew had stood it up in half an oil drum full of sand. Sturdy enough for her almost to swing on, if she'd been able, but under instructions *not* to use the step ladder, she contented herself with making up the garlands for Andrew to hang, and working her way through the large box of decorations to throw out all the broken ones. The gardener had delivered seemingly vast amounts of holly and laurel, even a smallish bunch of mistletoe given to her personally with a nod and a wink. Dear Albert, even in his sixties he still managed to look spry and effective.

At lunchtime Andrew emerged from the office, with Andrea in tow. 'You'll never guess, R, what came up in the e-mails this morning?' Andrea was grinning behind him.

'So? If I won't guess you'll have to tell me?'

'Two things. One from Sam – she's having Christmas in Africa before going out to Thailand in the New Year, and Peter will be with her; and the other is an offer – suggestion perhaps better - from a film company making a series for a commercial channel. They want to use the Barn, subject to coming down and checking us out, for one of the 'make-over' programmes? Seems someone was snooping around last month as a pretend client – probably that lanky girl in tatty jeans with the horn rimmed glasses.'

Roberta laughed and then pulled a face. 'Ouch! The twins can't cope! You and your girls. Do you really think we should? Involve ourselves with the telly? Lots of hassle. When?'

Andrea took over. 'I think it's too good an opportunity to miss. You won't have to spend any money on adverts for ages, and I dare say there'll be quite a good facility fee. I'll be happy to do extra if you want.' *Maybe I'll find a sexy bloke who'll fall for me?* 'I think it said 'sometime in the Spring' didn't it, Andrew?'

He was miles away, mind full of Samantha and her absence again. 'Hmm? Oh, yes. What do you think, R? Be after the twins are born. Maybe we'll be able to afford Hazel full time again?'

They'd reluctantly had to tell Mary they couldn't justify even an extra few hundred pounds every month for Hazel every day, not after suspending the B & B side of things while Roberta was pregnant. It had been a shame all round, but no way out. Now, with possibly an extra source of income over and above and the work involved it was clear to Andrew's accountancy brain there'd be some sense in getting her back.

Roberta perked up. She liked Hazel despite her odd little ways. 'Oh, lovely. Yes, if you all agree. Mary?'

'Aye, lass. Why not?' She'd been sad that Hazel could only do one day a week despite the acceptance of the reasoning. If having film crew types running around was the price for getting that girl back out from under her mother's feet she'd manage.

'Settled then. Can you spare time to deal with the tree and put the garlands up, Andrew? This afternoon?'

'So long as Andrea doesn't mind chatting up the Parkinsons at half two and the Smithsons at four? Eh girl?'

She pulled a face at him. 'On commission?'

'Cheeky! After promising a pay rise in the new year?'

The repartee was harmless. He'd managed to keep his distance even though the blouse today was one demoted from a party outfit and hence pointed a clear course for her cleavage.

The light had completely left the day, long before they'd finished. Andrea's clients had proved totally different, with the Parkinsons demanding and willing to spend but the Smithsons time wasters. Eventually she was able to close up the Barn and retreat thankfully indoors in time to be given the honour of mounting the fairy on the top of the tree. In reality it was less of the honour but more the chance to exhibit her underwear as she stood precariously on the top rung of the steps.

'Oi, you, stop peering.' Roberta poked him. As the direction of his gaze was diverted from the glories above to the amused smile on her face, he almost blushed and pulled a face at her. He let go the steps and Andrea felt them move, swayed, grabbed and fortunately missed clutching the tree before ignominiously toppling down into his arms, grazing a leg on the side of the steps as she fell. They both ended up in a heap on the floor, with Roberta unable to help herself bursting into laughter.

'There's no need to fall head over heels over the girl, Andrew. She may be expendable, but she's too pretty to damage. Come on, up, the pair of you. The tree looks fine.'

Andrea struggled to her feet, smoothed her skirt down and rubbed her shin; glad she'd not broken the skin. Andrew straightened himself out and lay flat on the floor. That way he could still see a wonderful pair of legs straddling him, as her hands reached down and hauled him up. Her narrowed eyes said it all. *Not here, not now.* She'd forgiven him.

True, the effect was very Christmassy once the twinkling lights were turned on, the best Roberta had seen since she'd been here first as a silly twenty year old. She and her ex had never bothered much with the Christmas thing but now she felt totally different. Even if the twins couldn't see, she felt it was the start of a future family tradition.

Mary had the mince pies warming and the teapot full and waiting. She'd heard the frolics in the hall and guessed something of the going's-on. Mr Andrew at his tricks with that Andrea girl again. She didn't miss much, though not too worried. None of it was serious and Roberta would stamp on young Miss Andrea if it got out of hand.

Two weeks later Christmas Day was heralded by the first snow fall of the winter. Magic, pure magic, snow on Christmas Day. Roberta struggled out of bed to look, alerted by the strange clear light of the reflected white through the curtains. She felt a stab, a twinge, and rubbed her side. Still a fortnight according to the system, but she wasn't so sure. Her bump had moved progressively downwards and it was far more of a waddle to reach the window.

'Oh, *Andrew!* Look, darling! It's so pretty!' The snow had fallen onto frozen ground, and the trees were decorated, the lawn a pristine sheen of icing. Not a sound, the world held its breath, before on the stroke of nine, the first peel of bells of the day reached into the countryside and told them, 'Christmas, and the coming of a Baby'.

Not *a* baby. Two.

Christmas lunch was postponed. It had been planned as a quiet one, just for two. Mary was going to be at home, Andrew more than capable of serving up the meals she'd prepared. They would have a celebratory 'business' dinner in the New Year, after the babies were born. Well, they couldn't wait until the New Year. They wanted in, and there was no stopping them.

'I don't know when we've had as rapid a first delivery, Mr Hailsworthy. She's been a very good girl. I make no secret of it, we

285

were a bit concerned, given she was expecting twins, but no, everything's fine.' The consultant obstetrician, called in from his otherwise peaceful day at home, hadn't really minded as she had always been a model patient and anyway, twins on Christmas day, even though it was close on midnight now, was good. Andrew had gripped her hands, listened to her screams with justified concern, given her all his support and encouragement as he watched first a little girl and then a baby brother carefully managed into the world. Now she was sedated, regaining her strength, but still he held her hand. *His.* A family, a brand new family.

'Thank you. I'm relieved. Surprised it's all happened so quickly, but you've all been great. And that Roberta's really okay? No complications?'

'None. I think we're lucky they weren't too large, being twins, so she's had an easier time. No, she'll be fine. Now I'm going home. I'll see her tomorrow, but she should be clear to go home after the day. We don't keep these young mums in any longer than we need to. You all organised at home?'

Andrew thought of the nursery they'd had to adapt when twins were evident, and grinned. 'Yes. Sort of. We'll cope.'

'I'm sure you will. Well done, the pair of you. Good night then.'

With Roberta still sleeping quietly, he had no reason to stay. With reassurances from the ward sister that all was well, he took another look at his new swaddled up offspring, and went home. It was strange, lying in the big double bed all on his own, alone in this large house. He couldn't sleep, not at first. The memories of the year pulled at him, the walk into the raw country that had brought him face to face with all this. London, Ireland, the Open Day, Sam coming home, Andrea, the farce that had been the death throes of the Brewery, Mary, June, bless her, Andrea . . .

No new snow had fallen; the tyre tracks and the footprints were still echoes of yesterday. He phoned the hospital. She'd had a good night, the twins were squalling their heads off and yes, he could visit whenever. He phoned Andrea.

'*No! Last night?* Oh, Andrew – you should have let me know! Oh, good for her! Everything all right? When is she coming home? Can I . . . ?'

He nearly laughed out loud at her enthusiasm. 'Wait till I get her home, Andrea. Maybe today, but I don't want visitors too soon. Why don't you come over day after tomorrow?' With her ticked off his mental list the next call was to June.

Her's a more muted response. 'I'm so pleased for you both, dad. Is Roberta all right?'

'She's fine, June, thanks. The maternity ward people were quite impressed how simple it all was.'

'Did you . . .?'

'Yes. Marvellous, actually. Don't you . . .?'

'Of course, dad. Any names?'

'Hmmm. Don't know if I ought to say just yet. They were five pound ten and six two, by the way. Oh all right. The girl's Aubrietia Bridget, and the boy Christopher David. Roberta wants me to agree they are 'Hailsworthy'. She's very firm about that. You realise I don't even know what her maiden name was?'

'No, dad, I don't. I like the Aubrietia. You'll have to think about the boy though.'

'Why?'

'Would you like to be known as CD? Seedy? Come on, dad, surely you thought that one through?'

'Oh Lord! We'll have to reverse them. David Christopher. Yes, perhaps it does sound better. Well done. When are you coming over?'

'That an invite or a command?'

'Invite. William?'

'Oh no, he won't want to indulge, not his scene and I rather think I'm either going to have to resort to devious means or resign myself to being regarded as barren.' She went on, a deceptively light-hearted tone which didn't fool him. 'You want me to tell mum? You know she's flying out to Thailand at the end of the week?'

'So she said. I hope all this won't drain her. I know she's

pretty tough, but it's a funny old place. You want kids don't you?'

'Dad, don't. I'll ring you. Love to Roberta.'

She'd gone. He got himself showered and changed, and then Mary turned up. One person he was going to have real pleasure in surprising.

'Miss Roberta not up yet?'

'I doubt it.' He tried to keep a straight face and failed; watched the gamut of expressions chase across her homely features.

'She's not . . .?' and the concerned look changed to amazement. 'You mean . . . ?'

He nodded, 'Yesterday, Christmas present. Two of 'em. Aubrietia Bridget at five ten and David Christopher at six two. All three fine, Mary. I'm sorry we didn't do justice to all your lovely cooking but really there wasn't much choice. At least I didn't have to go through a do-it-yourself exercise. Can you sort out the debris? I really do need to get over to the hospital.'

She'd held out her matronly arms to him and he found himself hugged well and truly. 'Eee, lad, I'm so pleased for 'ee both. It'll be the makings of her, having children of her own. You knows about her family?'

'No, not really, Mary. She'd never said and I didn't want to rake up the past. Surprisingly I've never felt the need.'

'Well, sit yoursen down, lad. It's time you knew. Best afore you gets her back, then there's nought to worry over.'

Andrew sat himself down, his spine beginning to tingle. Mary plumped herself opposite and took a deep breath, coming straight to the point. 'She's my daughter.'

He gulped, felt his heart leap. This wasn't, couldn't be, true? How could she be Mary's daughter? Shock, amazement, incredulity, incomprehension, total surprise. There'd been nothing, *nothing* to show that, in all that had happened over the near year he'd been involved, *in love* with, living with her, and nothing had remotely suggested the possibility. It couldn't be, not with that sort of mistress/servant style of relationship?

'I know, lad. You canna believe it. Well, she doesn't know, and now's the time for her to be told. I couldn'a bring mysen to tell her afore. But with two grandchildren . . .' she was wiping tears from her eyes, 'it was a mistake, you ken. There's many a time I could have been heartily ashamed of it, but now she's such a pretty girl and so successful I'm just *so* proud of her, how can I be ashamed of bringing her into the world?'

He shook his head slowly. Roberta's mum, Mary? That explained a lot, how protective she was, how she was always here, and the way the two blended in what they did. It would have been uncanny if he'd really thought about it, which he hadn't, being too wrapped up in his own relationship with her. But how come she'd let him fool around with Roberta? Because she'd been a 'fallen woman' herself? He had to say it. 'She's a lovely girl, Mary, any mother would be proud of her.'

She went on. 'It was her father. Such a dashing romantic man, and I fell for him. He'd not had much of a life with Henrietta, you ken. She couldn't conceive, seemingly. He and I . . .' her voice broke, quavered, but she swallowed and went on, 'well, I fell for a child, and he wanted it to be his. It nearly broke him, but finally Henrietta agreed that they would adopt her. I stayed on as a housekeeper. Roberta was five when Henrietta died from meningitis. Christopher . . .'

This time she couldn't stem her tears.

Andrew found himself weeping in sympathy, unable to quell his emotion, but with his mind in a total turmoil. Though he and Roberta had edged around the subject of her family past a time or two it had never seemed to be that important and neither had a penchant for looking back.

Mary sniffed loudly, caught her dress hem to wipe her cheeks and through the tears she had an embryonic smile for him. 'Ee, lad, we're a right pair.' She got to her feet and went out of the kitchen. He heard her down the end of the corridor where her little room was, to return within minutes clutching a tatty yellowed envelope. She pulled out a card-mounted photograph. 'Yon's Roberta's father. Henrietta,' she pushed a finger at the slight figure of the girl holding onto the man's arm, 'her's was the money, you ken, and the London house. His was the family. Italian, his mother, why she's got the looks. I was in service, a lot prettier, good deal slimmer in them days. Old fashioned, they was. Very much in the social whirl. Christopher looked after me when they could have just let me go. Then when Henrietta died, I had my girl to look after as best I could without ever letting on. That was the deal, and even when Roberta's father died I couldn't let on. He was good to me. Reckon he'd have married me if he could. Roberta's alus known me as a housekeeper, we've been such pals. Reckon it've spoilt things to tell 'er. Now's different; she's got you, and the twins, and *I's so proud of 'ee all.'* She held out the ageing photograph. Andrew took it and looked at the man, seeing dark, almost saturnine features, the litheness that was Roberta, trying to ally that with Mary's more buxom ampleness. Hard to imagine what the household must have been like, but it certainly fitted with the London address. 'What did he do?'

Mary laughed. '*Do*? Not a lot, my lad. They owned a fashion house and lived it up. Roberta was alus dressed to kill, went to balls, all the social functions, public school girl afore, and then swept up in the crazy life till that man married her. I was agen it, you ken, but couldna' say ought. Her father died two years after, that's when she took over the London house but the fashion business had gone. She started the Interior design thing instead. I came here with her after that, after Christopher died. Heart, you knows. Diabetic, he was.'

'What was her maiden name, Mary? She's never said, but to be honest I've never asked or worried about it, strange though it may seem.'

'Tower. Her grandfather was Count Tour. She called him '*Con Tor*' in her childish way. He came over for a few weeks each year when Henrietta was alive, even though he was in his eighties. Lovely man.' Her eyes went still and far away, remembering. After a moment's silence between them she snapped out of her reverie. 'Hey, lad, you best go fetch the lass home. And the bairns. Then us'll have a grand evening. Go on with 'ee'

'Do you tell her, Mary, or do I?'

'She's your girl now, Andrew. You tell her.'

NINETEEN

Before setting off for the hospital Andrew showered and changed and made sure he had the little red velvet box in his pocket. Then he kissed his future new mother-in-law and drove carefully to see his new children.

Roberta was sitting up with one infant at her breast and the other in a cot alongside and an attendant nurse trying to demonstrate the principals of breast-feeding. She didn't see him until he was half way down the little ward, and nearly dropped her charge, *'DARLING!'* It was as much a shout as anything and the whole roomful of new mums were made aware of her enthusiasm. *'Love you!'*

Her beaming smile and flashing eyes told its own tale. The nurse took the infant she was holding and waited until Andrew had greeted her patient in the approved new father manner, before offering him the bundle.

'Which . . .?'

'Aubrietia. Abby for short, Andrew. Chris is still asleep. He can't half yell. They'll all be glad to see the back of us.'

'How're you feeling, darling?'

She whispered at him, 'Sore. I had them make sure I was going to be back to normal *properly* for you. I've got some exercises to do. Tits won't be quite the same though, not after these two have had been at me day and night. Guess we'll get them on bottles as soon as it's right and proper. Have you told everyone?'

'Some. Mary's over the moon. I didn't realise Christopher was your father's name.'

She looked at him strangely and he wondered at the spasm of alarm on her face. 'Mary?'

'Yep. She's been filling me in on some of the family history.'

'Oh! So you know there's a bit of hot blooded Italian in me, then?'

'Yep. No wonder I fell for you. I'd always fancied Sophia Loren.'

She giggled. The nurse alongside went red and Andrew raised an inquisitive eyebrow. 'She's Lauren, Andrew, and brilliant with the little ones.'

'Hi, Lauren. Do you take on some contract work on the side? Spend an hour or two at our place?' The girl just smiled at him; she'd heard it all before.

'Hoi, mate, I'm not having you add to your harem just because she's a Lauren. Leave her alone. And don't drop Abby.'

He wouldn't, not in a million years. The little puckered up face with eyes tight shut was gearing up to holler, having been previously introduced to a soft warm source of comfort that her current holder didn't seem to possess.

'Give her here. Before Chris wakes up. I can't handle two at once.'

'Why not, you've got two taps?'

She scowled at him, and he loved her. Lauren laughed.

Once she'd completed the refuelling exercise and the twins had been settled back into their respective cots, she swung herself out of bed and walked, gingerly, with him down to the day room at the end of the ward. Then he could kiss her properly and absorb the womanliness of her. A mother, a lovely, happy girl with two beautiful infants, and all his.

'Happy?'

'Hmmmm.' She snuggled into his shoulder. 'Can't wait to get home. They think best tomorrow. Can *you* wait?'

'Needs must, my darling. I have something for you.' He slipped his hand into his pocket and withdrew the little box, cupped in his hand to obscure the view of it until he'd one handedly opened the lid before showing it to her.

He gently withdrew his loaned signet ring from her finger,

took the new one, carefully matched for size, from its burgundy cushion. In silence she took the ring from him and slipped it on her engagement finger. It sat perfectly. Twin diamonds.

There was no need for words with the depth of her love in her eyes.

* * *

The following morning he came for her at ten o'clock and drove his new family carefully home. Mary was waiting on the steps, with Hazel hovering in the back of the hall. In solemn procession they trooped up to the nursery and introduced the twins to their new abode. Chris, true to form, yelled, whereas Abby merely opened her brown eyes, puckered her face in what could have been a smile, and promptly went back to sleep.

It took Roberta half an hour to feed the twins and show Hazel how to burp them, before she went thankfully back into their bedroom and showered, changed into a slinky dress to improve her feelings and bolster her courage before going to find her man. The sitting room was as cosy as ever. 'Pre lunch sherry, Andrew?'

'Unless you want champagne?'

'Save that for the christening. No, sherry's fine. Where's Mary?'

'In the kitchen.'

'Call her, Andrew, please,' the die was cast, now or never. 'It's important.'

He looked at her, trying to fathom that expression. Enigmatic, that's what it was, with hints of deep seriousness alloyed with a twitch of a smile. This was his *real* woman who'd given birth to *his children*. Deep inside his soul there was awe and a wonderment that they'd travelled this road so far, had not found anything like a dead end or a nowhere, *au contraire,* she was stronger and he was irrevocably linked to her. The vacillations of the ten, eleven, months at an end but with another fascinating twist to their saga; Mary and how would Roberta come to terms with her relationship?

Such deep thoughts, staringly deep, blankly directed at his girl; she frowned and motioned him with her head. Abruptly he spun around to do as he was told. Why this?

'Mary – come and share a sherry, please. Roberta asked.'

She checked the oven, flung her cloth at Hazel and followed him.

Roberta made Mary take a glass as well. Still with that enigmatic half-smile she raised hers and Andrew's perplexity came to an end.

'To the best Mum a girl could ever have. The best granny two little people could ever wish for. Andrew, meet my mum.' Now she was really smiling, coyly and mischievously at the same time.

Andrew looked first at Mary; she'd gone white, and sat down heavily, then to Roberta and he shook his head.

'You *knew?* 'Her mother, Mary, asked in total surprise.

'I knew. Ages ago, when you made such a fuss over Michael. I couldn't own up, I'd promised father. We were such good pals, Mary; I didn't need to change things. I knew you cared, the way you've *always* looked after me, and if we'd altered the relationship I felt you wouldn't want to be paid, or have a house of your own like you do, so I played a game. As so did you, *Mum.* I was going to tell Andrew first, sometime when it seemed right, but then when the twins came along it didn't seem fair to deprive them of having a proper granny, so I promised myself this was the first thing I'd do when I got home. Mum?' She took the ten steps across the room, and took hold of Mary's toil-worn hands. 'Will you forgive me?' Mary stood and hugged her daughter.

'Lass. Oh, *lass!* There's nought to forgive.' The tears were there, but she wiped them away. 'To think we've played the game for so long without each other knowing! And I'd saddled Mr Andrew with the job of telling 'ee what you'd already found out – ee, lad, I bet you's relieved!'

The colour had come back and she reached for her glass. 'To us!'

'To us!'

'You'd better drop the Miss Roberta, Mr Andrew bit, Mary.' Andrew, immensely glad and yet quite stunned by this turn of events, couldn't think of anything else sensible to say.

'Aye. But I'm happy with staying Mary to you both. *Mum* sounds a bit daft; though I won't say no to being a *'Granny''*

Roberta was one step ahead. 'You might want to come back under the Manor roof, mum – Mary – if you want to be a full time Granny. Unless you want to keep your own place?'

'Lass, I *like* my little house. No, I'll stay there, though I don't mind staying the nights while you gets the twins under way. You'd best go see to them, my girl.'

'Yes, Granny,' she said meekly, winking at her Andrew.

It was going to take a fair bit of time to acclimatise themselves, all of them, to the change in domestic arrangements. Lunch round the kitchen table as declared equals for the first time, with a bemused Hazel included. Roberta could not have been happier. Nearly all her deep hidden problems ironed out, apart from getting a proper legal father for her offspring. That would come, she was sure. Happiness, pure unadulterated happiness.

The first of the afternoon telephone calls was Andrea. Could she pop up? Then June, looking to confirm that she could come up tomorrow and stay a couple of days? Andrew was concerned Roberta wouldn't get over tired, but she, indomitable as ever, pooh-poohed the idea.

'I'll be fine. I want to enjoy being a new mum, Andrew, and show off. We'll have to put something in the papers, you know.' Reflectively, she mused, 'Shall we ask Hazel - or perhaps her mother – if she could stay here for a while, act as sort of nursery maid? Provided mum agrees?'

And Andrew could see that she was getting intense pleasure out of calling Mary 'Mum', as if it was a beautiful new concept, which it was, of course. 'You're a lucky girl, my darling. I always thought there was something special between you two, and now I can see something of a likeness, despite your Italian flavour. He must have been a special person, your father.'

'He was. He meant absolutely everything to me, Andrew. I'm so sorry I didn't really know Henrietta, though. But there, if he'd loved mum as well . . .' she tailed off and went into a trance. 'Bit like you, really, responding to the girls. P'raps that's why I fell for you, seeing my father in you.'

'And *Con Tor?*'

'Grandpop? He was special too. I can see him now. Upright, impressive, beautiful way with him, clear as clear eyes. I know I wasn't very old, but I can *remember*, Andrew. *Compte-tours*. Light the fire, my darling. It's getting cold.'

Then he had to reach for her, wrap his arms round her and gently hold; getting more the feeling she was so very, very, special. A love child in her own right, given birth to two little people for the sake of their loving, a union forged out of happenstance that was growing stronger with every twist and turn. 'You're very special, darling. Your father and grandfather would be proud of you. I know Mary is. I'm proud of you too. And very much in love with you.'

She looked down at her ring, the twin diamonds catching the first blaze of flames from the fire, sparking the truth of this. 'And I you, my love. Bless you for giving me our children.'

Mary found them, still standing together in quiet contentment. 'Andrea's here. You not heard the car then?' Her smile was for the delight in them in being deaf to all but their belonging. 'I thought not.'

Roberta eased herself free of Andrew's arms. 'I'd best fetch them down then. I'll feed them first. 'Bout twenty minutes Andrew, keep her amused,' and escaped upstairs unseen with her mum.

Mary had already taken Andrea through into the kitchen, where Andrew found her alone, greeted her with a 'Happy Christmas' kiss. 'You look very festive!' She'd tied her hair up with a tartan ribbon and was wearing a soft red woollen dress. 'Good enough to eat.'

'Thanks, you're not looking too bad yourself, for a new daddy. What's it like, Andrew, being a father all over again? You know I'm jealous?'

'Of me, or Roberta?'

'Both of you. Wish it had been me. I'm feeling rather broody. Entirely your fault. Kiss me?'

The want was in her eyes, her softness under that dress too feminine. She was too close, her stance too wide and her kiss too clinging. The reaction was inevitable and she must be feeling him, pressing her belly up against his growing hardness. Her whisper in his ear, just that soft *'Andrew'*, was a passion-inducing drug. *'Need you!'*

This was crazy. That he had to kill this passion thing stone dead was crystal clear. He should break away from her, tell her to behave, grow up, take a cold bath or even slap her, but he could not. Not Andrea, for he'd loved her physically, offered her comfort before, and damn the girl, he felt for her, cared for her as a daughter but she wasn't a daughter, she was a woman.

'Andrea, I can't. Not now.' Easing away, seeing the hurt in her eyes, *'Can't you see?'*

'You've taken me before, when *you* needed me. Roles reversed. *I need you. Just once?'*

'I . . .' Footsteps, and she moved back, brushed her lips with the back of her hand and smoothed her skirt down. Andrew wasn't sure if her lipstick wouldn't show and looked at her despairingly. She shook her head slightly as if to say, don't worry.

Roberta, with a child on each arm wore a beaming smile. Now he felt a right proper heel, almost wishing he had slapped the wanton girl. Andrea froze, just momentarily, and then held her arms wide and Roberta offered her a bundle. 'Say hello to Chris, Andrea. Be careful, he's just had a whole breastful. Here, daddy, you have your little daughter.' She handed the other bundle to Andrew. The world slid round him, back into true focus. Was he an Adam with Eve playing her role; serpent-like sinuosity in slinky red trying it on? Yes, oh yes, he could have moved on the girl, captivated her breasts, absorbed the shape and feel of her under that dress, felt for her and welcomed the rush and insistence of penetrating into the dark lusciousness of her desire, giving in and taking the wildness of a woman in heat.

He felt sick and had to sit down, carefully, nursing Abby's fragility with a tenderness he'd never have thought possible. Her mother's amber flecked eyes followed his actions, saw the pain, instinctively understood, and her heart went out to him. She'd had her need, her want, aeons ago and she'd succeeded in assuaging that yearning, moved on, and any hurt had been calloused over by the months of living and loving, to being an infinitely stronger structure of togetherness she'd never thought possible. Yet the damage she'd done to his life must still be there; where she'd cut into his soul then so might another woman. And *this* woman, nursing *her* child, had already weakened whatever resolve might have been formed; Roberta could smell her desire. Abruptly, she took Chris back.

Andrea didn't comprehend. 'He's gorgeous, Roberta. Can't I hold him a while longer?'

'I don't want him to be sick all over that lovely dress. You look fabulous, Andrea,' and she meant it. 'Let me get you a pinafore. Unless you have Abby. She's a sweetie, hardly ever sicks, just dribbles; mind you, dribble can pong a bit too. You wouldn't want that either. Hang on a mo.' She gave Chris to Andrew so he was holding both and Andrea saw the expression of love on his face for the two little mites, scraps of humanity so dependant on their parents and something changed within her. She took several deep breaths to calm her racing emotions. She'd never had a panic attack, unless being molested by Fred was one, but something was going on inside her she wasn't sure about; searching blindly behind her for the stool with a hand she found it and attempted to sit down, but her balance was wrong and she fell, crashing down heavily on her shoulder onto the floor.

'Andrea!' Roberta was there, kneeling beside her, sliding an arm under. 'Oh, my dear girl! Let me help you up.' Andrew was helpless; he had his hands full and could only watch. As Roberta tried easing her up, Andrea brought her knees up and attempted to stand, but something was wrong. The stool, balanced precariously against the table, fell over with a crash that startled the two babies and Chris started to yell. She clutched at her shoulder, trying hard not to let tears show. She was hurting, and the left arm just wouldn't work.

'R, be careful, it looks as though she may have dislocated her shoulder. Andrea, don't try and move it. Prop her up against the table for now. How did you do that, for heavens sake?' He saw the expression on her and felt a tug at his emotions.

Mary and Hazel, upstairs sorting the rooms out, must have heard the commotion and had come running; Hazel relieved Andrew of his precious burden and Roberta let Mary and Andrew lift Andrea up between them, instinctively grasping hands between them to support her and carry her through to the sitting room, propping her on to the settee. It seemed like an hour but happened in less than ten minutes.

'I'll call an ambulance,' Roberta was all concern, but Mary was looking and feeling.

'Ouch!' Andrea winced at the stab of pain.

'Steady, lass. Reckon we can sort this. Andrew, lad, you just hold her, nay, *here*. That's right. Now . . .' holding onto the upper arm and another hand against the side of the injured girl's chest, she somehow jerked and pulled and Andrea screamed.

'Hey, Mary, what're you doing?' Andrew was alarmed. Roberta had her fingers at her mouth and Hazel, with two infants balanced precariously, closed her eyes.

'There now, that's sorted. No need to bother other folks. You'll have a bruise or two mind, but your shoulder's back in place. Cup o' tea? Give those bairns back to their parents, Hazel, my girl, and let's get summat organised.' Patting Andrea on her head, she smiled at her daughter. 'You ken I did that nursing course? First Aid and then some? Mind you, it's as well you didn't break your collarbone. Can you move that arm, now, lass?'

Andrew realised he was still holding her and couldn't help himself, bent down and kissed her cheek. 'You're okay?'

She tried, gingerly, and yes, it moved. She rubbed the shoulder. It wasn't too bad, but her head was feeling muzzy and the room seemed out of focus, walls swimming . . .

'She's fainted. Put her head down, Andrew, between her knees. Mary – that tea?'

'Aye. Not surprised, she'll be in shock. Put that rug round her, Andrew. Hold her.'

It was Andrew holding me, hugging me close, whispering 'it's fine, Andrea, you're only shocked, you're fine, dearest girl, come on now!' I felt his kiss on my cheek and the strength of his arm, and knew I was okay. If only – but it was foolishness. I'd love him to bits, he knows that, but he's Roberta's, lucky girl. So I'm going to have to let him go, 'specially after seeing that look in his eyes when he held those little ones. Deep breaths now. One, two, three. Try my arm. Ouch! No, it's going to be all right. Pull my skirt down, it's all rucked up, showing my knees. Oh, Andrew! Kiss me again?

He kissed the girl again and watched her eyes open. She was going to be fine. Mary had the tray brought in and Roberta was pouring. 'Here, Andrea, dear. Try this. I know it's got sugar in, but you've been in shock.' Having sorted Andrea her attention went back to the twins. 'Hazel – back upstairs for those two please. Mum, how about dinner?'

Andrea's eyes flew wider open. 'Mum?'

Roberta laughed. 'That woke you up. Yes, Mum. She and I have been playing silly games for years, but what with the twins and all, we decided to come clean. She started all this by flirting with my sexy father. Like Mother, like daughter. See where it got me?'

'Get on with you, Roberta! I'll not stay to listen. Dinner at seven.' Mary went, head in the air.

Roberta followed Hazel upstairs and Andrew was left alone with Andrea again. She wasted no time. 'I'm sorry, Andrew. I've been a selfish cow, expecting you to fall over me again. I saw you look at the twins. You won't let Roberta down now, not now, not ever again? With me?'

He shook his head. 'I shouldn't even think about it, but you're too nice a girl. We've been playing with each other, Andrea. Playing a different game. We both know it wasn't serious – don't we?' Her look was enigmatic. 'You're *not* serious, are you?' The repetition was getting to her, and her eyes seemed to glisten. She wasn't going to cry, was she?

. . . I've been a silly, silly girl, allowing my emotions to run fast and loose. And I was going to be so, so good, but then he just got to me. And now look where I am, hurting with it all. What am I going to do? Pretend?

Impasse. She was just too sexy, that was the problem, and past the point where social discretion would have kept them politely apart, so how on earth were they going to withdraw behind their respective moral and ethical barriers without wrecking normal relationships? He couldn't think. Was she going to answer him or continue to stand there, looking so woefully wistful?

'I'd better go. Andrew, I'm sorry. You'll still be a friend?'

'Silly girl! You work here, and I love you for everything you are and do, much more than being just 'a friend', provided we keep to conventions? Can we do that?'

She nodded, a slow and gentle nod. 'You're too good, Andrew. I'll try. Promise. Give my love to Roberta and the twins. I'd like to see them again when I've got some emotions under control, if I may.'

He had to laugh. 'You're fine, Andrea. You'll survive. You did long before we bumped into each other. Sure you want to go? You don't need to. Mary will have included you in dinner numbers.'

'No, I'd best go. Thanks all the same. It's a bit late, Andrew, but 'Happy Christmas' – or should I say 'Happy New Year'? Roberta's given you a wonderful Christmas present.'

'Heavens! Thanks for reminding me; I've got one for you. Forgotten in all the excitement. Hang about.' The little box was in his office drawer. Three minutes, there and back. 'Here you

301

are. With *our* love and woefully inadequate thanks, Andrea. You may open it if you wish.'

Her tummy muscles twitched. This was unexpected but nice. Undoing the holly paper the velveteen box gave the game away. It must be jewellery. Snapping the lid open revealed a necklace, a coil of beautiful silver rope with a semi-precious stone in the elegant pendant. Beautiful, oh so beautiful, and definitely her. Oh yes, *he'd have* chosen it for her!

. . . *Every time I wear this I'll feel wonderful. Was this a leaving present or a promise? Who knows? I love him for this!*

'It's beautiful, Andrew! You shouldn't have. Thank you, *thank you!*' She couldn't help it, and anyway she had a good excuse. She took those steps and flung arms round his neck, winced at the pull on torn muscles, but kissed him none the less. Fully, believably, and lovingly. Then she drew back. 'I'll see you. Take care, Andrew.'

The room felt empty, cooler and the fire had ebbed. Mechanically, he re-stoked it, put the guard in place and went upstairs. 'Andrea's gone.'

Roberta was feeding again, under her mother's watchful eye. Hazel was nowhere to be seen but he guessed she'd retreated to the guest room they were letting her use for the next few days. 'Gone? Why – I thought she'd stay for dinner?'

'Too emotional. Still. I gave her our present. She loved it, gave me a socking great kiss and went. Hope her arm doesn't play up driving home.'

'Nay, she'll be fine, lad. Sore, mebbe but it shouldn't hurt. Not much, any road.' Mary heaved herself off the dressing table stool. 'I'd best get on with dinner, then.'

Now they were on their own. Roberta treated him to her quizzical 'come on, tell' look.

'I know. You realise she was still holding a torch?'

'Uh huh. Bloody obvious. You and her. You won't be tempted, will you?'

There was a wee bit of wistfulness in her voice, he thought, underneath that slightly crosser tone. She wasn't sure about him, even now, and maybe justifiably.

'Can I be totally frank and open about her, R? Clear the air?'

She changed Abby over from one side to the other. Chris was sleeping, thankfully. 'You may. It won't change anything. Andrew, in case *you've* any doubts. I love you, adore you, won't let go and neither will these two. So fire away.'

Perched on the still warm stool, hands under him, legs swinging, staring at the carpet, he started to put his thoughts into rational voice. Not an easy task, as well as covering some ground all over again into the bargain, but it would have to be done. Trying to be unemotional about the girl, too, as though he were dictating a statement.

Roberta listened, aware of the effort her partner was making.

'. . . so then I lost my head over her . . .'

'In the office, for heavens sake?' Roberta couldn't help it.

'. . .Yes. No joy for anyone. Just relieved physical necessity. Not since, I wouldn't . . .'

'But you might have?'

'. . . She's a very seductive lady . . .'

'And I'm not?'

'You've been pregnant.'

'So?'

'. . . I've told her I'm keeping within bounds from now on. She saw me look at the twins earlier, said she'd been *'a selfish cow'* - her words, and that she was sorry. So, between us, I think we've called a truce . . .'

'A truce suggests it may resume.'

'I don't think so. You, the twins, mean the world, Roberta. I wouldn't want to renege on my feelings for you.'

'Hmmph.' She carefully detached a somnolent Abby and put her over the cloth-protected shoulder, patting her gently. The baby girl belched happily. *'Good girl!'* She laid her back in her cot and adjusted her dress. 'Did I really know what I was letting myself in for when I did an Andrea on you, Andrew?'

Then she laughed, a merry, giggling laugh, so infectious he couldn't help smiling at her, and then laughing himself. Suddenly they found themselves entwined, and her kisses were infinitely sweeter. In between gasps for air, she managed *'I love you!'* and he said *'I've been an idiot!'* and she said she agreed with him and they laughed some more and then it was perfectly all right between them again.

'Mind you, Andrew, I could do a Samantha on you as well. Give you a licence and then go away out of reach, just to see what would happen. You haven't anyone else lined up have you? Like that girl Lauren?'

'You wouldn't dare!'

Appearing to reflect for a while made him concerned, she could see. 'You're right. I wouldn't.' Whatever made her add, 'I still might give you a licence if you're good,' she couldn't work out. Maybe it was because she loved him too much.

TWENTY

The strange Christmas went; it was with a big sense of anti-climax they took the beautifully decorated tree out of the hall and tucked all the two hundred or so Christmas cards away. The New Year progressed and before they knew where they were the days had begun to open out, bringing fresh green shoots of daffodils above the dew-dampened grass. The taste of Spring was in the air, the few sharp frosts merely adding to the magic of the Manor's mornings. Andrew loved these fresh, bright starts to the day. Roberta was blooming despite her constantly interrupted nights, for between her mother's help and Hazel's involvement she was allowed plenty of time to catnap during the day. The twins were thriving, filling out and showing signs of outgrowing the first sets of baby-gro's, much to Mary's delight. With Roberta restored to full working condition, Andrew was a happy father and a satisfied partner in every respect; after the declaration of intents expressed on the day after Boxing Day all seemed to be on an even keel; Andrea was pleasant, still approachable but now even more professional and the office ran like clockwork.

The first of the new series of weekend courses was going to take place in February and the only matter of consequence outstanding was the television interest. They had been very patient and understanding after being told why they couldn't possibly be allowed anywhere near until the business Principal had hatched. *'That'll add some zing,'* was just one cryptic comment amongst a collection of goodwill noises.

All through the past two months Samantha had been very quiet. She'd gone out to Thailand for a short while, but now an e-mail said she was apparently due to go to the Middle East and Andrew couldn't prevent himself expressing his concern to both June and Roberta.

'Dad, she'll be looked after, I'm sure,' was June's comment on her last visit. She'd taken to coming up every other weekend; after her first visit she'd fallen in love with the twins and couldn't keep away. Roberta wasn't quite as confident but daren't show her concern to her partner. All she really wanted was for the divorce papers to be finalised.

It was one Tuesday morning when Marjorie rang. 'Is Andrew about? Next Friday, Roberta, though don't tell him I told you.'

She went haring off to the Barn where he was pulling out the worst of the old design layouts ready for her to install another new concept. 'Marjorie on the phone, Andrew.'

He looked at her ardent expression. 'Silly girl – we've a phone here, why didn't you buzz?'

She'd omitted to use the facility so thoughtfully installed all those months ago in her excitement. 'Sorry! *Come on!* She's waiting!'

'All right, all right. I'm coming.' He stepped back off the little dais and found himself pulled out of the building and across the grass. 'What's all the excitement?' *As if he didn't know.*

He picked up the phone. 'Marjorie?'

'Andrew. Just to let you know I should have the Decree Absolute on Friday.'

'Oh. Right. Thanks. You'll let me know?'

'Certainly. Be in touch.'

'Yes, right. Thanks. 'Bye.'

That was it then. Over. All twenty odd years of a marriage, written off. Gone, as if nothing had ever happened. Just an empty, fusty house, a few sticks of furniture, some photographs and a mind full of memories. Roberta was looking at him.

'Andrew?'

'It's over, Roberta. Sam and I. Divorced. Nothing left.' He

felt strangely drained, empty and grey; not the enthusiastic dance up and down sort of reaction she was obviously expecting. 'Sorry, R. Give me a few moments?' He walked out of the office, picked up his coat and stick from the hall and set off up the fields. She watched him go, and worried.

'June? It's Roberta. Have you got a moment? . . . Your father's heard about the divorce. I think it's unsettled him. He's gone off walking. He won't do anything silly, will he?'

'I don't know, Roberta. My guess is there's still a lot of emotion bottled up. Do you want me to come up?'

'Would you? Sorry to impose like this, but . . . '

'No, Roberta, it's all right. I'll pop up, be about lunchtime. Twins okay?'

'Yes, fine, thanks. You're a great girl, June. A real *Andrew* girl. Thanks, I'm very grateful.'

June had to smile at the phone. Being called after her father. She went slowly upstairs to William's den. He'd scarce know she'd gone, poor lamb.

Andrew's feet led him instinctively over the old path, up towards the ancient bench where he could sit and just quietly absorb the countryside. From here he had seen Roberta fall off her horse, a year past and gone. If she'd not fallen? If he'd not bothered to go to her aid? *If Sam hadn't gone off that morning he may not have gone out anyway.* But fate had intervened in the humdrum, and changed every aspect of his life. The same old catalogue of events, emotions, every nuance of the happenings that had led him down this path circled round his brain looking for a way forward; for the next step. But wasn't there a next step already mapped out? He and Sam would still be friends, still communicate one way or another; June - and Peter, to a lesser extent - would be always present in his life. Roberta would expect a wedding, and soon, he knew, so the twins could have proper married parents. A few months ago he would have led her down the aisle like a shot, now it was feeling like just another chore. He'd *got* to rekindle that feeling which had led him into that pantomime wedding gesture under the tree last summer; smiling at the recollection, the joy in her then; at the look she'd given him when she'd slipped that engagement ring on. Then the time when he'd come back from the hospital after the twin's birth and learnt about Mary's strange life. The revelation on the relationship hadn't brought the cataclysmic effect on life at the Manor it could have done, it had just happened; they'd adjusted almost overnight, happily it was if it had always been like that. Well, in a way it had. Mary had always seemed like a mother – to them both, once he'd been accepted. He wondered what thoughts she'd had once it was clear he and Roberta had – er – slept together. He grinned inwardly. That first time was scarcely 'sleeping' – and he had a shrewd idea the twins had been the result of that first frenetic coupling if time scales were anything to go by, though the Irish trip and that afternoon under the trees up on the hill would have been an equally wonderful event for conception. The remark made by Ken – 'all the love in the land '- sprung into his mind. And those first couple of days in London; he hadn't known then it had been her childhood home where Mary had presided over the household near thirty years ago. If Christopher's wife Henrietta had been able to conceive, would Roberta have been born? Was she conceived in the same room where he and Roberta had been so passionate – their first time away together? How come Mary still had that strong vernacular way of speaking even after all the years in that elegant household – though she *could* speak well if she'd a mind?

Well, it was all water under the bridge. Come Friday he'd be a free man. With a house to sell. Sam had been very good about the money – but then it wasn't as if they'd been acrimonious about the divorce, more a rationalisation of the state of play. Would she – *had she* - found someone else? Did he care? In a funny way he did, though why when he'd got Roberta – and for that emotive period there had been Andrea. She was being very demure nowadays. Oh, what the heck. He was feeling the cold, parked up here like some seated scarecrow. He'd been up here for over an hour. So back to the ranch. Which ranch? A year plus ago it'd have been back to Samantha. Now the Manor. Was this really what he wanted? No elation at the change; some sadness. The ties between them were still there, he and Sam. June and Peter living proof. If he didn't go back, would Roberta *really* miss him? Would Sam care if he gave it all away and ended the relationship? Had it been the right thing to do? The oft-repeated phrase came back; i*n sickness and health . . . till death do us part . . .* was that the proper way out? P'raps Roberta should have broken her neck when she came off that horse, maybe as Michael had intended. God, what *was* he thinking? And as if the phrase triggered a miracle, the clouds parted briefly and a burst of sunlight crept down the contour of the hill and lit up the Manor roof.

Heaving himself off the bench and stretching, he decided to go back via the longer route. Get some blood flowing; work off some energy, clear the brain, whatever. He shrugged his coat firmly into place and set off. He'd get back for lunch.

June didn't bother to knock nowadays; she simply walked in, feeling so much part of this extended family, after all the twins were half brother and sister, weren't they? William hadn't even turned his head away from the screen, merely nodded and said 'okay, give my regards to your dad'. She'd felt a smidgeon tearful about that; wondered if he really loved her, and suddenly saw herself as another Andrew with a partner like her mother. *Oh Lord!* At least it had been an easy trip, no hold-ups, thank heavens.

She walked on through the hall and on into the kitchen. They were all there, and it was so wonderful to feel part of the happy family atmosphere. 'Dad not back yet?'

'Nope.'

'Shall I go look for him?'

'Not unless you want to. Not sure which way he went, though my guess is up the hill. There's an old seat which overlooks this place.'

'I'll go. I don't mind the walk even if I miss him, after the drive. How long?'

'He's been gone nearly three hours now. Rather too long really. Lunch in another, say, three quarters of an hour. Just time to get up there and back. Got your phone?'

She had, and pulled her thicker coat out of the car boot. At least she'd sensible shoes on.

She found the bench, but no sign of him. The path led on alongside the tall hedge towards the wood, so that seemed the sensible way to go. On reaching the wood edge she reflected carefully on the next move. Back, hoping he'd got home by another route; on into the wood – there was a sort of path – or round the edge. Playing a bit of a scouting game she scanned the soft ground for clues and reckoned his footprints – fresh, no erosion by last night's rain – led on into the wood. She'd give it ten minutes or so, just to see.

'Blessed pigeons!' She didn't realise she'd spoken aloud, but the birds were crashing away through the branches. If he'd been this way the birds would have already flown, so where did he turn off? She spun round, and backtracked.

The wood had given him a bit of a respite from the cooling effect of the mid day breeze. It wasn't unpleasant but fresh enough to feel relief getting out of the draught. Generally he'd have gone along on the straight path through, but with mind so upskittled from its norm by the un-eradicable thought of such a forthcoming dramatically positive change in his status, he deviated and went up the edge, keeping just inside the trees. He'd not come up this way before and it was proving a steeper climb than he'd anticipated, pushing branches aside and struggling to maintain his footing on the side of the drainage ditch running downhill. The exercise, logically, was making him sweat and he needed to loosen his jacket; from cool to warm by a quarter of an hour pull uphill. Looking back he could scarcely make out where the Manor nestled into the valley below, but it was there. His domain. Well not exactly, but as good as. Somewhere down there were his two brand new children and his replacement wife – how much of a change would there be after the divorce was finalised? Would there be *any* change? There must be some, surely? Perhaps Roberta would become, what – less or more possessive? More sure of herself maybe, not that she was in any way insecure. No, life would probably go on just the same, so why was he feeling so uneasy? His earlier thoughts worried him.

This was daft. Best go back now; he'd been out too long. They might even be worrying about him. More than Samantha would have done. That thought caused a wry smile. What would happen if he slipped and had an accident; who would rescue him like he'd rescued Roberta that time? Then maybe it would be ordained, a solution to his dilemma. No! Not many folk wandered this way, so he'd best be careful going back down the hill, in fact it may be the better option to go down the field. Pushing his way through the hawthorn scrubby hedge onto the plough, and gingerly treading from tussock to tussock to avoid getting his feet all snarled up with the soft mud, it took a fair bit of time, so it was with some relief he eventually got back to the access track to become suddenly aware he was not the only person in this neck of the woods. A girl, looking vaguely familiar?

June heard rather than saw him first; slightly laboured breathing and the plodding squelch of his head down watched footsteps on the muddy ground, before he stepped out onto the stoney track. She'd stopped to listen; rewarded by the release of pent up suppressed anxiousness; an almost sexual orgasmic expellation of breath, steaming around as his physical reality broke into her reverie. 'Dad!'

'*June!*' Why and how was this? Not a mirage, a mental conjuring of unconsciously demanded need but actuality in smiling familiarity hurling towards him to capture arms around and kiss, daughter's lips pressed firm and longing. '*Hey?*'

'Roberta's worried.' She drew back, reddeningly aware her kiss expressed love with needy undertones. 'She rang; I came.' She kept hold of his hands, searched the smile for understanding. 'You're okay?'

'Ah. Friday. Sam?' Pulled her closer, lovely hair smoothed against his jacket and the scent of her over scored his slight error, 'your mother. Yes, I'm okay. Now.' Held her eyes as that loveliness of her upturned to him, bent and kissed again. 'You're a lovely daughter. Let's go find some lunch.' She'd set the seal on his concerns with the depth of that kiss, blown away the worries with her physically expressed emotions. Bless the girl. He'd survive.

Coming up the steps and back into the Manor's comfortably familiar hall revisited the memories of that other time, the *first* time; girl at his shoulder, muddied boots, same season of the year; the magic of the place unchanged, wrapping itself around him as jacket off, shoes left on the mat, the creak of the corridor door and Roberta flinging herself at him. June went through to the kitchen out of the way, happy and happy for the two of them.

'Why . . .? – No, silly of me. I understand. Come and have lunch,' simplistic acceptance and no recriminations, just a hug and a kiss and the flash of the smile. Friday would come and go with the same inevitability that blew scrap plastic into a hedge and startled a horse.

He was home. He'd travelled the contours of his emotions, his strengths - and weaknesses; explored uncharted territory, taken some knocks but survived; three – no, four, girls had joined his search for diverse aspects of life and each had achieved a different goal. Sam would have no ties, she'd find a new partner, of that he'd no doubt; and she'd risen to meet her challenges to become a complete person; Andrea – gorgeous girl – there would be someone out there who'd appreciate her qualities sooner or later and she'd know how essential it was to keep faith; June, beloved daughter (hopefully William might wake up one of these days and make her a mum) had saved him from despair; Roberta, that deliciously scheming wonderfully complete person who had so sexed up his life, well, she had chased him round the hill, caught him and happily unmasked her mother, *wonderful!* He took her hand and squeezed, no need for anything to be said; the telepathy between them enough.

The hill had been conquered. All contours explored.